IN
ANOTHER
LIFE

ALSO BY C. C. HUNTER

WEDNESDAY BOOKS
NEW YORK

IN
ANOTHER
LIFE

C. C. HUNTER

IN ANOTHER LIFE. Copyright © 2019 by Christie Craig. All rights
reserved. Printed in the United States of America. For information,
address St. Martin's Press, 175 Fifth Avenue, New York, N.Y. 10010.

www.wednesdaybooks.com
www.stmartins.com

Designed by Anna Gorovoy

Library of Congress Cataloging-in-Publication Data

Names: Hunter, C. C., author.
Title: In another life / C. C. Hunter.
Description: First edition. | New York : Wednesday Books, 2019. |
  Summary: Told in two voices, high school seniors Chloe Holden and
  Cash Colton try to determine if she is his foster mother's daughter,
  Emily, who was kidnapped at age three.
Identifiers: LCCN 2018044545| ISBN 9781250312273 (hardcover) |
  ISBN 9781250312297 (ebook)
Subjects: | CYAC: Adoption—Fiction. | Secrets—Fiction. | Foster
  home care—Fiction. | Kidnapping—Fiction. | Divorce—Fiction.
Classification: LCC PZ7.H916565 In 20219 | DDC [Fic]—dc23
LC record available at https://lccn.loc.gov/2018044545

Our books may be purchased in bulk for promotional, educational, or
business use. Please contact your local bookseller or the Macmillan
Corporate and Premium Sales Department at 1-800-221-7945, exten-
sion 5442, or by email at MacmillanSpecialMarkets@macmillan.com.

First Edition: March 2019

10 9 8 7 6 5 4 3 2 1

To my hubby, whose faith in me never wavers. Whose praise for my work is a big motivator. Who brings in take-out food so I can work late, and who has the coffee on when I wake. I love you, babe. Thank you for being my rock.

Acknowledgments

So many people need a nod of appreciation. My fans who inspired the name for Chloe's dog, Buttercup: Heather Renee Contreras, Lori McVicar, Janine Crawford, Melissa Ownsbey, and Peyton Lapato. My agent, Kim Lionetti, who knows the right thing to say. My editor, Sara Goodman, who had some great ideas on how to make this book better. My assistant, Kathleen Adey, who helps me get it all done. My friend JoAnne Banker whose knowledge of adoption helped me kick-start this book. Thank you, everyone.

IN ANOTHER LIFE

1

"What are you doing?" I ask when Dad pulls over at a convenience store only a mile from where Mom and I are now living. My voice sounds rusty after not talking during the five-hour ride. But I was afraid that if I said anything, it would all spill out: My anger. My hurt. My disappointment in the man who used to be my superhero.

"I need gas and a bathroom," he says.

"Bathroom? So you can't even come in to see Mom when you drop me off?" My heart crinkles up like a used piece of aluminum foil.

He meets my eyes, ignores my questions, and says, "You want anything?"

"Yeah. My freaking life back!" I jump out of the car and slam the door so hard, the sound of the metal hitting metal cracks in the hot Texas air. I haul ass across the parking lot, watching my white sandals eat up the pavement, hiding the sheen of tears in my eyes.

"Chloe," Dad calls out. I move faster.

Eyes still down, I yank open the door, bolt inside the store, and smack right into someone. Like, my boobs smash against someone's chest.

"Crap," a deep voice growls.

A Styrofoam cup hits the ground. Frozen red slushie explodes all over my white sandals. The cup lands on its side, bleeding red on the white tile.

I swallow the lump in my throat and jerk back, removing my B cup boobs from some guy's chest.

"Sorry," he mutters, even though it's my fault.

I force myself to look up, seeing first his wide chest, then his eyes and the jet-black hair scattered across his brow. *Great! Why couldn't he be some old fart?*

I return to his bright green eyes and watch as they shift from apologetic to shocked, then to angry.

I should say something—like, add my own apology—but the lump in my throat returns with a vengeance.

"Shit." The word sneaks through his frown.

Yeah, all of this is shit! I hear Dad call my name again from outside.

My throat closes tighter and tears sting my eyes. Embarrassed to cry in front of a stranger, I snatch off my sandals and dart to a cooler.

Opening the glass door, I stick my head in needing a cooldown. I swat a few stray tears off my cheeks. Then I feel someone next to me. Dad's not letting this go.

"Just admit you screwed up!" I look over and am swallowed by those same angry light green eyes from a minute ago. "I thought you were . . . Sorry," I say, knowing it's late for an apology. His look is unsettling.

He continues to glare. An all-in-my-face kind of glare. As if this is more than a spilled slushie to him.

"I'll pay for it." When he doesn't even blink, I add another, "I'm sorry."

"Why are you here?" His question seethes out.

"What? Do I *know* you?" I know I was rude, but—hotness aside—this guy is freaking me out.

His eyes flash anger. "What do you want?" His tone carries an accusation I don't understand.

"What do you mean?" I counter.

"Whatever you're trying to pull, don't do it."

He's still staring me down. And I feel like I'm shrinking in his glare.

"I'm not . . . You must have me mixed up with someone else." I shake my head, unsure if this guy's as crazy as he is sexy. "I don't know what you're talking about. But I said I'm sorry." I grab a canned drink and barefoot, carrying sticky sandals, hurry to the front of the store.

Dad walks in, scowling.

"Careful," a cashier says to Dad while mopping up the slushie just inside the door.

"Sorry," I mutter to the worker, then point to Dad. "He's paying for my Dr Pepper! And for that slushie."

I storm off to the car, get in, and hold the cold Diet Dr Pepper can to my forehead. The hair on the back of my neck starts dancing. I look around, and the weird hot guy is standing outside the store, staring at me again.

Whatever you're trying to pull, don't do it.

Yup, crazy. I look away to escape his gaze. Dad climbs back in the car. He doesn't start it, just sits there, eyeballing me. "You know this isn't easy for me either."

"Right." *So why did you leave?*

He starts the car, but before we drive off, I look around again and see the dark-haired boy standing in the parking lot, writing on the palm of his hand.

Is he writing down Dad's license plate number? He's a freak. I almost say something to Dad but remember I'm pissed at him.

Dad pulls away. I focus on the rearview mirror. The hot guy stays there, eyes glued on Dad's car, and I stay glued on him until he's nothing but a speck in the mirror.

"I know this is hard," Dad says. "I think about you every day."

I nod, but don't speak.

Minutes later, Dad pulls over in front of our mailbox. Or rather Mom's and mine. Dad's home isn't with us anymore. "I'll call you tomorrow to see how your first day of school was."

My gut knots into a pretzel with the reminder that I'll be starting as a senior at a new school. I stare out at the old house, in the old neighborhood. This house once belonged to my grandmother. Mom's been renting it to an elderly couple for years. Now we live here. In a house that smells like old people . . . and sadness.

"Is she home?" Dad asks.

In the dusk of sunset, our house is dark. Gold light leaks out of next door, Lindsey's house—she's the one and only person I know my own age in town.

"Mom's probably resting," I answer.

There's a pause. "How's she doing?"

You finally ask? I look at him gripping the wheel and staring at the house. "Fine." I open the car door, not wanting to draw out the goodbye. It hurts too much.

"Hey." He smiles. "At least give me a hug?"

I don't want to, but for some reason—because under all this anger, I still love him—I lean over the console and hug him. He doesn't even smell like my dad. He's wearing cologne that Darlene probably bought him. Tears sting my eyes.

"Bye." I get one slushie-dyed foot out of the car.

Before my butt's off the seat, he says, "Is she going back to work soon?"

I swing around. "Is that why you asked about her? Because of money?"

"No." But the lie is so clear in his voice, it hangs in the air.

Who is this man? He dyes the silver at his temples. He's sporting a spiky haircut and wearing a T-shirt with the name of a band he didn't even know existed until Darlene.

Before I can stop myself, the words trip off my tongue. "Why? Does your girlfriend need a new pair of Jimmy Choos?"

"Don't, Chloe," he says sternly. "You sound like your mom."

That hurt now knots in my throat. "Pleeease. If I sounded like my mom, I'd say, 'Does the whore bitch need a new pair of Jimmy Choos!'" I swing back to the door.

He catches my arm. "Look, young lady, I can't ask you to love her like I do, but I expect you to respect her."

"Respect her? You have to earn respect, Dad! If I wore the clothes she wears, you'd ground me. In fact, I don't even respect you anymore! You screwed up my life. You screwed up Mom's life. And now you're screwing someone eighteen years younger than yourself." I bolt out and get halfway to the house when I hear his car door open and slam.

"Chloe. Your stuff." He sounds angry, but he can just join the crowd, because I'm more than mad—I'm hurt.

If I weren't afraid he'd follow me into the house all pissed off and start an argument with Mom, I'd just keep going. But I don't have it in me to hear them fight again. And I'm not sure Mom's up to it either. I don't have an option but to do the right thing. It sucks when you're the only person in the family acting like an adult.

I swing around, swat at my tears, and head back to the curb.

He's standing beside his car, my backpack in one hand

and a huge shopping bag with the new school clothes he bought me in the other. Great. Now I feel like an ungrateful bitch.

When I get to him, I mutter, "Thanks for the clothes."

He says, "Why are you so mad at me?"

So many reasons. Which one do I pick? "You let Darlene turn my room into a gym."

He shakes his head. "We moved your stuff into the other bedroom."

"But that was my room, Dad."

"Is that really why you're mad or . . . ? He pauses. "It's not my fault that your mom got—"

"Keep thinking that," I snap. "One of these days, you might even believe it!"

Hands full, chest heavy, I leave my onetime superhero and my broken heart scattered on the sidewalk. My tears are falling fast and hot by the time I shut the front door behind me.

Buttercup, a medium-sized yellow mutt of a dog, greets me with a wagging tail and a whimper. I ignore him. I drop my backpack, my shopping bag, and dart into the bathroom. Felix, my red tabby cat, darts in with me.

I attempt to shut the door in a normal way instead of an I'm-totally-pissed way. If Mom sees me like this, it'll upset her. Even worse, it'll fuel her anger.

"Chloe?" Mom calls. "Is that you?"

"Yeah. I'm in the bathroom." I hope I don't sound as emotionally ripped as I feel.

I drop down on the toilet seat, press the backs of my hands against my forehead, and try to breathe.

Mom's steps creak across the old wood floors. Her voice sounds behind the door. "You okay, hon?"

Felix is purring, rubbing his face on my leg. "Yeah. My stomach's . . . I think the meat loaf I had at Dad's was bad."

"Did Darlene fix it?" Her tone's rolled and deep-fried in hate.

I grit my teeth. "Yeah."

"Please tell me your dad ate a second helping."

I close my eyes, when what I really want to do is scream, *Stop it!* I get why Mom's so angry. I get that my dad's a piece of shit. I get that he refuses to take any blame, and that makes it worse. I get what she's been through. I get all of it. But does she have a clue how much it hurts me to listen to her take potshots at someone I still sort of love?

"I'm going to sit out on the patio," she says. "When you're out, join me."

"Uh-huh," I say.

Mom's steps creak away.

I stay seated and try not to think about what all hurts, and instead I pet Felix. His eyes, so green, take me back to the boy in the store. *Whatever you're trying to pull, don't do it.*

What the heck did he mean?

I leave the bathroom, but before I open the back door, I stare out the living room window at Mom reclined on a lawn chair. The sun's setting and she's bathed in gold light. Her eyes are closed, her chest moves up and down in slow breaths. She's so thin. Too thin.

Her faded blue bandanna has slipped off her head. All I see is baldness. And—*bam!*—I'm mad at Dad again.

Maybe Dad's right. Maybe I do blame him for Mom's cancer.

It doesn't even help to remember that three weeks ago, the doctor ruled her cancer-free. In fact, her breast cancer was found so early that the doctors insisted it was just a bump in the road.

I hate bumps.

My gaze shifts to her head again. The doctor claimed the short rounds of chemo were to make sure there weren't any cancer cells floating around in her body. But until I see her hair grown back, and stop seeing her ribs, I won't stop being afraid of losing her.

When she was diagnosed, I thought Dad would come back, that he'd realize he still loved her. What's sad is that I think Mom thought he would, too. It didn't happen.

Mom's eyes open, she adjusts her bandanna, then stands up with open arms. "Come here. I missed you."

"I was only gone three days," I say. But it's the first time I left her overnight since she got cancer. And I missed her, too.

We walk into each other's arms. Her hugs started lasting longer since she and Dad separated. Mine got tighter when the big C stained our lives.

I pull out of her embrace. Buttercup is at my feet, his wagging tail hitting my leg.

"Has she redecorated the house?" Her tone is casual, but still loaded with animosity.

Just my room. Going for a conversational U-turn, I ask, "What did you do while I was gone?"

"I read two books." She grins.

"You didn't pull up your manuscript and try to write?" Before Mom and Dad's problems, Mom spent every free moment working on a book. She called it her passion. I suppose Dad killed that, too.

"No. Not feeling it," she says. "Oh, look." She pulls her bandanna off. "I got peach fuzz. I hear women pay big bucks to get this look."

I laugh, not because it's funny, but because she's laughing. I don't remember the last time Mom laughed. Are things getting better?

She moves over to the swing. "Sit down."

It sinks with her weight. Mom's shoulder bumps into mine.

She looks at me, really looks at me. Is she seeing my just-cried puffiness? "What's wrong, baby?"

The concern in her voice, the love in her eyes, they remind me of when I could go to her with my problems. When I didn't weigh every word to make sure it wouldn't hurt her. Because she already has way too much hurt.

"Nothing," I say.

Her mouth thins. "Did your dad upset you?"

"No," I lie.

Her gaze stays locked on me as if she knows I'm not being honest. I throw something out there: "It's Alex."

"Did you see him while you were there?"

Another lump lodges in my throat—I guess this subject is too tender to touch on, too. "He came by and we talked in his car."

"And?"

"And nothing." I bundle up that pain for another time. "I told you he's seeing someone else."

"I'm sorry, baby. Do you hate me for moving you here?"

Duh, you can't hate someone who has cancer. But now that the cancer is gone . . . ? Tempting, but I can't. Just like I can't hate Dad.

"I don't hate you, Mom."

"But you hate it here?" Guilt adds a sad note to her voice. It's the first time she's considered my feelings about this. I tried my damnedest to talk her out of moving—I even begged—but she didn't give. So I gave. I've done a lot of giving.

My vision blurs with tears. "It's just hard."

My phone dings with a text. I don't want to check it, thinking it's Dad texting to say he's sorry, and Mom might see it, then I'd have to explain. *He is sorry, isn't he?* I want to believe he realized giving my room to Darlene was a mistake.

"Who's that?" Mom asks.

"Don't know." My phone remains in my pocket.

It dings again. *Shit!*

"You can check it," Mom says.

I pull it out and hold it close. It's not Dad. And now that stings, too.

"It's Lindsey." I read her text. *Come over when you can.*

"She called earlier to see if you were home. Why don't you go see her? I'll fix dinner."

"I'll just text her," I say, knowing Lindsey will ask about my trip, and I don't know her well enough to dump on her.

"Okay." Mom pats my arm. "What do you want for dinner?"

"Pizza." I'm starving. I barely touched my lunch before leaving Dad's.

"Pizza? On an iffy stomach," Mom says. "How about tomato soup and grilled cheese?"

I hate tomato soup. It's sick food. Cancer food. We ate that every night of chemo. Then again, I suppose that's what I get for lying. "Sure."

Soup, a sandwich, and two sitcoms later, I hug Mom goodnight and head to bed. Both Buttercup and Felix follow me into my room. Or rather, the room I sleep in. *My* room doesn't exist anymore.

I grab my phone to see if any of my old friends, or maybe Alex, has texted me. Nothing's there except a message from Lindsey, reminding me to text her when I'm ready to leave for school.

I flop on my bed. Felix jumps up, snuggles beside me, and starts purring. Buttercup leaps up and lies at my feet. Phone still in hand, I swipe the screen to the selfies I took of me, Cara, and Sandy this weekend. We're all smiling, but not that big, natural kind of smile. All of us look sort of posed. Like we're faking something. Fake smiling. Faking friendship.

My finger keeps swiping until I find the older selfies with Cara and Sandy. We aren't posed, or phony looking. We're having fun. It shows in our expressions, our real smiles.

I keep going until I get to one of me and Alex. He's kissing my cheek. His blue eyes are cut to the camera, and I can tell he's laughing. I remember when it was taken. The first night we slept together. Tears fill my eyes, and my finger swipes faster. Images, snapshots of my life become nothing more than smears of color flying across my phone's screen.

I wonder if that's all life really is, just smears of color. A collage of sweeping moments in different shades and hues of emotions. Times when you're happy, sad, angry, scared, and when you're just faking it.

I toss my phone to the end of my bed and stare at the ceiling fan going around and around, and my emotions do the same. My eyes grow heavy, then—*bam!*—I'm not there staring at a fan. I'm trapped in a memory almost as old as I am.

I'm sitting on a brown sofa. My feet, buckled up in black patent leather shoes, dangle above dirty carpet. I'm wearing a pink frilly princess dress, but I'm not a happy princess. Deep heartfelt sobs, my sobs, echo around me. I'm a fish out of water. I can't breathe.

I sit up so fast, Felix bolts off the bed.

It's the only memory I have from before I became Chloe Holden. A few months before my third birthday. Before I was adopted.

Lately, the memory has jumped out at me. Haunting me, in a way. I know why, too. It's the sensation. The one of being plucked out of my world and planted somewhere else.

Not that it didn't work out. Back then, I lucked out and

was adopted into perfection. I had a mom, a dad, got a cat I named Felix, and eventually we got a dog named Buttercup. We lived in a three-bedroom white brick house filled with lots of laughter. And love. I had friends I grew up with. A boyfriend I'd given my virginity to.

I had a life. I was happy. I smiled real smiles in photos.

Then came Dad working late.

Mom and Dad fighting.

Dad's affair.

Mom's depression.

The divorce.

The cancer.

And then the move from El Paso to Joyful, Texas. Which, by the way, isn't joyful.

And here I am. Plucked again. So *plucked*.

But this time, I'm not feeling so lucky.

2

Telling myself this first day of school won't suck as bad as I think, I run my fingers through my thick dark hair that I spent half an hour straightening. After giving myself one last check in my dresser mirror, I text Lindsey and dart out.

Mom, swallowed in a too-big pink nubby robe, is sitting at the breakfast table and looks up. "I liked the red blouse."

"Yeah. But I like this one for today." I give her a hug. I look good in the red, but it felt too showy, like, *Look at me, I'm the new kid.* So I went for beige instead.

"Wish me luck," she says.

"Why? What are you doing? You going to start writing again?"

"No. I'm job hunting."

My first thought is that she should wait until her hair grows out. "Do you feel like working?"

"Yeah. I'm tired of doing nothing."

"Then good luck." I snatch my backpack, give Felix and Buttercup a quick rub, and leave, trying not to think about Dad asking if Mom is working. Trying not to think that I never got an apology from him.

Lindsey, wearing black jeans, a black blouse, black nail polish, and red lipstick, is waiting beside the driveway. Her hair, sandy blond with highlights, hangs down past her shoulders. She looks like she walked off a magazine cover.

"Aren't you stylin'?" I say.

She grins. "My plan is to make Jonathon sorry."

I heard all about Jonathon. Mostly referred to as "the no-good cheating dog." I saw him once or twice when we first moved here. It wasn't until they broke up that Lindsey and I started talking. I only recently told her about Alex, but we haven't come up with the perfect nickname for him yet.

If Mom hadn't dragged me across Texas, Alex and I'd still be together. I'm not sure I would've called it love, but I think I was bumping shoulders with it. When I left, we agreed we were going to do the whole long-distance-relationship thing.

That lasted four weeks.

"How was your visit with your dad and his live-in toy?" she asks as we walk to my car.

"Hell," I say, then change the subject. "You have a new guy picked out?" We get into my white Chevy Cruze.

"Yeah, David Drake. He asked me out last year right after I started dating Jonathon. He's funny, cute, and sweet."

On the ride, Lindsey talks about her class schedule and how she has three classes with Jamie. Jamie is her best friend, and was away over the summer. I worry now that since her BFF is back, Lindsey will drop me in a hot minute.

"I hope we have classes together," Lindsey says.

Most everyone had their class schedule emailed to them. I'll get mine after I visit the counselor. But since Lindsey isn't in honors classes, I doubt we'll have any together.

I pull into the school parking lot and hang the permit on the mirror. Mom guilted Dad into paying for the parking pass. My stomach starts cramping at the sight of strangers.

I look at Lindsey.

She's staring at me oddly. "Damn! You're nervous."

"A little, why?"

She makes a funny face. "I don't know. I thought you were fearless."

"Me? When?"

"Your mom has cancer. You had to move in twelfth grade, and you're, like, fine with it. I'd be a hot mess."

I tell her the truth. "I am. I just fake it." We jump out and grab our backpacks.

Only a few feet from my car, I feel people staring at me and waving to Lindsey. I lift my chin and pretend I don't care. Lindsey starts talking about where we'll meet up after school and tells me to text her when I know my schedule.

We're almost out of the parking lot when shouting erupts. We stop.

There's a big guy with light brown hair laughing at a younger sophomore-looking guy. The bully is holding a backpack up and making some wisecracks to the kid about being short.

The boy's face is red, like he's embarrassed and mad.

My heart goes out to the sophomore, who looks about as comfortable to be here as I am. I consider stepping in when someone else does. Someone with jet-black hair and shoulders a mile wide. I think he's a teacher; then—*crap!*—I recognize him. It's the weird psycho guy I rubbed my boobs on at the convenience store.

"Stop being an ass!" The psycho guy yanks the backpack from the jerk and tosses it to the younger boy. The kid catches the bag and runs for it.

"Look at him run," the jerk says, laughing. But damn—I hate bullies.

The weird guy mouths out something I can't hear. I take a step closer. Lindsey moves with me.

The jerk blows up. "Who the hell do you think you are?"

Lindsey leans in. "This is going to get interesting."

I don't look at her. My eyes are locked on the scene.

"Paul's the guy who took the kid's backpack," Lindsey continues. "He's a football player. The other guy is Cash. Cash came here only halfway through the last school year. He used to attend Westwood Academy, a private school where all the rich kids go. But rumor has it, he grew up in foster care and is a real badass."

"Paul is the one acting like an asshole." I try to mesh the guy who's standing up for the underdog with the lunatic I met yesterday.

"Yeah. Paul's a bit of a bully," she admits.

Paul edges closer to Cash. In spite of yesterday's encounter, I'm rooting for Cash. I guess I dislike bullies more than I do psychos.

Cash doesn't move, but his shoulders widen. Paul doesn't appear scared, but he should be. Cash is a good two inches taller than Paul. But it's not his height that makes him so intimidating. It's his body language. He *does* look like a badass. Even more of a badass now than he did yesterday.

"I asked you a question!" Paul yells. "Who do you think you are, Foster Boy?"

Cash's shoulders snap back. "I'm the one who doesn't have to pick on someone smaller than myself to feel important."

Paul moves in, puts his face in Cash's.

Cash speaks up. "Walk away while you can." His tone is dead serious.

"You walk away!" Paul says.

I think for sure Cash is about to draw his fist back. He surprises me when he says, "You're not worth the trouble." He turns to leave.

I don't know if I'm disappointed he didn't teach Paul a lesson, or impressed Cash took the high road.

He gets a few steps away when Paul lunges forward and shoves Cash's shoulder. "Coward," Paul accuses.

Cash swings around. "You're the coward for waiting until I turned my back."

"Well, I'm facing you now." Paul takes a swing.

Cash swoops to the left. Paul's fist hits air.

Everyone laughs. That fuels Paul on. He raises his fists to his face and starts dancing from foot to foot, like he's some professional boxer.

Cash brings his fists up to his chin. Everyone starts shouting. "Beat his ass! Teach him a lesson!"

Somehow, I know they aren't cheering for Cash. I'm not going to like this school.

I'm thinking we should leave, but like Lindsey, I'm glued to the scene. The two guys move in a circle. Paul swings again; Cash ducks. Paul growls.

I wait for Cash to make some smart-ass comment, but he doesn't. I get the feeling he doesn't want to fight.

Suddenly they're positioned so that Cash is facing me. Those liquid green eyes lift and meet my brown ones. He freezes.

That's when Paul takes another swing. His fist slams into

Cash's eye. He almost falls, but looking furious, he punches Paul—once in the gut, once on the nose. Paul falls down, gasping, and holds a hand over his nose. Blood oozes between his fingers.

"Stop!" someone yells. A man runs toward the group. This one really is a teacher. People start scattering.

"Let's go." Lindsey pulls me away. Right before I turn, Cash's gaze finds me again. His left eye is already swelling. I turn and follow Lindsey.

"That was weird as shit." Lindsey hurries toward the front of the school.

"The fight?" I ask.

"No. Him staring at you. Do you know him?"

"No," I say, and don't explain any further.

"Well, something about you stopped him in his tracks."

"I probably look like someone he knows." I recall telling him that at the store.

"Or he's got the hots for you. Every girl in school has tried to get his attention and failed. You get here, and he gets punched while he's checking you out."

"Maybe he wasn't staring at me," I say even though I don't believe it.

"Right." Lindsey rolls her eyes.

I glance at the school looming before me, and I want nothing more than to turn around and go home.

I'm waiting in the office to get my schedule from the counselor, Ms. Anderson, when I hear an angry voice behind me. "You broke his nose."

I'm almost certain it's the teacher who stopped the fight. I stare straight ahead. They walk past me. The teacher pushes through the swinging gate that leads to the back. Cash follows.

He's almost through the door when he turns around. His eyes, or I should say *eye*—one of them is swollen shut—finds me. Accusation shows in his expression. You'd think I was the one who hit him. I hear the teacher say something, and Cash turns around and follows him.

Weirded out, I see the desk clerk wave me forward. She pushes open the half door, and I follow her into the back, down a hall. We turn a corner and I see the teacher who broke up the fight. Looking pissed, he's talking to a dark-headed woman.

The desk clerk clears her throat.

The teacher and the woman look up.

"Chloe Holden." The desk clerk motions to me.

"Have her wait in my office." The woman grimaces. "I'll be right there."

The clerk ushers me in, and I take the chair closest to the door as she walks back out. I can faintly hear the conversation between the teacher and counselor. I lean back.

"No," the counselor says. "I'm saying look into it before making assumptions."

"I did," the man answered. "Paul Cane told me what happened, and three kids corroborated his story."

"Three of Paul's friends, no doubt," Ms. Anderson says. "Let me take care of this new student, and then I'll talk to him."

"You're wasting your time," the teacher says.

"Well, it's my time to waste." Her tone snaps.

Footsteps head my way. I sit up straighter and pretend I wasn't listening.

"I'm sorry to keep you waiting." She offers me her hand, but a frown still wrinkles her brow. "I'm Ms. Anderson."

I shake her hand. It feels awkward, but I already like her for standing her ground with the teacher. "I'm Chloe Holden."

She sits down behind her desk, then pulls a file from a stack of papers. "I got your school records from Lionsgate High. I saw your Preliminary SAT scores. Your grades are impressive. Your hard work will pay off."

I hear that a lot. I'm smart. But it's not really work. School stuff comes easy for me. In fact, in my old school, I usually missed one or two of the test questions so my friends wouldn't hate me. Being too smart isn't cool.

"You're planning to go to college, right?"

"Yes, ma'am," I say. "My parents both went to University of Houston, and I'm going there."

"With those grades, you could go just about anywhere. Have you applied for grants?"

I nod. At least Dad's getting a break on my college tuition.

"Well, I put you in all honors classes. Hopefully you won't get bored."

I give her another nod, my thoughts on what I heard her saying to the teacher in the hall.

"Your mom mentioned that she's going through chemo. And there's been a recent divorce."

Why would Mom tell her that? I sit frozen.

"If you ever need to talk about anything, I'm here."

"Thanks," I say. "I'm okay. Mom's okay. She's cancer-free now."

"Good." She looks at her computer. "I'm printing out your schedule and getting someone to shadow you for a few days until you learn where everything is."

I want to decline the escort, but don't want to risk losing my way around the school and making myself even more conspicuous.

She makes a quick call, then hands me my schedule from her printer. "Sandra will meet you in the main office."

I nod again, grab my backpack, and take two steps toward

the door, then turn around. "Uh. About what happened in the parking lot."

"What?"

"The fight," I say.

"You saw it?" She leans forward. I get the feeling she likes Cash, or perhaps she knows Paul's a bully.

"Yes, the guy with lighter hair, I think someone called him Paul, he was picking on someone younger. Had his backpack and was holding it up. The other guy, Cash, got the backpack for the kid. Paul started the fight. Cash even tried to walk away from it."

Her eyes widen with a smile. "Do you know either of them?"

"No, ma'am. I just saw it. And . . . someone told me their names."

"Thank you." She sounds relieved.

I step out and jerk to a stop, almost giving Cash another chest bump. Our gazes meet. Or my gaze and his half gaze. His eye is swollen shut now. But I swear that one eye is accusing me of something.

The words *Sorry I defended you* rest on my tongue. I don't say them.

I dart past him.

I feel him watching me. Like I felt him yesterday. Chills spider up my spine.

What is it with this guy?

3

Thirty minutes later, Cash Colton climbed into his Jeep. *Why did she defend me?* Then it clicked and he knew: *Because I was right.*

Bumping into him had been the perfect setup. *Always get them to notice you. Don't approach them. Makes them suspicious.*

It *was* all a setup.

Well, not all of it. The fight couldn't have been. No one could've known he'd come to the boy's defense. Cash wasn't even sure why he'd done it. Except . . . that kid used to be him.

Defending him, though, had to be part of her game. *Get them to trust you. Make them believe you're their friend.*

Good luck with that. Cash didn't trust anyone. Not even someone with nice breasts.

You couldn't con a con man—not when he knew every con in the book. He'd been trained by the best: his deadbeat—now really dead—father.

He drove like hell out of the school parking lot. After clearing him of wrongdoing, Ms. Anderson had called his foster mom, Mrs. Fuller. Being a doctor and the type of person she was, she insisted on seeing him herself before deciding if he needed medical attention. He was supposed to wait for her to come check on him before going back to his classes.

A block away from the school, he called her.

She answered, "On my way. You okay?"

"I'm fine. Don't come. I'm heading home now to get a few aspirins."

"Cash, Ms. Anderson wanted you to stay at school. You shouldn't—"

"Oh? I didn't know." Actually, he'd been listening to their whole conversation through the door and sneaked out before anyone could stop him. "I thought since she was talking to you, I was clear to leave."

"No, hon, you shouldn't be driving. You could have a concussion. How far are you from home?"

"Practically there," he lied again, and felt a pinch in his gut.

"You aren't dizzy, are you?"

"No."

"Okay, go ahead and get home. I'll call Ms. Anderson to let her know. I'll be at the house in twenty minutes."

"Please, don't come. I'm fine." He looked at the dashboard for the time. Eight forty.

"That's what you said two years ago, when your appendix burst," she said.

"And I'm still here. So I was fine, wasn't I?"

"After eight days in the hospital." She sighed. He heard a lot of that from her. Letting her down was the last thing he wanted. And as hard as he tried not to, he always did. His past followed him everywhere.

The Fullers had gotten screwed when they picked him.

Not that they'd have to suffer much longer. In two months, he'd age out of foster care. He didn't plan on bailing until after he finished high school. . . .

"Pull over and call me if you get dizzy."

"Got it." He hung up. Watching the time again, he passed the gated entrance into Stallion Subdivision, where the Fullers lived—where he occupied one of their bedrooms—and headed straight into Walmart. His eye throbbed.

He parked the Jeep, went inside the store, and headed to the bulletin board.

Every time he came here, he looked at it. The first time

he came across it, part of him had wanted to rip it down, thinking it would hurt the Fullers to see it. Later, he realized they'd been the ones to post it.

And there she was. Staring back at him.

Same eye shape. Same jaw. Same lips.

"Shit!"

That didn't mean it was her. Age-progression photos could be off. Photos sometimes lied. He knew that personally. But damn if this girl didn't look more like her in person than the photo the piece of shit gave Mrs. Fuller a year ago. And after Mrs. Fuller handed over three thousand dollars to the asswipe to find said girl, he conveniently disappeared. And he took a part of his foster mom's heart, too. She was just now getting back to normal.

If only Mrs. Fuller had confided in Cash, he'd have told her—told her how those kinds of cons worked.

Was this the same con man coming back for more? Probably. But this time, he'd upped his game. But this time, Cash knew about it. This time, Cash would stop it.

He glanced around to make sure no one was looking. Reaching up to take the image down, he heard the door swish open behind him. He jerked away and pretended to read a dog food coupon instead.

He stuffed his hands in his pockets, waiting for the person to wheel their cart out the door. Once the footsteps moved past, he refocused on the flyer.

There was a copy at the house, too. Tucked away in a file. But rummaging in Mr. Fuller's desk didn't feel right. Especially after he'd been caught doing it once before.

He'd been staying with the Fullers only a few months, a couple weeks shy of his fifteenth birthday, when he saw Mrs. Fuller, tears in her eyes, staring at the open file. Later, when she trusted him enough to leave him alone in the house, he went to find out what had made her cry.

He hadn't heard her walk back into the house that day. The second she saw him, he'd been sure she was going to yell; then she'd make the call to tell the social workers to come pick his ass up. Three other families had already sent him back. But she'd pulled a chair up beside him at her husband's desk and asked him what he was doing. He'd been honest: "I wanted to know what made you cry."

She'd sighed, sort of a low moan mixed with a whoosh of air—he'd soon come to know it was her signature unhappy noise—and she told him the story. She'd cried telling it, too.

Walmart's door closed. He snatched the paper from the board, folded it, pocketed it, and took off. Back in the car, he fired up the engine and checked the time. Damn. He had five minutes to beat Mrs. Fuller home.

And if she got there before him, she'd get upset.

While he couldn't be the person they wanted him to be, he worked hard not to upset them. He drove as if the devil gave chase. Sitting straight, he took extra caution since he could see out of only one eye. But he could probably drive blind. He'd had a lot of practice.

Another thing his old man had taught him. At only nine, he was the designated getaway driver when his dad robbed convenience stores. *Gotta earn your keep, boy.* It had been seven years since he'd seen the man's face, but his voice still rang in his head.

He parked in the driveway, unlocked the front door, and poked in the security code. He took the stairs two at a time to his room and hid the flyer in his desk. After running back down, he grabbed two aspirins, chewed them up, and dropped his butt on the sofa. Felix, the ancient red tabby, meowed to be picked up. Poor thing was blind as a bat. He picked him up and gave him a gentle stroke. He'd barely leaned back on the sofa when the door opened.

"Cash?" Mrs. Fuller's voice, almost melodious, called his name.

"In the living room," he said.

She walked in and he saw her frown. "Oh, goodness."

Once she stepped closer, she lifted his chin with two fingers. He tried not to flinch. It's not that he had a thing about being touched. It was her. It hurt when she touched him. Not a physical pain, but an emotional one.

"I think you need X-rays. Just to—"

"No." He pulled back. "It's a black eye. I get them all the time."

There came the sigh. "Have you iced it?"

"A few minutes at school."

She darted into the kitchen and returned with a bag of frozen peas. Her expression was determined. He suspected the X-ray matter wasn't settled.

"I'm not going to the hospital." He took the peas.

Sad air left her lips again, and she sat in the chair across from the sofa. They stared at each other. He compared her to the girl. There were a lot of similarities. But not the eye color. Mrs. Fuller's eyes were blue. Con girl had brown eyes with green and gold flecks in them.

Mrs. Fuller patted her knees and rocked a few times. That usually meant she had something rolling around her head and wanted to talk. Something serious.

He waited.

"Ms. Anderson told me what you did. Standing up for that kid."

He nodded and continued to wait. There had to be more.

"I'm proud of you, but I just wish you could have done it without fighting. You're better than this." Disappointment flashed in her eyes. He flinched.

His father's beatings hadn't hurt this much. He hated—loathed—letting her down.

There were all kinds of words lodged in the back of his throat. *I tried to walk away. He hit first.* But he'd learned a long time ago not to defend himself. People were going to think what they wanted to think.

"Sorry," he offered.

"You can't get kicked out of another school."

And that wasn't my fault either. He lifted his chin. "Did they say they're kicking me out?"

"No. When I called back, Ms. Anderson implied you wouldn't be in trouble. Several kids spoke up and defended you."

"Several?" He'd been shocked as hell that even one had. Then he recalled having seen Jack when the coach broke up the fight. He and Jack weren't exactly friends, but they'd been assigned last year to do a science project together and they'd actually gotten along.

"That's what she said. But if it happens again, they're not going to go easy on you."

He nodded again. "You can go back to work. I'm fine."

"It's okay. My PA is taking over my patients today."

But it wasn't okay. The Fullers didn't deserve to have to deal with his shit. To have the loss of their daughter used against them, to be reminded of that pain. What they deserved was to have their real kid back. But what were the odds that Emily Fuller wasn't six feet under?

But that didn't stop con men from preying on the Fullers. He would know. He'd lived with one. He'd been one. He and his dad had pulled a similar scam once after his dad had spotted a kid on a bulletin board who looked like Cash. His dad did a little research. The sad woman who'd posted that flyer was always eating lunch in the park by her work. They went there every day for a week. Cash's job had been to stare at her. Get the mark's attention. Bait the hook.

She finally bit. She approached them.

Dad was good. He played the part well. He told the sad story of how he didn't know Cash's last name. That this was his long-lost sister's kid—though he'd never even known she had one—and then she'd up and died and left the kid to him.

It took another day before she shared her own sad story with them. Only hers was true. She'd had a boy who went missing at age four. Cash looked a lot like him.

"Come here," the woman had said. She had tears in her eyes. With trembling hands, she'd touched him. He remembered he'd flinched then, too. "Are you David? Do you remember me? Is that why you were staring?"

"I don't know," he'd lied. Lied just like his daddy had told him to. Then his dad had poked at his shoulder to remind him to finish his part. Six years old, and he already had to earn his keep. "Did you have a black dog with a white smear on his nose?"

The memory of how desperate that woman had been still haunted Cash sometimes. She hadn't hesitated to give his dad the money so he'd go and get Cash's DNA tested. Of course, that never happened. That night they drove out of Little Rock, Arkansas, five thousand dollars richer. Probably the woman's life savings.

"That was wrong. I'm never doing that again," he'd told his dad. That had been his first black eye. It hurt. But he was certain the woman had hurt more.

No way in hell was Cash going to let that happen to the Fullers again.

He needed to find answers.

———

"Hey, sweetheart. How was it?"

Mom's waiting on me when I walk in that afternoon. I was hoping she'd still be out job hunting. I'm in no mood to be grilled.

"It was okay," I say.

"Did Lindsey introduce you around?"

"Yeah. I met Jamie, her best friend. She's nice." And she was, but I noticed how she kept telling me stories of her and Lindsey as if trying to prove something. As if wanting me to know I'm the new one—that Lindsey was her best friend.

I'm okay with that. It's just nine months.

I notice Mom is waiting for more. "Lindsey also wants me to hang with them in a couple of hours. Jamie's coming over." If I were in El Paso, I'd be hanging with Sandy and Cara. We'd be comparing stories of our classes, our teachers, the guys who look better this year than last.

But I'm not in El Paso. I'm here. And now, so I won't seem so pathetic, I'm going to go be the third wheel at Lindsey's and feel lucky I've got that much.

"How was your day?" I ask. "Did you find a job?"

Her smile widens, and it's nice to see it.

"You did?"

"Yeah, I went to my doctor's office, Dr. James, my oncologist. There's two doctors in the office. I told him I had an RN degree, and he practically offered me the job. They have to do background checks, and I have to interview with the other doctor, but it sounds as if I've got it."

She's smiling, happy. I hug her.

When we pull apart, she's still grinning. "It's going to work out." She cups my cheeks like she's done since I was a child. "Us here. We're going to do fine."

I nod, wanting to believe it. And seeing her happy, I almost do.

The next day, I decline the escort at school. I'm sure I've got it down. Wrong. I get turned around and I'm late to my second-period American Lit class, feeling like I have a neon sign blinking NEW GIRL on my back.

Unfortunately, that feeling never goes away. And I've spotted who's staring: Cash. He's beginning to freak me out. I'm counting down the minutes till class ends.

Between classes, I go to my locker to change out my books. I'm arm deep when I feel someone standing beside me. My heart drops. I think it's Cash.

Wrong.

I look up to meet a pair of flirtatious light blue eyes belonging to a cute boy I'd noticed in American Lit. "Need help finding your next class? Need a date Friday night?"

I return the smile. My heart takes a flattered dip.

"I'm David Drake."

"I'm . . ." My name sticks to my tongue while I try to figure out where I heard his name before. Then—*bam!*—I remember. And it's not good.

David Drake is the boy Lindsey is after. Shit. "I'm . . . not interested." I ease away to reclaim my personal space and focus on my locker.

"I thought your name was Chloe."

"Seriously." I give him another glance, without a smile.

His grin stays strong. "I can be an acquired taste."

"I'm not acquiring."

"Boyfriend back home?"

"Yeah," I lie, and push back my hair. "We're practically engaged."

He puts his right hand against his chest. "Did you hear that? You just broke my heart."

I shake my head, and it rattles free an idea. Before I can

figure out if it's a good or bad, I go with it. "You know, I've heard your name from a girl who's into you."

"Who?"

"I can't say, but . . . word is you asked her out last year."

His brow wrinkles. "Sara?"

I don't answer.

"Lisa?"

I frown.

"Katie? Paula? Anna? Lacy? Carol? Jackie? Hannah?"

My mind reels.

"I'm joking," he says. "Since I asked only two girls out and one of them rides to school with you, I know who it is. But I thought she was with Jonathon."

I worry that I should've kept my mouth shut, so I just shrug and turn to leave. Why do I always want to fix things?

I've taken only a few steps when I see Cash again, two lockers down from mine. He's not looking at me, but I'd bet my best bra he was listening.

Then I see Jamie standing across the hall. She looks away really fast and walks off. Somehow, I know she saw David talking to me.

Frigging great! She's probably heading to find Lindsey right now.

Cash waited until he saw Mr. Alieda leave his classroom for a quick bathroom run and he entered the science lab. He hurried over to the two terrariums lining the wall. Students would be coming in any second. One tank held a boa, the other had live snake food. Opening his empty backpack, he slipped on a glove.

The mouse stood on its hind legs and looked at Cash, its whiskers twitching. "Here's the deal: I help you, you help me. You get a chance at freedom. I get . . . answers. Maybe."

Cash gently caught the mouse and placed it into his empty backpack. After putting the top back on the terrarium, he headed to the office.

It wasn't the best diversion plan he'd ever made, but it was a plan.

This morning when he'd gone in to schedule a meeting with Ms. Anderson, he'd fumbled around choosing a time until he found out that Ms. Anderson had lunch between eleven and eleven thirty. Perfect. That's when he had lunch, too.

All he needed was three minutes in her office. Three.

He could wait and come back tonight to get in, but if he got caught . . . ? Breaking and entering came with jail time. Freeing a helpless mouse was a forgivable offense.

Walking into the office, he saw three girls waiting to talk to the front office clerk. This might work.

He eased behind the girls, unzipped the backpack, and set it down on the floor. It took the mouse about four seconds to run for freedom.

Pulling his bag back up, he said, "Is that a mouse?"

Just as he'd planned, chaos followed. The mouse ran under the counter. The desk clerk screamed and tore out of the office. While the girls continued squealing, Cash headed into the back, staring downward as if looking for the creature.

Once in the hall, he darted to Ms. Anderson's door and pulled out his paper clip. But he found the door open. Great.

He moved into the room, shut the door, and went straight to the desk where he'd seen Chloe Holden's file.

With his ears set to listen for any footsteps outside the door, he yanked open the file. He didn't read it. He'd do that later.

He snapped the first image, turned the paper, and took a second. One more page flip and he closed the file, set it back on top of the stack, and turned to leave. He eased open the door to listen for anyone coming.

Voices sounded. He recognized Ms. Anderson's voice.

Then women's heels came tapping down the hall.

Shit. He was caught.

4

"Cash!" she squealed, and came to a sudden halt when she stepped through the door.

"Hey." He sat in the chair across from her desk and forced himself to relax. To look innocent. Sometimes the only move left was fake it till you make it.

"What . . . are you doing here?" she asked.

He turned and looked at her. "I have an appointment." He kept his expression in check even when panic had his palms sweating. Honestly, if it didn't mean disappointing the Fullers, he wouldn't care if he got caught.

She looked at the clock on the wall. "That's in twenty minutes."

"That's not what the office told me this morning." He set his expression to show confusion. *They might not believe what you say, but they'll almost always believe what they see in your eyes.*

"I'm sorry." He stood. "I'll come back. I just . . . when I came in, I was a few minutes late, and no one was at the counter out front. I didn't want to keep you waiting. So I just came back. I thought you might be in the . . . restroom or something." He cut his eyes down as if embarrassed.

"No. I was . . . in the teacher's lounge." Her shoulders relaxed. She was buying it. The blood rushing in his ears slowed down. He wouldn't have to hear Mrs. Fuller sigh today.

He took a step to the door. "Okay, I'll just go and—"

"No. Now's fine. They must have told you wrong. This is my lunch period."

"Well . . ." He was dying to read the file. "I don't want to mess up your lunch."

"No, stay. I already ate."

He sat back down. She settled behind her desk. When he noted the way she was staring at him, his panic picked up again. Not staring like she knew he was lying. Or that she had a clue what he'd been up to. But like she wanted to fix him.

How many times had he sat across from a counselor's or psychologist's desk and had them try to get in his head? As if they thought by getting him to spill his guts, they could make him better. They couldn't.

No one could change his past. No one could change what had happened. Or the terrible things he'd done. Talking about it only made it worse.

"Do you know why I wanted to see you?"

"I assumed because of the fight," he said.

"Well, yes, but I also wanted to just . . . see if you're okay?" She focused on his bruised face. And talk."

Yup, here it came. He inhaled. "Ms. Anderson, I don't mean to be disrespectful. And if you want to talk to me, dish out a punishment for the fight, I'll sit here and take it. But I really don't want to talk about other things."

She looked down as if to collect her thoughts. "Okay,"

she said, but took a few seconds to resume. "I heard what really happened with the fight. I'm sorry."

"Me, too," he said.

"Bullying isn't allowed, period. What Paul was doing was unacceptable. I was told that you even tried to walk away."

He shrugged as if it weren't important, but he felt validated. He didn't get to feel that way very often.

"But I don't think you know your own strength. I'm sure you didn't mean to hit him that hard."

Yeah, I did. The asswipe had pounded his fist into Cash's eye socket. He'd wanted to hurt that son of a bitch. But he didn't say that.

She shifted in her chair. "Thank God, Paul's nose wasn't broken."

He had to work to hide his disappointment.

"Point is, I know how teenage guys are. And I know he hit first. But we need to make sure this doesn't happen again."

"I won't get in his face," Cash said.

"But what if he gets in yours?"

Cash didn't answer. He couldn't. To say he wouldn't defend himself was a lie. And believe it or not, he didn't like lying.

"Look. In two months, you'll be eighteen and Paul will still be seventeen. If a fight erupts, it could come with serious consequences for you."

Air caught in Cash's lungs. "So you want me to leave school?" This was exactly what the Fullers didn't want. Getting him graduated from high school was their goal.

Her eyes widened. "No. I just want you to be aware so you can avoid any legal complications."

He nodded. "I'll keep that in mind. Can I go now?"

If her expression was any indicator, she heard the emotion in his tone. "Just one more thing."

He braced himself.

"My parents were killed in a drunk-driving accident when I was eleven. They were the drunks. My grandmother didn't think she could take me on. I grew up in foster care."

That wasn't what he'd expected her to say. "I'm sorry." He meant it, but he still didn't want her in his head. Didn't want her story in there either. Didn't want to get anywhere close to caring about anyone else. Caring for the Fullers was bad enough.

"So am I," she said. "What I'm trying to say is that I know about growing up in a world of dysfunction. If you ever want to talk, I'm here."

Yeah, I'll do that when Satan starts serving snow cones with cherries on top in hell. "I'll remember that." He got up and walked out.

I walk into the lunchroom. The smells, the crowd of strangers, and the noise have me wanting to pull my head into a shell.

I look at everyone sitting side by side. They don't hear the noise, because they are part of it. They don't see strangers; they see friends.

Five minutes later, I'm feeling lonely and pathetic while eating my cardboard pizza.

Then someone drops down beside me. It's Lindsey. Her arms are folded over her chest. She looks upset. At me.

Just like that, I know why. She heard about David's visit to my locker. "I don't like him," I spill.

"You sure?"

"Positive. I like dark hair and brooding types." If I could delete the last part, I would, because that sounds too much like the one-eyed brooder who's creeping me out right now.

She looks up. "But it doesn't matter. David likes you."

"No. He doesn't even know me. I'm just new, and 'new' to guys is the same as flies to shit. Or, as my mom refers to it, it's the 'new cow disease.' Bulls see a new cow, and they immediately want it. Their nostrils flare, they paw at the dirt and drool."

Lindsey settles in the chair, looking more defeated. "I don't want a bull who goes after new cows. I've already done that."

I didn't mean to discourage her. "You can't judge David. He's not your bull yet. When you get him by the horns, brand your name on his ass, and he'll come when you call him, then if he chases a new cow, you can take him to the slaughterhouse. You can have him sold as dog food and pickle his balls."

Lindsey laughs. "Pickle his balls."

"Hey, that's my mom's dream. To have my dad's cojones floating in a jar while my dog, Bo, munches on his ass."

We laugh; then Lindsey's smile melts away. "So why do we do this? Why do we fall in love if all guys are cheating bastards chasing down new cows?"

"Because there's maybe one or two who aren't like that," I say, and the hurt of being an offspring of a man who has a severe case of new cow disease grows heavy in my chest, but Lindsey and I share a sad smile.

And just like that, it hits me. In a matter of minutes, I've gone from being an alien in a strange world to being a part of it. I'm putting down roots.

My friendship with Lindsey is moving past the awkward stage and heading to the part where we mesh, laughing at things that aren't really funny to help each other.

It feels good, but there's a part of me that wants to lift my feet and clip the roots because I know it's going to hurt when I'm pulled out of this life to go to college. Hurt like it hurt when I was plucked out of El Paso.

I stop laughing and Lindsey follows suit. I let out a sigh. Lindsey looks at me. "Your mom really said she wants to pickle your dad's balls?" She's not saying it like it's funny anymore. She's saying it like she knows it hurts me.

I nod. "Doesn't your mom take verbal stabs at your dad?"

She seems to consider it. "A little, but . . . They've been divorced fifteen years. She probably did and I don't remember."

I know she's saying that just to make me feel better.

"Shit," Lindsey says.

"What?" I ask.

"There's Jonathon. In the black T-shirt. Flirting."

I remember seeing him a couple of times this summer. He has sandy brown hair and is sort of good looking, but not really. "David's hotter."

Cash got permission to visit the library during study hall. Phones were frowned upon there, but last year, the librarian did a lot of looking the other way. If you were quiet and didn't cause waves, she pretty much left you alone. *Know the rules before you break them* was another lesson his old man had taught him.

He pulled up the images on his phone and zoomed in so he could read about Chloe Holden.

The first piece of information he collected was her birthday: November 18. Emily was born on November 6. But if kidnapped, they'd be sure to change that. The second piece of info was that she was smart. Her scores on the PSAT were higher than his. But if she was working a con, she'd have to be smart.

Then he learned her parents were recently divorced. If they were really her parents?

He read a note Ms. Anderson had written. *Mother, JoAnne*

Holden, has cancer. Well, allegedly. Cash "had cancer," too. His dad had shaved his head and eyebrows and posted pictures of him on a GoFundMe page.

As far as his dad was concerned, there wasn't anything off-limits. He'd even put Cash on a strict diet the month before so he'd look sick.

Cash read some side notes from her old school. She played soccer.

That was just the tidbit he needed. He jumped over to Google to find the name of the soccer team from her high school. He found it, and then went to search for images.

It took five minutes of clicking on links before he found her. He stared. Of the three girls in the image, Chloe—if that was her real name—stood out. She was taller, curvier. Hotter.

Not that he hadn't already noticed. Hell, he still remembered how she'd felt against him. But he could stare at an image with appreciation in a way he couldn't do in person. Or the way he tried not to do in person.

Too many times, she'd caught him staring. Not all those times were ones where he was checking her out like a guy checks out a girl. Sometimes he was comparing her to Mrs. Fuller. And damn if he didn't see the resemblance even more in these photos.

Clicking off that image, he searched for her Instagram account.

He found one, but she hadn't posted anything in the last three months.

If this was a con, she'd have kept up the posts, wouldn't she? Or maybe not.

The images and posts he could see appeared real. He checked out her photos. There were several of her with a guy, Alex. Hugging. Kissing. Looking happy. In one, she was sitting on his lap.

Lucky bastard.

He remembered what she'd told David Drake about her boyfriend: *We're practically engaged.* The lie sounded in her voice and in her body language.

He saw that Alex had commented on one of the photos, "You look hot, babe." He clicked on the link to his profile, hoping the pictures wouldn't be set to private. They weren't. And . . . Ha. There it was. The truth. A picture of the guy with another girl. Posted last week. He looked back at the older photos and found one with Chloe at soccer practice.

So, it looked as if she really was from El Paso. Not that this ruled out a con. He'd just scratched the surface.

5

The bell rang the following Monday. I've now completed one week at the new school. I don't like it any better, but I hate it less. Or maybe I'm just getting used to it. Used to being the new kid. Used to Cash Colton staring at me like I ate his last cookie.

Used to not having a dad. He hasn't even called me.

I'm halfway out of school when I realize I forgot my history book. I backtrack to get it and run into Lindsey.

"What's up?" I ask.

Lindsey nips at her bottom lip. "I'm . . . I'm going to go home with Jamie. She wants to talk about her ex-boyfriend."

I knew Lindsey's plan for us becoming the musketeers was doomed when the plans for us over the weekend fell through. This is why moving in the twelfth grade sucks. You can't just become friends with someone. You have to be approved by *their* friends.

"See you later." I even smile.

"Yeah." She turns, then turns back. "I feel bad. I asked if—"

"It's okay. You two have history and haven't been together all summer. I get it. Really, it's okay."

She walks away, still looking guilty. I feel bad for making her feel that way.

By the time I grab my book and get outside again, the parking lot is emptying out. Most of the cars are lined up at the exit to leave. Horns are blowing. School's-out laughter leaks from windows and makes me feel lonelier.

I pull my keys out of my backpack and hit the clicker. Once I'm behind the wheel, I notice my car's sitting funny. Off-kilter. Kind of how I feel.

I jump out, my gaze flying to my back tire. My flat back tire.

"Shit!"

I reach for my phone to call Dad. Then stop. Dad's no longer available to help me with this stuff. And—*bam!*—I remember how right after I got my driver's license, and right before Dad's affair came out, he taught me to change a tire. He made it a game, and we timed ourselves to see who could do it the fastest. For every time I won, I'd get ten dollars. We had a blast. I ended up winning thirty dollars.

Now that memory feels tainted because I wonder if Dad knew he was going to bail. Knew I wasn't going to be able to count on him.

Pulling back from feeling sorry for myself, I focus on the positive: At least I can change my own tire. Dropping my backpack, I go open my trunk.

"Need a hand?"

I catch my breath. Cash is leaning against a Jeep parked beside me, as if he's been there all along. How did I miss him?

"I can help." There's no accusation in his eyes or tone now. I don't think there is. I've never been so bad at reading people—or is it that I've never met someone so good at staying unread?

"No. I can do it. Thank you." This guy unnerves me, for numerous reasons.

"I've got some Fix-a-Flat. It'll just take a second."

"Some what?" I ask.

"Fix-a-Flat. It inflates your tire and seals up any possible leaks. Then you can drive on it."

"That's okay. I have a spare."

He moves in. Butterflies wake up in my stomach. "You can change a tire?" He tucks his right hand into his jeans pocket.

I lift my chin. "You don't think girls can change tires?"

He seems to consider my question. "I think most girls don't want to change tires."

"Well, this girl is fine with it."

I lean into my trunk and loosen the nut to get to my spare. I don't hear him move. Is he planning on watching me. Annoying. But fine. Maybe I'll get the nerve to ask him my questions.

"You're new?" he says.

"Yup." I pull the tire up and drop it on the ground. Then I get my jack out.

"Where are you from?" he asks.

I set the jack down and reach for the wrench. Only then do I look back at him and work up some courage. "What did you mean at the gas station, about me pulling something?"

He doesn't appear shocked by the question. "You were right. You look like someone I used to know."

"But obviously, you've figured out I'm not her, so why have you still been staring at me?"

His green eyes crinkle around the edges, and his lips turn up in an amazing smile. "Why do guys usually stare at girls?"

"Because they're perverts?" I say, remembering the old-cow-disease chat with Lindsey.

He laughs.

I'm caught off guard by the sound, and oddly enough he looks surprised as well. As if he doesn't laugh that much.

We stand in silence and stare at each other.

"Like who?" I ask.

"What?"

"Who do I look like?" I kneel to put the jack in place.

"She's dead." His voice sounds solemn.

I look up at him. "Sorry."

"Me, too."

He kneels beside me to see where I have the jack, as if he thinks I'm screwing up. His leg brushes mine. It's innocent, but it feels intimate. His scent, like wild grass, fills my nose and chases away the smell of oily tires.

"So what brought you here?" he asks.

My mind's busy savoring his scent, and it takes me a second to answer.

"What brought *you* here?" I counter, trying not to think about the tingle radiating from his jeans-covered thigh.

His left eyebrow over his black eye lifts, and his jaw clenches. "You don't like to answer questions, do you?" It sounds like an accusation.

"Obviously, neither do you." I fit the wrench on the nut and go to turn it. It won't budge. *Shit.*

"Can I help?" He shifts closer.

"I got it." I readjust and put my weight behind it, remembering how Dad showed me to lean into it. My weight's not enough. Crap. Whoever put this tire on did a number on it.

"Now?" He moves even closer.

"What?" Frustration leaks out with the one word.

"Can I help now?" He's smiling again. "I promise not to think less of you."

"Not funny," I say.

"Sorry." His lips tighten his smile, but it lingers in his eyes.

I relent and move over. "These tires are brand-new. I shouldn't even have a flat."

He moves in, and with one turn of his wrist, one bulge of his biceps under the gray sleeve of his T-shirt, the nut comes loose.

He glances over at me. Even with his lingering shiner, his smile sets off alarm bells in my head. One of those crooked grins that leaves his mouth and goes right to my stomach and wakes up more butterflies. The kind Alex used to give me.

"You loosened it up for me." He moves to the second nut. I go back to watching his muscles bunch up again. The butterflies are having a parade.

After several beats of silence, he looks up. "I didn't fit in at my last school."

"Oh." Because he gave, I do the same. "My parents got a divorce."

"And Joyful just seemed like the place to move?" He continues working on the tire.

"No. My grandmother lived here. She passed away, but Mom still owned her house."

"So you used to live here?" The question seems weighty, but I'm too busy watching his muscles to consider it.

"No." Then I realize it's a lie. I lived here a few weeks after I was adopted. "I mean, yeah, but I don't remember."

"Why wouldn't you remember?"

"Because I wasn't even three when we moved."

He stops working the wrench and gives me a long look. "Okay."

"'Okay' what?" My tone's short and sharp.

"Okay, I believe you."

"But why would you think I'd lie? What is it with—?"

"Everyone lies."

"I don't!"

He lifts his brow over his black eye again. "You lied to David about still going out with Alex."

"You were eavesdropping?"

"Guilty." His gaze collides with mine.

I press my palms on the asphalt pavement. "How do you know Alex's name? I didn't tell David."

He continues removing nuts from the tire. His calm freaks me out. You don't drop a bomb like that and go back to fixing a tire!

"Answer me!" I hit his leg with my foot.

He continues working. "I checked out your Instagram. Your photos are visible to the public. You should probably be careful about that." He looks at me; his expression is unreadable.

I frown. "But how do you know we broke up?"

"Because there's an image on his page of him and another girl. And I don't think you're the type who'd put up with that shit."

I'm not sure how to react to that. Everything is jumbled up in my head. "What are you, some kind of a cybersleuth? Or a stalker?"

He goes back to working on my tire. "More of a sleuth."

"Why are you sleuthing around the internet about me?"

"I thought we covered that earlier."

"Because I look like someone you know?"

He nods.

"But if the person I look like is dead, why would you need to—?"

"She has a sister." His tone is somehow different. Is he lying now? His eyes meet mine. "I thought she might try to hurt someone I care about."

There's so much honesty in those words, in his gaze, that I believe him. Or I think I do. "Why do I believe you one minute and not the next?"

He goes back to removing the last nut. "I don't know. Maybe because you have trust issues." He pulls the tire off and puts it down on the other side of him.

His tone was teasing, yet . . . He puts the spare on and tightens up the nuts. He lowers the jack and then pulls it out.

He's right. I have trust issues. That's what happens when your birth family gives you away and then the father who chose you decides he'd rather make house with someone new.

"You are hard to figure out," I say.

"So are you." He holds his hand out to help me up.

I almost reach for it, then stop.

"We could remedy that," he says. "There's a place up the street that serves coffee, chai tea, or whatever you'd like to drink."

I get up, without his help, and dust the grit off my hands by swiping them on my jeans-covered butt.

"What do you say?" he asks.

I look at him, my head spinning. "I'm still debating."

6

The tire trick worked like a gem, but it would've been easier if she'd let him use the Fix-a-Flat.

He got out of his car and saw her do the same on the other side of the parking lot. Her phone rang. Holding up one finger, she answered it.

"I don't know. But I'm driving on the spare. Yeah, just a few minutes," she said. "Okay." She hung up and slipped her phone in her backpack. "My mom."

He almost asked how her mom was doing, but stopped himself. "You live close to the school?" he asked, even though he'd gotten her address from the file.

"About a mile. In Oak Tree Park Subdivision. You?"

"Farther out," he said. "Stallion Subdivision."

"The one with the horse statue and a pond in front?" she asked.

He nodded and wondered if she judged him because he lived in the rich neighborhood. Some of the other kids at school threw it in his face last year.

Going in, she checked out the menu, and ordered a peach tea. He ordered a Coke. When he tried to pay for hers, she refused and handed over her credit card. Drinks in hand, he led the way to a table toward the back.

"This is a nice place," she said.

"Yeah. I used to wash dishes here when I was fifteen."

"Now?"

"I work part-time at a garage. Changing tires and such." He smiled. "So, you like Joyful?"

"It's okay." That sounded like a lie.

"Where did you move from?"

She lifted a brow. "You didn't find that info when you were sleuthing me out?"

He leaned back in the chair. "Okay. El Paso. Do you miss it?"

She told him how the two towns differed. It was small talk, but he hung on to every word. Afterwards, she sipped her tea and stared at him over the paper cup. "Now it's my turn."

"Your turn?"

"You dug up info on me behind my back. I'm going to do it the proper way and ask."

"So you're all proper-like, huh?" he said, trying to sound casual and change the subject.

She didn't answer. And he got the feeling she was still ticked about the whole Instagram thing.

He hated questions, but he knew this game well, and if he didn't give something, she'd clam up. "Okay. What do you want to know?"

She stared at her tea as if mentally combing through a list.

He wondered what she already knew about him. So much of his private business was already out there. He remembered Paul calling him out as a foster kid, as if it were something he should be ashamed of. Little did anyone know, he was much more ashamed of his life before he became a ward of the state.

"Why didn't you fit in at the old school?"

He shrugged. "They're rich kids, privileged. They think they can't be held accountable for their actions. And the school seems to think that, too."

She ran a finger down her cup. "So what made you leave?" She stared right in his eyes, as if looking for a truth.

Yup. He knew the game. *Tell them something personal.*

They'll think they know you, and will answer questions easier.
Normally, this was where he'd make some crap up, but for some reason, he didn't feel like faking it.

He tightened his shoulders. "I didn't leave. I got kicked out."

Her eyes flickered. "What did you do?"

Hadn't he been ready for this? It still hit a nerve. "Why do you automatically assume I did something?"

Her brows pinched. "Because you said you got kicked out. You don't get kicked out for nothing."

"Right. But you assume it's my fault."

She stared at him. His gut said he was giving her a hell of a lot more than he'd wanted to.

"I'm not assuming. I'm asking."

He hesitated, angry for not faking it, but he couldn't back out now. "You want the truth? Or do you want me to pretty it up for you?"

"The truth." Yet the way she moved back in her chair said she preferred pretty.

He gave her the middle-of-the-road version: "Three of their football players were taking advantage of a girl. I stopped them. When I was done, one guy had a broken jaw."

She gasped. "Was it your girlfriend?"

"No. The girl didn't give a shit about me. Which should've meant I didn't give a shit about her. But I did. Those guys lied and said I just barged in, wanting a fight."

"But what about the girl? Surely she—"

"Denied it to the cops."

"But how could she . . . ? Why?"

"She was embarrassed. And besides, she really wanted to make cheerleader and thought if she told, she might not make the team. She was sorry I got in trouble for helping her." He exhaled. "But I know it's common. Victims not wanting to say anything."

"Yeah, but . . ." Chloe put her palms on the table and leaned forward. She looked angry. It should have felt good, but it didn't. He felt exposed.

"It's still messed up." Her mouth thinned.

"Yeah, it was." Maybe it did feel a little good.

They both leaned back in silence, as if they both needed a time-out. He knew he did.

When she looked up, he took the lead. "So, my turn?"

She blinked. "I guess."

Are you trying to con the Fullers?

He couldn't ask that. "Why were you upset at the convenience store?"

She looked taken aback, but then sighed. "You want the truth? Or do you want me to pretty it up for you?"

He grinned, liking that she really listened. "The truth."

"I was pissed at my dad."

"For?"

"How much time do you have?" She smiled, but there was a sadness to it.

"All day," he replied, and meant it. He needed to figure her out. But a little voice said that wasn't all.

He liked watching her talk, her expressions, and how she moved her hands.

Liked listening to her voice, though he could do without the glint of sadness in her eyes.

"Up until a year ago, he was, like . . . the best dad ever. The dad who'd take me and my friends to school dances. When he picked us up, he'd take us out to eat at two in the morning. Then—" She paused. "—then he cheated on my mom with someone only seven years older than me. Now she's living with him. He's making a fool out of himself, trying to act younger, dyeing his hair, using gel. Oh, and he let her have my room for her gym. She has a Thighmaster and these weird machines where my bed used to be."

Her voice inched up. "She wears skirts up to here!" She lifted her hand up high. "And a neckline down to here." She placed her hand low on her breasts. His gaze went there, but he didn't let it linger, even though he wanted to. "Oh, and he told me he would call me the first day of school and he didn't. Because he's too busy screwing Tight Ass."

Cash laughed, but when he saw her painful expression, he pulled it in. "Sorry. That sucks."

"Yeah. It sucks." She pushed her drink away, then sighed. Sighed just like Ms. Fuller did when she was disappointed. A deep sad sound that hurt him to hear. A sound that made him want to believe her.

She looked up, and he could see her holding back tears. "Sorry I unloaded on you. So not cool."

"Hey, I asked."

"I have to go," she said abruptly, and was out the door in a flash.

Still wondering what had happened, he watched out of the window as her car drove off. When he looked down, he saw her credit card still lying on the table.

An hour later, he'd finished his homework at the coffee shop and decided to buy a little time before running by Chloe's house to give her the credit card.

He dialed the Fullers' home phone and was surprised when it was Mr. Fuller who answered. "Hey, I was going to call you. Is everything okay?"

"Yeah," Cash answered. "I stopped off at a friend's to do homework. Is it okay if I show up around six?"

"Sure. It's just you and me tonight. Susan had an emergency at the hospital. I thought we'd go out and bring her something back. Maybe pick up ice cream, too."

"It's that kind of emergency?" Cash's chest tightened.

Mr. Fuller was a general practice doctor and didn't have that many emergencies. Mrs. Fuller's crises meant she either lost a patient or one was in bad condition. She always took it hard.

"Afraid so," he answered.

Cash wasn't so close to Mr. Fuller, but he couldn't deny how much the man loved his wife. For that alone, Cash respected him.

Some of the distance was Cash's own fault. After eleven years with his dad, and some not-so-great foster dads, he'd resisted a father figure. Mr. Fuller made an effort, though. Last year, after Cash had started taking college classes and dating older girls, Mr. Fuller gave him the sex talk and a pack of condoms.

"You want barbecue or pizza?" Mr. Fuller asked.

"I think she likes barbecue better."

"Sold. Don't be later than six. I want to be back before she gets home."

"Why don't I just meet you at the restaurant?"

When Cash hung up, he considered how all the Chloe stuff would affect Mrs. Fuller. If he went to them now, and it turned out Chloe wasn't Emily Fuller, that could bring back all the pain of losing her the first time, like it had when that guy conned her last year. Cash couldn't say anything to them until he was sure.

Mom and I are waiting for my tire to be replaced. The television in the waiting room is talking politics. We are thumbing through magazines. I remember when Mom used to go through magazines to find characters for her books. It's sad she stopped writing.

I look over and she's staring at a magazine, wearing her faded bandanna. Normally, she wears a wig when we go out.

Not today. I can't wait for her hair to grow back. For her to gain weight. I'm tired of her looking like the walking dead.

"Did you eat lunch today?" I flip the page.

She looks up. "Yes."

"What did you eat?"

"A sandwich. I think."

"With chips?"

"No."

"You should have eaten chips."

She grins. "Are you the food police?"

"No. I'm your daughter who thinks you're too thin. Seriously, you need to eat more. We should go out for an early dinner. Something fattening."

"Pizza?" She grins.

"With extra cheese."

"Deal."

"And you're having a beer."

She chuckles. "I can't drink with my meds."

"What meds?"

"The pill I take for three years that helps keep cancer away."

I sit up straighter, a pain lodging in my chest. "Do they think it'll come back?"

"No." She bumps me with her shoulder. "The medicine is to assure it doesn't."

I nod, suddenly worried.

"Holden?" A man wearing coveralls walks in from the garage.

"Here." Mom stands.

"Good news. There's nothing wrong with your tire."

"But it was flat!" I say.

"Well, sometimes a tire can go low due to change in temperature, but since that hasn't happened, I'd say someone let your air out."

"Why would someone do that?" Mom asks me.

"I don't know." Then I recall Cash standing beside my car. He wouldn't, would he?

"Could be worse," the mechanic says. "They could have sliced your tires."

At four thirty, Chloe still wasn't home. The same at five. Finally, at five thirty, Cash saw her car and pulled into the drive.

He grabbed her credit card and slipped it into his front pocket. Stepping up on the porch, he saw a big window with the curtains open. He peered in. A woman was sitting at the dining room table. She was wearing a bandanna, but beneath it, there wasn't any hair. Her cheekbones were too prevalent. Her eyes sunken in.

The sight yanked him back to when his dad had shaved Cash's hair and eyebrows for a photo. He'd lost ten pounds, going hungry for almost a month; then his dad put makeup beneath his eyes to make him look even worse. It worked. His dad had been proud of the money people donated to save his sick boy.

But this woman wasn't wearing makeup. His chest hurt for Chloe. Was her mom going to pull through? He even hurt for Mrs. Fuller. This was the type of patient she saw. The kind who died on her no matter how hard she tried to save them.

Taking a resigned breath, he knocked. The woman's gaze found his in the window. When she stood, she looked even thinner.

The front door opened, and he introduced himself. "Hi. I'm Cash. I go to school with Chloe. Is she home?"

The woman smiled. "Come in. I'm JoAnne Holden, Chloe's mom. She's in her room." She called out, "Chloe?"

He walked inside. A red tabby cat, just like Felix, jumped down from a chair.

"Would you like something to drink?"

"No. Thank you." His palms felt sweaty. Was he just nervous to meet the mom? Or was it that this woman could've been the one who kidnapped Emily Fuller that made him uncomfortable?

Chloe walked in. Her posture was tight, her eyes accusing. Weren't they past that stage?

"Let's go in the backyard." She darted past him.

He nodded at her mom and followed Chloe through the living area and onto a back patio.

She swung around. "Shut the door."

He did, but the look in her eyes said he'd better find an escape route.

"How did you know where I live?"

Her question brought a whisper of relief. He had this. "You told me you lived in Oak Tree Subdivision. I drove around until I spotted your car. I brought this to you." He pulled her credit card out of his pocket. "You left it."

She took it, suspicion still tightening her eyes. "Did you let the air out of my tire?"

The question came out punchy and hit him right in his solar plexus. He'd known this might come up, and his plan had been to deny it. That was still his plan, but now it felt weak.

"Your tire didn't have a leak?" Did that sound convincing? Shit, it hadn't. He should've sliced the tire, but that would've cost her money.

"No." Her hand settled on her hip. "Did you let the air out?"

"Why would I do that?" *Answer a question with a question. It throws people off.*

"I don't know. But someone did it. And you were there."

She wasn't easily thrown. "And I fixed it. I don't like changing tires that much. Wow, you really do have trust issues, don't you?"

From her expression, he gathered that was the wrong thing to say. "Yeah, I do. And right now, I don't trust you."

"Fine. Go online to make sure I didn't use your card." He shoved the card at her, then left through the outside gate.

What was messed up was that he felt hurt she didn't believe him, even though she was completely right not to.

7

It was eleven when Cash's stomach decided he needed dinner. He hadn't had much of an appetite after he left Chloe's and had spent most of the evening up in his room after meeting Mr. Fuller to pick up barbecue.

When he quietly walked downstairs and opened the fridge, he saw Mrs. Fuller sitting in the dining room—in the dark. Felix, her cat, was stretched out on the table, and she was slowly stroking his fur. Her back was to him, but she had to have heard him come in.

He went and stood beside her. She put Felix on the floor and wiped her cheeks before she looked at him.

"I'm sorry," he said.

She nodded. "Everyone is."

He sat down beside her. "You save a lot more than you lose."

She offered him a teary-eyed smile. "She was only a few

years older than you," she said. "A few years older than Emily. I wanted to save her." She inhaled. "It's hard losing any patient, but when they're young . . . I think if I could save them, then it might make up for . . ." She put her fingers over her trembling lips.

"Make up for what?"

She shook her head. "It was my fault. I was so busy with school. It was my day to watch Emily, but I called the nanny and asked her to take her."

"That doesn't make it your fault," he said sharply.

"I know. I'm just feeling sorry for myself. And tomorrow is . . . fifteen years since Emily went missing." She paused. "I hate that I couldn't save her."

Fifteen years. He wasn't even sure which one she was talking about not saving. The girl with cancer or her daughter. She patted her eyes and looked up at him. This close, he saw her pain-filled expression.

He put a hand on her arm. Where the words came from, he didn't know, but they left his lips. "You've saved me."

"Have I?" Her voice shook. "Sometimes I worry you haven't really let us close."

"You're closer than anyone has been." And it was so damn true.

She smiled through her tears. "Thank you. Is it too much to ask for a hug?"

He shook his head, even when he wished he could avoid it.

They stood, her arms surrounded him. He didn't move; the emotional pain went deep. His throat tightened.

She let him go quickly, as if sensing it was hard for him. "We love you like our own child."

You shouldn't. "I know." But they deserved their own daughter, and if he could—if at all possible—he was going to give her back to them.

I'm getting ready for school the next morning when my cell rings. Sure it's Lindsey, I answer it. I'm wrong.

"How's my baby girl?" It's the man who owes me an apology. Suddenly I want him to know he hurt me. It seems there's nothing left of the dad I knew. The guy who used to take me out for Indian food because Mom doesn't like it, the guy who used to hug me so tight, the guy who taught me to change a tire. He's gone. Gone.

"How's my girl?" he asks again.

"Fine."

"How's school going?"

"That's funny." But I'm not laughing.

"What's funny?"

"I thought you were going to call the first day of school to check on me."

"Oh." Guilt rides his one word. "I'm sorry, hon. It's been hectic."

This is where I should say it's okay and let him tell me how much he misses me. I can't.

"Good to know everything comes before me."

"Chloe! Don't say that."

"Why? It's true. You gave Darlene my room. You say you'll call, but you don't. What's next? You going to renege on paying child support?"

"What? Is your mom going around bad-mouthing me?"

"Yeah, but she has been for a while. What's different is that I'm finally realizing everything she says is true."

I hang up and start crying. But it kind of feels good. He deserved that.

Seeing the time, I realize I have to leave. I dart past Mom so she won't see I've been crying.

When I walk outside, Lindsey is waiting by my car. "What's wrong?"

"Everything."

She gives me a shoulder bump. "This may sound terrible, but now you're not faking it so well anymore, and I like you better."

I look at her like, *What the hell?*

"Before, you acted like Superwoman. I felt bad telling you my problems because you'd think I was pathetic." She goes around to get in the car.

"What are your problems?" I ask, to avoid looking more pathetic. I get behind the wheel. "Besides the cheating dog?"

She settles into the front passenger's seat and looks hesitant. "I won't bore you with details, but . . ." She comes off scared and serious. "My mom's gay."

I look at her. "I know that."

Her mouth drops. "It's that obvious?"

"Yeah. Your mom's girlfriend is always at your house, and when they watch TV they hold hands. Why's that—?"

"A big deal?" she finishes my sentence. "It's not. I'm happy she's found herself and found Lola. About two years ago, she got depressed. Then until seven months ago, she was on antidepressants, lonely, and miserable. She's so much happier now. And I'm so okay with it. But . . . not everyone is. And I'm afraid—"

"You shouldn't care what they think. Who your mother loves isn't anyone's business. I have family that's gay. It just doesn't matter."

Her eyes tighten. "You don't get it. It's not that I care what they think. I'm afraid the next time someone says something about her, I'm going to come unglued and jump their ass. That's my mom! I hate that the world judges her."

I smile. "Good. Who said something about her?"

"Clare, one of Jamie's cousins. It was right before Jamie left for camp. I didn't know Jamie had told her until she started saying how weird it must be for me. I just walked out. I didn't even say goodbye to Jamie. Later, I was so mad at myself for not defending my mom that now I'm champing at the bit for someone else to say something."

I cut her a look. "Tell you what. When someone says something, come get me and I'll help you give 'em crap. I'm getting good at it these days."

Lindsey sighs. "I'm so glad you moved next door."

I can't say that back, because I still long for my other life, but I smile. Right then, I know I'm not just Lindsey's sidekick. Like it or not, I've got myself a good friend. So I decide to confide in her about Cash and the tire incident.

"What if he just did it to have a reason to talk to you?" she asks.

"If he wanted to talk to me, he could've talked to me. He's not shy."

"You don't know that. He might not be as confident as he comes off."

Did I freak, because of my own insecurities? Because I didn't think he could possibly be interested in someone like me?

Did I automatically jump to the wrong conclusion, like everyone else? Remembering the story of how he'd been thrown out of his last school, because people believed the worst of him, I start feeling guilty.

"I'm such a bitch," I mutter, and Lindsey laughs.

Cash had decided to apologize. He'd do whatever it took to get back into Chloe's good graces. He needed answers, and the only way to find them was to get close to her. He had to find out if she was Emily Fuller.

He didn't know exactly what he needed to prove or disprove it. But his gut said he'd know it when he heard it. And he wasn't going to hear shit if she pushed him away.

He'd seen Chloe once at her locker, but before he got to her, she disappeared in the hall crowd. Walking to the American Literature class that they shared, he looked left and right, hoping to spot her. When he approached the door to the classroom, he saw her standing there, waiting.

Their gazes met and she started toward him. He wasn't close enough to read her expression. But tension pulled at his stomach.

She stopped in front of him, then waved him away from the door. "Hey. I—"

"Look, I—"

"Go ahead," he said. *Always let the other person talk first. Your game plan may have to change.*

She bit down on her lip. "I'm sorry. I shouldn't have accused you. That was rude." She glanced up. Her apology brightened her brown eyes. He saw the flecks of gold and green. Were they the same color as Mr. Fuller's?

Resting on his tongue was his own apology. When had dealing with girls gotten so impossible?

Instead, he nodded. "It's okay."

"No, it isn't." She paused as if it was his turn to say something, but he was too busy feeling like shit because he was guilty and should've been the one apologizing. She turned to leave.

"Wait." He caught her arm and felt that emotional jolt again. Like touching a live wire. But it faded and all he could feel was how soft her skin was. "Can we get together this afternoon?"

"Yeah." She smiled and didn't move.

It took a second to realize he still held her arm. He was even rubbing his thumb over her skin. But damn, he liked touching her.

He reluctantly let her go and followed her into class. Touching her might come with a spark of pain, but what came next—the warm, feminine softness—made it worth it.

8

After school, Cash drove to Chloe's house, but parked down the street. Waiting, he felt a tight ball of nerves in his gut. He'd been planning to suggest they meet at the coffee shop. Something about Ms. Holden gnawed at his stomach lining. Seeing her so sick, and questioning if she'd been the one to kidnap Chloe, made it difficult.

He wondered how hard it was on Chloe, seeing her mom so emaciated. And here he was going to compound Chloe's issues if he told her she was possibly Emily Fuller. He found himself thinking it'd be easier if she wasn't the Fullers' kid.

He wouldn't have to lie to her.

Chloe's car pulled into the drive.

He watched in his rearview mirror as Chloe's friend slipped a backpack over her shoulder. He'd noticed her last year. She wasn't one of the bitches.

Chloe got out of the car. Cash liked watching her, especially when she didn't know he was watching. She seemed somehow . . . different from other girls. When she'd run into people in the hall, she said excuse me. Most didn't. She smiled at other students—not just the popular people, like some girls did.

He also saw the guys looking at her. He couldn't blame them. He looked, too. It's just some of the guys were jerks.

Only when Chloe spotted his car did Cash get out.

"Come on in." Her hair swayed around her shoulders, and the red shirt clung to her breasts.

He followed her into the house.

"Mom," Chloe called out. "Cash's here. We're going to sit out back."

Cash heard her mother say something from a bedroom.

Chloe dropped her backpack on a dining room chair. "I'll bet your house is a lot nicer."

"Not really," he lied, because to say differently sounded rude. But until he came to live with the Fullers, this house was nicer than any he'd lived in. Hell, for six months, he and his father had lived in a shack in the woods without running water, electricity, or a bathroom.

He followed her through the house and saw some framed pictures on the sofa table. There were several of Chloe when she was like three. One of them called to him, like he'd seen it before. It was Chloe holding a red tabby cat. He picked it up. Was he imagining it, or was it almost the exact photo Mrs. Fuller kept in one of the extra bedrooms? He wished he could photograph it to compare them.

He looked up and realized she was watching him. "You were cute."

"Right." She motioned him outside. He recalled the last time he was here, she'd given him hell about the tire. Hopefully, not this time.

Once on the patio, a yellow medium-sized dog, of an unrecognizable mixed breed, came running up and barking. Not a threatening bark, but playful. Cash petted the animal.

"No. Don't jump up, Buttercup." Chloe moved to sit on the swing. He got the feeling she expected him to do the same. He lowered in the seat, purposely leaving several inches between them. But even that was too close. He could smell her. A fruity and flowery scent. Not perfume, but lotion and maybe lip gloss, because he noticed her mouth looked shiny.

The dog put his paw on Cash's leg. "She's cute."

"He," Chloe said.

"You named a boy Buttercup?"

"He was yellow. I was seven."

Cash chuckled. "You probably took away his manhood, too."

She lifted a brow and petted her dog. "Only after he got a neighbor's dog pregnant. And it was at my birthday party, too. My entire school class attended. I had a jumping house, a clown, and sex education."

He laughed and realized he did that a lot around Chloe. Then what she'd said landed. He hadn't really thought about what her childhood would've been like, but it didn't sound bad. Did people who threw elaborate birthday parties kidnap children?

He'd never had a birthday party. He'd had only one birthday cake before he got to the Fullers'. Now it was like clockwork. Cake and presents. And Mrs. Fuller always took the day off and cooked him anything he wanted. If he didn't tell her what he wanted, she cooked the things she knew he liked. Was that what Chloe had?

Realizing the silence had grown awkward, he said, "Sounds like a good birthday."

"It was memorable."

"I don't care!" Chloe's mom's raised voice leaked out from behind the closed back door.

Chloe frowned.

"Well, I've only said the truth!" Her mom's voice carried again.

"Shit." Chloe bolted up from the swing. "Be right back." She tore off inside. The dog sitting next to him whimpered. As the door closed, he heard Chloe say, "Mom! Cash's here."

Her mom's voice exploded again. "Maybe you should have thought about that before you started screwing someone who could've been her sister! Yeah, I said that. You're a piece of shit. And she's a bitch!"

"Mom! Stop!" Chloe's voice rang louder.

"Goodbye!" her mom yelled out, and then . . . "Did you tell your dad I was bad-mouthing him?"

Cash put his feet down to stop the squeaking motion of the swing so he could hear what came next. "I . . . can we talk about this later? Cash's here."

"Why would you tell him *anything* I said?" her mom yelled.

Chloe's voice came next. "I didn't mean . . ." Pain sounded in her voice. The same kind of pain he'd heard yesterday when she told him about her father.

"That man's a bastard! And you can tell him I said that!"

A door slammed inside. Cash ran his hands down his jeans and wondered if he should leave.

Chloe stepped back outside.

Her face was red. She had her arms crossed tightly over her chest as if angry or embarrassed. Maybe both.

She met his eyes. "Look, I'm going to give you a piece of advice—leave and forget about me. You don't want a part of this dysfunctional crap."

He didn't move, searching for something to say that would make her feel better. "I've lived in far worse dysfunction. This is just divorce problems."

She came over and dropped down on the swing. "I'm sorry."

When she turned her face up, he saw tears webbing her long dark lashes. "Seriously, it's okay."

"I'm a mess. You don't want . . ." She bit down on her lip.

"No. They're the mess. You're just an innocent victim."

He couldn't believe he was recycling some of the old psycho crap that had been tossed at him when he was in the hospital after being shot. The psychologist was there when he woke up. He remembered asking her, "Am I going to jail?"

She'd tried to console him. "No. You didn't do anything wrong."

He remembered sticking out his chin, willing to take his punishment. "Yes, I did."

"You aren't a bad person. It was your dad who did bad things. You're young, you did what you had to do to survive."

Next to him, Chloe shook her head. "No. I'm not innocent this time." Again, she bit down on her lip. "Dad called this morning, and I said something I shouldn't have. I was wanting to hurt Dad, not Mom."

He wasn't sure what provoked him to do it, but he placed his arm over Chloe's shoulders. A jolt of pleasure went through him but pain came with it. The pain left.

She let out that sad sound again—one so much like Mrs. Fuller's, it reminded him why he was really here. Before he could move his arm, she leaned against him.

He tried not to flinch. "It's still on them. Not you."

She looked up. They were so close that he could count her lashes. And that gave him a front-row seat to the hurt in her brown eyes.

"You're pretty good at this," she whispered.

"At what?"

"Knowing the right thing to say."

"That's odd. I usually suck at it." He forced a smile,

feeling every inch of her that came against him. Feeling all kinds of rightness, but wrong, too.

"Did your parents get a divorce?" she asked.

Air caught in his throat. The last thing he wanted to do was talk about his past. "No. They're dead."

"What happened? Sorry, I shouldn't . . ."

Buttercup bumped against his knee holding a yellow tennis ball in his mouth. He pulled his arm free and tossed the ball for the dog. "Your mom seems really angry."

"She's more than angry. She's bitter."

Chloe looked at the door, and her expression went sad again. "I can't blame her, except . . . it hurts to hear her constantly belittle my dad. I know he deserves it. But—" She dropped her face in her hands. "Blast it. I'm doing it again."

"Doing what?"

"Barfing my problems all over you."

He grinned. "I can handle a little barf."

She laughed and leaned back. They were even closer now. He inhaled. "Is it cancer?"

"Yes."

"Is she going to be okay?"

The anger in her eyes shifted to sadness. "Doctor said she's cancer-free. But I just learned . . . it could come back." Chloe paused. "I can't wait until she stops looking like . . . she's dying."

"I'm sorry." He almost told her Mrs. Fuller was an oncologist, but talking about the woman he thought could be her mother felt wrong.

Their eyes met. Locked. Her mouth came against his.

He jerked back.

She flinched. "I'm sorry."

"No. I just. I wasn't . . ." He couldn't look away from her mouth. Then he leaned in. His senses went on hyperalert. He became aware of everything. How she tasted. A little salty, like tears. How her lips felt. Soft, warm. Moist. How she'd inched closer and her breasts pressed so sweetly against his ribs. He wanted her closer, to let his hand circle her waist, to slip his hands under her red shirt to feel skin in the places he hadn't gotten to see.

Realizing how wrong it was, he ended the kiss, but managed to do it slowly.

She smiled. "That was nice."

"Yeah. Real nice."

But holy hell, he was getting in too deep. This could end badly.

Cash parked in the garage, walked into the house, and punched in the number to shut down the alarm. He'd left after they kissed the fifth time. Five. He kept telling himself he needed to stop, but he couldn't. Not when she sat so close, so willing, looking up at him with warmth mingled with sadness. She needed to be kissed and he needed to kiss her.

He bolted up the wooden steps and went down the hall to the bedroom where Mrs. Fuller kept all the memorabilia of the daughter she'd lost. Photographs, stuffed animals the child had played with, books he imagined Mrs. Fuller read to her. The dresser still had some clothes in it. It was like a museum dedicated to her daughter.

When he turned on the light, he found the bed was unmade. He'd bet Mrs. Fuller slept in here last night. She did that when she was dealing with something.

He walked to the shelves that held books and framed photographs. He found it. An image of Emily Fuller holding a kitten. Not just any kitten, but Felix. The red tabby almost identical to the one in the photograph at Chloe's. Equally identical was the girl.

He picked it up.

Mrs. Fuller had told the story of how Emily loved Felix many times. They'd found the kitten as a stray. Hence the reason Mrs. Fuller loved the cat so much. Was this part of the puzzle? Or did all decent parents have pictures of their kids with their pets? But how could these two girls look so alike? And was it a coincidence that the kittens looked alike, too?

He pulled out his phone to photograph it.

9

Aware of every little noise I hear from Mom's bedroom, I stick the leftover pizza in the oven, hoping the smell of it cooking will draw her out. Cash left an hour ago, but Mom hasn't shown her face. Is she crying? Moping? Pissed?

Part of me feels like demanding she come out. She's acting like an angry kid.

When did I turn into the parent of this relationship?

Oh yeah, when she got cancer. Or maybe even when Dad left.

I take my frustration out on the lettuce, tomatoes, and carrots I'm chopping. Felix meows and circles at my ankles.

With my hands on automatic, my mind wanders. I'm caught between angst over Mom, and walking on clouds at being kissed by Cash. Kissed five times. I initiated the first kiss. I mean, his mouth was so close and I just did it. But the other four are on him.

I can close my eyes and feel his lips against mine. I savor

the memory and the . . . the brand-new feelings blossoming in my chest. Hope. Excitement. Anticipation.

Since Mom and Dad started having problems, I've felt like someone stole my joy. But maybe it wasn't stolen, just suppressed. Maybe . . .

Mom's door off the hall opens. She walks into the kitchen bringing a cloud of depression.

"I'm heating the pizza," I say.

"I'm not hungry."

"You have to eat." Yup, I'm the parent.

Our eyes meet. I see hurt in her sunken eyes. What joy I have in my chest wilts like a flower left in a vase with no water, and I feel guilty. "I didn't tattle on you to Dad. He called this morning and I was angry."

"At what?"

"He told me he'd call the first day of school and didn't. When I called him out on it, he asked if you were bad-mouthing him and if that was why I was being ugly. I told him that, yes, you'd been talking bad about him but that wasn't the problem. It was that I was realizing everything you said was the truth. I didn't mean . . ."

She sits down. "So he said he'd call and didn't?"

This isn't helping. Now she's going to get mad again. I borrow some of that anger. "Don't do this."

"Do what?"

"Get mad."

"How can I not be mad? Look what he's done to me!" She yanks off her bandanna.

"What happened to you being happy the other day? Telling me that it was all going to work out?"

"Your father happened!" Tears fill her eyes.

Tears fill my eyes, too. I sit down beside her. "Mom, you need help. You need counseling or something. You might have survived cancer, but this bitterness is gonna kill you."

Without a word, she goes back into her bedroom.

I shut off the oven, stomp off to my room, and slam my door.

Neither of us eats dinner.

The next morning when I step out of my room to pee, Mom calls my name. She's sitting in the kitchen, swallowed by her pink nubby robe. "Can we talk?"

I try to read her mood. Is she still angry? Still depressed? When I get closer, I pick up something else. Guilt.

"Sit down." She motions to the table.

I sit across from her. The dark circles under her eyes are darker. She's not sleeping.

"I'm sorry," Mom says. Tears rim her green eyes. "I had a bad day yesterday. The doctor's office was supposed to call back about the job, and they didn't call. I'm worried they changed their mind. And the medicine I'm taking causes flulike symptoms. I started feeling sorry for myself then your dad called, and I lost it." She takes my hand. "I'm sorry I had a meltdown in front of your friend."

While I wish I could believe everything is okay now, I can't. This isn't her first apology.

"I love you, Mom," I say. "And I forgive you. But you need to get counseling."

"I just had a bad day."

I stiffen my shoulders and tell myself I'm the parent. "It's more. You stopped writing. Stopped living. Stopped eating. You haven't just had a bad day—you've had a bad year. I see commercials that says there's all kinds of medicine for depression."

"Honey, I don't need—"

"You do, Mom." I look her right in the eyes.

She hesitates, then begrudgingly says, "I'll see if it's covered by our insurance."

It wasn't a yes, but it wasn't a no either.

I finish getting ready, hug her, and remind her to call the insurance company. When I go outside, Lindsey's by my car. She'd texted me last night about an hour after I'd barricaded myself in my room. I begged off going to her house, but I did call her. I didn't tell her about Mom—I wasn't ready to talk about it—but I did tell her about Cash. About us kissing.

When she sees me, she grins. "Still floating on cloud nine?"

"Just cloud seven." I get into my car.

Lindsey pops into the front passenger's seat. "I can't believe you're dating Cash Colton. He's the hottest guy in school."

"Whoa! I'm not dating him. Not yet."

When I pull out, I see Mom looking out the window. Make that cloud six.

"Okay, let me rephrase," Lindsey says. "I can't believe you're making out with the hottest guy in school."

"Five kisses isn't making out."

"Hmm," Lindsey says. "I think it is. Let's see what Google says." She grabs her phone, and in a few seconds, she's silently reading and laughing.

"What?" I ask.

"Well, according to the Urban Dictionary, there are several meanings for 'making out.' Just kissing is one. Kissing with tongue is another." She looks at me. "Did you get tongue with Cash?"

"A little," I say.

"Oh yeah!" She refocuses on her phone. "Oh, here's another: 'Petting, dry humping, or removing articles of clothing.'"

"We did not remove any clothes!" I laugh.

She continues. "Listen to this one: 'Anything that doesn't include penetration.' Penetration? That sounds so naughty."

That brings a snort out of me, and afterwards I ask, "So when are you going to approach David?"

"I'm not. If he likes me, he'll approach me." Lindsey buckles her seat belt. "Guess who texted me last night?"

"Who?"

"Jonathon."

"The cheating dog?" I start driving.

She nods.

I put the brakes on too suddenly at a stop sign. The car jerks forward. "No," I say adamantly.

"'No,' what?"

"No, you're not getting back with him! He treated you like shit."

"But—"

"No buts! I wouldn't be your friend if I let you get back with him."

She drops her chin to her chest. "You're right."

"Talk to David today!"

"Maybe," she said.

"No maybes. Do it! And I'm not even saying to date him, but just . . ."

"Just what?"

"Feel the buzz of knowing it's possible. Find your girl power and stop thinking you need Jonathon to make you happy. Sometimes I think we need to know another guy likes us to make us feel good about ourselves. Sometimes we just need to know we could have a guy to realize that maybe we don't even need one."

"Is that what you're doing with Cash? Finding your girl power?"

The question rolls around my head. "Maybe. I don't know yet." But when I think about him, I can feel there's more.

———

Cash walked into school early. He told himself his eagerness to get there had nothing to do with Chloe.

Nearly all he thought about last night had been her. Wondering if she was Emily. If she'd enjoyed kissing him as much as he enjoyed kissing her. Was she going to hate him when he told her what he suspected?

When he turned down the hallway, he saw her. He slowed down and watched. Watched the way her hair shifted across her back as she unloaded her backpack into her locker.

He moved in and stood beside her. "Hey."

She turned and smiled. "Hi."

"Hi." His gaze went straight to her lips and he wanted to kiss her. He'd never been one for public affection, but he could tell it would be easy to change his mind.

Realizing that staring at her lips was awkward, he saw the math book she held against her breasts. But letting his gaze linger there would be even more awkward, so he spit out the words, "Going to calculus? Do you have Mr. Williams? I have him fourth period."

He knew she had Mr. Williams, since last night he'd read and reread the file he photographed in Ms. Anderson's office.

"Yeah," she answered. "He seems okay. What do you have first period?"

"History." The bell rang.

"I should go," she said. "I'll see you in American Lit."

"Yeah." He leaned in. "I enjoyed yesterday."

She smiled, and those soft brown eyes glanced up at him through her lashes. "Me, too."

She eased away. He watched her move down the crowded hall. The black jeans she wore fit almost as well as the blue jeans she wore yesterday.

He stayed there watching until his view was obstructed by other students.

Considering he was in mostly honors, it was odd that they had only one class together. Just bad luck. Or maybe it was because he took auto tech.

Last year, when he'd set up his classes, Ms. Anderson tried to talk him out of it. "But I can't keep you in all honors classes if you take auto tech. You could take another math to be better prepared for college courses."

He explained that he planned on taking college math on his own time before he graduated. And he was. Tonight was the first class.

"So, you're going to college?" She'd asked as if she didn't expect he would. Now that he knew she'd been in the foster system, he was kind of disappointed that she'd automatically thought the worst of him. Regular people did that, not people who understood.

Or maybe she understood too well. Most foster kids who came through the system ended up in jail. When he'd read that statistic, it hurt. He thought about the few foster kids he'd actually liked. Not that he'd stayed in touch with them. Doing so was almost impossible given the number of times he'd moved.

As he made his way to history class, he recalled Ms. Anderson's next question. She'd asked, "Then why take auto tech?"

He'd told her. "Because I like it."

And he did. But another truth was, once school was over, he didn't plan on taking handouts from the Fullers. If something happened to his car, he'd better be prepared to fix it.

Plus, the garage was giving him bigger jobs now that they knew he was in auto tech, and he hoped to work for an auto shop while he went to college.

It bothered him that the Fullers bought him the Jeep.

They convinced him the cash they received from fostering him had paid for it. But he knew better. And he was determined to pay them back.

After lunch, I go to my locker to get my books. Locker open, I pull my phone out of my purse and send Mom a text. *Have you called insurance?*

She needs to know I'm not dropping this.

I'm waiting to see if she'll answer when I feel someone standing beside me. I'm all smiles, thinking it's Cash. But when I look up, I see the face of a bully with a very bruised nose. The nose Cash gave him.

"Hey," he says. "I'm Paul Cane. Quarterback."

I look at my phone again, hoping he'll go away. He obviously thinks I should be impressed with his football position. "Yeah?"

"Chloe, right?" he asks.

"Yeah."

"I thought I'd do you a favor."

That has me lifting my gaze.

"I saw you hanging out with that Cash guy. You probably haven't heard, but he's a foster kid."

This rolls over me like lemon juice on a deep paper cut. "So?" I hear the sharp edge to my one-word response, and I hope he does, too.

He must have, because he appears disappointed. "I know some kids who go to Cash's old high school, and rumor has it, he's bad news."

I send him one of my tight, not-pleasant smiles. "Good thing I don't waste my time on rumors, then."

His gray eyes darken. "They say he killed his dad. Shot him right in the heart."

That sends a jolt through me, but I don't dare show it. "Like I said, I don't pay attention to rumors."

I start to walk off, but he catches my arm.

"You should." His tone is the same pompous one he used with the sophomore he'd been bullying. As if he's smarter, superior. But I see him for what he is: a jerk.

I glare at his hand and pull away.

Shoulders tight, I slam my locker a little too hard. It clanks, and the echo bounces down the hall. People turn and stare.

As I start walking, my mind starts racing. Could Cash have killed his father?

10

When the last bell rings, Lindsey meets me at my locker and we walk toward my car. I'm disappointed that Cash didn't meet me. All day I've thought about what Paul said. Not that I believe it.

I know Paul's a jerk who'd say anything to hurt Cash. And if Cash knew what he said, he'd be upset. Which is why I'm not telling him.

As Lindsey and I get close to my car, I see him leaning against it. I recall with clarity how it felt to kiss him. A smile works its way to my lips and then to my eyes.

Nope. He's no murderer.

"You want me to hang back?" Lindsey asks.

"No," I say.

We walk up, and all I can see is Cash. How his green eyes are watching me watch him. How he's almost smiling. "This is Lindsey."

Cash does the polite thing and says, "Hi. I saw you around last year."

"Yeah." She pulls out her phone. "I need to text . . . someone."

She moves around to the other side of the car. I know she's just giving us some privacy, and I appreciate it. I walk closer. "I hope your class goes okay tonight."

"Yeah," he says. "I just wanted to say bye."

I look up at him. His black eye is fading. A brush of wind stirs his dark hair from his brow. I wonder if he wants to kiss me again. I know I want to kiss him, but I used up my gutsiness when I kissed him first yesterday.

"Is it okay if I text or call you later?" he asks.

"Yeah." We trade numbers.

"You can call me, too." He brushes a hand down my arm. I know then he's not planning on kissing me. But the touch somehow leaves me just as breathless.

I stand there and watch him walk away. He turns once and smiles. This feels so good.

"No kiss?" Lindsey asks after we get in the car.

"No." I offer a grin and almost tell her how amazing I feel.

She sighs. "Do you know how crazy this is? Seriously, girls were, like, throwing themselves at him, and he ignored them."

"Crazy," I say, and insecurity hits. I know he said I look like someone, and that's what started this, but if Cash could have any girl he wants, what's he doing with me?

I push that thought aside and look at Lindsey. "Did you talk to David today?"

She smiles. "I did."

"And?"

"I found some girl power," she says. "And if he asks me out, I'm going. I don't know what it is about him, but I like him. He's refreshing."

"Good." As we wait in line to exit the parking lot, a knock sounds on the front passenger-side window. It's Jamie.

Lindsey rolls down the window.

"Hey," Jamie says to Lindsey, not even giving me a nod. "You want to ride home with me and do homework together?"

"Uh . . ." Lindsey looks at me as if she feels bad.

"Go," I say.

"Okay, then," Lindsey says.

I watch Lindsey jump out of the car and walk off with Jamie, telling myself I'm not jealous. The car in front of me moves up another space. I do the same. I look in my rearview mirror and see them laughing. *I'm not jealous*, I repeat, but it stings a little anyway.

Cash left Chloe, worried he should've kissed her. He headed to his Jeep. She looked like she wanted to be kissed. Maybe he'll text her and say that he wanted to. Yeah. Then he wondered again if any of this was wise. How mad was she going to be when he told her the Emily thing? It's not as if liking her had anything to do with that. He hadn't planned on liking her.

Surely, she'd understand.

But he needed to tell her soon. Real soon. He didn't know what he was waiting for. More proof?

He got to his Jeep and saw the driver's door. Anger boiled in his gut as he stared at the thin line etched down the side of the car. Some asshole keyed his Jeep. And he'd bet that asshole had a fat nose, too.

He stood there clenching and unclenching his fist. He wanted to find that bastard and teach him a lesson. Then he remembered Mrs. Fuller's sad sigh.

While he knew Paul did it, he had no proof. Just as he'd had no proof about the rape. Who'd believe him? No one. If he went after Paul now, he'd be accused of starting the fight. He'd get in trouble. Might get kicked out of school again.

"Shit!" He forced himself to get in his Jeep. He sat there gripping the wheel so tight, his fists hurt. Somehow, some-way, he had to teach that asswipe a lesson, without getting in trouble.

I pull up in the driveway and sit staring at the old house. I'm afraid to go in. Afraid that there'll be mama drama. I'm tired of drama.

Mom told me that this was the first place they'd come after the adoption. She'd been so excited to show me off to her parents. Why don't I remember that? Instead, my only memory is staring at that dirty carpet and my black leather shoes. Sad, alone. Scared. I wonder if I was missing my real parents that day. I wonder why they didn't want me any-more.

I wonder why the hell I'm spending time thinking about this. It always ends up with me feeling sorry for myself. Feeling pathetic. And I don't want to be that girl.

I grab my backpack and get out of the car.

Walking into the house, I prepare myself for another standoff with Mom. She never answered my text about call-ing the insurance company.

She's in the kitchen. Dressed. That's a good sign. But with her clothes two sizes too big, she reminds me of a poorly dressed mannequin.

After stepping into the kitchen, I set my backpack on the table. Mom's smiling, and I can't help but wonder if this is a ploy. "How was your day?"

"Great!" she says.

"Did you start writing again?" She used to be really happy on a good writing day.

"No. I got a call from the doctor's office. I have an interview tomorrow to meet with the other doctor. I freaked out over nothing."

"That's great, Mom."

I hate to rain on her happy parade, but I have to ask. "Did you call the insurance company?"

Her smile dims. "I did. They are sending me an email with a list of counselors."

"Isn't there just a website you can go to?"

"Yes, but it's being updated, so she'll send it to me when they have it up."

I don't know if this is a stall tactic, but I don't know how I can argue with it. "Good. I just want—"

"I need to go shopping," she interrupts. "I wore the only nice outfit I have for the first interview. And since today is September fourth—" She blows me a kiss. "—I thought we could celebrate. I'll buy you an outfit, too."

I forgot the day.

When I was younger, September 4 felt like a second birthday. Gifts and cake. It's the day they adopted me. We always celebrated. Last year, after Dad moved out, he sent me flowers.

I give the kitchen counters a quick check. No flowers. Maybe they'll come later. Or maybe Dad forgot, too.

Mom's still grinning. "Where would you like to eat?"

I force myself to look interested. I think I'm still pissed at her for embarrassing me in front of Cash, but I do the right thing. "There's that Italian place off Main Street."

———

Home by eight that night, I hug Mom, tell her I had fun helping her pick out an outfit, and say thank you for the blouse. I bypassed getting another pair of jeans, because I know money's tight.

Actually, I did have an okay time. Mom was . . . almost normal. We didn't mention Dad, the phone call, or the insurance. We ate chicken marsala and tiramisu, and she talked about growing up here. She even mentioned a few of her old girlfriends, and I suggested she try to contact them.

On the way home, she asked about Cash. *Is he your boyfriend? What do you know about him?* My answers—not yet and not much—were short and meant to shut her down. Since Lindsey mentioned how all the girls practically threw themselves at Cash, I've been questioning his interest in me. Besides, five kisses do not make a boyfriend, and I don't feel like going into the he's-a-foster-kid talk. But it does make me think about how little I know about him.

After grabbing a bottled water, I head off to my room to do homework and to figure out what I'm going to text Cash. Or why he hasn't texted me.

I hate that I feel like this. Why can't I just text him? I worry I'll say something stupid and he'll stop liking me. I worry he hasn't texted, because he ran into some really pretty college girl.

Yup, I'm an insecure little twit. I always blame it on the adoption. Knowing my real parents gave me away. Sometimes I want to find them and ask why.

I fall back on my bed; Felix crawls on my chest. I listen to his purr, and it's calming. I hit my picture app and take a close-up shot. I have only half his face, but it's neat looking.

I finally push him off me, roll over onto my belly, and text, *How was class?*

Immediately, I see the three little dots appear. I smile and wonder if he was about to text me.

Cash: *Boring. Teacher was late.*

Me: *Sorry. You still at school?*

Him: *No. What did you do tonight?*

Me: *Went out for Italian food with Mom.*

Him: *Is she in a better mood?*

Me: *She's no longer a banshee.* ☺

Him: *Good.*

Felix crawls on my back and kneads my shoulders. I pause and stare at the phone. Should I say goodbye now?

Him: *I wish I'd kissed you in the parking lot.*

I laugh and squeal.

Me: *Me too.*

Him: *Can I see you tomorrow afternoon?*

I don't want to bring him here again.

Me: *How about I meet you at that coffee place after I drop Lindsey off?*

Him: *That works.*

Me: *Need to do homework, but cat won't leave me alone.*

Him: *The Fullers' cat is like that.*

I get a sad feeling that he doesn't think of the cat as his and he didn't refer to the Fullers' house as his home. I wonder if things are bad there. I want to ask but don't know how.

Instead, I attach the picture I just took of Felix and a note.

Me: *Meet Felix.*

Stretched out on the bed, Cash read the text. He shot up. *Shit! Her cat's name is Felix?* He tried to remember if he'd told her the name of the Fullers' cat. He hadn't. He hadn't even talked about the cat until now. *Right?*

Him: *Your cat's name is Felix?*

Her: *Yes.*

Him: *Who named it?*

Her: *I did. I was young. 3 or 4. Why?*

Shit! He bounced out of bed, paced the room.

But, damn it, if this was a con, it would be the perfect way to pull it off. Keep dropping hints until . . . It wasn't a con.

He stood there, his finger poised above the phone, not knowing what to type. What to say. He finally typed.

Him: *The Fullers' cat is named Felix.*

Her: *Great minds think alike.*

Him: *Yes.*

Her: *Did you name it?*

He sat back down, and emotions zip-lined through him, hitting nerves. He typed: *No. He's old.*

He had to tell her. Tomorrow. He'd show her the age-progression photo. Would she be angry? Shoot-the-messenger kind of anger? Would she be pissed he'd kept this from her? Would what they had end?

"Probably," he answered aloud. But he didn't have a choice.

11

"What are you doing?"

Shit. Cash looked up through his windshield. It was five in the morning, and he'd thought he could do this without anyone knowing.

Mrs. Fuller, still in her bathrobe, stood in the doorway of the garage. What time did she get up?

He hadn't told the Fullers about his car getting keyed. So now explaining why he was installing a camera in his car was going to be awkward. He had about one second to decide if he should tell the truth, or lie. Lying didn't seem right.

He got out of his Jeep. "I'm installing a camera."

"A camera? Why?"

"Yesterday someone keyed my door."

"What?" Frowning, she walked over and looked at the driver's side of his Jeep. "Why would someone do this?"

"I'm thinking it's the boy I fought with. But I can't prove it. So, I thought if I caught him again, I could be sure." What would he do if his plan worked? Oh, he had a few ideas. Most of them involved his fist, and all of them would land him in a shitload of trouble. But that was a bridge he'd cross later.

"Did you report it?"

"No."

She tightened her lips. "Why? The school needs to know this."

His gut knotted up. "Please let me handle it."

She stiffened. "And get into another fight with him?"

"I won't fight," he said, knowing that was going to be a hard promise to keep. "I don't know for sure he did it. It could even have happened at the college." That was a lie. "I don't want to accuse anyone without proof. If anyone does anything else, I'll know who."

"And what are you going to do when you know?"

"I won't start a fight. I promise."

She sighed that sad sound, and his chest shrank, knowing he was letting her down again. "We need to report it to the insurance. I'm sure it's covered."

"It's fine. I can live with this." Never mind it felt like he couldn't.

"You shouldn't have to. I'll let Tony know, and you and he can decide how to handle it."

Crap! He should've lied.

"Where did you get the camera?" she asked.

"At an auto store. I paid for it with my own money."

She released another slow breath. "You have our credit card. You could've used it."

Yeah, he had it, and never used it. Never would. He'd never take advantage of the Fullers more than he had to.

"Since you're up, join me for breakfast. I'm making toast and eggs."

He wanted to decline, but knew she'd be upset if he did. "Sure."

"Five minutes," she said.

He got the camera going in three minutes and went inside.

"Mr. Fuller not up?" Cash asked.

"He doesn't have a patient until nine, so he's sleeping in," she said.

"You want juice?" he asked.

"Please."

As he got to the counter, he saw what was lying there beside Mrs. Fuller's purse. His breath caught. "What are you doing with this?" He looked at the age-progression photo.

"Someone took the one that was at Walmart. I printed an extra."

He looked up at her as she was cooking eggs.

"Don't say it. I've already heard it from Tony." She set the skillet off the stove. "I know the chances of ever finding her are practically nil. I get that the picture that man showed me is probably a fake, I do. But what does it hurt to keep one up?"

She hugged herself. "I'd love to know who removed it."

Guilt tugged at his chest.

She pulled toast out of the toaster and set it on a plate. "Did they think it looked like someone? My mind goes all over the place. What if it's the person who took her? Everyone thinks she's dead. I get that." She put the toast on the table. "But what if she's not?" She looked up. "I'm not obsessing over it. I just . . . What would it hurt to keep the image up?"

He saw the hurt in her eyes and wondered if she and Mr. Fuller had argued over it. Cash had heard them arguing after they were conned. Mr. Fuller wanted her to let it go. She accused him of forgetting their daughter. "I'm sorry."

She frowned. "I know. Don't make a big deal out of this like Tony did. I'm fine."

She wasn't fine, Cash thought. She'd lost her child. Why was it that after fifteen years, Mrs. Fuller still longed for her girl, but his real mother had just gotten up one morning and walked out?

He heard his father's words: *She didn't give a shit about you.*

My alarm rings and I stumble toward the bathroom, still half asleep. Lights are on in the living room. The scent of coffee flavors the air. I slow down enough to peer around the corner and spot Mom, without her bandanna, sitting on the sofa. She's wearing that too-big robe and has a photo album in her lap. She turns a page. Something about the slowness of that turn sets the mood.

And it's not good.

Hoping I'm wrong, I go pee. Then I step out and move

into the living room, purposely adding a cheeriness to my tone. "Morning."

She looks up. I emotionally cringe at the tears in her eyes. I hope the insurance company emails that list of counselors today.

Moving closer, I feel like I'm walking into a bubble of sadness. My gaze shifts to the album. I'm expecting to see a picture of Dad, even though I think I confiscated and hid all his pictures when I found her yanking them out of the album and ripping them up. But it's not Dad's image she's staring at.

It's my grandmother when she was younger. I remember her.

Mom dusts a tear off her cheek. "I dreamed about her."

As I sit beside Mom, the sofa sighs. I stare at the image of a woman with light brown hair, light green eyes, and a bright smile. For the first time, I realize how much Mom looks like her. Yet, I haven't seen Mom smile that big in a long time.

She turns the page. There's a picture of both my grandparents. Mom was an only child, and they didn't have her until late in life. I'm told her father died soon after I was adopted.

Grandma died when I was seven. She always came and stayed with us at Christmas and during the summers. Back then, Mom worked full-time at the hospital and Grandma watched me. I remember her always eating and giving me tangerines; she even smelled like tangerines. She always read to me at night, and her hugs were extra tight. She called me Bug. I hated bugs, but I knew she meant it with love.

I also remember waking up one morning and finding Mom sobbing in the kitchen. Dad was holding her. He let go of Mom and pulled me aside and explained that Grandma had gone to heaven and Mom was sad. I remember crying that day, too. I had loved my grandmother. I was going to miss her tangerine hugs and the funny faces she made when she read to me.

But right now, because I came so close to losing Mom, I want to cry again—but for Mom this time. I can imagine all too well what it feels like to lose a parent.

"Was it a good dream?" I ask.

"Yeah. We were cooking. Peeling potatoes and laughing. I still miss her."

"I'll bet you do." My heart swells. I touch her head. "Hey, I see hair. Real hair, not just peach fuzz."

"Yeah, I noticed it, too." She smiles, but her eyes look tired.

"How long have you been up?"

"Since three."

"Go back to bed," I say.

"Nah. I've got to emotionally prepare for my interview."

"Oh yeah." I squeeze her hand. "Good luck."

"My interview isn't until four thirty. I'll see you before I go. I'm going to need you to remind me that I don't have anything to worry about."

No. No. No. I'm meeting Cash. The words sit on the tip of my tongue, but I can't push them out. "Sure."

Damn. Damn. Damn. I'm muttering under my breath twenty minutes later as I swipe some gloss over my lips. Why can't I just tell her good luck now? My mom needs a life, and until she has one, it's going to be hard for me to get one. The thought of leaving for college seems impossible. I get this image flashing in my head of growing old with Mom.

I stare at my face in the bathroom mirror and wonder if depression is contagious.

Truth is, I was probably depressed before school started. But having someplace to go every day, and maybe the excitement of finding Cash, and maybe even becoming better friends with Lindsey have made my life feel brighter. Better. Less bitter.

It gives me hope that Mom will feel the same way about her job. Between that and the counseling, maybe I'll get my mom back.

I hear Buttercup whining at the bathroom door. I open it and he's standing there with his leash in his mouth. "Sorry, buddy. I gotta go to school. Maybe this afternoon." And that's when I realize that although I might not be able to meet Cash right after school, Mom's interview will last long enough for me to see him while she's gone.

"You liked Cash, didn't you? It's okay if he joins us, right?"

Buttercup's tail wags. Ah, there is hope after all.

It was early when Cash got to Chloe's house. She'd told him to arrive at four thirty, so he parked four houses down and waited. His nerves were so tight, his shoulders hurt.

He touched his front pocket, where he'd put the folded progression photo.

How was he going to explain this? Would she be pissed? Would knowing this clue her in to all his other lies? The tire? The counselor's file? He kept telling himself he'd play it by ear, but his ear wasn't in the mood to play.

Needing something to do, Cash deleted video footage off the memory card of his car's camera. He'd gotten nothing today. But it might take a while before they got disappointed that he wasn't reacting and try again. That's what they wanted. A reaction. Paul wanted him to start a fight. So he could say, *See, Cash started this one* and *the last one.*

He wasn't going to give Paul what he wanted. In fact, today he went out of his way to walk past Paul and his friends, smiling the whole time.

He could tell it irritated the shit out of him, too.

Patience is the key. Wait people out. They'll screw up. They always do.

Down the street, he saw Chloe walking her mom to her car. Before her mom got inside, Chloe hugged her. He remembered her mom had a job interview today.

The scene struck him as odd. As if Chloe were the mom, not the daughter. All the more reason for Cash to worry the Emily thing could backfire. Her first reaction could be to defend her mother. No, he wasn't going to come out and accuse her parents of kidnapping, but it was implied.

His gut said to put it off, but would any time be a good time to tell her?

Chloe watched her mom drive off. When she turned to go back inside, her gaze shot down the street. She put her hand over her brow to block the sun and stared. Crap. She'd seen him.

He started the engine and pulled in front of her house.

Feeling like a Peeping Tom, he got out shrugging, trying to knock off the guilt. "I was early and didn't want to bother you."

"You didn't have to wait in the car." She didn't look upset. He realized he'd earned her trust. And now he was about to destroy it.

A smile brightened her face. A breeze stirred her hair. It was the perfect weather to go to the park. "Come in," she said. "I'll get Buttercup."

He followed her inside. She turned and looked at him. It was the first time they'd been alone since they kissed. Did she expect him to kiss her now? He wanted to. He'd thought about those kisses so much, the memory was tattooed on his brain. But it didn't seem right to kiss her again while he was still keeping this huge secret.

She called her dog. A bark came from the backyard, and she let him in. "You want to go to the dog park, buddy?"

She collected a leash and connected it to her dog's collar, then stopped. "I'll run and get a blanket to sit on."

While she ran to her room, he moved over to the family photos on the sofa table. He found the one with a young Chloe holding her cat. He realized another coincidence. Chloe and Emily were both wearing pink. He took out his phone to snap a pic, but heard footsteps and pocketed his phone again.

A red tabby cat followed her. He looked at the animal curling itself around her ankles. The two Felixes were identical. Was that why the young Chloe had given them the same name?

"Felix?" he asked.

"Yup. He's a sweetie." She dropped the blanket on a nearby chair and crouched down to pet the feline. The shirt she wore had a scooped neckline and it gave him a view. He should look away but couldn't.

"Felix, meet Cash," she said.

Chloe stood and he barely managed to shift his focus onto the cat. He grabbed the blanket, and as they walked out, she leaned close. The jolt of both pleasure and pain hit. In spite of the spark of discomfort, he loved touching her.

When they got to the park, Buttercup jumped out. Cash caught the leash, and Chloe grabbed the blanket. The park was mostly empty. They found a partly shady spot, and she spread out the blanket.

"Should I take the leash off him?" he asked.

"Yeah. He stays close." He sat down next to her and freed

the dog, who froze in place as if mesmerized by the ball in Chloe's hands.

She tossed it and he ran. Chloe grinned. "I apologize in advance. He's going to drive us crazy. He has a ball obsession."

"That's okay," Cash said. "I'm getting a Chloe obsession, so I can relate."

She laughed. "I think I'm getting a Cash obsession, too."

"Good," he said.

Smiling, she looked up at the sky. "It's a nice day."

He followed her gaze to the blue sky scattered with white puffy clouds. "Yeah."

She leaned back on the blanket. Her scooped neckline rose just high enough that he could look at her without gawking—her dark hair was strewn around her head, and the soft afternoon sun lit up her face.

He wanted to kiss her and skip the conversation.

Her brown eyes found his. "Did you ever find shapes of things in the clouds when you were a kid?"

"Find what?" he asked, so busy staring at her that he'd missed what she said.

"You know, like elephants or dragons. In the sky. Right now, I see a horse." She pointed up.

He tried to follow her finger. "All I see are clouds."

She laughed. "Use your imagination. Don't you see the head and the legs and the tail behind it?"

He tried. "Sorry."

"Mom and I used to go into the backyard and stare up for hours, trying to find things. She'd bring a bag of Skittles, and whenever one of us found something, we'd get a red one." She grinned.

"Why red?"

"Because they're the best. They're sweet, a tad sour, and taste like a reward."

He forced a smile and again tried to connect the personality of a kidnapper to someone who cloud-watched with her kid. Something felt off.

"Do you remember your parents?" she asked.

The question took him off guard. Buttercup came running back. Cash took the ball, grateful for the short reprieve, and tossed it again. "Not my mom. My dad, I do."

"What was he like?"

He looked back up at the sky. *A sorry piece of shit.* "I think I see the horse."

When he looked back at her, she was frowning. "You do that a lot."

"What?"

"Change the subject." She bit down on her lip. "You don't like talking about them, do you?"

"Not really." He inhaled. "Chloe, I need—"

"I feel like you know everything about me and I know nothing about you."

"I don't know everything about you," he said, trying to skirt the conversation.

"You know my dad's a cheating jerk. You know my boyfriend was named Alex and my mom had cancer."

"What kind of cancer?" he asked, and to his credit, he'd wondered about that. He'd heard Mrs. Fuller talk about the cancers that were harder to beat.

Chloe sat up. "Breast cancer." She pulled one knee close and hugged it. He could tell it was hard for her to talk about her mother's illness.

"But she's cancer-free now, right?"

"Yeah. It was caught early. My grandma had breast cancer, so Mom got yearly mammograms. She was afraid she had the cancer gene."

"Gene?" he asked.

"There's a breast cancer gene that's hereditary. She was tested and doesn't have it."

"I'm sure you're relieved," he said, not knowing what else to say.

"Well, since she's not my biological mom, it didn't affect me."

Her words ran around his head. *Not my biological mom.* Buttercup came running up. He dropped the ball beside Cash. Cash ignored it. "She's . . . not your real mom?"

"No. I'm adopted." She pulled her other leg up. "And there I go again, telling you about me. Since you know about Alex, tell me about your ex-girlfriend."

Chloe was adopted? Does that mean . . . ? "Adopted?"

"Don't change the subject. Tell me about your old girlfriend."

He had to focus to answer. "I dated a girl for a couple of months when I was sixteen."

"From the private school?"

"No, she lived in Langly."

"How did you meet her?"

"Her parents have a lake house next to the Fullers' vacation home, but . . ." *Not my biological mom.*

"What happened?" Chloe asked.

"She met someone else." He needed to tell Chloe right now.

Before he could push out one word, she continued. "Did you care about her?"

"No. Some. We only dated two months."

"And that's the only girlfriend you've had?" The tone said she wasn't letting this go.

"This summer, I dated a few girls at college."

"Older girls?" Her eyebrows rose as if it were a bad thing.

"Just by a year."

"Are you still dating them?"

"No. Chloe, I need—"

"How long have you lived with the Fullers?"

Buttercup butted the ball against his leg. He tossed it again.

"Right at three years."

She rested her hand on his arm. Her touch sent a spark of pain right to his chest. But then just as quickly, the spark turned sweet.

"How old were you when your father died?"

He put a finger to her lips. "Stop asking questions." His tone rang a little sharper than he liked. "I'm trying to tell you something."

She frowned. "Okay."

Great. He'd already pissed her off, and he hadn't even begun yet. He ran a hand through his hair. "I'm just going to show it to you."

"Show me what?" She tilted her head to the side like a curious puppy.

He pulled the folded progression photo from his pocket and handed it to her. She opened it.

She studied it, then looked at him. "What's this?"

He didn't see the recognition he expected in her eyes. His heart slammed against his breastbone. "It's an age-progression photo of Emily Fuller."

"Fuller, like your foster parents?"

He nodded.

Her brow tightened. "I still don't get why you're showing it to me."

"It's you. Can't you see it?"

She glanced at the photo again, eyes wide. "It's not me."

"It looks just like you."

"No. I mean, maybe a little, but not . . . really." She studied the image again.

He watched a crease appear between her brows. Was she seeing it now?

Now she looked concerned. "They . . . gave their baby up for adoption?"

12

"No," Cash says.

I'm trying to wrap my head around what he's saying. I look back at the photo. No, not a photo, but a drawing. Or a computer drawing. One of those shown on detective shows. I see the resemblance, but it isn't that close. Is it?

"Then it isn't me. I was adopted."

He looks apologetic. "She was kidnapped."

His words echo in my ears, and my response comes immediately. "And I wasn't."

"How old were you when you were adopted?"

"Wait. You think . . . ? This is crazy."

"I know it is, but just answer me. How old were you?"

"Almost three."

His eyes tighten as if that proves something. "Do you remember your real parents?"

"No. But you're not listening. I was adopted."

"Chloe, Emily Fuller went missing two months before her third birthday."

An uncomfortable feeling builds in my chest. "I was adopted. Not kidnapped."

"There's more." He takes out his phone, pulls something up, and gives it to me. "Look."

With one hand I'm holding the picture; with the other I'm holding his phone. Suddenly they feel heavy.

I almost don't look at the screen, then I do. It's the framed picture of me as a toddler with Felix. "Why did you take a picture of this?"

"Chloe, that's Emily Fuller. I snapped this picture at the Fullers'."

"No, this is the photo at my house." I look back at the image and realize I'm wrong. In the picture at home, I'm standing beside a swing set. "Okay, I look like her, but that doesn't—"

"The cat's name is Felix."

"Huh?"

"You said you named your cat Felix. The Fullers' cat is named Felix."

Air catches in my chest, a big bubble that crowds my organs. "A lot of cats are named Felix. There was a cartoon—"

"Your parents moved away right after they say they adopted you."

They say? That bubble became painful. "You think that my parents kidnapped me? You're nuts!"

I look at the photo again, and my thumb accidentally swipes the screen. The image changes. I blink and stare. It's a form. But it has my name on it.

"What's this?" I hold out the phone.

Guilt fills his eyes. "Your school files. I needed to find out if . . ."

"Find out what?" My backbone stiffens.

"I thought you could be trying to con the Fullers."

"Con them? What do you mean?"

"If you looked like their daughter, then maybe you were trying to get money from them."

I draw in a gulp of air, adding to the bubble. I shake my head. Nothing is making sense. I sit there, feeling the sun on my skin and his accusation under my skin.

"You think I'm trying to get money from them? What kind of a person would do that?" Then I remember what Cash said to me that day at the convenience store. *Whatever you're trying to pull, don't do it.*

"People do shit like that." His expression is almost angry. But he doesn't have a right to be angry. I do.

"That's what this—" I move a hand between us. "—is all about." I glance at the picture of the form. It has my address on it. "You didn't ride around my neighborhood looking for my car that day. You knew where I lived."

He doesn't answer. He doesn't have to. His expression tells the truth.

"You . . . You did let the air out of my tires!"

"I needed to get close to you to figure out—"

"None of this is real!" Anger swells inside, I can't contain it. I toss his phone at him and lunge to my feet. "You're insane."

He springs up, too.

I push my palms into my eye sockets; I see blackness, then flashes of light. "Oh God. I kissed you." I pull my hands away from my face and stare at him. "You . . . You don't even like me."

"That's not true. I kissed you back and then I kissed you four more times. I didn't mean to . . . fall for you, but I did."

I snatch up Buttercup's leash. "I'm going home."

"Chloe, don't. Let's talk."

"No." I hold up my hand. I call Buttercup. When he comes, I put the leash on him.

I take one step. Cash catches my arm. "I'll drive you."

I yank free. "No. I'm walking." I need to be alone. I

need . . . I don't have a freaking clue what I need except to be away from him. Away from his absurd accusations.

I hear him call my name, but I keep putting one foot in front of the other. I was adopted. Not . . . No. It isn't true. It can't be. I don't believe it. Then I remember the one memory: me sitting on a dirty sofa, looking at dirty carpet. I remember feeling so lost. So abandoned. So scared.

I continue walking. My knees are shaking, or is it the ground beneath me that's quaking? My whole world is shaking. This can't be true.

I walk fast. Buttercup keeps up. The sound of his paws hitting the street fills my head. Every time I hear a car, I'm afraid it's Cash.

My phone dings. I ignore it. As I get closer to home, I see Jamie's car in front of Lindsey's house. The two of them are on Lindsey's porch steps. I don't want to talk to them.

I realize I'm still holding the picture Cash showed me. I wad it up, start to toss it away, then change my mind and stuff it into my pocket. I dart off the sidewalk when I'm in front of my house.

"Chloe?" My name's being called from next door.

I ignore it and keep walking. Digging into my pocket for the key, I make the porch steps and pray they'll give up.

They don't. I hear them coming up the steps behind me. *Please go away.* I realize I'm crying.

"What's wrong?" It's Lindsey's voice, but I heard more than one pair of footsteps, so I know Jamie is with her. Jamie doesn't even like me. I don't want her to see me bawling like a baby.

"I can't talk now." I open the door, usher Buttercup in, shut the door in their faces, and I run into my bedroom. I fall on the bed, hug a pillow tight enough to kill the stuffing. Felix jumps up on the mattress trying to cuddle.

I don't believe it, I tell myself. So why am I so upset?

I tell myself it's because I made an idiot out of myself when I kissed Cash.

My phone dings. I ignore it.

Five minutes later, it dings again.

And again.

And again.

I yank it out of my pocket to cut it off, but I see there's a message from Mom.

Oh, freaking great! I swipe it to see what she says, knowing I can't be like this when she comes home.

Got Job! Filling out paperwork. Picking up Chinese for dinner. See you in an hour.

I hear a knock at my door. Shit! Is it Cash?

I go look out my window where I can see the street. His car isn't there, but I can't see who's on the porch from this angle.

My phone beeps again. It's Lindsey. *Worried. You okay?*

I text back. *You at the door?*

Yes.

Alone?

Yeeessss.

I wipe my face, pull myself up by the bootstraps, and walk to the front door.

"What's wrong?" she asks as soon as I open the door. She doesn't wait for an invitation; she comes inside.

"It's crazy," I say.

"What's crazy? Did Cash do something?"

I pull out the wadded picture from my pocket and flatten it. "This doesn't look like me, does it?"

She takes the crinkled paper, stares at it, then stares at me. "Yeah. What is it?"

My chest tightens. I move to the living room and drop down on the sofa. My body feels extra heavy as it lands. "You were supposed to say it doesn't."

She sits beside me. "Sorry. You should have told me that before you asked."

I take a deep breath. I still want to cry, but I hold it in. I look at Lindsey. "You can't tell a soul."

"I won't."

"Cash thinks . . . He thinks I'm the missing daughter of his foster parents."

She stares at me as if I don't make sense, which gives me a little hope. Because it doesn't make sense. It can't be true.

"What?"

"She was kidnapped."

Lindsey's eyes round. "He thinks you were kidnapped?" She makes a snorting sound that's half laugh, half disbelief.

"Yeah. It's crazy. I don't think he ever even liked me. He thought I was trying to swindle his foster parents out of money. Oh, and get this! He did let the air out of my tires."

"What?" she repeats. Then she looks back at the picture. "Okay, this does look like you, but . . . that's crazy."

"I know. I mean, yeah, I was adopted but—"

"Wait?" She leans closer. "You were adopted?"

"Yeah."

Her eyes go wider. "Okay, but when were you adopted, and when did this girl go missing?"

I frown. "Around the same time."

She looks at the picture again. "Shit." When she glances up, I can see in her eyes that she's starting to believe it.

"It can't be true. My parents aren't kidnappers!"

She makes a face and gives the photo back to me. "Have you looked it up on the internet?"

"Looked what up?"

"The kidnapping?"

"No." I stand up. "But I am now." I run to my bedroom, where my laptop is plugged in.

"Do you know the kid's name?" Lindsey asks, following me.

"Yeah." I sit at my desk and set the photo aside. My phone dings. Probably Cash. I ignore it and type into Google's search engine: *missing child Emily Fuller.* Typing out the name, I get chills, as if it means something to me. But it can't mean anything. Then I hear the name in my head. *Emily. Emily. Emily.* There's a familiarity about it that I hate but don't understand.

I click on the first link, but there are, like, a dozen. The link opens. It has a picture of a little girl. A little girl who looks a hell of a lot like me when I was young. I start reading. "Missing September 3, 2004." My breath catches. I was adopted September 4.

Lindsey is reading over my shoulder. "You weren't adopted until you were three?"

"Almost three, yeah," I answer.

"This is weirder than shit." Her voice echoes.

I look at Lindsey. "It's not me. It can't be."

My phone dings again. "Shit." I pull it out. I see Cash's name and cut it off.

Right then, the doorbell rings.

Lindsey turns as if she plans on answering it.

I grab her. "No. I don't want to see him."

"Cash?" she asks, and moves to the window. "There isn't a Jeep. There's a van with a flower shop logo on it."

The doorbell rings again. I move to the front door and open it. A man stands there, flowers in his hands.

"Chloe Holden?" he asks.

It's one of those questions I shouldn't have to think about, but now I do. Actually, I've thought about it a lot in my life. Thought about who I really am. Who my parents really were.

Thought about what I could have done wrong so young to be given away.

Suddenly, I know who sent the flowers. And I start crying again.

An hour later, Mom's talking nonstop. We're sitting in the kitchen. I take a bite of the cashew chicken she brought home.

"They loved me!" She's excited. Happy. Which is why I hid the flowers in my room. I almost threw them away. I had them out of the vase, holding them above a trash can, but I couldn't do it.

He's my dad. And . . . he's not a kidnapper. This whole thing is a mistake. So why am I not telling Mom?

I open my mouth to do it, but nothing comes out. Because it might upset her? Because maybe I'm not convinced it's nothing? The dates. The cat named Felix. The picture. Crap.

"He told me that having had cancer, I could offer real support to the patients."

I'm trying to listen, but she's at the point of repeating herself. I'm looking up, then down, fork in hand, as I chase a cashew around my plate.

"It's the perfect job for you." I catch the cashew, stab it, and put it in my mouth. I chew. I swallow. I don't even taste it.

Mom drops her fork. "Don't eat too much. I bought rocky road ice cream."

"Yum." I push my plate away and fake another smile.

"I don't start until the other nurse leaves. Which could be two or three weeks. I wish it were now. " She reaches for my plate. "Did I tell you I bought some of those Boost drinks? I weighed myself this morning. I've lost ten more pounds."

Yeah, because you don't eat when you're upset, and you're upset 80 percent of the time. "You should drink, like, three a day."

"Two."

I look at her and I'm afraid to ask, but I have to. Because even though she's happy now, I'm scared that something small, like the vase of flowers hidden in my room, could change that. "Did you get the counselor names yet?"

"Yes. And I made an appointment, too."

I'm shocked. "Really?"

"Yeah. And it's tomorrow." She points her fork at me. "They had a cancellation."

"Good."

She looks at me, all motherly. "You feeling well?"

"Yeah."

"You look puffy."

My stomach tightens. "I'm fine. I took Buttercup for a walk. I think it's allergies."

She continues to stare. "Did your dad call again?"

"No." Shit. She knows I've been crying. And I can see the happiness drain from her eyes at the mere mention of Dad.

She keeps staring. "You sure?"

"I haven't spoken with Dad." That confession sparks a bit of guilt. I should have called him after I got his flowers. I didn't.

"What upset you?"

"Nothing. I'm fine, Mom."

"What's got you so upset?"

Cash looked up at Mrs. Fuller standing in the kitchen doorway. Thursday was Mr. Fuller's late day, so it was just the two of them. And because he'd skipped dinner, she was certain something was wrong. It was.

He wanted to head to his room and finish his homework, but they had a rule: If she was home, he wasn't allowed to go to his bedroom until eight. Even if he had homework, he was expected to do it downstairs.

She thought that was what was wrong with teens today. Kids spent too much time in their rooms and not enough time with family.

Never mind that she was *not* his family.

It was a stupid rule.

"I'm not upset. I told you I picked up a hamburger."

She frowned. "That explains why you didn't eat. But why do you look so downtrodden?"

Because I hurt Chloe. He should've thought it through better. He should've . . . "It's the homework. I hate doing math problems."

She sat down. "I can help. I'm not as good as Tony, but—"

"No." He glared at the book.

He felt her staring.

"Something is upsetting you, Cash."

"I just need to finish this."

She reached over and lifted his chin and looked him right in the eyes.

Her touch hurt, like Chloe's had hurt today.

"I care about you." She stared as if trying to read his soul. He didn't want anyone seeing what was there.

"Stop trying to psychoanalyze me."

She dropped her hand. "The other night when you came into the dining room, I was hurting and you helped me. I don't think I said thank you."

"You're welcome," he said, unsure why she was bringing that up.

"I want to do the same for you." Her sigh filled the room. "But you don't come to us with your problems. You push us away. I want to make things right."

You can't make it right. "I told you I'm fine." Eventually, he was going to have to go to them about the whole Chloe/Emily thing, but not with Chloe pissed. And not until he was 100 percent certain he was right. On the drive home, he'd thought about Chloe's words. *You think I was going to try to get money from them? What kind of a person would do that?*

His kind. He'd done it. He remembered the dark pain he saw in the eyes of the woman he'd lied to about being her son.

He had to make sure he was right about Chloe's being Emily before he told the Fullers.

He had to get Chloe unpissed so they could figure this out. But how, when she wasn't even answering his texts?

"You aren't fine," Mrs. Fuller said. "It's as if you don't think we care. We love you."

He dropped his pencil. "Stop." The same frustration he'd used with Chloe leaked out.

"Stop what?"

"This. I'm sorry I can't be what you want me to be." He slammed his book shut.

Mrs. Fuller's shoulders dropped. "What do you think I want you to be, Cash?"

The answer spilled out of him. "Your son! I'm not your son!"

Hurt flashed in her expression, and he wanted to kick his own ass.

He looked at the clock on the oven. "It's five till eight. Can I go to my room?"

She nodded.

He walked out, but not soon enough. He heard her disappointed sigh.

Damn it! He couldn't do anything right.

13

I pull up at the school the next morning. Lindsey talked the whole way here. Asking me questions I don't know the answers to. But I don't get upset, because they are questions I need to be asking myself. Did Emily Fuller have any birthmarks? Were there any suspects? Descriptions of the suspects?

I didn't go back on the computer last night. I couldn't face it. Instead I read. I stayed up and read an entire novel about vampires and shape-shifters, because the story was so far removed from my life. *I* wanted to be removed from my life. Because my life is a freaking Pandora's box, and if I open it, I'm scared what I might find.

I park and look up at the school buildings. I'm tired. I think I slept an hour, maybe. Thank God, it's Friday. I reach for my purse and backpack and realize I can't face this either. Can't go through the day pretending everything is fine. Can't face Cash. I haven't even found the courage to read his texts yet.

"Uh, I'm skipping school," I blurt out.

"Really?" she asks.

"I want to read about Emily Fuller." Why is it that every time I say the name, I get this feeling of déjà vu? *Emily. Emily. Emily.*

"I have a test," Lindsey says, "but—"

"No," I say. "I need to be alone." Did that sound rude? "It's not you. I have to digest this whole thing. I need to read all those articles."

"Isn't your mom home?" she asks.

"I'll go to the library."

She looks concerned. "You sure you don't need me?"

I nod. "I'll pick you up after school."

"No. I'll get Jamie to take me home." She hugs me. "It's going to be okay."

How? I want to ask. The only way I can think it's going to be okay is if I learn none of this is true. And even then, it isn't okay. My life's a freaking mess.

Mr. Fuller had finally gotten around to talking to him about his car being keyed. The talk almost made Cash late for school. He lied about not knowing where his car got scratched. Mr. Fuller insisted on reporting it to the insurance, but wasn't forcing Cash to report it to the school. However, he had to offer the same promise to Mr. Fuller that he'd given to his wife. That if he got something from the camera, he'd handle it without using his fists. Keeping that promise wouldn't be easy, but Cash intended to try.

Mr. Fuller hadn't mentioned anything about Cash's rude behavior with Mrs. Fuller. Mrs. Fuller might not have told him. Probably because she feared her husband would kick Cash out. Didn't she know they'd be better off without him? He felt like shit for hurting her. Why had he turned into a bastard?

Stress. Worry about Chloe. Being pissed at Paul for keying the Jeep that the Fullers gave him. The Jeep he didn't deserve. The Jeep that was the only new and perfect thing he'd ever had in his life.

He suffered through his first class, desperate to see Chloe. He waited by American Lit to catch her before she went inside—hoping she'd talk to him. She never showed.

Before the bell rang, he headed over to the East Hall, where Lindsey had her locker.

"Hey," he said when he'd spotted her.

Surprise tightened her eyes. "Hey."

"Do you know where Chloe is?" he asked.

She frowned. Not a good sign. "I hope like hell you aren't playing games with her."

Now it was his turn to be surprised. "What do you mean?"

"You know what I mean! She's got a lot on her plate right now, losing her boyfriend, her parents' divorce, and her mom's cancer, and you throw the whole you-were-kidnapped thing at her."

He hadn't told Chloe not to tell anyone, but he was shocked she had. "I need to talk to her. Where is she?"

"She skipped school. Said she needed to read everything she could find on the kidnapping."

"Did she bring her laptop?" he asked.

Lindsey's brow wrinkled. "Huh?"

"Did she have a laptop?"

"Why would—?"

"Her mom's probably home, so she wouldn't go back there. If she didn't bring her laptop, that means she's at the library."

Lindsey's expression confirmed it. "I didn't tell you that." Her words chased him down the hall as he disappeared into the crowd.

It feels as if the silence in the library is stalking me. Every few minutes, I look over my shoulder, afraid someone is looking at what I'm reading, seeing the images, seeing me. For reasons I can't understand, I'm afraid. And not just of the truth. It's a monster-under-the bed kind of fear.

I try to shake it off. Staring at the computer, I can't believe there are so many articles about Emily Fuller's kidnapping. Even if it's a coincidence, I can't help but wonder why Mom and Dad didn't see the pictures or news media and think I looked like Emily.

I finish the eighth article. My heart's swollen and raw. When I breathe, it bumps against my rib cage. I fight to keep from crying. I click on a video, and slip on the earphones from the side of the computer. Before I hit the start button, I stare at a woman's face on the screen. Her dark hair, blue eyes, and facial features keep my eyes locked on her. I don't want to see it, but I do anyway. I look like her.

My breath catches. All my life, I've tried not to wonder what my biological mom looks like. I've tried not to be resentful, because I have a mom, a mom who loves me. But I never could get over the fact that my birth mom didn't love me. That she just passed me along to some agency to be given away. And in that one memory of me sobbing, I know I'm missing her.

I've always told myself it doesn't matter that she gave me up, but the abandonment has always been there, crowding out the happiness in my heart. Always making me wonder what's wrong with me.

But what if I wasn't given away? What if she wanted me after all?

In my head, I see an image of Mom, mostly bald, and too thin in her pink nubby robe. Why is it I feel disloyal to her? A knot forms in my throat. I hit play.

"Please, please don't hurt my baby." Her voice rings in my head like music. Is it familiar or is my mind playing tricks on me? "She's a good girl," she continues. "She's happy and sweet and smart." There's so much pain in the woman's voice that it seeps out of the computer and into my skin, into my chest—it curls up like a super-tight ball of rubber bands that's about to unfurl. "Please don't hurt my baby. Please send her back to me. I can't breathe without her."

Tears fall down her cheeks. Tears are falling down my cheeks. I don't even bother to wipe them away. It hurts. It hurts so bad.

How could this be? It's too crazy. It's absurd. This has to be a freaking mistake.

Someone sits down beside me. The fear attacks me. A scream rises in my throat. I jump up, then through watery vision, I see Cash.

I yank off the earphones.

"Chloe, please let's talk."

I grab my purse and my notes that I've been taking, and rush out the library door. It's just Cash, but the fear hangs on. The monster under the bed is out there. Chills like spider legs crawl up my spine.

I hear footsteps behind me. Just Cash, but I hear my heart beating in my throat, still hear her voice pleading. There's a swishing sound in my ears. Tears are wet on my cheeks. Fear, unfounded, unexplainable, follows me out.

I make it to my car and realize I have to look for my keys. Before I get my hand into my purse, Cash is standing in front of me.

"We have to talk!"

The ball of rubber bands in my chest starts popping free. One. Two. Three. *Pop, pop, pop.* They sting.

"How did you know I was here?" I ask.

"You weren't at school."

I blink. "Did you go to my house? If you told my mom any of this!" I put my palm on his chest. "If you did—!"

"I didn't."

"She has enough shit. You aren't going to tell—"

"I won't. Believe me."

I shake my head. "Yeah, it's not like you've ever lied to me or anything!"

He holds out his hands. "You're right. I lied. I made a mess of this. I didn't know how to tell you. I'm sorry."

I start going through my purse, looking for my keys.

"But, Chloe, I know you have questions, and I can answer a lot of them."

I shake my head once more. "It's a mistake," I say, and I wish I believed it more. I wish the name Emily didn't pull at some cord inside me. Wish the woman's voice in the video didn't keep washing over me. Wish this crazy fear would go away. "It has to be a mistake."

"I know it's hard. And maybe it is a mistake. But let's find out."

"How?" I ask him, my voice too loud. "What do you want me to do? Go to my mom and ask, 'Hey, did you kidnap me?'" I grip my hands into tight fists. "Haven't you seen my mom? She doesn't freaking eat, because she's so damn depressed. It'd kill her!"

I go back to digging in my purse. "Where are my damn keys!" My heart's racing so fast, it's vibrating in my chest.

I move to the hood of my car and dump my purse contents on top. My wallet, my phone, a compact, a tampon, and some loose change all fall out, and half of it rolls off the hood. I stare at my things, here, there. I don't see my keys. I must have left them in the library.

I grab my wallet, the only thing I can't live without, and start back into the library.

He walks beside me. "Chloe, please. Come sit in my Jeep, and let's just talk. We can figure this out."

I face him. "Maybe I don't want to figure it out."

His green eyes stare at me. "You're upset. You're crying, and if you go in there, they'll think something is wrong. Go sit in my Jeep. I'll find your keys."

The calm in his voice gets through. I brush my hand across my face.

"It's right behind you." He reaches in his pocket, and I hear a beep as the Jeep unlocks. "Go. I'll find your keys. Okay?"

I do it. I don't know why, but I turn around and crawl inside his Jeep. I lean my head back and close my eyes. But then I open my eyes thinking someone is standing outside my window. There's isn't anyone there.

I sit there and breathe. Just breathe. In a few minutes, I hear him getting back in the car.

I lift my head up. "Did you find them?"

"Yeah," he says, but he doesn't have them in his hand. "Can we talk? Please."

I want to insist he hand over my keys, but logic intervenes. "I don't know what to say."

"Then let me say I'm sorry again." He sounds so sincere. "I don't know how I could have handled it differently, but obviously I screwed up big-time."

"No shit, Sherlock!"

He grins, then wipes it away and looks guilty.

The sound of cars passing and life happening echoes outside his Jeep, but inside, it's silent. I take another breath and try to chase away the wad of panic growing inside me. "Seriously, how did you find me here?"

"When you weren't at school, I asked Lindsey. She said you wanted to read about the kidnapping. I figured with your mom home, the only place to do that was in the library."

I nod, then pull the visor down and look at myself in the

mirror. He's right. I look upset. I rub my fingers across my face and wipe at least some of the smeared makeup away. Then I stare at my features and remember the face on the video. Her face. My mind goes back to everything I just read. Tears fill my eyes.

I fall back against the seat. "My parents wouldn't have kidnapped me." I look at him.

I can see he has doubts. But how can I be upset with him when there's this tiny part of me that . . .

"Then let's look into the adoption. Do you know the name of the agency?"

"No," I say.

"Do you know if they were local, from around here?"

"I think so."

"Is there any way you could find the name of it? Does your mom have papers or anything?"

I vaguely recall Mom coming across them once when she was looking for some paperwork involving my grandmother's insurance policy. But it was a long time ago.

"Yes, but I don't know if she left them at my dad's."

He nods. More doubt. "Maybe you can look around the house?"

"Yeah."

"What about your birth certificate?"

"She has that. She used it to get me registered for school. But I've seen it. It lists me as Chloe Holden and my adoptive parents as my parents. And I'm born on November eighteenth."

"What county were you born in?"

"I don't know." Something occurs to me. "You haven't told . . . them, the Fullers, have you?"

"No. I think we should know for sure before we tell anyone. If they thought you were Emily and then . . . you weren't, that'd hurt them."

I close my eyes a second. Curiosity bites. "What are they like?"

He looks at me, and I see pity in his eyes. "They're . . . nice. Too nice. Strict. Too strict." He exhales. "They're better than most people. A lot better."

I hear so much in his answer. Love, respect, and something else I can't put my finger on, but I'm dealing with too much to ask. Truth is I have so many other questions of my own. One of the articles said they were both going through medical school when their kid was taken. I want to know what kind of doctors they are. If they've ever said anything to Cash about Emily. Do they still miss her? Do I have any of their mannerisms? But I'm afraid I'll fall apart if I ask. So I don't.

"Do you not remember anything before you were adopted?" he asks.

I almost tell him about the snapshot memory I have, but I'm too raw to talk about it. "Barely."

"You were watching the video. Did Mrs. Fuller look familiar?"

"The voice . . ." A lump of emotion forms in my throat. "I can't believe it. It has to be wrong."

"Then let's prove it's wrong."

"How?" I close my hand into a tight fist.

"There's a file in Mr. Fuller's desk where they keep copies of all the articles. I'll try to get to it and take pictures so we can have copies of everything. It might help. You try to find the adoption papers."

"And what if I can't find them? I'm not going to ask—"

"We'll figure it out."

"You believe they kidnapped me, don't you?" The pain inside me swells.

"I don't know what I believe," he says. "But together, we can find the truth."

My fist clenches tighter. "I don't know. Maybe it's not a good idea."

"Chloe, if you're Emily and your parents kidnapped you, they deserve—"

"They did not kidnap me!"

"Then why is this not a good idea? You want answers, don't you?"

I do. I think. "Maybe I don't."

"How could you not want to know the truth?"

"My life's so freaking messed up already." More tears form. "I have to go." I get out of his Jeep, stare at my car parked next to him, then remember he has my keys. I just stand there.

I hear him as he gets out of the car. He walks in front of me. "When you want to talk, call me, okay?" He looks concerned, and part of me wants to fall against him and cry on his shoulder.

Instead, I nod.

"I work tonight at the garage, but I get off around eight. We could go grab a pizza."

"No," I say.

He hands me my keys.

They're heavy. My heart feels heavy with the possibility that I'm Emily Fuller. That they never gave me away. That some monster, the monster under the bed, took me from them.

I get in my car and pull out of the parking lot. I don't have a clue where I'm going, but I drive anyway.

14

Cash watched Chloe drive off. *That went like shit.* What was he doing wrong? How could she not want answers?

Then he remembered the DNA test at home that he'd never taken. The Fullers had gotten it for him last year, in case he wanted to look for his mother. His father had always told him his mother just up and left—abandoned him. Mrs. Fuller questioned that story: "You don't know, your father could have taken you from her, like someone took Emily."

Sure, Mrs. Fuller had a point, but Cash still didn't send it in. He'd been afraid of the truth. Afraid how he'd feel about the truth. Was that what Chloe felt? Sometimes what you didn't know was scarier than what you knew. Even if what you knew was already pretty damn scary.

He stayed in the parking lot a good thirty minutes, just stewing. Not knowing if he should head back to school or just go home.

Driving home, he felt the hollow pit in his stomach that food normally filled. He'd skipped dinner last night and breakfast this morning, and he was starving. He pulled up to a convenience store with a McDonald's. Walking by the candy aisle, he saw bright red bags of Skittles and remembered Chloe talking about the red Skittles. *They are sweet, a tad sour, and rewarding.*

He grabbed four packs.

I spend the rest of the day curled up in a Whataburger booth. The bright colors, the cheerful crowd, chases away the crazy fear from earlier. Struggling to stay awake, I start going through all my old friends' Facebook pages, seeing how everyone in my old life is doing great while mine's insane. I even go to Alex's page. He's added several pictures of him and Cassie.

Then I look up some of my favorite authors, and order another vampire book for when I can't sleep. Next I read some online articles about how to know if a guy is just dating you for sex.

I wish there were an article about a guy just dating you because he thought you were possibly the child of his foster parents. *Grr!* Then while thinking about Cash, I go to the unread messages he sent me yesterday.

I have fourteen of them.

One *Don't shoot the messenger* text.

Two *I'm sorry* texts, one for sending the *Don't shoot the messenger* text.

Three *You left your blanket* texts. Two of them adding, *Can I bring it to you?*

Seven *Call me* texts in different variations.

And one very long, you-got-it-wrong text that read: *You're wrong about me not liking you. I thought you were beautiful from the time you slammed into me and spilled my slushie. And you did slam into me. Then I saw who you looked like and I tried not to think you were beautiful. But it didn't work. Then I got to talking to you and you were funny, and smart, and still beautiful and I couldn't help but like you. The only reason I didn't kiss you first was because I was scared it could get messy with what I was about to tell you. And it did get messy. But I still like you. And I want to kiss you again. And again.*

That text got to me. Damn it. I like him, too. And if my life weren't such a train wreck, I'd be jumping up and down, I liked him so much.

My phone dings and comes with a picture of the word *Hi* written out in red Skittles. The next text says to call him when I feel like talking. And then: *I know this is hard.*

Emotion crowds my tonsils. I grab my cold fries, spell out the word *Hi,* take a picture, and text that I'll call him tonight.

His response is another photo: a Skittles smiley face.

Yup. I really like him.

At the same time school would've ended, I drive home in a much better mood than when I'd left, but the moment I walk into the house and see Mom, tears in her eyes, sitting at the kitchen table with the flowers I'd hidden in my bedroom, my mood spirals downward.

"Why would you lie to me?"

"I didn't," I say.

"You didn't tell me you got these."

"That's not lying."

"Well, you made me lie! I called your dad and gave him hell for forgetting to send you anything. He swore he sent them. Then I found them. Why wouldn't you tell me?"

"Because I was afraid it'd upset you. Like it's doing." My heart's pounding, and I don't need this right now. When can I raise my hands in the air and scream *Enough!*

"You can't keep things from me!" she snaps.

"I wasn't—"

"He's mad you didn't call him. He accused me of turning you against him. He's coming up tomorrow to see you. But I don't want to lay eyes on him ever again! He's a piece of shit." She storms off into her bedroom.

I drop my purse and backpack on the kitchen table and plop into a chair. I guess I'm going to assume that the counseling session didn't go well.

My chest tightens, my throat knots, but I'm cried out. I

just sit there and try not to follow my mom into a deep dark hole where only depression lives.

That night, I've been texting Lindsey. She wanted me to come over, but I begged off.

I'm about to call Cash when Mom knocks on my door.

She pokes her head in. I see the apology in her eyes. "Can I come in?"

I nod.

She moves in and sits on the edge of my bed. "I'm sorry. Again."

I nod. *What am I supposed to say? I don't forgive you. I'm tired of this shit. Did you kidnap me?* The last question whispering through my mind hits hard.

"Thanks for the macaroni and cheese," she says.

I'd made it earlier and left a plate on the stove. "Did you drink one of the Boosts?"

"No, but I will." She touches my hand. "I'm a terrible mother."

Right now she is. But before Dad dumped her, before cancer, she was awesome. So I shake my head no. Of all my friends, I've always known I was the luckiest when it came to parents. Could I have felt so loved if they were the type who'd kidnap a child? I don't think so.

I realize Mom's staring. "How did counseling go?"

"Hard. I was told I harbor a lot of anger."

"You do."

"I'm going to start going once a week. I'll get better."

"What about medicines?" I ask.

"We're going to try without them at first. I'm going to start walking every day."

I try not to be pessimistic, but I want to scream, *Walking isn't going to cut it!*

"He also thinks I'll improve when I start work. You know, get out and have something besides cancer and your low-life father to think about."

The low-life comment stings, but at least she's seeing someone about it.

"And if you don't want to see your dad, you don't have to."

My mind races. I don't want to see him, but I don't want Mom feeling she has the power, consciously or sub-consciously, to dictate whether I see him or not. "I'll be okay."

Disappointment flashes in her eyes. But she nods. "I found a good movie. A comedy. The doctor suggests I start laughing more. You want to watch it with me?"

"Yeah. Let me make a call first."

Her tone tightens. "Your dad?"

"No. Cash." I'll deal with Dad when he gets here, but just thinking about it fills me with dread.

"Do you *like* him, like him?"

"Yeah." Admitting it is hard.

"Just be careful. Men can stab you in the back." Mom walks out.

Such warm, welcoming motherly advice. I drop back on the bed. I think about Cash and remember how it hurt when my dad left. Remember how it hurt to walk away from Alex. I remember I'm supposed to go away to college next year. I remember the one memory of when I was young, of being yanked out of my life. I hate that feeling, and if I let myself get close to Cash, I'm going to feel that way again. I'm already going to feel that way with Lindsey.

There are a whole lot of reasons to protect my heart, to not let myself fall for Cash. Reasons that don't even include what he believes about my being Emily Fuller.

I hear his question from earlier.

How could you not want to know the truth?

My phone rings. Thinking it's Cash, my heart flips. It isn't Cash.

I check to make sure Mom closed the door before I answer.

Then, "Hey, Dad."

"Did you have a good night?" Mrs. Fuller asked when Cash arrived home from work and walked into the kitchen. His plan was to head upstairs to start on homework and to decide whether he was going to take the initiative and call Chloe, or wait and let her do it.

"Okay." Cash remembered he and Mrs. Fuller had parted ways badly last night. "Can I fix a sandwich?"

She frowned, and he knew why.

"I meant to say, I'm going to fix a sandwich." She hated that he asked, said it was a sign he didn't see this as his home. She was right. He didn't belong here. Yeah, he appreciated the hell out of the Fullers, but he couldn't help but wonder if they wouldn't change their mind about him if they knew all the things he'd done alongside his father. Wouldn't they realize he wasn't worthy of their generosity?

"Better," she said. "But if you're interested, I saved you some pizza in the oven."

"Very interested." He pulled the box out of the oven and set it on the counter. "Thanks." He picked up a slice and sank his teeth into the soft, semi-warm cheese and pepperoni pizza.

"You're welcome." She smiled. She liked pleasing him, so much so that it bothered him sometimes. "There's salad in the fridge. I can get it out."

"No. Just pizza, thanks." He talked around the bite of ambrosia in his mouth.

She pulled a plate from the cabinet and waved him toward the table. "Sit down and eat. We'll chat before you go and hide in your room."

He wondered if that was a complaint about last night. Either way, he grabbed the box and moved to the table.

"Where's Mr. Fuller?" he asked before going in for a second bite.

"He's swimming laps." She motioned to the backyard, where the pool lights lit up the patio. "He ate five pieces of pizza."

She pulled over the bowl of Skittles he'd left on the table when he texted Chloe. "Did you get these or did Tony?"

"I did."

She shook the bowl for a second. "Where are the red ones? They're the best."

He swallowed the bite of pizza. "I ate them." It was a lie. They were in a baggie upstairs.

She set the bowl down. "You never told me how your college class went."

"It was fine. The teacher's boring, but I don't see a problem." He finished off his first slice and grabbed another one. She handed him a napkin. He set the pizza down and wiped his mouth. "How was your day?"

"Okay."

"Did you save someone's life?"

"Working on it." She looked down in the Skittles bowl, pulled out an orange one, and put it in her mouth. "You know, Tony and I were talking that you may want to quit working to focus on school since you're doing the college course and finishing high school."

"No, I'm fine. I only go on Wednesday night for the college class." He savored the second piece. She watched him finish it off. He reached for a third.

She frowned. "It's not as if we don't think you can do it. It's . . . think how much easier it would be if you just concentrated on your studies."

"I like working." He took another bite. "This is good," he added hoping for a conversation changer.

"Colleges look at your GPA. You're doing great. But just a few more points, and you could get into—"

"I'm fine." His plan was to go to junior college for a while and then transfer to the University of Houston. The foster program grant would cover it. But he didn't want to talk about colleges tonight. They'd already butted heads when he told them he was going to use the scholarship that the foster program offered. Because, blast it, he already owed them for the Jeep. He didn't want them paying for college.

"You could go anywhere you want."

"It's late. I wanted to get some work done." He snatched up the plate and dropped it into the open dishwasher. "Thanks for the pizza." As he walked past the table, he grabbed another slice.

"Cash," she said his name, sounding a bit impatient.

Taking another bite, he turned, expecting her to start naming off schools. Good schools, expensive schools. He started talking around the lump of pizza in his mouth. "Look, I need—"

"We want to adopt you."

He heard the words, but they didn't compute. The bite of pizza, halfway down his throat, bounced against his Adam's apple. His mind raced. His heart hurt. He remembered telling her he wasn't her son.

Was that why she was doing this? Did she think he wanted this?

It was the last thing he wanted. His goal had been, always

been, pay them back and get out of their lives so his problems wouldn't keep landing on their doorstep.

"No. Bad idea." He hurried up the stairs.

"Why?" she called after him. "Why is it a bad idea?"

He didn't answer.

15

Ten minutes into the movie, and the second condom joke,
Mom decides it isn't funny or appropriate. Actually, it was
funny, or it had been when I watched it with Alex a year ago.
I remember all the times we went to his house, climbed in
his bed, and watched movies. And did other things.

His parents owned a real estate company and worked
late. We had his house to ourselves until around eight. I
honestly think if his parents had worked normal hours, we
wouldn't have had sex.

Mom cuts the movie off and we watch *Law & Order*. I
almost remind her that she's supposed to be watching something funny, but I'm afraid she'll flip out again. So I keep
my mouth shut. It's a rerun. I've seen it. But not wanting
Mom to feel abandoned, I stay and pretend to watch. What
I'm really doing is going over the phone call I had with Dad.

He came right out and apologized about not calling me
the first day of school, claiming he'd had a bad week. I
wanted to ask if it had anything to do with his new live-in
girlfriend.

He didn't say anything about giving my room to Darlene, but he told me he loved me and that he knew he wasn't perfect. I couldn't disagree. But as sad as it was, I think that was part of the problem. Before, he had been perfect. Then Darlene happened. She sucked all the perfect out of him.

He reminded me that I was his daughter and Mom shouldn't try to turn me against him. I couldn't disagree on that one either.

He said he needed to see me and missed me. And that like it or not, he was my dad and he wasn't letting Mom come between us. I almost asked, *What about Darlene?* Was he letting her come between us?

I managed to keep that in and agreed I'd have dinner with him tomorrow night. But only after I confirmed it would just be us. I heard the tightness in his voice when I asked, too. I don't know if he'd planned on bringing Darlene, but he agreed to come alone. Still, I'm looking forward to our dinner about as much as I do getting my period.

I grab the photo album that Mom left out. I flip through the pages. I don't think I've ever seen this one. I'll bet this was one of Grandma's. Until we moved here, most of Grandma's stuff was boxed in the attic.

I study the black-and-white images of Grandma and Grandpa and Mom when she was little. Pictures of her as a child, looking happy. I turn the page and find pictures of me.

Me really young. Me holding a present with a big bow on it.

Me not looking happy even though I'm holding a gift. There are a couple of pictures that have been edited, meaning Mom took her scissors to them and cut out Dad.

Mom sees me looking at the album. She points to one of me with my grandparents. "That was the first time you met them."

I study the image. My younger self is staring at the camera as if begging for someone to save me. The look on my face reminds me of the look on the animals' faces that you see in that long, heart-wrenching fund-raising commercial. Dogs who are abandoned. The fear I had pushed away slams into me again.

Then I see a bruise on my cheek. *How did I get that?*

"We'd just got you and came straight here from the adoption agency."

My pulse's fluttering at the base of my neck. "How did I get that bruise?"

Mom's looks at the picture. "They said you fell on the playground. Why?"

I don't know, I really don't, but fear has the hair on the back of my neck standing. Then I realize this is my chance to ask questions. "So you adopted me from around here?"

I stare at the album, not wanting her to see me waiting with bated breath for her answer.

"In Fort Landing. Two towns over. I remember I put you in a car seat and I rode in back with you."

I look up. She's got the smile she gets when she talks about me when I was little. A smile that says love. It's so not the look of someone who remembers kidnapping a child.

I don't know if you can call it relief, but something releases in my chest. Something that reaffirms what I'd sworn was true. Mom and Dad didn't kidnap me. I know this. I'd bet my life on it. "How long did it take for the adoption?"

"Eight months. The longest eight months in my life."

I gaze back at the picture of my younger self. I have curly dark hair, and my eyes look too big for my face. "I look scared."

"You were nervous. Confused. You'd lived with a foster family for several months. You'd grown attached to them."

My heart does another flip-flop. If that's true, if I lived

with a foster family, then I'm not Emily Fuller, because she'd been taken the day before I was adopted.

"They said it'd take you a while to adjust."

I swallow. "Did it?"

"Yeah. I slept with you for almost a month because you'd cry at night. I'd hold you and sing to you."

I think I remember her singing. My chest hurts almost as if I'm feeling what I felt then. What I felt in the one memory that haunts me. Confused. Scared. Unsure. Abandoned. Unloved. "Did I ever tell you anything about before?"

"Just that you wanted your mama and daddy. Broke my heart. I kept telling you that we were your mama and daddy now. It wasn't long until you were all smiles."

A question fills my head. The one I've secretly wondered. "Did the agency tell you why I was put up for adoption?"

Mom looks surprised. And I'm surprised, too. Surprised that I've never asked before. Then, just like that, I know why I didn't. Not knowing felt safer.

"They said your mom was young and not married. She wanted to keep you, but then it got so hard financially. We felt so lucky to have you. So blessed. We'd tried to get pregnant for several years. Your granddad met a couple who'd used this agency. It wasn't too expensive. They placed a lot of slightly older biracial children, who are difficult to find homes for."

I was told I was part Hispanic, which shows through my light olive coloring and brown eyes. "Was my mother Hispanic or my dad?"

"I don't know."

I turn the page. There's an image of me with a doll. One of those that's supposed to look like its owner. We're dressed alike. It has brown curly hair and big almond-shaped brown eyes. The doll's smiling, and in this picture, so am I. I wonder how long it was after I was adopted.

Mom grins. "You loved that doll. We went to this store where we had to adopt it. You carried her everywhere."

"I don't remember it," I say. I recall the box of toys I saw in Dad's attic when we were moving. "Do I still have it?"

"No. We left it at a park only a few months after you got it. We went back for it, but it was gone. You cried for weeks, wanting Emily back."

My breath catches. "Emily?"

"Yeah, that's what you named it."

It was ten that night when Cash's phone rang. He bolted from his desk, where he was half-assed doing his homework and half-assed fretting over what Mrs. Fuller said, and praying she didn't decide to try to finish the conversation. Because he didn't know how to finish it.

Why is it a bad idea?

His only answer was to ask why she thought it was a good idea. They'd done more than expected. Didn't they know how hard it was to live up to their expectations? Did Mrs. Fuller not remember how disappointed she'd been when he was kicked out of Westwood Academy? Or a year earlier, when he'd been accused of stealing a car in their neighborhood because he was the foster kid?

Or even when he got in the fight with Paul? His past wasn't going away. Hell, they didn't know half his past. He'd robbed old people of their social security checks. Stolen cars. Once while his dad had been working on this elderly couple's house, Cash had gone in and stolen their bank cards and the woman's antique necklace, a gift her husband had just bought her for their fiftieth anniversary.

He saw Chloe's number on the screen. "Hi."

"Sorry it's late. It's been a crazy night."

"Your mom didn't find out you skipped school, did she?"

"No. You?"

"No."

She got quiet, then blurted out, "Look, I'm certain my mom and dad didn't kidnap me, but . . . I'm thinking someone did. And you're right. I want answers."

"Good." Pause. "Did something happen to change your mind?"

She told him about learning where the adoption agency was, that she'd been placed in foster care for a month, and about the doll she'd named Emily.

He hated the pain in her voice. "We'll find out the truth."

"How?"

"I think we need to talk to the nanny." He sat down on his bed.

"Nanny?"

"Emily was with a nanny when she went missing."

"How do you know that?"

"Mrs. Fuller mentioned it. And since you got here, I went online and researched it. I also read some of it years ago in a file they have. They have other stuff in the file, too. Like police reports and stuff. I'm going to try to get to the file again. But I have to wait when I know they aren't home. But as soon as I hang up, I'll look and see how many adoption agencies are in Fort Landing. It's bigger than Joyful. It might have more than one."

"There's three," she said. "I checked. Only one has been open since I was adopted, A New Hope Adoption Agency, but that doesn't mean it's the one."

"Yeah." He leaned against his headboard. "I'll start trying to find the nanny."

"How?"

"Internet."

"I found my birth certificate. It says I was born here."

He heard her sigh, and it sounded so much like Mrs. Fuller that he felt it in his gut. "We'll figure it out."

"You say that like you believe it."

"I do. I'm good at figuring things out. Solving puzzles." *Every con is a puzzle—you just have to figure out what pieces go together.* He paused. "I work tomorrow, but I get off at five. You want to get together? We can get something to eat and talk."

"I can't. My dad's coming into town."

Is she just saying that because she doesn't want to see me? "Sunday?" His grip on his cell tightened.

The line went silent.

"I need to ask my mom, but it shouldn't be a problem."

He remembered what Chloe had said about her dad. "You okay with seeing your dad?"

"No. But it doesn't matter—I don't have a choice."

"You always have a choice," he said. Even he'd had one when he was with his dad.

"Not one that wouldn't cause problems."

"Haven't you ever heard? You have to break some eggs to make an omelet."

"So you're an egg breaker and I'm a peacemaker. I'm not sure we're compatible."

He laughed. "I break eggs only when I have to."

"When have you had to?" she asked.

"What do you mean?"

"When's the last time you stood up for something? Besides that kid the first day at school."

"Tonight," he said, then regretted saying it.

"What happened?"

He decided he could tell part of it. "Mrs. Fuller wants me to quit working at the garage."

"Why?"

"She says it's too much with the college classes I'm taking and regular school."

"You're taking college classes?"

"Yeah. On Wednesday nights. Just to get a jump start."

"That does sound like a lot," I say.

"I can handle it. Besides it's not really the time. She's scared I'll change my mind and decide to work at the garage and not go to college."

"But if you're already taking college classes, why would she think that?"

"Because I'm also taking auto tech, and I'm not signing up for some fancy college."

"What college does she want you to go to?"

"Rice or Harvard, for all I know."

"Why don't you want to go to a good college?"

"Because it has to be a state college for my grant to pay." The moment he said that, he wished he hadn't. It sounded like a handout.

"You have a grant?"

He hesitated. "Through the foster program."

"That's good," she said.

"Yeah," he lied. He kept telling himself that when he was out of school, he'd pay the state back as well. All his life, his dad had done nothing but take from people. Cash had taken from people. He wanted to change that.

"You got college plans?" he asked to change the subject.

"University of Houston, probably."

"I'm considering that one, too. But why 'probably'?"

"Right now I can't see leaving Mom the way she is."

"But she's over the cancer."

"She's not over the divorce."

He remembered Chloe saying her mom was depressed. "How bad is she?"

"Depends when you ask. Earlier today, I would've said really bad. Tonight, she's better. At least she's getting help now."

"A doctor?"

"Yeah. Today was her first time. I'm hoping it'll help."

"Yeah." Cash didn't hold much stock in shrinks. He'd been forced to see one for a year when he went into foster care. The only thing he'd gotten out of it was how to better hide his emotions.

If the doctor had said it once, she'd said it a dozen times. *None of what you did was your fault.* But it had been. He'd known it was wrong when he'd done it.

"She's got a job, so I'm hoping that'll help, too. But she doesn't start for a few weeks."

"What kind of work does she do?"

"Nursing."

"Is that what you're going to take in college? Medicine?" And if she was the Fullers' kid, wouldn't that be appropriate?

"No. I'm thinking journalism. English degree."

"You want to be a writer?"

"No. My mom used to write. She wrote several books. Had an editor from one of the big publishing houses in New York ask for revisions on her last one, but then Dad went crazy and she stopped. Thankfully, she's still reading."

"You like to read?" he asked.

"Yeah."

"What do you read? Love stories?" he asked to tease.

"Of course." She laughed. "I'm on a paranormal fantasy kick right now. You read?"

"I used to read more when I wasn't working. But yeah."

"What have you read recently?"

"I read *The Outsiders* and a couple of Stephen King

books over the summer. I tried to read *Fifty Shades of Grey*, but—"

"You read *Fifty Shades of Grey*?" She laughed some more. "And you gave me a hard time about reading love stories?"

16

Her laughter had Cash's chest instantly feeling lighter. "I said I tried to read it. I never finished the first chapter."

"I can't see you buying it or checking it out of the library."

"I wouldn't," he said, "Mrs. Fuller read it, and one day I went into their library and picked it up. You didn't read it?"

"No." Her tone went high, dishonestly high.

"You're lying. You read it."

She laughed with guilt. "Okay, me and my friends were curious."

"And what did you think?" He readjusted his pillow behind his back.

"I can see why you didn't make it through the first chapter. What are you planning on taking in college?"

He noticed her conversational turn. "Probably a business major. I'm still undecided, too." He paused. "So what else do you do besides read naughty books?"

She laughed again. "I don't know."

"You run or anything?"

"If I'm being chased."

Now he laughed. "I mean for exercise."

"I know. I used to play soccer."

"You were the prettiest one on the team, too." He re-membered the image of her and several classmates practic-ing in bathing suit tops. She'd looked amazing.

"How? Oh yeah, you stalked me on the internet."

"I didn't stalk you. I checked you out."

"What's your Facebook address?" He heard her typing something into the computer.

"I don't have one. Not a real one."

"You have a fake Facebook account? But not a real one."

"Yeah."

"Why?"

"Because . . . I like stalking people on the internet." It was a joke. She didn't laugh.

"Seriously?"

"At the other school, I heard some of the kids were talk-ing about me on Facebook. I wanted to check it out . . . anonymously."

She didn't say anything for a few seconds, then, "Do you run?"

"I try to. But this summer, I did more swimming."

"Are you on a swim team?" she asked.

"No. The Fullers have a pool. And I went to their lake house a lot."

"You don't play sports?"

"I like watching them. But never played."

"Really? With your size, I'd think some coach would have had you playing football years ago."

"They shy away from foster kids. We move a lot."

"Did you?"

"What?" he asked.

"Move a lot before you lived with the Fullers?"

He ran a hand over his face. Why had he brought up the foster program? "They were my fourth home."

"Was it bad?"

Not as bad as with my dad. "Not really."

"How old were you when your father died?"

He wanted to change the subject, but she'd accused him of doing that at the park. "Eleven."

"How . . . how did your father die?"

Shit. This was the downside of getting close to a girl. They wanted your life history.

The line went silent.

"You don't have to tell me if you don't want to."

He almost said *good,* but opted for, "It's a long story, and it's late."

"Yeah. I should let you go."

He felt her pulling away. When he wanted to pull her closer.

"He died in a car wreck." It was true. Cash had wrecked the car. But it was the bullet in his father's friggin' chest that'd killed him.

"Were you in the car with him?"

"No."

"I'm sorry." Emotion came with her apology. "When my mom got cancer, I was so scared of losing her. I don't think I could have handled it. That must've been so hard."

He hated hearing her sympathy. He didn't deserve it. And neither did his son of a bitch father.

Saturday afternoon, I'm at Lindsey's, helping her figure out what to wear on her date with David. I'm thrilled they are dating. But I'm struggling to work up some good vibes. Mom's been down all day. I barely got her out of her room to eat.

Seeing her depressed makes me feel guilty for agreeing to see Dad. Oh, I know it's not fair that she makes me feel that way, and honestly, I don't think she *wants* to make me feel that way. But she does and I do. Add that I'm not looking forward to seeing Dad, and it's understandable that my mood isn't much better than Mom's.

"I like this blue blouse better," I say to Lindsey.

"It's not too plain?"

"No, it shows off your girls."

"It doesn't show them off too much, does it? I don't want him to think I'm trying to get him in the backseat on the first date."

I laugh. "It doesn't say 'let's hop in the backseat'; it says 'notice me a little.'"

"And 'notice' is good, right?" She frowns. "I don't know if I'm ready for this."

"You're ready," I say.

She looks at me in the mirror. "I wish it were a double date. Can't you call Cash and see if you two can go with us?" She turns.

"I can't. I've got my dad tonight, remember?"

"Oh." She frowns. "Sorry."

"Me, too." I drop on her bed and vow not to whine. I did enough of that last night, when we talked after I got off the phone with Cash. Sandy, one of my old friends, was a whiner. "Besides, I'm not really dating Cash."

"You're going out Sunday. Plus, you made out with him on your porch swing."

"Yeah." I smile, remembering, and if I could just think about that instead of the other stuff, I'd be happier. "But I don't know if it's a date, or just us figuring out if I'm Emily Fuller."

She rolls her eyes. "After that text he sent about wanting to kiss you?"

Yeah, I'd shown her Cash's text, too. "You're right. I guess you're not the only one who's nervous."

"I just pray if he tries to kiss me, I won't think about Jonathon. He emailed me this morning. Asked me what I was doing this weekend."

"You didn't email him back, did you?"

"Yes, but only to say I was busy. I had to hint that I wasn't staying at home mourning him."

"Did he ask what you were doing?"

"He did. I didn't answer." She grins.

"Forget about him," I say. "Tonight is going to be fun."

She drops down on her bed. "Should I tell David my deep, dark secret?"

"What secret?"

"That my mom's a lesbian? Or is that not first-date information?"

"Why would you need to tell him?" I ask.

"Because if Lola is here, he might figure it out like you did."

"You wouldn't feel the need to tell him if your mom were heterosexual. So why tell him this?"

"Because not everyone thinks it's normal like you."

"I don't think you need to make a big deal about it."

She smiles. "Thank you."

"For what?"

"For coming over. For saying all the right things. I asked Jamie to do it, and she said she and her cousin were getting pedicures."

"No big deal." I wonder if Lindsey realizes she just told me I was her second choice. It sucks being someone's second choice. But hey, it's better than no choice.

"Are you going to ask your dad about the name of the adoption agency?"

"If I can find a way to bring it up in the conversation."

"Why don't you just ask him?"

"Because I don't feel like explaining that I might be a kid who was kidnapped!" I snap.

She runs a brush through her hair. "Do you really not remember anything about your life before?"

I tell her the one and only princess-dress memory.

"What about the kidnapping? I mean, you'd think that would've been traumatic and you'd remember it."

"I don't." Fear brushes against me "I tell her about the picture with the bruise on my face. Of the fear I can't explain."

"Okay, that is creepy," she says.

"Yeah."

"You know you don't have to tell your dad about the kidnapping thing. Just say you've been thinking about the adoption."

"Yeah." But like I told Cash, I'm a peacemaker, not an egg breaker. Then again, the last few times I've spoken with, or seen, Dad, I've come unhinged. But the whole kidnapped thing is different. Bigger. And if I learn I'm really Emily Fuller, there won't be a bowl big enough to hold the eggs that'll break.

My phone dings with a text. Thinking it's Cash, I feel a thrill ride my rib cage and pool in my chest. It's not from Cash.

It's Mom.

Make sure your dad knows not to come inside the house. I don't want to see him! And ask him why he hasn't paid your car insurance yet.

A crazy thought hits. Not about Mom, but Dad. About forgiving Dad.

Maybe I won't be able to forgive him until Mom's okay. Maybe I won't be able to forgive Dad until Mom forgives Dad.

That might be, like . . . never.

That feels wrong, but it might be true.

I drop back on Lindsey's bed. "I hate my life."

Working a little late, it was six when Cash was washing up to leave work. His phone dinged with a text. Hoping it was Chloe, he grabbed his cell. He hadn't texted her today for fear she'd bring up his dad again, but he'd decided to text her later.

He hoped she'd be up for another late call. Other than talking about his past, he'd enjoyed talking to her. He smiled about the whole *Fifty Shades of Grey* conversation.

He looked at his phone. It wasn't Chloe. The text was from Mrs. Fuller. Dread hit. He'd gotten out of the house this morning without seeing her. He didn't have a clue how she was going to react to his *bad idea* comment about being adopted.

He read the text.

Tony and I are in a curry mood. Can you join us at Kiran's Café?

He wanted to decline, but maybe going out to eat would be easier than facing her at home.

He texted back. *What time?*

Seven?

Sure.

She sent back a smiley face. She texted a lot of smiley faces. He knew it was a sign that she cared. He also liked getting them.

With an hour to kill, he decided to run to the bookstore. Talking with Chloe about reading had him eager to pick up a book. Perhaps he'd find one in the fantasy genre so they could talk about it.

———

Mom's snuggled up with a book and Felix when I walk out of the bathroom after getting ready to go out with Dad.

She looks up. "You look nice."

"Thanks." All I did was comb my hair and put on mascara and lip gloss, but I know this is Mom playing nice, and I appreciate it. I check the time, and it's almost six thirty. Leaning down, I pet Buttercup, who's wagging his tail as if he thinks we're going on another walk.

"Do you want me to bring you something back to eat?" I ask Mom.

"No! Wouldn't want to eat anything your dad bought." She's already out of nice. "I'll fix something."

"Why don't you write?" I say.

"I might."

What do you want to bet she doesn't? She probably won't eat either. I checked today, and she drank only two of her Boosts, total. What happened to drinking two a day? I swear, she's even thinner now.

"Later." I grab my purse and walk out, feeling guilty for leaving her alone.

Sitting on the porch steps, I see a truck stop next door. Then Jonathon, the no-good cheating dog, gets out. He sees me and nods. I nod back, but not in a friendly way. I know Lindsey left thirty minutes ago.

I listen to him knock and ask for Lindsey. I hear her mom answer. "She's out."

"Can you tell her—?"

The door snaps closed. I smile. Lindsey's mom doesn't like the cheating dog either.

I'm still smiling when I hear footsteps. *Oh shit!*

I look down the street, praying I'll see Dad's car roll up. But nope.

Then Jonathon is in front of me. "You're the new girl at school, right? Chelsea?"

"Chloe," I say.

"You and Lindsey ride to school together?"

"Yup." *Where are you, Dad?*

"Do you know where she's at?"

Decisions. Decisions. I could tell him she's on a hot date. Or I could . . . "Nope."

"Do you know who she's with?"

Decisions. Decisions. I go with the truth again. "Yes."

He frowns. "But you aren't going to tell me, right?"

"It's not my place."

"You know, I'm not nearly as bad of a guy as she told you I was."

Right. So you didn't cheat on her? I think it, but don't ask.

He leans against the porch post. "Where did you move from?"

"El Paso," I say, wishing he'd go away.

"You like it here?"

"No." When I look up, he's ogling my boobs. As if the guy has a chance in hell.

He scuffs his shoe against the porch. "Well, since I'm not doing anything and you aren't doing anything, maybe—?"

"No." Dad's car pulls up. I stand. "Bye!"

When I get into the car, Dad's head is dipped down, staring at Jonathon, who is looking at us as he walks back to his truck. Considering Dad's driving a red convertible and is wearing spiked hair, Jonathon probably thinks my dad's my date. *Ew.*

"Who's that?" Dad asks.

"No one." I push back my dislike for Jonathon and confront my angst over Dad. He needs to lose the spiked hair.

"You already have a boyfriend?"

"No." Then I remember Cash. "Maybe."

"Don't you think that's a little soon?"

I shake my head.

"Why didn't you introduce us?" He sounds like a concerned father. Why does that annoy me? Then I realize why. He lost the right to parent me about boys or sex stuff when he started screwing Darlene.

"First, because that's not him. Second, because . . . just because." I shut my mouth. I don't want to argue.

He stares, and from his expression, I can see he's thinking the same thing. "It's good to see you." He reaches over and squeezes my hand. "We haven't done a father–daughter date in a long time."

If you missed me so much, how come you sent flowers a day late or didn't call me when you said you would? I swallow the question. No breaking eggs tonight. But I've thought about Lindsey's remark about asking Dad some "vague" questions about the adoption agency. I might do it.

Dad starts talking. "I Googled Indian restaurants in Joyful. There's one, Kiran's Café. You up for butter chicken?"

We talk about safe subjects, riding to the restaurant. The weather. The last book I read. He's trying to make conversation, but he's using up subjects so fast, I'm afraid we'll run out.

"How're Brandon and Patrick doing?" I ask about Dad's cousin and his husband, thinking those are safe subjects.

"Don't know. I haven't seen them in a while."

"Why not?" They used to come to the house at least once a month, plus holidays. Brandon, a chef, would cook.

"We've been busy."

We being him and Darlene. My next thought falls out of my mouth. "They don't like Darlene?" That shouldn't make me happy, but it does. "Or does she not like them?" That possibility ups my Dad angst. Since both my dad's parents died in a car cash right after Mom and he were married, Brandon is Dad's only family.

"You shouldn't let Darlene break up your family." Then again, he let her break up our family.

Dad's expression flinches. "It's not like that." The lie colors his tone.

In a few minutes, Dad parks and we enter the restaurant filled with the rich scent of curry, cumin, and turmeric. My stomach growls but my heart goes straight to hurting. I'm transported back to all the daughter-and-daddy dates in the past. Back to when spending time with Dad was one of my favorite things. We'd laugh. Talk soccer. Talk movies. He'd ask about school, my friends, my life. Not like he was checking up on me, but like he wanted to know everything about me because *I* interested him. Because *I* was important to him.

I miss that. I miss him. The old him. The old us. A knot lodges in my chest.

We're seated at a front table. The waiter, a tall, older Indian man, hands us menus. Dad's looking around like he's confused. He takes the menu, but glances at the waiter. "Did this used to be Pauline's Pizza?"

"Yes," the waiter says. "My brother bought it seven years ago."

"I thought so."

The waiter takes our drink orders and leaves.

Dad looks at me. "Your mom worked here. I used to eat

here every Friday night, because there was this guy who worked on Fridays who liked her." There's a look on his face as if the memory's good; then, just like that, he blinks and that touch of happiness vanishes. He pulls up the menu as if to hide behind it. I can only speculate, but I swear his reminiscing of Mom hurt him. Or maybe remembering how badly he's hurt her is what stings.

Then again, I swear Dad doesn't know how badly he hurt her. Or me.

Is it terrible of me to want *him* to hurt? Maybe it's normal, but it feels wrong. Everything feels wrong. Being here with him feels wrong.

He sets down his menu. "You want to order the usual? Butter chicken and lamb vindaloo, and we share?"

"Yeah," I say.

"You want anything else?"

"Maybe," I say, thinking the more food we have to eat, the less we'll have to talk.

The waiter brings our drinks. "Ready to order?"

Dad looks at me. "Let's order those two things first, and if you see something else, we can order that, okay?"

I nod. Dad orders.

When the waiter walks away, Dad and I are back to staring at each other. "So school's okay?" he asks.

I think he wants me to say it's okay so he can feel less guilty. "I'm surviving it. Barely." I'm not letting him off the hook that easy.

He tells me about running into Cara and Sandy in the music store. Because Dad never went into the music store unless I begged him to, I figure he was with Darlene. I imagine my old friends' shock at seeing Darlene. I wonder why neither of them texted me about it.

They probably thought it'd hurt me. Embarrass me. It does.

"I'm hungry," Dad says when a different waiter walks past with plates of food.

"Me, too," I lie. I'm not sure I can eat. All those smells that at one time brought on feelings of love now bring on queasiness.

We get quiet again. Dad's phone dings with a text. He reads it. I wonder if it's Darlene. Nope. Not hungry. The restaurant noise picks up. Forks hitting plates. Cooking noises from the kitchen. Low conversations. I hear the hostess asking someone how many are in the party.

"Three. Thank you," the patron answers. Those three words strike a familiar chord.

I look up. A whoosh of air leaks out of my mouth. It's Cash with a man and a woman. The woman from the video, but older. The man has dark hair. And brown eyes. Brown eyes like mine.

I stare at his face.

Then I stare at hers.

Are they my parents? Do I have their DNA? Was I taken from them?

Part of me wants to run to them; another part wants to run away from them.

Cash must feel me staring, because his gaze shifts to me. His eyes round in an *oh shit* way.

I grab the menu on the table to cover my face.

"Right this way," I hear the hostess. Footsteps move away. My heart's thump-thumping in my chest. I hear the swish of blood flowing in my ears.

I lower the menu and see Cash trying to get the Fullers to sit with their backs to me.

Panic, like liquid, rises in my chest. My lungs refuse air.

"Did you find something else you want?" Dad asks.

I cut my eyes toward Cash's table, and then back to the door. "I can't do this," I say, not meaning to say it aloud.

"Do what?" Dad asks.

I stand up, not so fast as to call attention to myself, and head toward the door.

"Chloe?" Dad calls. I don't look back.

I push the door open. Hot air surrounds me. I still can't breathe. "Shit!"

I go and lean against Dad's car. My heart is slamming against my rib cage. And that's when it hits me. I have to know. I have to know if they are my parents. I have to know if I wasn't just given away like I didn't matter. Like I wasn't loved. I grip my fists.

Then I hear footsteps. Dread knots my stomach that they saw me, that all of this is going to happen now. As ready as I am, I'm scared. I look up. It's Dad.

His steps eat up the pavement and bring him and his frown to me.

"What the hell?" he asks. His shoulders are tight, his expression pinched; his frustration is a cloud around him.

His anger sparks my own. My mind races, and the only thing I can think to say is what I've already said. "I can't do this."

"Do what?"

"Have a father–daughter date like everything is normal when it's not." The second the excuse is out of my mouth, it's no longer an excuse. It's true. "You left me. I didn't matter to you." I feel abandoned by him, like I felt when I was three. Then out of nowhere, I hear a voice, *Your mama and daddy don't want you anymore.* Where the hell did that come from? Tears fill my eyes. "Can you open the car? Please!"

Dad's expression hardens. "I divorced your mom, not you!"

"It doesn't feel like it," I counter.

He stands there, still angry, still frustrated, and still the man I blame for so much of my pain. How can he not be ashamed of himself?

"Let me go pay for dinner." He clicks the car open.

I slide into the passenger seat and try to make myself small just in case anyone else comes out of the restaurant. How odd is it that I'm out here arguing with my dad when my real dad and mom may very well be inside that restaurant.

I start sweating, but I don't care. I sit there, windows rolled up, and feel the heat. Then it hits again. The fear. I want to run. I'm afraid.

I close my eyes, press my head back on the headrest, and try to breathe. Time passes. One minute. Two. Three.

Five.

Eight.

What the hell is Dad doing? Oh God. Did the Fullers see me and confront Dad?

My phone dings with a text. I pull it out. It's Cash.

Him: *You okay?*

Me: *No. What's happening?*

Him: *Your dad's getting the food to go.*

Me: *Did they see me?*

Him: *No.*

I hear the car door opening. I get another wave of fear. I push it back. Dad, looking pissed, hands me the big white bag.

He crawls behind the wheel. But he doesn't start the car. "You're my daughter. My little girl. I can't lose you, Chloe!"

Tears fill my eyes and I look out the window. The smell of Indian food fills the car, the smell of father–daughter dates. I suddenly don't like that smell.

He starts talking again. "I know I was supposed to call and I screwed up. And, yes, I didn't realize it was your adoption date until late. So your flowers didn't get to you on time. I'm human. I'm not perfect, Chloe."

My chest burns with anger, hurt, desperation. Some of it for now. Some of it from the past. I still don't look at him, but I say, "You used to be perfect. You used to remember things. I used to matter to you."

I hear him bang his hand on the steering wheel and say a four-letter word. After a second, he says, "You still matter to me."

Then there's only the silence of us in the car. All I hear is us breathing and my heart breaking.

"Other parents get divorced," he says as if that's justification. "Fathers and daughters across the world work things out. Why can't we?"

His question hits, and the answer rises inside me and becomes like the volcano he and I built for my fifth-grade science project. "I guess their moms didn't get cancer!" My voice rings loud. "Their dads didn't leave their daughters to take care of everything. To face their mom puking for weeks on end. To deal with the thought of their mom dying!"

Words spill out of me. I can't stop them. I'm breaking eggs left and right. I don't care. It feels as if I don't say this, something inside me will break.

"Mom got cancer! But it felt like I got it, too. I'm the one who cooked tomato soup and grilled cheese sandwiches for her because she couldn't eat anything else. I was the one who sat on the bathroom floor with her sobbing because her hair fell out. I was the one who had to be strong when I didn't feel strong. Me, Dad!" I slap my chest. "Me! Damn it! She needed you. I needed you! But you were too busy dyeing your hair and getting a new wardrobe and screwing Darlene to care!"

He grips the steering wheel and looks away from me. He sucks in air. Holds it. Holds it longer. Then he looks at me again. I see everything in his eyes. Guilt. Pain. Even love. And that hurts most of all.

"I . . . I'm sorry. I didn't . . . I screwed up. I screwed up so bad, baby."

I breathe in, and the sound is shaky. I'm shaky. My whole world is shaky.

Dad starts the car and drives off. My lap is hot from the take-out boxes in the bag. The smell seeps out. I want to toss it out the window. I don't ever want to eat Indian food again.

He drives toward my house. He pulls into the subdivision. But he doesn't turn down my street.

"Where are we going?" I ask.

"I don't know. But I can't let you leave this car until . . ."

"What?" I ask.

I hear him swallow. "Until you . . . forgive me." His voice is uneven.

"Then we're going to be in this car a really long time!" I tell myself not to feel bad that he's hurting.

He pulls into the park. The one Cash and I came to when he told me about Emily.

He parks under some streetlights.

"Chloe, I don't know what I was thinking. Actually, I wasn't thinking. You were growing up, dreaming about college and boys. Your mom was all about her writing, dreaming of a new career. And I . . . I didn't have dreams. I felt old and tired." He took a deep breath. "Then I met Darlene, and . . ." He stopped talking.

"And you loved her more than me and Mom?"

He breathes in. "No. There's no excuse for what I did. I see that now. It's so freaking clear. I was a bastard. I don't deserve your love. I don't deserve your forgiveness. But I can't lose my little girl. Please . . . forgive me."

His pain is so real, I feel it. I don't speak for almost a

minute, because I don't know what to say, but then words pour out of me. "I haven't refused to see you. But forgiving you isn't easy." I swallow. "I still love you, but sometimes I wish I didn't."

He nods. "What can I do to help? I'll do anything. Tell me. Does your mom need money?"

"I don't . . . think so. But she did tell me to ask why my car insurance wasn't paid."

"It wasn't paid?" he asked.

"She said it wasn't."

"But Darlene said . . . I'll look into it. What else can I do?"

"Nothing." Hearing Darlene's name makes me angry all over again.

My phone dings with another text. I don't look at it. I'm guessing it's from Cash.

We sit in the silent, hot car.

"We brought you here that first day we got you," Dad says.

I look at him, not understanding. He continues, "When we picked you up from the agency, we came to see your grandparents and then we came here. I put you in the swing. I remember thinking how delicate you were. How small, even though you weren't a baby. I was scared, thinking I was responsible for taking care of you. I put you in a swing, but I was afraid I might push too hard and not catch you if you fell. You seemed scared. I wanted to do something, anything to prove to you that I was an okay guy." I hear his voice catch. "I fell in love with you then. I swore I'd never let anyone hurt you, and now I'm the ass who's hurt you. I hate myself for it."

I don't say anything.

"I know it's going to take time for you to forgive me, but

I'm not going to disappear from your life. I love you," he says.

It's crazy, throughout all of this, I never doubted he loved me. I just couldn't fathom how he could have loved me and done this.

I also know he's hoping I'll say it back. Say I love him. But I've said it once. That's all I can do.

18

"Chloe?" Dad slips his hand in mine.

His touch brings a jolt of pain. I almost pull away, but don't because I know it'll hurt him.

We sit there. I remember what I wanted to ask him tonight. "What was the name of the adoption agency?"

"What?"

I pull my hand free. "The name of the adoption agency? It was in Fort Landing, right?"

"Yeah. I think it was . . . New Hope or something. Why?"

I shrug. "Just curious."

"Are you wanting to—?"

"No," I say. "And don't say anything to Mom. I'm afraid it'd hurt her."

"I won't."

After another bout of silence, he opens his car door. "Come on," he says.

"Where?"

"Let's go swing. You used to make me do it all the time."

"No," I say.

"Humor me. You told me once that swinging was as good as flying."

I almost tell him no again, but I remember how hurt he sounded a few minutes ago, so I get out. It's dark, but the moon's full and bright. The night's so quiet, I hear our footsteps. We walk to the swing set with the highest swings. We each take one, leaving an empty one between us. He looks too big to be in a swing. I feel too big. But the pain between us somehow feels smaller.

I swing. Legs back. Legs front. I stare at the big ball of moon, at the stars twinkling down. The motion, the back-and-forth, feels somehow cathartic. It does feel like flying.

A whoosh of air brushes past me as Dad starts to swing. As he goes forward, I go back. We aren't on the same rhythm. I realize it might be a while before I feel the ease of the father–daughter relationship that we had before.

I don't know when I'll be able to forgive him, but this is the first time I've felt he regretted anything. It doesn't fix it. But it's a start. Maybe it won't ever be like before, but I hope we'll find a new rhythm, a new way to a father-and-daughter place that doesn't hurt.

I guess breaking eggs can be a good thing.

When I walk into the house, there's no food smells drifting from the kitchen. Mom didn't fix dinner. I walk into the living room, hoping she's awake.

She is. She's on the sofa, reading. Not writing. I stand there, remembering how I felt when I saw Mrs. Fuller—as if I'd been cheated out of something—of a mother's love. Yet I have a mother. And as flawed as she has been this last year, she loves me. I know that. And I love her.

She looks up, and I suddenly feel guilty. Guilty for feeling she wasn't enough, guilty for whining about taking care of her to Dad. Yeah, it was a bitch. It was terrible, but not nearly so hard as it was on her. And if I'd been the one to get cancer, she'd have done the same thing for me. Only she never would've complained. My chest clutches.

I pull my cell phone out. "What toppings do you want?"

"What?"

"I'm ordering us pizza."

"I thought you went out to eat?"

"I didn't eat anything," I say.

"Why?" she asks.

"It didn't smell right."

"Did you have an argument?" She sits up straighter, as if preparing herself to get angry.

"I want Canadian bacon and pineapple," I lie, because I know she loves it. "Something a little sweet and a little bacony. Sound good to you?"

"Yeah. What was the argument about?"

"Do you want a salad?"

"You aren't going to tell me?"

"You know what I think we should do?" I ask.

"What?" She sounds a little frustrated.

"Order the pizza and then give that movie you rented another shot."

She makes a face. "It was inappropriate."

"Maybe. But humor is sometimes inappropriate. And we both need to laugh."

"You've seen it?"

"Yeah. But I want to see it again."

"Who with? Who did you see this movie with?"

I frown. "Promise you won't get mad?"

"Alex?" When I don't deny it, she looks shocked, but not so much angry.

"Yeah. And we laughed our butts off. And you need to laugh your butt off. So we're eating pizza and watching the movie. And we're going to laugh at condom jokes. Got it?"

She appears surprised at my tone. "I guess I don't have a choice."

I remember Cash saying, *You always have a choice.* But for Mom, this is the right choice. And I'm glad she's not arguing. I've argued enough tonight.

When Cash and the Fullers got home, he wanted to take off to his room.

"I think I'm going to read." Mrs. Fuller headed toward the master bedroom. Cash got to the stairs when Mr. Fuller said, "Cash, grab us two beers from the fridge, and let's talk outside."

What? "A beer?"

"I know you've drunk one before."

"I don't drink that much." He'd seen his dad do it too much.

"I wouldn't offer you one if I thought you did. I'll wait outside."

Cash grabbed two Bud Lights. "What did I do?" he asked, but his knotted gut said this had to do with his *bad idea* comment about being adopted.

"Thanks for meeting us for dinner. Susan was afraid you wouldn't."

Mr. Fuller twisted the cap off the beer. Cash did the same.

"She loves you." Mr. Fuller lifted his beer and took a long sip.

"Too much." Cash took a sip.

"You can't love too much," Mr. Fuller said.

Cash disagreed. "This is about her telling me she wanted to adopt me, isn't it?"

Mr. Fuller set his beer down. "We don't understand. Why would you not want that?"

"I'm going to be eighteen in six weeks. I don't need someone taking care of me."

"Everyone needs family, Cash."

No, they don't. "Look, it's not like I don't appreciate what you've done."

"We know that, Cash. That's just it. You do appreciate it. We can tell. And other than fighting issues, you're a good kid. Heck, you even put up with Susan's rules, some of which are ridiculous. And I know that's because you care about her. That's why I don't understand why you wouldn't want this."

Cash shrugged. "I don't know what to tell you. I just don't think it's needed."

Mr. Fuller sipped his beer. "Do you know what she's afraid of?"

"No." Cash turned the cold bottle in his hands.

"That on your birthday, you'll pack up your stuff and walk away, and we'll never hear from you again. And—damn it!—she's still suffering from losing one kid. She can't lose another."

Hurt swelled in Cash's chest. That's why he hoped Chloe was Emily. "I'm not planning on moving until I graduate."

"And then what?" Mr. Fuller asked.

"I need to be my own person."

"When have we tried to make you something you aren't?"

"All the time," he said, his tone firm. *You want me to be your son.* "You got upset when I signed up for auto tech. You want me to go to some fancy college. And Mrs. Fuller wants me to quit working at the garage. Which I'm not going to do."

"Is it wrong of us to want you to go to a better college? You're so smart, Cash. You have higher SAT scores than either I or Susan did. You could be anything you want. Why would you settle to be a mechanic?"

"There's nothing wrong with being a mechanic. And I'm going to college, just not the one you want."

"But we've got money—"

"I've got a grant!" Cash stood up.

"Cash, son, please, sit down."

I'm not your son.

When Cash didn't sit down, Mr. Fuller continued, "I'm begging you, don't hurt her more than she's already been hurt."

"I'm trying not to." He shot off upstairs, barely refraining from slamming the bedroom door.

In his room, his phone dinged. A text from Chloe. He'd texted her earlier and asked if they could talk.

Her reply: *Can't tonight. Let's talk tomorrow.*

"Shit!" He tossed the phone on the bed. He could've really used a distraction. He could've used a laugh. He could've used hearing her soft voice. He wanted to tease her more about reading *Fifty Shades of Grey* and tell her about the book he bought.

He wanted . . .

He wanted . . .

He wanted . . .

It was eleven when I went to bed. Mom and I laughed. A lot. I think I put on a good show, but in truth, I laughed more for Mom than anything else. Now I can't sleep. Nothing feels so funny.

I keep seeing the Fullers in my mind. Her face at the

restaurant. His face. His eyes. The man who could be my father.

I keep wondering if I'm Emily. And if I am, what would my life have been like if I hadn't been taken from them? In another life, would I still be me? Since they're still married, would I have skipped out on the pain of my parents' divorce? The pain of Mom's cancer? Would I have gone to private school and now be planning to go to some fancy college? Who would I be if I hadn't grown up thinking . . . thinking I'd been given away? That I'd done something wrong. How much better would my life have been?

That leads me to feeling guilty again. As if wanting answers, wanting to know my real parents loved me, makes me ungrateful for the parents I have.

Pushing that thought away, I start going over all the things I told Dad. All of it's true, but I remember the tears in his eyes, the pain my words caused him. Even knowing he deserved it doesn't make it feel right.

The craziest thought hits. What if Dad had an accident on the way home? What if I lost him! I remember him saying he loved me while we sat in the car. He needed to hear me say it back, and I hadn't. What if that was my last chance to say it?

I know, I know, I'm crazy for thinking shit like this, but I think it anyway, and this ball of emotion—of grief, of guilt that I shouldn't feel—sits on my chest like a big, pink elephant.

I grab my phone to text Dad. Then I realize he's not home, I realize his home used to be mine and now it's Darlene's home. I slam my phone down and draw my hands into fists.

I think about texting Lindsey, but I'm sure she's still out with David.

At twelve, I grab my phone to text Cash. I want to tell him that I know it's the right adoption agency. I want someone to tell me that I shouldn't feel disloyal for needing answers. Or maybe I just want to talk. To him. Last night, on the phone with him, had been nice, fun. It made me forget how messed up my life is.

It didn't matter that he's helping find out if I am some missing kidnapped child. Didn't matter, because the teasing, the flirting, the wanting to know more about him. That was fun. That was normal.

I needed more normal.

I start to text him, but envision him asleep in bed. I even envision him without his shirt. I've never seen him shirtless, but I can imagine how nice it'd be.

Right then, my phone dings with a text. Bolting up, I grab it.

It's him. *You awake?*

Me: *Yes. You want to talk?*

Him: *No.*

Me: *No . . . ?*

Him: *I want to see you. I'm outside your house.*

Me: *My house? Right now?*

I run to the window. My heart races.

I see his Jeep. And more than anything, I want to see Cash.

19

I turn to go to the door but hear the old wooden floors squeak under my bare feet. I stop and realize I'm just wearing boxer pj bottoms and a matching T-shirt.

Am I decent?

Yes. Other than being braless, but the top isn't tight.

My next thought is of Mom hearing me.

I run back to my window. It doesn't have a screen. I'm unlocking it when my phone dings again.

Him: *Does this mean you don't want to see me?*

Me: *I'm opening my window.*

I hear his Jeep door open and close, and I see Cash. The heaviness in my chest lifts like fog dispersing.

He looks so good, walking toward my window. Toward me.

"I'm afraid I'll wake up Mom, going to the front door," I whisper.

He looks up. "Do you want me to come in?"

"No, I'll come out." I glance down. It's only, like, a three-foot drop. Considering I'm five-seven, it's nothing. I put my top half through the window, straddle the ledge, then turning, I put my other leg out. I'm leaning forward, perched on the windowsill. All I need to do is push off the ledge.

"I'll catch you." His words sound so sweet. I want to be caught.

He reaches up, and I push off. His hands end up under my T-shirt on my naked waist, and his touch feels so good, so warm, so sweet. I instantly feel butterflies.

When I land, I catch my breath, not from the jump, but from his touch. He pulls me closer, or did I move in?

We kiss. His smooth lips glide across mine. His hands rest on my waist, and his thumbs make small circles on my bare skin, right under my rib cage. My hands move to his waist.

I lean closer. My breasts, minus a bra, come against his solid chest. A thrill, a sweet tingling waves over me.

"Wow." He pulls back.

"Yeah." I grin. "I wanted to text you."

"Why didn't you?"

"I thought you'd be asleep."

"Couldn't sleep," he says.

"Me neither."

"Bad night?" he asks.

"Yeah. You?"

"Yeah. But it's better now." He dips down and kisses me again. This time, his tongue slips between my lips; his mouth tastes minty, as if he popped a breath freshener.

When the kiss ends, we're both breathless.

"You want to go somewhere?"

I roll my eyes. "I'm in my pajamas and barefoot."

His eyes lower to my feet. "Cute."

I curl my toes in the warm grass. "My feet?"

"All of you," he says. "You want to sit on the porch?"

I hear a meow. Felix jumps up on my bedroom windowsill. "No," I say, and the cat jumps back into my room. Cash closes the window.

"Maybe in your car," I say, not wanting anyone to see me in my pj's, kissing a guy on my front porch.

"Yeah." His hand drops from my waist and slips inside my palm as we walk to his car. I lace my fingers through his.

"What happened?" I ask, remembering his *bad night* comment. "They didn't see me, did they?"

"No. Just more of the same shit."

"You mean quitting your job and going to a better college?"

"Yeah," he says.

"Sorry."

We get to his Jeep. "You want to get in the backseat?"

I remember Lindsey's comment about not wanting David to think she wanted to get in the backseat.

"Just to talk," Cash says as if he's reading my mind. "And kiss." He looks embarrassed. "Not . . . you know."

"Yeah." I smile because I believe him. He's not here to try something that I'm not ready for.

I lift up on my tiptoes and kiss his cheek. "Thank you."

"For what?"

"For coming here."

He opens the back door and follows me into his car. The console between the seats is down. I slide only halfway in so I'll be close to him. He settles beside me and shuts the door.

"Sheep," he says.

"Huh?" I ask.

"You have sheep on your shorts and shirt."

I look down. "They're pajamas."

"I know." Smiling, he pushes my hair off my cheek. "Oh, here." He pulls something out of his pocket. It's a plastic bag.

I grin. "Red Skittles. Thank you." I put one in my mouth. Then put one in his.

"What made your night bad? The restaurant thing?"

"Part of it. I'm an egg breaker now."

"What?"

"Remember I accused you of being an egg breaker while I'm a peacemaker?"

"Yeah. What did you do?"

"I came unglued. Told Dad what I thought of him leaving me to deal with Mom and the cancer."

"Good." His caring tone sends a sweet pain right to my chest. "What did he say?"

"I think he finally realizes what a jerk he was."

"Did it feel good?" Cash asks.

"No. Not really. I hurt him." I bite down on my lip. "He cried. Begged me to forgive him."

"And you forgave him," he says almost as if it were a bad thing.

"No. I told him it wasn't easy. But I told him I still love him."

"You're a better person than I am," he said.

I see something in his eyes. "Who do you need to forgive?"

"A lot of people."

He kisses me again. I get lost in the feel of his mouth against mine.

In a few minutes, we're stretched out on the seat, facing each other. We kiss and kiss and kiss. I have my hands on his chest; his are still at my waist. He moves up under my shirt to my back, and he starts easing to my front. To my breasts.

Then he jerks his hands out from under my shirt and buries his face in my neck. I feel his breath against my cheek. I open my eyes. The car's windows are fogged up. He lifts his head and I see his eyes. Pupils dilated. I know he stopped to keep his promise. And I almost wish he hadn't.

He smiles. I smile back.

"I needed this," he said. "You make me . . . forget the bad stuff."

"Yeah." I kiss him again, but I end it quickly. Deep down, I know we need to slow down. I know what comes next. And while it feels so right, I'm not really ready for next.

I touch his lips. "You make me feel so . . . normal."

"Normal?" He grins against my fingers. "For a girl who reads love stories, I think you can do better than that."

I laugh. "No, I mean, I'm not Chloe whose mom has cancer or is depressed. Or Chloe whose dad's a cheater. Or Chloe who might be a kidnapped girl. I'm just a normal girl, feeling amazing things while kissing a hot guy."

"I like the 'hot' part," he says.

"I like the hot guy."

"You're awesome." He runs a finger over my cheek.

I remember what I wanted to tell him. "You were right. It's A New Hope Adoption Agency that my parents used."

"How do you know?"

"I asked Dad."

"Did you tell him—?"

"No, I said I was curious and told him not to mention it to Mom."

Cash nods. "We should go talk to them. Ask to see your paperwork."

"Would they let me see it?" I sit up.

"You're not eighteen, but you'll be eighteen soon, so who knows. Maybe they'll give you something for your parents to sign."

The kissing magic starts wearing off, and I remember what I'm facing. "I want to do this. I do, but . . ." I remember hearing Mom laugh tonight. "I can't ask my mom to sign anything. It might make her even more depressed."

"I could forge her signature."

"That's illegal."

"Not as illegal as kidnapping."

Yup, the magic's gone. "My parents didn't kidnap me. They adopted me."

"I don't mean . . ." He hesitates. "Before we go, we

should know everything we can. I'll try to get ahold of the file. It might be Monday."

I nod.

His green eyes meet mine with caution. "When I asked you if you remembered anything before the adoption, you said, 'barely.' What do you remember?"

"It's not even a whole memory. I'm sitting on a sofa. It's light brown, and it's stained. I'm crying, scared. I'm wearing black patent shoes. The kind that buckle. The carpet's dirty. And I'm wearing a princess dress. I'm even holding a tiara."

"Was someone with you?"

"I don't know. All I know is I'm scared."

"Like you were kidnapped?"

"I don't know, but that feeling, that same fear, I sometimes feel it out of the blue." My throat knots. "Or maybe it's that my mom just dropped me off at the adoption agency. What if we're wrong? What if this is all a coincidence? And my real parents just didn't want me?"

He frowns. "That's a lot of coincidences. Your living here. Your cat's name. The date Emily was kidnapped and you were adopted. Your doll."

"Yeah, but it could still be that."

His shoulder shifts closer to mine. "We'll figure it out."

I close my eyes, and I remember almost hearing someone telling me that my mama and daddy didn't want me anymore. Did that happen, or was that just what I felt? And the bruise . . . ? "Do you think if the Fullers had seen me, they'd have recognized me?"

"Yeah. You look just like that picture."

I lean against him. "This is so hard."

"I know," he says.

Right then, a car stops in front of Lindsey's house. I look

up as the headlights go out. "That's Lindsey coming home from her date with David."

I lower myself in the seat and pull him down. He lifts back up. "Uh-oh, they're on the porch. He's going in for a kiss."

"Stop snooping." But then I lift up and watch David kiss Lindsey.

"That's sweet," I say, hoping Lindsey isn't thinking of Jonathon.

"This is sweeter." Cash pulls me down and kisses me. And he's right. It is sweeter.

We kiss until we see David's car leave. Then I say, "It's late."

"Yeah." He walks me back to the window and opens it.

I measure the climb up. "Getting in is going to be harder than getting out."

"Pull up and I'll give you a push." He takes the Skittles from my hands and sticks them in his pocket.

I put my hands on the ledge and pull up. His hands come against my butt, and he gives me a shove. I land halfway in the window. Suddenly, I find it funny. I laugh and look back. "You can get your hands off my butt now."

"I was just helping," he says, and grins.

I climb the rest of the way in, then turn and look at him. He hands me my candy, then pulls himself up on the ledge. His shoulders fill up the window space, his biceps bulging, his green eyes on mine.

He gives me a brief goodbye kiss. "Sweet dreams."

"You, too."

I watch him walk back to his car. I run my tongue over my lips to savor his taste. Even with all the shit I have going on, for the first time, I'm beginning to feel the joy in Joyful, Texas.

20

After breakfast Sunday morning, Cash texts and says he'll be here at eleven to pick me up. I hurry and get ready, and at a little after ten, I run over to Lindsey's. I say hello to Lola and her mom as Lindsey escorts me into her bedroom. As soon as the door closes, she says, "He kissed me twice while we were at the game room playing pool."

"And once when he walked you to the door," I drop down on her bed.

She looks shocked. "You were spying on me?"

"No. I was in Cash's car when he brought you home."

"Cash? I thought you went out with your dad."

"I did, but at midnight, he texted me and said he was sitting in his Jeep outside my house."

"And . . . ?" she asks.

"It was sooo good." I'm smiling, thinking of every tingle and thrill. How his hand felt on my bare back, but I don't want to share those things. It's almost as though if I share them, they won't be so special. They are my secret. "But tell me about your date."

She went through the entire date, about how she beat David at pool, and how they laughed about it, then added, "Oh, guess who came here last night?"

"Jonathon," I say. "I was waiting on the porch for Dad when he pulled up." I told her about her mom shutting the door in Jonathon's face. Then I tell her about him coming on to me.

"Jerk. He came to see me and then asked you out."

"He didn't say a date, but—"

"But he meant it. Ugh! That asshole!"

"Yeah. He is."

She smiles. "Are you still going out with Cash today?"

"At eleven."

"Do you want me to help you pick out something to wear?"

I make a face. "I was planning on wearing this."

"Stand up."

I do. She studies me, and I suddenly feel incredibly insecure. I remember Cara and Sandy always giving me fashion advice.

"Jeans look great. But go with your red blouse and black boots. And more lip gloss and mascara."

"Okay." It makes me feel a little better that I wore that outfit to school, and I'm not totally fashion impaired. I pull my phone out to make sure I keep track of time.

"Did you ask your dad about the adoption agency?"

"Yeah." I tell her the whole Dad story. The Fullers at the restaurant story. She's glued to my every word, whispering "Shit!" and "Crap!" every few minutes.

Then I tell her about Cash wanting to photograph all the paperwork that the Fullers had on Emily. "He says we should go talk to the agency."

"What are you going to do if you learn you really are Emily?"

The question is simple, but suddenly it doesn't feel that way. "What do you mean?"

"Are you going to go live with them? Don't you think they'll expect you to? I mean, you are about to go to college, and they haven't seen you in . . . fifteen years?"

The question hits me like a soccer ball to the chest that I didn't see coming—it knocks the breath out of me. *Live with them?*

Lindsey keeps talking, something about not wanting me to move, but I'm barely listening.

I hadn't thought about what the Fullers would expect from me. Not physically. Not emotionally. Am I supposed to immediately love them like I love Mom and Dad? What if they blame me for not remembering them? For not finding my way home earlier? What if they *do* expect me to move in with them?

When Cash came down the stairs Sunday to head over to Chloe's, Mr. Fuller walked out of the kitchen. "Hey, you want to go for a jog with me?"

"Can't. I'm meeting the study group again. I told Mrs. Fuller."

Mr. Fuller nodded. "What's her name?"

"What?"

Mr. Fuller laughed. "No guy showers and smells like toothpaste before going to study. And you smiled all the way through breakfast. What's her name?"

Cash wanted to deny it, but then gave in. "Chloe."

"Is she pretty?"

Shit. Why had he told him? "Don't . . . don't tell Mrs. Fuller."

"Why? She'd be thrilled."

"She'd want to meet her and—"

"Why wouldn't you want us to meet her?" Mr. Fuller's brow wrinkled in concern.

"Because we're not at that stage."

The man leaned in. "What stage are you in?" When Cash didn't answer, he said, "Do you need . . . protection, because . . ."

"No." Cash realized his huge screwup in telling Mr. Fuller

Chloe's name. When the truth came out, he'd realize Cash had been dating his daughter.

"Look, I know what happens after you've been dating awhile, so . . ."

"I gotta . . . go." Cash left.

Driving to Chloe's, he allowed himself one minute of worrying how his dating her would play out. Hell, if she was Emily, the Fullers would probably want her to date better.

The farther he got from the Fullers' house, the less he worried about that and the more he thought about Chloe. About how wonderful last night had been. He'd barely slept, remembering every touch, every laugh, every brush of her body against his. He'd never felt like this. Yeah, he'd been with girls. Enjoyed being with girls. But it wasn't the same. This was more intense. Yet somehow more comfortable.

Almost to her house, he realized he wasn't looking forward to seeing Chloe's mom. His gut said she didn't like him.

Pulling up in front of Chloe's house, he pushed back his concerns. *People are just like dogs, they can smell your fear!*

When he walked onto the porch, he saw Chloe's mom through the window. She was wearing too-big jeans, a T-shirt, and a bandanna. She looked sick. God, he hoped her doctor was right about her being okay. He knocked. Ms. Holden opened the door.

"Hi." He offered what he hoped was a fearless smile.

"I'm coming," he heard Chloe call out.

"Come in," Ms. Holden said.

"How are you doing?" He walked into the living room.

"Okay." She studied him with that look again. As if he wasn't good enough. And she was right, but . . .

Chloe walked out frowning and practically rushed him out the door.

"Everything okay?" he asked.

She glanced back at the house, as if worried her mom would hear. "No."

No? They got in his Jeep. "What's wrong?"

"I don't know if I can do this."

Her words sank to the bottom of his chest. "Did I do something wrong last night?"

"No. I mean the Emily thing."

"What happened?"

She fell back against the seat. "I just don't know how the Fullers will react or what they'll expect from me."

He started driving. "You said last night you wanted to do this."

"I do, but . . ."

"They'll be ecstatic to have found you, and I don't know what you mean about what they'll expect."

"Where are we going?" she asked.

"To the park, to talk." Silence followed them until they arrived. When he turned off the engine, he looked at her. He wanted to kiss her, but it didn't feel right. "Why are you worried about this?"

"It's just . . ."

"Are you scared your parents are the ones who kidnapped you?" As much as he wanted to believe it wasn't them, and even as much as her perfect childhood didn't paint them as the type to kidnap children, he had doubts.

"No!" she snapped. "I told you my parents wouldn't do that."

"Then what is it?"

She exhaled. "What if they blame me for not remembering them? For not finding my way home? Or what if they expect me to automatically love them like I love my mom and dad? I don't know them."

"Blame you? You weren't even three years old. And they'll be so happy you're alive that they won't judge you for what you feel."

She wrung her hands in her lap. "What if they try to make me go live with them? I can't leave Mom. I won't."

"You're almost eighteen. No one can make you do anything."

"They could still try and—"

"Why don't we not worry about that now. Let's figure out if you're really Emily first."

She bit down on her lip. "Only if you promise me something."

"What?"

"That even if I end up being the Fullers' child, it's my choice if I want to tell them."

"What? Are you saying you might not tell them?"

"I just don't know how my mom's going to take it. I need to know the truth, but I can't let this hurt her. And . . ."

"And what?" he asked, seeing her eyes tear up.

"I feel . . . disloyal. As if wanting to know my real parents is like saying they weren't enough. As if everything they've done for me didn't matter."

"You're not saying that."

"I know, but Mom's hurting so much right now."

Cash stared at her. "You're just scared."

"Yes, I'm scared. This whole thing is screwed up."

"Okay, I get it, but you can't keep this from them." Damn it, Chloe wasn't seeing the whole picture. "You think the Fullers aren't hurting? Do you know how many times I've heard her cry? If you're their daughter, they deserve to know. They've done nothing wrong."

"Neither did my parents," she said. "And I'll tell them eventually. I might even tell them when we find out. It's just . . . if Mom is still like this, then I want to make sure she can handle it." She sighed. "Please, Cash. Promise me you'll leave that up to me."

21

He gave me his word. But I can tell he wasn't happy doing it. We leave the park and go to Whataburger. We order and are just sitting down when my phone dings with a text.

It's from Dad. I swipe it. An image appears. It takes a second to figure out what it is, but when I do, it pulls my heartstrings.

It's my room. My room! He moved my things back. Then I read the text: *Paid car insurance. Sorry it was late.* I smile, but tears fill my eyes.

"What is it?" Cash asks.

"My dad gave me my room back." I try to blink away my tears. "Sorry."

"For what?"

"You've seen me cry how many times? I know boys hate that." I make a face.

"I don't mind. Not if a girl has a real reason. You've got a lot of stuff going on right now." He looks down at his drink and turns his straw. "Did you not cry in front of Alex?"

I recall when Dad left and even when Mom got cancer,

I mostly bottled everything up inside. Only once did I really lose it in front of Alex. It was when Mom was diagnosed. He'd picked me up, and when I got in the car, I started crying.

He hugged me real awkward-like and said he'd understand if I didn't want to go to his house. Which was his way of saying he was okay if we didn't have sex. At the time, I saw that as support. But now I recall how he took me home an hour after that. It was as if he didn't know how to deal with my being upset.

I compare that to how I've lost it in front of Cash several times. Then I remember how I apologized for barfing my problems all over him. What was it he said? *I can handle a little barf.*

Glancing up, I realize Cash is waiting for an answer. "No. Alex didn't rate too high on giving or being sympathetic."

"I knew I didn't like him." There's a tease to Cash's tone, but also a touch of truth.

Our cheeseburgers and fries come.

I eat a fry and feel ketchup drip onto the corner of my mouth. I grab a napkin, but Cash reaches over, swipes it away. Our eyes meet, hold. The memory of kissing him last night, of his hands on my bare back, brings a warmth to my chest. And from the heat in his green eyes, I know he's thinking about it, too.

The following Sunday, I'm getting dressed to go out with Cash again. This week I've been caught in a roller coaster of emotions. Worry about Mom, about Dad, about being Emily. I've even started waking up feeling afraid. Almost as if I'm reliving something. I try hard to ignore that. No use going to the past to find problems. A past that may or may not be nothing more than a child's imagination. I have plenty of problems in the present to hash over. That said, when I'm with Cash, I'm walking on clouds.

Because Mr. Fuller took some time off work, Cash wasn't able to get his hands on the file until this morning when the Fullers went out for breakfast. Cash is more upset about the delay than I am. Not that I don't want to do this, but Mom's not getting any better. I even offered to walk with her, but she said no.

"Where are you going?" Mom asks when I step out of my room.

"I'm hanging out with Cash. I told you yesterday."

"I forgot." She reclines on the sofa.

She's forgetting a lot lately.

I hear Cash pull up, and because Mom's still in her pajamas, I meet him outside.

We kiss when I get in his Jeep. "You okay?" he asks.

He's good at picking up on my moods. "Yeah. Just Mom. She's still down."

"Sorry." He heads to the print shop. "I downloaded everything on a stick. Their printer has a memory card on it."

Their printer. I look at him. "You always say 'their house' or 'their printer,' as if it's not yours."

"It's not mine," he says as if he doesn't understand what I mean.

"I know, but it's as if . . . Are you not comfortable there?"

He hesitates. "I'm comfortable."

"But you don't feel at home, do you?" And if he doesn't, I know I won't. Not that I'd go live with them, but is that the type of people they are?

The question seems to annoy him. "They are taking care of me for the state."

I try to grasp what he's saying. "So they treat you like a foster kid?"

He frowns. "I am a foster kid." His tone yanks at my heartstrings.

He pulls up at the store and parks. Then he looks at me. "They don't treat me badly. They're too good to me. I just don't belong there."

"Why don't you belong?"

He stares out the windshield. "They deserve their real kid. They deserve you."

"We don't know I'm Emily."

"Okay, they deserve someone like you. Someone good."

"You aren't good?"

His frown deepens. "You don't get it, because you haven't been in foster care."

She had been, according to her mom, but she didn't remember, so it didn't count.

"This is the fourth family I've been with. You learn not to start thinking of it as your home, because things change."

A lump forms in my chest. "I can't imagine growing up that way."

"It's not . . . I'm just explaining why things are different. The last thing I want is for you to start feeling sorry for me. I hate that." He gets out of his Jeep.

I do the same. "I don't feel sorry for you," I lie.

We walk to the back counter. "Can I help you?" the young guy asks me.

Cash speaks up. "I need to print some copies off my memory stick."

"Yeah." The guy's gaze stays on me. "I can do it for you."

"No. I got it," Cash says. "I've done it before."

The guy nods and finally looks at Cash. "I'll turn on number one."

In a few seconds, Cash connects his memory stick to the computer and types on the keyboard. The printer starts spitting out papers.

Cash slips his hand in mine. "You want to go grab something to drink, and we can go through them?"

"Sure. But I need to be home by four. I have some homework."

"You should have brought it. We could've done it together."

"Yeah. But I don't want Mom to be alone that long."

"Okay." The computer stops printing. Cash gathers up the papers and takes his memory stick.

"I can check you out," the guy behind the counter says.

"I'll pay up front." As we go, Cash whispers, "I needed a chisel to get his eyes off you."

"What?"

"That guy had the hots for you."

"Did not," I say.

Fifteen minutes later, we sit at a small diner and he pulls the papers from the envelope and puts them into two stacks. "I got two copies so we can each have one."

I watch the stacks grow with what looks like copies of newspaper articles. Some of them have baby pictures of Emily Fuller. I'm shocked again at how much they look like the images that were in my grandmother's album.

He finally has two equal stacks, but he's holding one extra sheet. "Crap. We're missing one."

"You think it spilled out of the backseat?"

"I hope so." He sounds concerned.

"Is it a problem if we lost it?"

"No, it's just . . . you should never leave crumb trails?"

"Crumb trails?"

He glances up. "Just something my dad used to say."

It's the first time since we met that I've heard him mention his dad in casual conversation. "Do you miss him?"

"Huh?" His brow tightens.

"You mentioned your dad, and I . . . I wondered if you still miss him."

"No." His tone is brust.

I remember Paul mentioning the rumor that Cash had killed his dad. I didn't believe it then, and Cash told me his father died in a car crash, but for some reason, he hadn't seemed . . . mournful.

"Was he a good father?"

"No." He studied the sheet in his hand.

A sharp pain hits my chest. "What did he do?"

Cash looks up. "If there was a rule book on how to be a good father, he never read it."

I want to ask for specifics, but my gut says he doesn't want to give any more. I guess if something really bad had happened, I wouldn't want to talk about it either. Then again, something kind of did. I was either given away because someone didn't want me, or I was kidnapped. Either way, it's bad.

Cash studies the stacks of paper. "There has to be something in here to help us."

"What are we looking for?"

"I don't know. Something that might . . . trigger your memory."

I flinch remembering waking up afraid. Do I want my memory triggered? I do. I don't. I rub the back of my neck.

"What's wrong?"

"I'm scared, but it's nuts. I'm not scared for me today. It's as if I'm terrified for me when I was young. It doesn't make sense."

"I think it does." He rests his hand on mine. "Sometimes the past haunts you."

I look at him and I get a glimpse of his pain. "What haunts you?"

He shakes his head. "Let's get working on this. My gut

says something in here will show us where to look for answers." He picks up a sheet. "Remember I told you we needed to talk to the nanny?"

"Yeah." I lean a little closer.

"I was reading one article on the computer that implied the police suspected she was part of the kidnapping."

"Was she arrested?"

"No, they didn't have proof. What's weird is that she even described a man who she said spoke to you at the park that day. I'm guessing the police didn't believe her. I'm hoping to find something in here that helps us find her because with her name, Carmen Gonzales, she might as well be Jane Smith. And I want to either call her or, even better, go see her to ask questions."

The thought scares me. "But if she was part of the kidnapping, she won't tell us anything."

"If she refuses to talk, that'll tell us something."

"But isn't she going to wonder why you're asking questions? You can't tell her about me."

"I won't. I'll make something up. Like maybe my sister went missing at the same time and I'm looking for any similarities in the kidnapping. Or I had a foster sister who thought she was Emily Fuller and she's in California now and I told her I'd look into it."

His answer stops me. "Wow. You're good at—" I almost say *lying*. "—coming up with stories."

"I told you we'll get to the bottom of it."

I pick up a sheet that has a picture of Mr. and Mrs. Fuller on it. Some of them are the same articles I read at the library. "I used to wonder what my real parents looked like. And when I'd meet other kids who kind of looked like me, I'd wonder if they were my siblings. If my parents gave me away, maybe they gave other kids away. Up until I was, like, eight or nine, every time Mom or Dad would get upset with me, I'd worry they'd give me away like my other parents."

I breathe around the heavy lump in my chest and realize that was probably what Cash felt like all his life, too.

"So you always knew you were adopted? It's not like they just told you one day?"

"I don't ever remember *not* knowing." My mind takes me back, back to a collage of I'm-adopted memories. Most of them painful. "In the second grade, my teacher was pregnant. One day, I came home crying because she seemed so happy to have the baby in her belly, and I was afraid my mom couldn't love me as much as my teacher was going to love her baby, because I was never in her belly."

"What did your mom say?" he asked.

"That a person loves with their heart, and you don't have to be in someone's belly to be in their heart. She asked me if I loved her less because I knew I wasn't in her belly."

He dropped his hand on mine. "Sounds like she said the right thing."

Tears fill my eyes. "Yeah, she always said the right thing. They love me. But . . . I still questioned it. There was always that empty spot." I put my hand in the center of my chest. "When Dad left and Mom and I came here, I felt it even more." I swallow. "I think that's what I want to come from all this. To not feel this spot anymore."

He squeezes my hand. "We can do it."

His tone is so caring, his smile so assuring, that I know I never got this from Alex. I lean forward and kiss him. He kisses me back.

When it ends, we're both smiling. I put my hand on his chest. "What can I do to help fill your spot?"

He looks surprised. "I don't have one."

I don't argue with him, but I know it's a lie. I'm pretty sure his spot is bigger than mine.

Part of me wonders if this isn't some of the attraction between us. Why I defended him to Ms. Anderson. Why I agreed to meet him at the coffee bar. Maybe wounded people are subconsciously drawn to each other.

That would explain why Alex couldn't understand. Maybe people walking around with empty spots instinctively recognize each other's pain.

I want to help him fill his empty spot, too. I remember the red Skittles text messages and his buying them for me, and how that made me feel . . . happy.

"What's your favorite candy?"

"Red Skittles." He grins.

"That's mine. What's yours?"

"Those soft caramels."

"Favorite band?"

"The Black Keys."

"Favorite thing to do?" I ask.

He smiles and I know he's thinking *sex*. I hit him in his chest. "Besides that."

He laughs. "Kiss you."

"Favorite thing to do that doesn't involve me. And if you say kiss someone else, I'm going to hit you."

His grin widens. "Lie in bed, listen to music. It's like a reward after I've been successful at something, like a boatload of homework, or acing a test."

"What's—?" He puts his finger over my lips, as if to stop me from asking another question. "We should be reading these. It's almost three."

"I know," I say. "But there's so much I want to know about you, and this feels good."

"Yeah, it does." He touches my face.

I look at the stacks of papers. "We're about more than this, right?"

"Hell yeah."

I wave a hand to the papers. "That scares me."

"I know," he says as if he understands.

"This—" I wave a hand between us. "—kind of scares me, too."

"Why?" Concern fills his eyes.

"Because I'm an insecure twit sometimes. Because I've had my heart broken twice. Once by Alex and once by my dad. Because I'm scared of losing people, and maybe it's because—" I wave to the papers again. "—I lost people I loved a long time ago."

"I wouldn't hurt you." He pauses, then says, "If you're not a little bit afraid, you're not doing something right." He said it like it was a quote from Einstein or Freud.

"Who said that?"

"My lousy-ass father, but he had that one right."

"How bad was he?" I hurt just asking the question.

"Bad enough." He looks down, letting me know he's not saying more. I want to insist it isn't fair that I'm barfing my problems on him and he's not sharing. But something tells me it wouldn't help.

I pick up the first sheet of paper. He picks up one. We start reading.

"It says here that Emily was born on November sixth. I was born on November eighteenth."

He looks up. "They could easily have lied."

"Yeah." I continue reading. Emotion fills my chest as I read the pleas from the Fullers to the kidnapper to bring their baby home. I find myself staring at Mrs. Fuller's face again. The uncomfortable feeling has me remembering being on that dirty sofa. I'm so scared, and I'm hurt because . . . I close my eyes and I hear that voice again. A man's voice. *Your mama and daddy don't want you anymore.*

And for one second, I swear I see his face. Red hair. Dark

eyes. He scares me. I don't like him. Then I remember the bruise in the photograph. I get chills.

Cash touches my arm, but I gasp as if . . .

"You okay?" He pulls his hand away.

"No. Yes. I think . . ."

"What?" he asks.

"It's as if I remember other stuff, but it's not all there."

"What kind of stuff?"

"Someone telling me that my mama and daddy don't want me anymore. Part of me is so scared to remember, but another part . . . if I was really kidnapped I want that person to pay for it. He hurt me. He hurt the Fullers.

Right then I know: I may not be ready to tell Mom, or even Dad, but I need answers. And I need them now.

"Can we go to the adoption agency tomorrow?"

22

Monday, at one o'clock, we pull up in front of A New Hope Adoption Agency. I texted Lindsey last night and told her I was skipping school again. She asked if everything was okay. I texted back. *I'll explain later.*

Cash and I met and spent an hour at Whataburger. He kept telling me what I should and shouldn't say. *You're just here wanting to meet your birth parents. I'm just a friend here to support you. You're supposed to act cool, not desperate.*

But now, staring at the building, all I'm feeling is desperate. "I'm gonna screw this up," I tell him when we get out of his Jeep.

"No, you're going to be fine. Just remember what I said."

"But I'm shaking." I hold out my hands to show him. "I don't think I can do this."

He squeezes my arm. "It's okay. You'd be nervous if you were just here to ask about your birth parents."

I bite down on my lip. "If they kidnapped me, they'll lie. Why did we think this is going to work? It won't."

"If they lie, I'll be able to tell."

"How?" The one word comes out too strong.

"I'm good at reading people."

"No one can read people that good."

"I can. My dad taught me. Look, if they're behind the kidnapping, they'll be nervous and I'll know."

"If? You don't believe they're behind it? You still think my parents did it," I accuse him.

"That's not true," he says. "At first I did. But not anymore."

I realize I'm overreacting because I'm so nervous. "I'm sorry. I'm just scared."

"It's okay. I'm with you."

He takes my hand and we walk inside.

"Can I help you?" A woman wearing a green suit stands up behind the counter. She's about my mom's age.

I force myself to talk. "Yes." I walk forward and put my hands on the counter to keep from falling over.

"My name's Chloe Holden. Your agency handled my adoption, fifteen years ago. I was hoping to get some information on my birth parents."

"Oh. Well . . . Normally, this is handled through lawyers."

"She's representing herself." Cash's tone is confident.

"Do you have an appointment?" The question sounds curt.

"No." I'm ready to bolt.

"We're here. Surely we can talk to someone," Cash insists.

"Let me see if Mr. Wallace has time."

We wait twenty minutes before being led into a conference room.

It's a small room that holds a long, dark wooden table and a strong odor of Febreze. I realize I half expected the room to have a dirty brown sofa and stained carpet. Nothing is dirty. It's almost too clean, too sterile. But the air-conditioning is on in the room and hums cold air.

When the woman walks out, I hug myself.

"It's going well." Cash leans in and whispers, "There's a camera, so don't say anything."

I nod. He squeezes her hand. We wait. And wait. And wait. A clock on the wall ticks off the time. One minute. Two. Three. *Tick. Tick. Tick.*

Cash offers small talk. Telling me about a trip he and the Fullers took to Hawaii. I try to listen, but my mind races. "What's taking them so long?" I'm losing my nerve.

He doesn't answer because heavy footsteps sound outside the door. I catch my breath.

It's as if time slows down when the door opens. My heart thumps against my breastbone, I hear blood gushing in my ears, and I feel it. I feel the memory taking over my mind. I'm young, and exploding inside me is the pain of abandonment. My throat is raw as if I've cried too long. I'm afraid, afraid of strangers. Afraid of the man . . .

My fingers grip the arm of the chair like I'm at the dentist. I hate dentists.

Cash puts his hand over mine as if offering confidence.

I stare at the big man with thick salt-and-pepper hair. Did it used to be red? He has dark eyes. Like the guy I imagined. He's wearing a dark suit, but it's the red tie that pulls my eyes to it. I force my gaze up to his face. Air catches in my throat. Am I looking at a kidnapper?

I can hear the voice again. *You're getting a new mama and daddy.*

I don't want new ones! I hear my younger self scream.

Cash felt the tension coming off Chloe in waves. The big man had a yellow pad with some scribbled notes. His gaze locked on Chloe as if trying to remember her.

The man moved his large frame closer and leaned over the table. "Hello." He offered his hand to Chloe. "I'm Mr. Wallace."

Cash stood up first.

His meaty hand slipped into Cash's. And the first thing Cash noticed was his damp palm.

Never let your palms sweat. It's a sign you're up to no good.

"My receptionist didn't get your name," Mr. Wallace said to Cash.

"Cash Colton," he said. "Chloe's friend."

"Yes." He pulled his free of Cash's grip.

Chloe stood and offered her hand to the man. He leaned in, and when he did, Cash read the note on the pad. *Chloe Megan Holden. November 18.*

"It's a pleasure to meet you, Ms. Holden." Mr. Wallace took the seat across from them. "Do you have ID?"

Nervous at them seeing Chloe's license with all her information, he waited until she got it out and then took it from her and held it out, his thumb over her address.

The man didn't say anything. "How can we be of help today?"

Cash waited for Chloe to speak. He was about to fill him in, but she found her voice.

"I'd like information about my birth parents."

"I see," Mr. Wallace said. "We handled your adoption?"

Why was he asking a question he already knew?

"Yes." She fidgeted in her chair.

"Do you have a copy of the paperwork?" the man asked.

"Not on me." Chloe sounded apologetic.

"How old are you?" Mr. Wallace pulled at his tie.

Like you don't know. You got her birthday written down, idiot.

I'll be eighteen November eighteenth."

Mr. Wallace picked up a pen. "Are your parents aware of your interest in finding your birth parents?"

"Yes. They're just busy."

The man nodded. "Well, I can certainly understand your need to get answers, but unfortunately, with you not being eighteen, I can't proceed until I have your parents' consent."

Cash watched the man straighten his tie again, and his eyes darted back and forth.

Watch their hands and eyes—it'll tell ya if someone's lying.

"But it's only two months," Chloe said.

"I'm sorry." Mr. Wallace shifted.

Cash noticed the droplets of sweat on the man's brow.

"Is there some paperwork they can sign to save them from coming here?" Chloe asked, sounding slightly less nervous.

"I'm afraid they or a lawyer will have to show up." The man's tie got another tug. "I hope you didn't drive a long way to come here only to be disappointed."

It wasn't a question, but it was implied. The man wanted to know where Chloe lived. Before Chloe felt compelled to answer, Cash jumped in. "Thanks for your help." He glanced at Chloe. "We'll come back with Chloe's parents."

Mr. Wallace's eyes flinched. "It would be best if you made an appointment. Then we'll look at your file and see if it's even possible to release information."

"Why wouldn't it be possible?" Chloe's confidence now sounding.

"It depends on the type of adoption. If it was a closed adoption, we—"

"It wasn't closed. My parents said anytime I wanted information, I was allowed."

"Of course. I won't know until I look at your file."

And there it was. The first lie. "We should go." Cash stood up.

"That was a waste of time," I say the second we step outside. My chest feels heavy and I'm still shaking.

"No, it wasn't." Cash reaches for my hand.

"We didn't get crap." The only thing keeping me from crying is knowing I've done it way too often around Cash.

"He's lying."

I remember him saying he's good at reading people, but seriously . . . "How do you know?"

"His palms were wet when he shook my hand, and—"

"So were mine." I walk faster to keep up.

"Yeah, because you were nervous. Why do you think he was nervous?"

His words zip around my head as I try to believe them.

He clicks his Jeep open, then looks back at the building as if he thinks someone is watching. I turn, and see the blinds shift as if someone was peering out.

"You think they're watching us?" I lower my voice.

"Yeah," his voice seethes. "Shit. I'm an idiot. I shouldn't have parked here."

I get into the Jeep. He walks around and does the same.

I sit, trying to absorb what he just said. Then I shake my head. "He couldn't have lied. He didn't tell us anything."

Cash dips down to look at the building again. "He said he never looked at your file."

"Why do you think he did?"

"He had your full name written out on the yellow pad and your date of birth. You never told him either one. He's hiding something. We just need to figure out what."

Cash drives off.

I'm still trying to digest what Cash means, when he says, "We need to get our hands on the adoption papers." He looks at me. "Did you look everywhere in your house for them?"

"Not . . . in Mom's room."

"Is your mom going anywhere today?"

"I don't know."

He frowns. "Next time she's out, you look for them, okay?"

"Yeah. But how will that help?" Frustration leaks out.

"I think it should say if it was an open or closed adoption." Then he says, "Shit."

"What?" I ask.

"I read that if an adoption is through the state, like CPS, then it's closed."

"But my mom always said I could find my birth parents."

"Maybe she just said that to make you feel better."

"I don't think so."

He squeezes my arm. "It's going to be okay."

"Then why does it feel like it isn't?" Tears fill my eyes.

"I'll figure this out." He turns and looks at me. "We need to get our hands on your file."

"How? They won't give it to me."

"Then we take it."

"Take it?" I shake my head. "What do you mean?"

I hear him exhale. "Let me handle this."

"Handle what?"

"How to figure this out."

"You said 'take it.' You can't break in or anything."

"Let's concentrate on reading all the paperwork from the Fullers' file. I'll keep trying to find the nanny."

"And if you can't find her?"

"We'll figure it out."

I arrive home at the same time I would have if I'd gone to school. Mom's sleeping on the sofa. She's still in her pajamas. She didn't get out for a walk today either.

I wish they'd call her to work already.

I try to wake her, but she mumbles something about how she needs to sleep. I do my homework. Later, I fix us both a grilled cheese. She eats only half, refuses to drink one of her calorie-laden shakes, then tells me she's going to her room to read.

I stay up watching *Law & Order*, hoping she'll eventually join me. She doesn't.

I finally go to bed and pull out the paperwork from the Fullers' file. I face away from the door so if Mom walks in, I can hide them. I read the article about the nanny telling the police about the man who spoke to Emily that day at the park. I get chills when I read her description. Red hair. Brown eyes. Could it have been Mr. Wallace?

I recall the image of the face I got a glimpse of in my mind. Did the two men look alike? I don't think so, but I'm not sure.

My phone dings with a text from Cash. *Want to talk?*

I text back yes. He calls. I stuff the papers back in my backpack just in case Mom wakes up and pops in.

"You okay?" His concern flows through the line.

"Yeah," I say even when I'm not sure it's true, and drop back on the bed.

He tells me about his job at the auto shop and his friend Devin, who works there. He's a couple years older than Cash, but Cash relates to him because Devin spent some time in foster care, too. I tell him about Cara and Sandy back home. How it's sad when I went back home because our friendship had felt forced. Then he tells me to get on YouTube, and we listen to music together. He picks a song and then I pick one.

It's good. It's easy. It has nothing to do with what happened today. Nothing about my adoption or me being kidnapped.

We stay on the phone almost an hour. At the end of our conversation, he tells me he plans to read the rest of the Fullers' papers, and it all comes back. The uncertainty. The fear. The questions.

"Did you read some more?" he asks.

"A little." I close my eyes not wanting the conversation to go there. "I'll read more tomorrow."

"You sure you're okay?"

"Yeah," I lie again, but I think of the face I imagined, and fear rides my spine all the way up to my neck, and I feel a headache coming on. "Just tired."

We hang up. Exhausted, physically and emotionally, I fall right to sleep. And I stay asleep until I'm jolted awake by Mom yelling out my name.

I jackknife up. Mom's standing on the side of my bed. A storm of emotions swirls inside me. I can't catch my breath. I feel like a fish out of water, gasping. My lungs finally open. I suck in air.

"You okay? You were screaming."

My face is wet with tears. "A nightmare," I mutter.

"About what?"

"I don't remember." Then I do. I remember him yelling at me to go to sleep on that dirty sofa. I remember crying so hard. I didn't want to be there with him. I wanted my mama and daddy. I kept calling for my mama.

How much if any of that is true?

I swallow tears and desperation. Then I wrap my arms around her and cling to her.

"You kept saying, 'My mama does love me.' Then you kept calling for me."

Not you.

I release her. "I'm sorry I woke you."

"It's okay. Scoot over, and I'll sleep with you."

I do. Mom curls up beside me, even shares my pillow. She runs her hand through my hair the way she always does when I'm sick.

"You're right. I do love you." Her words are meant to comfort.

I swallow another round of tears.

"I love you, too." I curl up close to her. Images of the dream tickle my mind. I know I should reach for them, try to understand, but I'm too shaken. I push the dream away. And in that second, that desire to just accept her affection, her comfort feels like déjà vu. I've done this before. I've tried to forget the monster memories, the loss of someone else, and accept her. Accept her love and try to stop loving someone else.

Rodney Davis pulled into the back of the adoption agency. His ex-wife had called and said her brother, Jack Wallace, had damn near ordered him to show up here after he got off work. Rodney didn't normally follow orders. But then again, maybe Jack needed something that could possibly put a few bucks in his pocket. Working as a security guard didn't quite earn him the living style he liked, so any chance of making a few extra bucks appealed to him.

He went to the back door. When he found it was locked, he knocked.

The door swung open almost immediately. Jack stood there. His hair stood on ends, his suit wrinkled, and his face almost as red as his tie. High blood pressure probably because he'd put on at least fifty pounds since Rodney last saw him. But damn Jack looked like an old fart.

"What's up?" Rodney asked.

"Your screwup has finally caught up with us!"

"What screwup?"

"How the hell can you ask that? You know what screwup."

Yeah, Rodney pretty much knew, but . . . "That's from fifteen years ago. How could it be a problem?"

"She's looking for her parents! That's how!" He gripped his hands in tight fat fists at his side.

Rodney rubbed a palm over his chest. "Tell her they don't want to meet her. Or tell her that they're dead."

"She still might want to meet the rest of her family. And with today's access to DNA, she'll figure it out! I knew this would come back to haunt us! We're screwed. And it's on you. If you'd gotten the kid from Mexico like you said you were, none of this would've happened. None of it!"

"We're not screwed!" He refused to be screwed. Because this kind of screwed meant jail time. He'd done time eight years ago and decided he didn't like it.

Hell, if this shit came out, they could accuse him of killing the kid. He hadn't killed her. Hadn't touched her. She just died. So he'd done what he had to do. Got rid of the body and replaced her.

Damn. He wasn't going back to jail.

"What's her name?"

"Why?"

"What's her name?" He took an aggressive step forward.

"No. I shouldn't have called you. I'll take care of it. You already screwed this up."

He grabbed Jack by the neck, curled his hand around his throat, and slammed him against the wall. "What. Is. Her. Name?"

When he didn't answer, Rodney tightened his grip.

"Chloe Holden," Jack squeaked out.

"Her address?"

"I don't know."

Rodney tightened the grip once more.

Jack reached for his hand. "I said I don't know." His voice came out weak, airless.

Rodney loosened his hold a bit.

"All I have is her name and the license plate of the guy who drove her."

"What guy?"

"Another kid. He said his name was Cash Colton. That and his license plate are all I have."

Rodney believed him, but held onto the man's neck. "You gonna give it to me?"

Jack, his eyes so wide that it looked like his eyeballs might pop out, nodded.

Rodney released him. The man grabbed his neck and moved away from the wall. "I'll give it to you. But you don't have to do anything yet. She's not eighteen yet. I'll do what you said, I'll tell her the parents don't want to see her. I'll make it convincing."

"Just give me the information. Give me everything!"

23

It's ten o'clock on Wednesday night, and I'm in bed, looking over the Emily paperwork to see if I missed anything and waiting for Cash to get home from his college class so he can call me.

Yesterday after school, Cash and I hung out at Whataburger reading the Emily articles. We discovered a lot of things we didn't know. For example, the kidnapping actually happened in a park in Amigo, Texas, three hours from here. We don't know why Emily was there, but the article stated she was with her nanny. Another one said the Fullers hadn't been aware the nanny was taking her to Amigo. That makes me think the cops were right. The nanny was behind the kidnapping.

Then we found an article that named the nanny as Carmen Vaca Gonzales. Discovering the name Vaca will help narrow down the three dozen Carmen Gonzaleses in the surrounding towns.

Cash started a new search on her last night. He says if he finds an address, he plans on going there.

But he still believes Mr. Wallace was lying. I told him about the dream, about the man in it not looking like Mr. Wallace. Yet Cash insists the agency is behind it.

Me, I don't know what to believe anymore. But after I spill my guts to Lindsey, she thinks Cash is right. So maybe they're both right.

Not only is it two to one, but also I'm learning that Cash is really good at detective-type work. He picks up on things in the paperwork that I don't, like how none of the documents say I was wearing a princess costume. I wonder if that memory is even true.

Even as crazy as this makes me feel, I'm still on top of the world about Cash and me. I see him at school every day. We talk on the phone every night. Last night, after Whataburger, we went to the park and got in his backseat and kissed, and talked, and laughed. I asked him more silly questions about himself.

I now know a lot of nonsensical facts about Cash Colton. His favorite color—and yes, at first he said brown because it was the color of my eyes, but I called bullshit on that one. He admitted he liked blue. "Not blue eyes," he insisted.

I know his favorite vegetable is green beans. Peas make him gag.

I know he broke his arm when he was nine. When I asked him how, he claimed he fell from a tree, but my gut says he was lying. I think his dad did it. And even now, thinking about it makes me glad the man's dead.

I close my eyes. I don't think I've ever thought that about anyone. But I hate Cash's father. Somehow I'm sure the pain I see in Cash's eyes, the pain he works so hard to hide, comes from his dad. Cash's time in foster care probably didn't help. But whenever he mentions his dad, I see his eyes go darker and kind of blank—as if he hates remembering.

I've tried to ask questions about his father, but Cash either changes the subject or says, "I don't like talking about it." If I insisted, I think he'd talk, but I know people have to want to share. I just wish he wanted to share with me.

My phone dings with a text. I roll over, hoping it's Cash, but nope, it's Dad. He's been texting every day. Just to say hi. I haven't forgiven him, but I'm glad he's trying. I'm glad he gave me back my room. I hope it doesn't smell like Darlene.

I read Dad's text.

Goodnight Sunshine.

I go to send an emoji. I almost chose the one with a smile and a tear, because when he uses those sweet nicknames, it reminds me of how great things used to be—and how they aren't so great now. But I don't send the tear. I keep that little pain inside me. I send one with a real smile, hoping soon I won't debate which emoji to send.

I hear Mom's footsteps outside my door. I panic, grab the pillow, and put it on top of the papers. My biggest fear is that Mom will find them. I've even been taking them to school with me.

A knock sounds. My heart knocks with it.

She opens the door. "You awake?"

"Yeah." I see one of the papers on the edge of my bed. It's one of the newspaper articles, and it has a picture of Emily Fuller. My heart starts racing to the *Jaws* theme. If I try to hide it, she might see it.

If I don't? She might see it.

"I couldn't sleep," Mom says. "I'm making hot chocolate. Want some?"

"Yes!" I jump off the bed and rush to the door, moving Mom back into the hall. I'd've agreed to eat a cockroach if it got Mom out of my bedroom.

I sit at the kitchen table as she makes hot chocolate. She's too quiet, and I'm sensing something's off. I'm afraid of what it is.

She's still having good and bad days. I can tell the difference. Good days, she's dressed when I come home from school, and I know she actually walked like the doctor told her to. Bad days, she's still in her pj's. Today was a pajama day. Which means she didn't follow the doctor's orders.

"Did you walk today?" I ask, hoping she'll be more inclined to do it if she knows I'll ask.

"A short one." It's a lie, and I didn't expect that. When did she start lying?

So you wore your pajamas to walk? I bite my tongue. "When do you go back to the doctor?"

"Friday."

"Maybe you should talk to him about taking something for the depression?"

She frowns. "Marshmallows?"

"Sure," I say. She drops small white bits of fluff into the cups and sits down beside me. I wait for her to tell me what's on her mind, hoping it's not terrible.

My phone rings in the bedroom, and I know it's Cash.

"You want to go get that?" she asks.

"Nah."

She looks at me. "You think it's your dad?" The way she says *dad* sounds like a four-letter word.

"Probably Cash," I say.

"I don't like him very much."

You don't like anything. Is this what you brought me out here to talk about? This isn't gonna be pretty, because right now, Cash is the only good thing in my life. Well, Lindsey, too—but Cash has turned into my touchstone.

"He's a good guy," I say, but if she knew what brought us together, she'd disagree.

"Does your dad know you're dating?"

"Kind of."

"Did he even give a shit?"

I take the Dad insult on the chin and sip at my hot chocolate; the sweet, gooey marshmallow cream coats my lips. "He thought it was a little soon, but he didn't say I couldn't." I don't mention that I wouldn't have listened to him if he did.

She turns her cup in circles. She breathes in. "What do you think of him marrying his little home breaker?"

I gasp. "He's marrying Darlene? He told you this?"

Then—*bam!*—I wonder if that's why he moved my things back to my room, hoping I wouldn't be so upset. *Forget my room, Dad. This is bad!*

The sweet foam on my lips no longer tastes so sweet. Everything tastes bitter. I mean, it can't be. Dad's got the new cow disease. Surely, Darlene's newness will wear off! It's not that I dream of my parents getting back together. Not after how much he hurt Mom. But . . . No! Just no!

It's as if just the thought ruins the unsnapped photos of my future. Birthdays. Father's Days. My wedding.

Darlene will be in those photos.

It hurts like hell that she's living with him, living where the memories of us used to live, but *marriage*? He can't do that!

But he can. He can do what he wants. He already has. He left Mom to deal with the cancer. He left me to deal with Mom's cancer.

"Did he tell you to tell me? Is that what this is about?"

"No."

"Then how do you know?"

"He has a charge to Borne's Jewelry on his Visa."

I'm trying to understand. "You don't know it's an engagement ring?"

"It's five thousand dollars," she says. "Your father had a rule—he never spent more than a thousand dollars on jewelry, except for my wedding ring. And he spent only twelve hundred on my ring. I guess he loves her more." Bitterness laces her voice.

Emotions bombard my mind. I try to get out one straight thought. And I do. I look at Mom. "How do you know what he charged on his credit card?"

"He never changed his password." Mom must read my mind, because she says, "If he didn't want me snooping, he should've changed them."

"That's wrong," I say. But Dad's getting married is worse.

"Why don't you call him?" Mom says. "See if he'll tell you. We have a right to know, don't we?"

Now I know why I was summoned out for hot chocolate. She wants me to call Dad. She wants me to be pissed at Dad. I am pissed at Dad. But I'm pissed at her for wanting me to be pissed.

"I'm going to bed!" I bolt from the chair and leave her and her anger to drink hot chocolate alone.

Rodney held the phone away from his ear.

"I'm telling you I'm taking care of it!" Jack's loud voice over the phone sounded like it might crack.

"I don't like how you take care of things." Rodney sat in his car. He'd gotten the information back on the license plate he gave his coworker. The Jeep was owned by a Cash Colton, co-owned and listed on the insurance of Anthony Fuller. Probably a stepdad.

Being a security guard had its perks. The first one being that a part-time guy working for the company was a cop. And when Rodney explained his niece had seen this car following her and they wanted to make sure it wasn't an old boyfriend, he'd been happy to assist.

"I got an address on the boy."

"That boy isn't in on this!" Jack said.

"No, but he knows where the girl is."

"No, Rod. Don't do anything."

Rodney ran his hand over the steering wheel. "Quit pissing in your pants. I'm just going to follow the kid until he leads me to the girl."

"This is wrong, Rod. Wrong. I'm serious. I'm handling things. I got it figured out. I can do this. Besides, the girl hasn't called or brought her parents in. She might even drop it."

"And if she doesn't?" Rodney stared down at the address. Joyful, Texas. Hmm. Joyful. Whoever heard of that? Hell, when this was all done, maybe he'd move there. Between this issue, his two ex-wives demanding money for kids he didn't even see, and his girlfriend acting like a bitch, demanding he move out, he could use some joy.

"I told you, I have it figured out. I'm going to write a letter like it was from the girl's mom. Make it so she won't try to contact her. Nobody has to get hurt. So don't do anything."

Rodney scrubbed his hand over his five-o'clock shadow. Dare he trust the old fart? Especially when it wasn't Jack's ass that could wind up with a murder charge? Then again, if all this could be made to go away? Tempting.

"Okay, I'll stand back, but if I find out you're holding back on me, it's going to be your ass I'm after. I'm not going down for this. Got it!"

He hung up.

Then he looked down at the address again. Hell, he could go home and fight with Peggy, or he could go do some legwork. Just in case things went bad. Then again, it was late. Maybe he'd go home and see just how piss-poor of a mood Peggy was in.

"Sorry, I was in the kitchen with Mom," I say when I call Cash back an hour later. It took that long to get over being pissed so I could talk.

"Is everything okay?" He obviously hears the frustration in my voice.

"No."

"What happened?"

I realize I'm doing it again, dumping my woes on him when he won't share. But I don't stop. "I need you to do something."

"What?"

"You know that fake Facebook page you have?" Buttercup jumps on the bed.

"Yeah."

"Can you befriend someone and tell me what's on their page?"

"Who?"

"Darlene." Felix rubs his face on my cheek.

"Your dad's girlfriend."

"Yeah."

"What are you looking for?"

"If Dad asked her to marry him."

"Yikes," he says.

"Yeah." I run my hand over my dog's fur.

"You don't think she's pregnant, do you?"

Air catches in my chest. "No! Oh God, I haven't even thought about that. Shit!"

"Breathe," he says.

"Why would you say that?" I slam back into my pillow.

"I wasn't . . . Sorry. Why do you think they're engaged?"

"Mom's been snooping on his credit card accounts. Dad bought something at a jewelry store."

"That doesn't mean it's a ring."

"It was five thousand dollars."

"Okay, so maybe it was. Why don't you ask him?"

"Oh, I'm sure he won't mind that my mom is breaking into his credit card account."

"Okay, I see your point. Do you know her Facebook ID?"

"Yeah, she sent me a friend request right after Dad and Mom got a divorce."

He laughs. "And she thought you'd friend her?"

"I never said she was smart." I give him Darlene's information.

"I'll send her the request and let you know if she accepts." He pauses. "Did you find anything else in the file?"

"No. I was reading it and Mom came in." I move back to my bed.

"She didn't see it, did she?"

"Almost."

"You sound upset," he says.

"I'm okay."

"You want me to come over?"

"It's late. Mom wouldn't like it."

"I can wait an hour, and you can sneak out the window." There's a tease in his voice.

I smile, remembering. "I don't think Mom's going to be sleeping tonight. If she caught me, she'd freak."

"I kind of think she already has tonight." He understands more about my night than I'm letting on.

"Yeah," I say.

Silence fills the line until he says, "I found the nanny."

"What?"

"I found her on Facebook. Then I found her number in the yellow pages."

My heart races. "Did you talk to her?"

"I called. Spoke to her niece. She said her aunt's in Mexico and won't be back for three weeks. She gave me her address. She lives about an hour away from here."

"Did you tell her what you wanted?"

"No, I said I wanted to talk to her about someone we both knew. I gave her my number and said she could call me. But the niece acted like she might wait until she's back."

Felix climbs up on my chest. Buttercup is licking my arm. They can sense I'm upset.

"We need to make a plan."

A knot forms in my throat. "I hate thinking about this It's giving me emotional whiplash. I feel sorry for the Fullers. I feel sorry for Emily. Then I remember I might be Emily. Then I feel sorry for my parents. Part of me wants to be Emily so it'll mean I wasn't thrown away. Part of me is scared to be Emily because I'm afraid wanting it means that I don't want the parents I have." My voice rises. "And yeah, right now with the whole divorce and depression shit, I almost don't want them, but . . . It's like a hurricane of different emotions hitting me all at once. And then there's you."

I take a breath. Close my eyes.

"Me?" he asks.

"Yes." It's like the night with Dad—I can't shut up. "You . . . know everything about me, and you never tell me anything. I know your past hurts you, and I want to help you the way you're helping me. Why don't you trust me?"

There's silence. One beat. Two. Three.

"I do trust you." Frustration tightens his voice. "You know more about me than anyone, other than the Fullers or previous foster parents who read my report."

"Then why don't you tell me the rest of it?"

Three beats of silence passes.

"You don't understand," he says.

"What don't I understand?"

"Damn it, Chloe! You're innocent. All the things that have happened to you aren't your fault. You didn't do anything wrong. You're perfect."

His words confirm what I've known all along: He doesn't feel worthy. "What do you think you're guilty of? Whatever it is, you're wrong. You were only eleven when your father died!" She immediately recalls Paul's words. *They say he killed his dad. Shot him right in the heart.* She doesn't believe it. She doesn't. Yet, she recalls his story about the car accident and how something didn't feel right.

"I was old enough to know better." Pain laces his words. Then, he says, "Shit. I got to go. Someone's coming."

I'd've believed it was a lie if I didn't hear Mrs. Fuller's voice saying, "I saw your light on. You okay?" The sound is muffled, as if he set the phone on his bed, but it's still audible.

"Just couldn't sleep," Cash says.

"Me neither. I was going to make some Sleepytime tea. You want some?"

"Sure," Cash answers. The phone clicks silent.

I'm left holding my phone to my ear. Holding questions in my heart. But knowing, knowing with everything inside me, that Cash isn't a bad person.

24

I head to school early on Thursday morning. I'm worried about Mom. She didn't get up. When I poked my head in before I left, she barely said goodbye. I wish she'd start working.

Glancing at the clock on the dashboard, I hope to see Cash before school. Remembering our conversation about his secrets, I'm nervous he's upset with me.

On the ride, Lindsey's talking nonstop. She's comparing David to Jonathon. David comes out looking better, but the fact that she's talking about Jonathon tells me she's not over him.

"So what do you think?" she asks.

I must've tuned her out, because I'm clueless to what she's asking.

"Sorry, I'm half asleep," I say. And I am. I didn't have another nightmare last night, but I woke up thinking about it. Thinking about the Fullers, the nanny, and the face. "What do I think about what?"

"Double-dating on Saturday night?"

"Oh," I say, but think no. Between my not wanting to leave Mom too much and Cash's schedule, I get so little time with Cash, and I'd like it to just be us.

"Please say yes."

Now I feel guilty. "I'll see what Cash says."

We get to school. Lindsey heads out to find David. I hang in front of the school, hoping I'll see Cash pull in.

When his gray Jeep arrives, I watch where he's parking and walk that way.

He's setting up his camera when I get there. He told me about his car getting keyed and how he suspects Paul and hopes he'll catch him doing it again on film. He also told me he promised both Mr. and Mrs. Fuller he wouldn't get into another fight. I'm worried about that. Cash is really pissed. He loves his Jeep.

He motions me inside.

I crawl into the front seat. "Hey."

He leans in and kisses me. The kiss feels desperate. When we pull apart, his gaze meets mine and I can read his mind, he's begging me not to ask about his past. And I won't. Because he has to want to confide in me. Being shut out still stings.

"Darlene accepted my friend request."

I'd been so worried about his secrets that I forgot about her. "Did you look at her page?"

"Yeah."

"And?"

"There's no mention of her being engaged, or any picture of expensive jewelry. Do you want me to pull it up on my phone?"

I hesitate. "Does she have pictures of my dad?"

"Yeah. And you're right. She dresses provocatively. You want to see?"

"Always nice to know my dad might be marrying a slut." I exhale. "No, I don't want to see it."

"You don't know it was an engagement ring." He reminds me.

"I know." My phone dings with a text. Of course, it's Dad. *Have a good day.*

I show Cash. He says, "I'm sorry."

I want to text Dad back and say something ugly, but I don't. Something ugly would eventually require an explanation. And because I know he'd be pissed at Mom for the credit card business, I can't. However, I don't answer Dad's text. I can't even bring myself to send an emoji.

I remember Lindsey's request about double-dating. I ask Cash about it. His expression says he doesn't want to. I'm about to let him off the hook, when he suddenly says, "It could be fun."

I'm in first period when I realize why Cash may have said yes. We won't be alone and he won't feel pressure to tell me his secrets.

Is he going to back out of going to the park this afternoon? Why can't he talk to me? He says he trusts me, but I'm not convinced.

The bell rings and I'm going to my locker when I hear

my name. I glance back and see it's Paul. I consider walking away, but my gut says he'll just follow.

He comes and stands in front of me. Too close. I step back. "What?"

"I have a party to go to tomorrow night. I thought you might like to come?"

I'm so shocked, it takes a minute to understand he's asking me out. "Uh . . ." I try to come up with a response, but when I can't think of one, I just spit out, "No."

"Why not?" he asks.

Because you're a bully. Because I don't like you. Because I'm dating Cash.

"You really dating that foster boy?" he asks when I don't answer.

I really don't like him. "Yeah."

"He went to juvie. He's no good."

I tilt up my chin, feel my lips thin in anger. "Obviously, I don't agree."

He leans in. "So you like bad boys." He puts his face in mine. "I can be bad."

I stare right into his eyes. "You're a dick." I step back.

"You'll be sorry," he says. "Take my word for it."

I watch him walk away, fist clenched, shoulders tight, anger making my head buzz. My first thought is to find Cash and tell him. Tell him I'm glad he punched the guy in the nose. My second is that I can't. Can't tell Cash. He'd confront him. There'd be another fight.

Mom's still in her pj's, stretched out on the sofa with Felix, when I get home from school. So she didn't walk. But at least she's awake. I recall abandoning her last night after she told me about Dad's jewelry purchase.

"Hey." It's sad how easy it is to push things under the rug.

"How was your day?" She sits up.

"Okay," I lie, my thoughts on Paul.

"Just okay?" Mom asks. "Something happen?"

"No," I lie again, and hand her a pack of Reese's Peanut Butter Cups.

"What's this?" she asks.

"I stopped by the store, and I know you like them." Buttercup barks at the back door. I let him in.

"Thank you." Mom opens the candy and sinks her teeth into it. "So good," she says around the mouthful of chocolate. I notice her eyes look bloodshot, as if she's been crying. My heartstrings are tugged. I need her to get better. I need to stop feeling as if I'm walking on eggshells every second I'm around her.

I need it because I want to ask her about the adoption. I want her to go with me to get the information. I want it, but looking at her now, I know she can't handle it.

"Did you eat lunch?" I crouch down to love on Buttercup.

"Yeah . . ." She doesn't sound sure.

I'll bet she didn't, and I decide to fix something fattening for dinner. Then I remember we're low on food. "Did you go to the grocery store?" I ask afraid it's a no.

"I kind of took the day off," she says.

She's been taking lots of days off.

"We can do it this weekend," Mom says. "You can make yourself a sandwich. This is my dinner." She holds up the candy.

I bite my tongue and remember when Mom cooked pot roast and parmesan chicken. When the house smelled like food and love. *I want that Mom back.*

"Cash and I are taking Buttercup to the park." I stand up. Buttercup hears the word *park* and starts dancing.

"Okay." Her tone lands on a negative note. I ignore it. No breaking eggs with Mom. Not when she's so broken. Besides, I seem to reserve that privilege for Dad, or at least sometimes. He texted me again right after school, and I ignored that text, too.

I go brush my teeth and grab a blanket for the park. When I get back, Mom's asleep.

I hear a car door shut and, thinking it's Cash, I grab the caramel candies I bought him and stick them in my pocket.

I put the leash on Buttercup. Then with the blanket, the ball, and dog in tow, I head outside to save Cash from seeing my depressed mom.

When I make the front porch, I see it wasn't Cash's car door I heard. It's Jonathon's.

He gives me a smirk as he's walking up to Lindsey's porch. I give him one right back.

I hear Lindsey's front door open, and she says something I don't understand. Then Jonathon walks in.

"Well, shit." I worry Lindsey's going to screw up a good thing with David. But I don't have time to fret, because Cash pulls up.

In fifteen minutes, we're at the park, sitting on a blanket. Buttercup, resting beside us, is already tired from Cash throwing him the ball.

We lie back on the blanket. His shoulder is against mine and he's holding my hand. I look over and he's staring up at the sky.

"I see an elephant." He points up.

I smile. "Where?"

"There. See the trunk. It only has three legs." He laughs. "But there're a lot of three-legged elephants out there, right?"

I stare up. "I see it."

"I guess you get this." He pulls out a pack of Skittles. He leans up on one elbow. "Let me find you a red one."

"I got you something, too." I pull the caramels from my pocket.

His grin widens. "You brought me candy." He says it like it's some big deal, like he didn't just pull out a pack of candy he'd brought for me.

"Yes." I open the package and remove one, and then I take the plastic off. "Open up." I put the candy in his mouth.

He moans with pleasure. "Sorry. But this is better than Skittles."

"Nope." I pull the bag from his hand and find a red candy.

We're lying there, eating candy, staring at the white puffy clouds. I remember Paul, and I almost feel guilty not telling Cash about it, but I know it might end badly.

I feel him staring at me. I lean my head to the side. "What?"

He eases over and his lips touch mine. The sweet and tart taste of Skittles and caramel blend with the kiss.

When we stop, our eyes open, meet, and hold. The park sounds float around us, people talking, a dog barking, Buttercup snoring, and a few birds singing, but somehow it feels like it's just us.

"It's not that I don't trust you, Chloe. It's that . . . this—" He waves a hand between us. "—this is so good. I like how it feels. I like that it has nothing to do with my past. What happened then is bad, and this is good. It's so damn good and I don't want that to poison this. Does that make sense?"

I stare into his green eyes, and I swear I see into his soul. I see the empty spot there. The one like I have. "Kind of," I say. "But I don't think anything could poison this."

He kisses me again.

My phone rings. I pull it out of my pocket and frown. "It's my dad."

"Answer it if you want," he says.

"No. I'm not ready to talk to him." We lie back and look up at the sky. "Did you look to see if Darlene posted anything about a ring?"

"Yeah. She hasn't."

We get quiet again, and I enjoy being this close to him. My hand is in his. His shoulder, his arm, his leg are pressed against me. I feel tingly all over and I wish I had more of him against me.

He stirs. "Yesterday afternoon, before I went to my college class, I drove to the nanny's house."

I swallow. "Why? You said she wasn't home."

"She's not. But just so I'll know where she lives. I thought about calling the niece again. But I don't want to sound too eager. It might make her suspicious."

"I think she's going to be suspicious anyway," I say.

"You don't know that." But he kind of frowns.

I roll over on my side and face him. "Are you going to be disappointed if I'm not Emily?"

"No. I'll be surprised, because I think you are, but not disappointed. Why would you think that?"

I inhale. "I don't know. It just feels like you want me to be her."

"Honestly, it would be better if you weren't. You know with my dating you, but . . . I think you're Emily." He touches my face. "How do you want it to turn out?" he asks. "And forget being afraid of hurting your parents."

I dig deep for my answer. "In one way, I want to be her— to know I wasn't given away—but in another way, I don't want to be her. I always used to think if I could figure out who my real parents were that I might . . . be able to figure out who I am. Now, it kind of feels like . . . that by discovering who I would've been in another life, I'll lose part of the person I am. I know that doesn't make sense, but—"

"It makes sense," he says. "But I don't think it's going to change who you are."

"Mom, I'm home," I call out when I walk into the house. I stand there, hoping I'll smell food cooking. I mean, yeah, I kind of knew it was a long shot, but hey, I could hope my mom suddenly woke up, went grocery shopping, and decided to be a mom.

Mom doesn't answer. "Mom?"

I move into the living room; the sofa's empty.

I walk toward her bedroom. The door's ajar. Mom's in bed, and the light's off.

"Mom?" I lean against the doorframe.

I get nothing. "I'm going to order Chinese for dinner."

Nothing. I could've spent more time with Cash.

My phone dings with a text.

I look at it. It's from Lindsey.

Please come over!

I noticed Jonathon's truck was gone when I came in. She's probably wanting to talk about his visit. But I swear, if she's thinking of going back to that creep, I'm giving her hell.

"Mom, I'm going to Lindsey's. I'll order Chinese when I get back."

Mom doesn't even move.

"Sounds good, Chloe. I'll see you when you get back," I answer as if I were her. Then I mutter, "Thank you for being the adult around here."

Angry, I head to Lindsey's.

Before I get off my porch, my phone rings. It's Dad again. Nope. Not dealing with that now. I'd rather deal with Lindsey and her Jonathon issues.

It was almost six when Cash pulled through the gate into the Fullers' subdivision. On Thursdays, it was usually just him and Mrs. Fuller. He'd texted her about an hour ago and let her know he might be running late. She'd texted him back, saying she was leaving the grocery store, and asked what he wanted for dinner. He'd told her to surprise him.

When he got to the house, there was a black sedan parked in the driveway. The garage door was open. Mrs. Fuller's car was inside, but the trunk was open and there were bags of groceries there. He thought she'd gotten home earlier. He grabbed some bags and headed inside. Stepping into the kitchen, he heard her talking in a high-pitched tone.

"I told you she was alive. I've known it! Oh my God, someone took down the age-progression photo that I put up in Walmart. It might've been her."

Mrs. Fuller's words, and the emotion in her voice, stopped Cash in his tracks. Dread swirled in the pit of his stomach. He quietly set the bag on the counter.

"Ma'am," a man answered. "Don't put too much merit into this. We're suspicious that this is another scam. Maybe the same guy as last time."

Cash froze and listened.

"But you said he saw her. You said—"

Saw her? Shit. Had someone seen the age-progression photo and recognized Chloe?

"Look, the clerk said it looked like the girl in the article that they were photocopying, but—"

Photocopying?

Damn it! This was about the missing copy from the print shop.

His dad's voice rang in his head. *Never leave a crumb trail.*

"Look, it's terrible, but this is probably just like last time."

"We don't know that," Mrs. Fuller said. "It could be her. Wait. You said *they were photocopying*? Who was with her? It could've been the kidnappers. They could still be holding her against her will. Did the witness give you a description of the man?"

Cash leaned against the counter. He was so screwed now. Crap!

"He got a better look at the girl than the guy. He thinks he was in his midtwenties, so it's unlikely it could be the kidnapper."

"What are you going to do? Please tell me you're going to look for her."

Desperation rang in Mrs. Fuller's voice, and it sank into Cash's chest. He remembered how she moped around for almost two months after the man conned them last time. But this wasn't some two-bit con hurting her. Cash had done it. He'd caused this.

Damn it! He had to figure this out. And fast. He wasn't waiting to talk to the nanny. He had to get his hands on Chloe's adoption papers. But how?

I stay an hour at Lindsey's, talking her off the Jonathon ledge. One minute she's listening to me and swears she's not going to see him, the next . . .

"I know he's bad news," she says. "But I still care about him."

"You cannot give in. He'll cheat on you again."

She frowns. "He said he wasn't hitting on you. He felt sorry for you."

Oh, right! And you believe him? She's worse off than I thought.

"I know I have to tell him no. But—"

"No buts," I say. "Seriously, I wouldn't be your friend if I let you get back with him."

She frowns. "Jamie says I should give him a second chance."

I sit there on her bed and try to think of the right thing to say. "Fine. Go back to him, but I'm going to tell you I told you so."

My phone rings. It's Dad again.

"Cash?" she asks.

"No. My dad."

"Did you ask him about the ring?"

"No." The phone stops ringing. I get a ding that he's left a message.

I look at Lindsey. "I should go. I need to order dinner."

She puts on a pout. "What am I going to do about Jonathon?"

I shake my head. "Cut him out of your life."

"Isn't that a bit harsh?" she asks in a pissy tone. "Your dad cheated on your mom, and you still see him."

Her words rake across all kinds of nerves. "Yeah, and you of all people know I still haven't forgiven him. Look what a mess he made of my life." I stand up. "Screw it! Do what you want! But don't tell me he wasn't hitting on me, because he was."

I leave. I'm almost to my house when my phone beeps again with Dad's message.

I stop on the porch to erase it. But instead, I put my phone to my ear.

"Chloe. Where are you? I'm worried about your mom. I called a couple of hours ago, and she wasn't making sense. Check on her and call me!"

Wasn't making sense? I haul ass through my front door. I run into her bedroom.

"Mom!" I scream. She doesn't answer. She's a dark, motionless lump in the bed. I turn the light on. And the first thing I see is the open bottle of pills on her nightstand.

"No!" I run to her. "No, God, no! Mom?" I cry.

25

I'm about to dial 911 when she mutters, "What?" Her eyes flutter open. She tries to sit up but falls back.

I look at the pill bottle. There's pills still in it.

"What are you taking?" I pick the bottle up and read it. It's Ambien.

"When did you start taking sleeping pills?" I ask.

She sits up, but wavers like she's drunk. "Why?" She's annoyed.

I read the label that says she should take only one at night. "How many did you take?"

She frowns.

"How many?"

"I'm a nurse. I know how many I can take."

"So you took more than it says?"

"Stop! Don't make a big deal out of this." She reaches for the bottle.

"No, you stop! Answer me! How many did you take?" I stare at her. I see the date the pills were ordered. "I can count them and find out."

She shakes her head. "Give me my pills!"

"No. You're abusing medication!" Tears fill my eyes.

"Do you know how scared I was when you wouldn't wake up? Do you even give a fuck about me?"

"Don't talk like that, young lady!"

"Oh no! You can't call me on my language when you're popping pills!"

"I'm not . . . I just needed to sleep!"

"How many did you take? And don't lie, because I'm going to count them!"

She finally looks embarrassed. "I took two, but—"

I shake my head. "There's no excuse!"

That seems to make her mad, but she can't be as mad as I am. "Why don't you go yell at your dad instead of me," she says. "He's getting married!"

"I don't care what Dad's doing. I care about what you're doing." I pour out the pills in my hand and start counting them, blinking back my tears. I count twenty. I read the bottle to see how many pills she had. "Mom, you had thirty pills. You've taken ten! Ten in four days!"

"I took a couple during the day." She wipes tears from her cheeks. "When I sleep, I don't remember what he did to us."

I grab the cap of the pill bottle and screw it on. "I'm taking these pills. You can ask me for one at night if you need it. Right now, you need to get up and eat something!" And she can fix it herself, too.

When she doesn't move, I say, "Get up. I'm not letting you do this to yourself or me! Tomorrow, you are going to get pills for depression from your doctor. If you don't have them when I get home, I'm calling the doctor myself!" I storm out of her room and into mine. I slam the bedroom door as hard as I can.

I throw the pills in my backpack and fall onto the bed. I start crying. I remember Dad's message. I go to text him, but I don't know what to say. Do I tell him the truth? Will he insist I go live with him?

Him and Darlene. His fiancée.

I'm so mad at Mom, I can't even be in the same room with her, but I can't leave her. And I cannot live with Darlene.

I dry my eyes so I can see to text. I type: *Mom's okay.*

Then I turn my phone off, grab a pillow, and let myself cry as long and as hard as I need to.

"Damn!" Rodney turned into the subdivision with the huge-ass horse statue and a sign. But it was one of those damn gated communities. So the little girl he'd grabbed all those years ago was dating well. He'd give anything if he found him some rich sugar mama.

He stopped. He'd need a passcode to get in. Then he looked hard and realized he'd need more than a passcode. There was a guard sitting in the little glass box.

Since he got off at ten tonight and Peggy had kicked him out last night, he'd decided to make the drive up to Joyful.

But now it looked as if it'd been a waste of time. He hit the steering wheel with his palm.

Right then, a pair of headlights splashed over his car—a vehicle was exiting the subdivision. The bar lifted. Rodney leaned against the wheel to get a better view.

For a second, he imagined it. He blinked. Nope, he wasn't imagining it. A dark gray Jeep was pulling out of the gate.

How lucky could he be? He let the Jeep get ahead of him; then he followed. Getting close enough just once to make sure it was the right license plate.

It was.

———

I wake to a tapping noise. I lift up, and my head hurts. My face feels puffy from crying.

The noise sounds again. I roll over. I'm sure it's just Felix chasing a toy. Then I hear Buttercup let go of a low growl. I open my eyes and a face appears in the window. I almost scream.

But then I recognize the face.

I toss my covers off me. Glancing down, I see my nightshirt. It's old, faded, and has the Little Mermaid on it, but I don't care. I open the window. Right now, nothing sounds better than being in Cash's arms.

"Come in." I back up.

He pulls himself up inside and looks at me. "What's wrong?"

I see myself in my dresser mirror. Mascara is smeared down my face. I start to explain, but trying to think of how to say it brings on more tears.

He wraps his arms around me. I plop my head on his chest and let myself cry.

"What happened, Chloe?"

I finally pull back and try to stop the tears. "Remember Dad was trying to reach me?"

He nods.

"Well, when I got home, Mom was in bed, I went to Lindsey's, and Dad kept trying to reach me. He left a message and said Mom was acting wierd. I ran inside and I couldn't wake her up." She lets out a sob. "There were pills on a bedside table. I thought . . . she was dead."

"Shit? Is she okay?"

"She finally woke up, but she's been taking too many sleeping pills. She took ten in four days. She was only supposed to take one a day. I got so mad."

"You should be mad!" he said. "That's stupid. What did your dad say?"

"I didn't tell him. I texted him that Mom was okay and cut my phone off. I didn't want to talk to him. Mom said he's marrying Darlene." I back up and drop on my bed. "I'm sorry, I should have realized you'd call me. I just . . . was upset."

"That's fine."

"I took the pills from her," I say. "And I told her if she doesn't get medicine for depression tomorrow, then I'm calling the doctor. And I will." I let go of another gasp. "I thought she was dead. And all I could think was that it was my fault because I didn't take Dad's call earlier."

"No." He drops down on the bed beside me. "It wouldn't have been your fault. Did you take her to the hospital?"

"No. She was pretty alert then. I made her get up and eat something. I heard her moving in the kitchen, so I'm pretty sure she did." I look at the clock, and it's almost one in the morning.

He pulls me against him and I don't feel so alone. "I'm so tired of worrying about her when I have this whole adoption thing."

He kisses me on my forehead. "I know."

In a few minutes, we're stretched out on the bed. I'm on my side. His arm is around my waist, and my head's on his chest. I'm aware I'm braless again, and something tells me he's aware, too. Not that he's doing anything wrong.

I lift my head and kiss him. He kisses me back. This feels so right, when everything else in my life feels so wrong. I know Mom is just down the hall, but suddenly I don't care. I deepen the kiss.

He follows my lead, but doesn't take it further. I want further.

I sit up and pull my nightshirt off. His eyes round. "Chloe . . . ?"

My gut says he's going to tell me to put it back on. I kiss

him before he can. His hands are on my bare back. It feels awesome. He's awesome.

He rolls me over; his mouth meets mine. His hands are on my breasts. I slip my hand under his shirt.

"No." He pulls away. I lie back on the bed.

He looks at me. At me shirtless. His eyes on my breasts. Then his gaze lowers to my pink panties. "We can't—"

"Why?" I feel rejected.

"No," he says as if he knows what I'm feeling. "You are so damn beautiful and I'd love to . . . But not like this. Not with your mom here." He looks around and finds my night-shirt.

Embarrassed, I close my eyes.

He lowers beside me. "Look at me."

I do.

"I want this so damn bad, but not when you're upset or when your mom might walk in on us." He kisses me then pulls back. His gaze lowers again. "Get this on before I change my mind."

I sit up. He slips it over my head. His hands brush over my breasts as he lowers the material down to my waist.

I lie back down. He lies beside me and pulls me closer.

"I'm sorry," I say. "I shouldn't have—"

"Don't ever be sorry for that." His voice hoarse. He lifts up on his elbow. "That was a gift, and one I'll cherish. And it's going to happen. Just not now."

I start crying again. He lies back down and pulls me against him. He keeps his hand on my waist. And I lie there, head on his chest, and listen to his heartbeat. It's strong, steady, and soothing. When I'm with Cash, my life doesn't feel so bat shit crazy.

The next thing I know, I'm stirred awake by his kiss.

"I have to go," he says.

I smile, not sure whether it's been an hour or three, but

I realize how good it was to sleep with him for this little bit, even if all we did was sleep. "Thanks for staying."

"Thank you," he says.

As I watch him climb out my window, a light airy feeling rises in my chest. And I know what it is. It's something I never felt with Alex.

I'm falling in love with Cash Colton.

Rodney leaned back against the headrest of his old Honda and stared at the old house. He'd followed the kid to another neighborhood. One with older homes and leaning mailboxes. The Jeep parked in front of a small house with a small porch, where a light attracted bugs. But instead of heading to the porch, he went to the front window. At first he thought the kid was a Peeping Tom. But no, the boy stood there only a second before climbing inside.

Whatcha wanna bet it's her?

Teenagers doing the dirty.

He thought to leave, but not knowing if it was her kept him there. Hell, he wasn't sleepy. All he had waiting for him in Fort Landing was a cheap hotel room. Why not just hang? His car was more comfortable than the damn bed.

An hour and a half passed before he saw the kid crawling out the window. He watched the Jeep leave. Then he waited another half hour. Easing out of his car, checking to make sure no one watched, he made his way up to the window.

A dog barked across the street, and he hesitated, waiting to see if the animal would run out. When it didn't, he eased up to the window. Cautiously, he came against it and looked in.

A night-light beside the bed glowed, and he saw a girl in the bed. Not that she looked like a girl, more like a woman.

Dark hair spilled over the pillow. She had on a nightshirt that clung to her curves.

He wondered if he crawled in whether she'd give him a roll in the hay.

But was it really her? Inching in, he studied her face and tried to remember what she'd looked like as a kid. Dark hair and brown eyes, light olive skin. He'd thought she was just another illegal kid.

But then she'd spoken perfect English. He remembered that worried him, but not enough to do anything about it. She'd been a little fighter. Had spunk. Screamed like a little banshee. But he'd only had to hit her once to shut her up. She listened after that.

He continued to study her. Yeah, that could be her. All grown up. His gaze fell to her curves again, to her long legs bare and out of the covers.

It would be a shame if he had to kill her. Maybe Jack would actually fix this. Maybe. But if not, he'd do what he had to. He wasn't going to prison.

All of a sudden, a bark echoed from inside the room and a dog jumped up. His paws landed on the window seal, his nose hit the glass, and he bared his teeth.

Rodney dropped down.

He was almost about to run when he heard the window opening. He crawled to the other side of the house and hid behind the neighbor's car. Crap.

"Cash?" a soft voice called out from the window. Rodney stayed where he was, and didn't breathe until he heard the window shut.

He was about to head back to his car when a light comes on in a window at the back of the girl's house. He peered around the car and saw a shadow move to the window. Another woman. Tall. But not curvy. Her mom, perhaps? Was she as good-looking as her daughter?

He stayed behind the neighbor's car another ten minutes before he made it back to his own car.

The next morning I'm finishing off my cereal when I hear Mom's bedroom door open.

I stop eating. Anger swells inside me all over again.

She comes and sits beside me at the table. "Chloe—"

"No," I say. "I don't want to hear how sorry you are, or how it's Dad's fault. This is on you."

"I wasn't trying to kill myself," she says in a scolding voice. And she has no right to scold me.

I stand up. "No, you were just abusing drugs." I lean down in her face. "What would you say if I'd done that, Mom? Can I borrow three or four to take tonight?"

Guilt rounds her eyes. "I'm sorry. I—"

"I don't want to hear it!" I stand straight. "If you want to make it up to me, go to your appointment and get some depression meds. If you don't have them when I come home, I don't know what I'll do. I love you, Mom, but I'm not going to watch you kill yourself."

"I wasn't—"

"Just do it!"

"I will. I promise." Her voice catches.

I walk out the door. I guess the gloves are off. I'm breaking eggs with Mom now.

Lindsey is standing by my car, looking at me almost the same way Mom looked at me. Damn, I forgot all about getting mad at her.

"Are you still giving me a ride?" she asks.

"Yes," I say.

"I'm sorry," she says. "I shouldn't have said that about your dad."

We get into the car. I look at her. "I'm sorry I exploded

like that. I do *not* like Jonathon. I don't think I was wrong in what I said, but neither is it my place to tell you what to do."

She frowns. "I know. I just wish you weren't right. We still friends?"

"Yeah." I almost tell her about Mom, but it just seems too heavy a topic for the morning. For the same reason, I put my phone on silent and head to school. But I feel it buzzing right now in my back pocket. Probably Dad.

I haven't even turned off the engine when I see Cash walking toward the car. He's smiling, and my heart swells. I know he's thinking about last night. And while I'm not sorry I did it, I'm embarrassed. I never was the one to initiate things with Alex.

Lindsey sees Cash. "I'll go so you'll get your morning kiss."

Cash says hello to Lindsey and then climbs in my car. He leans over the console and kisses me. It's sweet. It's somehow hotter than before.

"I didn't sleep a wink after I left." He touches my face.

"Sorry." I grin.

"Don't be. I put on some music and lay in bed and thought about you."

"About how terrible I am?" I duck my head.

He laughs. "You can be terrible with me anytime you want."

I bump his chest with my palm.

"How was your mom this morning?" he asks.

I told him about our argument.

After a few minutes, things get quiet and he says, "Something happened last night. I didn't tell you, because . . . you were already upset." His tone is dead serious.

"What?"

"Remember the photocopy of the article we left at the print shop?"

"Yeah."

He tells me about finding the detectives at his house, and I immediately start panicking. "What are they going to do?"

"All they said was that they were going to look into it."

"But how? What could they do?"

"They could put something on the local news. Ask people if they've seen you."

"Crap. People would recognize me." My stomach knots, thinking about how this would affect Mom. "My mom can't handle this right now, Cash. She swears she wasn't trying to kill herself, but I don't know for sure. She's a walking skeleton with no reason to live. Nothing but me. I'm all she has. And if she's thinking she's losing me—" I bat tears off my face.

"I'm not saying they'll do it. That's just the worst-case scenario."

"I hate this," I say, and a lump forms in my throat.

"What about your dad? Do you think you could ask him to go with you to the agency?"

"Ask him? I'm not even talking to him now! And I don't think he'd do it without telling Mom." Emotions swirl in my gut. "I thought she was dead. I can't risk making her worse right now. I just can't." The lump in my throat becomes a lump in my heart. A big ball of pain I don't want.

"Then can you at least ask him to find your adoption papers? If we had them—"

"How will I explain that?"

"I don't know, but we have to do something. Mrs. Fuller is—"

"You said you were going to talk to the nanny's niece again."

"I tried. No one is answering the phone. I left a message, but they haven't returned it."

"Then call again. I want to do this, but I can't hurt my mom."

He stares at me, and the sympathy I always feel from him isn't there right now.

"And then what?" he asks.

"What?"

"When you find out the truth? Are you going to tell your mom? Tell the Fullers?"

A surge of anger washes over me. "You promised it was my choice when I told."

"I know, but you don't get it, Chloe. Your mom isn't the only one hurting. Mrs. Fuller can't handle this either."

He gets out of the car and leaves me there to cry alone.

26

All day I was scared the police had released my photo and someone at school would recognize me. I'm hurting. I'm angry. At the world, even at Cash. He didn't even talk to me in American Lit, but he finds me right as I'm walking to my car after school. He doesn't say anything at first. Just hugs me. My anger melts away.

"I'm sorry," he says. "I didn't mean—"

"I know. I'm sorry, too." I lift up on my toes and kiss him.

"I'm going to figure this out," he says.

Lindsey walks up, and Cash kisses me again and leaves. Lindsey and I head home.

Mom's car is in the driveway when I get there.

I pull in. My palms are sweating. I wonder if it's because I'm nervous Mom didn't get her medicine or I'm worried that the cops have already put my face on the news.

Backpack over my shoulder, reminding myself Mom's sleeping pills are still tucked inside so I can't drop it on the kitchen table, I walk in.

I get a weird no-one's-home vibe. But her car's here. "Mom?"

She doesn't answer. I drop my backpack in my bedroom, then walk toward Mom's bedroom. The door's open. The bed's made. That's a first in a while.

"Mom." I tap on her bathroom door.

No answer. My heart skips a beat. My gaze goes back to her bed. I remember the longest seconds I ever lived when I thought Mom was dead. I'm about to start panicking. Then I realize that Buttercup isn't home either. She probably went for a walk.

Right then, the front door opens. I walk into the living room.

"Hi." Mom's unleashing Buttercup. She's wearing a wig and her one pair of jeans that actually fits. "How was school?"

"Okay." I stand there, waiting for her to tell me. *Please, Mom, tell me you got the pills!* "Mom?"

"I got my prescription. It's on the kitchen table."

I lean back until I see it there beside her laptop.

"One of the side effects is it may make me gain weight. So that's good. Oh, I have doctor's orders to start back writing, too."

At least part of the tightness I've been carrying in my

chest evaporates. She did it. She got the pills. I'm so relieved, a rush of tears stings my eyes. I blink. "You loved writing."

"I know. I read the first three chapters." She smiles. "It's actually pretty good. I thought I'd read it and realize it was terrible. But it's not."

"Weren't you almost done with the book when . . ." *When you realized Dad was cheating on you?* ". . . when you stopped writing?"

"Yeah, I only have two more chapters to finish. But I'm going to reread it first. I even went online and found there's a writing organization here. They meet on Thursday evenings. I think I'll go."

"That'd be good." I remember when Mom was involved with a writing group in El Paso. She was happy.

She looks down a second, then up. "I know this has been hard on you and it's not fair. I know I've promised before, but I mean it this time. I'm going to get better."

There's something about the look in her eyes. Call me an optimist, but I believe her. I hug her. It's tight. And long. I can't blink away my tears. Then a big sweeping wave of fear hits. If that age-progression photo shows up on the news, will that knock Mom back down?

Later, I sneak into my room to call Cash. "Did you get anything on your camera?" I ask. I know he's checking it every day and hoping to catch Paul. I'm hoping he does, too. The jerk hasn't said anything to me since he asked me out, but I still don't like him.

"No. But I'm not giving up. Every time I pass him in the hall, he just smirks at me as if wanting me to react." He pauses. "How's your mom?"

"She actually seems good." I lean back on the bed. Felix jumps up and curls up in my lap. "She wants me to go to dinner and grocery shopping with her. She's even reading the book she wrote, like she might start writing."

"Good," he says. "Maybe she'll get her shit together."

"Yeah," I say, and then ask, "How are things there?"

"No one's home yet. Which is odd, because they both get off early on Fridays. Felix is following me around like a kitten."

A crazy question hits. Would the Fullers' cat remember me if I'm Emily? I push that thought away. "You work tonight, right?"

"Yeah. At five."

"Remember we're going out with Lindsey and David tomorrow."

"I remember." He doesn't sound thrilled.

I pull my Felix beside me. "What are we going to do if they post that progression photo on the news?"

"If someone recognizes you, we'll have to tell the truth."

"What if they accuse my parents of kidnapping me? And won't the Fullers be pissed at you for not coming to them in the beginning?" My line beeps. "Shit," I say when I hear it.

"What?" he asks.

"My phone beeped. It's probably my dad."

"You have to talk to him sooner or later," Cash says.

I remember him saying I should go to Dad about the whole adoption thing or at least ask about my papers.

"You make it sound easy."

"I don't mean to. I know it's hard."

The phone beeps again, telling me I got a message.

"Go call him. We'll talk when I get off work."

Ten minutes later, I lie there on the bed, gathering my courage to call Dad. Then I hit the messages to make sure it was him.

It is. I listen to him insist I call him. He's worried. He loves me. I'm his daughter. He's worried about Mom.

Seriously! He's worried about Mom? He didn't care when she had cancer. I cut the message off and call him. He answers on the first ring.

"Chloe. I've been worried sick."

"Sorry, I didn't hear your call." I test my palms to see if they're damp. They are. Damn, Cash was right about the sweaty palms and lying.

"I called before school and texted five times last night."

"Sorry. I was . . . with Mom."

He sighs. "Is she okay?"

"Yeah."

"She was drinking last night, wasn't she?"

"No." I stare at my bedspread.

"She had to have been. She wasn't making sense."

I close my eyes. Felix rubs his face against mine. "She took some sleeping pills."

"Too many of them?"

"She hasn't been sleeping," I say, not answering his question.

He doesn't say anything. Silence lingers, and I wonder if he's feeling guilty, knowing he's the reason she can't sleep, the reason she has to take pills to forget.

All of a sudden, Buttercup barks and lifts his front paws on the window seal to look out. I remember him doing that last night, too. I thought Cash had come back, but he hadn't.

Dad continues, "I'm going to Fort Landing for a sales call on Wednesday. I'm going to stop in Joyful on my way back. Can we have dinner on Thursday?"

I hesitate. Will that upset Mom? Then I remember she'll be at a writer's meeting. Hopefully, anyway.

"Yeah," I say, and I think about telling him I want him to go to the adoption agency with me. Just the thought makes my lungs seize, air locks inside.

"Good," he says. "We can talk then."

Talk? That's when I realize he's probably coming to tell me about his engagement. "Just you?" I ask in a not-so-loving tone.

"Yes," he snaps.

And—*bam!*—I'm annoyed because he is. No, I'm more than annoyed. I'm pissed, and I'm back to that breaking-eggs point again. "If you're coming to tell me that you're marrying Darlene, you—"

"I'm not marrying Darlene!" Dad spits out.

"But Mom said—"

"Yeah, she told me that, too. And when I denied it, she called me a liar. Then she tells me she's seen my credit card bill. What the hell is she—?"

"You didn't buy Darlene a ring?"

"No. My credit card was stolen. There was all kinds of other stuff charged, too."

Relief comes as my lungs release air. "Really?"

"I wouldn't lie to you."

I want to ask if he's planning on asking her to marry him in the future but decide to be happy with what I've got.

Happy until Thursday, when deep down, I know I need to talk to him about the adoption. I just have to figure out a way that he won't tell Mom.

Cash was starving when he got home from work that night. He walked into the Fullers' kitchen. Opening the refrigerator, he saw a white carryout box with his name on it. Mrs. Fuller brought him dinner again.

He frowned, but was too hungry to turn it down.

He emptied what looked like chicken parmesan on a plate

and popped it in the microwave. While it heated, he ate a cold bread stick.

Then he heard voices and footsteps entering the living room. No, not just voices, angry voices. He stopped the microwave before it dinged.

"Don't you want to find our daughter?" Mrs. Fuller yelled.

"I loved her, too, Susan," Mr. Fuller said. "I lost my little girl. But I can't go through this again."

"Go through what?" Mrs. Fuller's voice shook.

"Watch you crawl back into depression. Lose you."

"Someone saw her!"

"No. Someone saw a girl who looked like her. It's a trick, just like the cops said. Just like the last guy you gave money to."

"We don't know that. And all I did was ask the police to get the video from Walmart to see who took down her picture last month. It might lead us to her."

Cash's stomach clenched. Why the hell had he taken down that photo?

"It would have been nice if you could've at least seemed supportive of me," she said.

"I was. I went with you to the police station, didn't I?"

"But if you'd insisted—"

Mr. Fuller moaned. "I didn't insist, because I knew they wouldn't do it. Just because something disappeared off a bulletin board, doesn't mean anything."

"They saw her!" Mrs. Fuller yelled.

Cash leaned against the counter. Damn. He'd caused this. This was his fault.

"All they had to do was look at the video," Mrs. Fuller said.

"For how long, Susan? You don't know when it went missing. It could have been months ago. The store's open seventeen hours a day, seven days a week."

"I'd have looked at them. I'd have stayed up night and day to find my little girl."

"This is what I'm talking about. What about work, Susan? What about your patients? What about me? And Cash. I thought you said he was your main goal, to prove to him that he's part of our family. If you get lost in grief again . . ."

Cash felt the sting of their words.

"I don't understand why you don't want to look for her!" Pain and desperation came with her words.

"She's gone, Susan!"

"No! She's alive!" Mrs. Fuller yelled. "A mother would know if her baby was dead."

Footsteps pounded up the stairs. Cash swallowed a gulp of guilt. Guilt for doing this to them. Guilt because he'd done this to a mother of a little boy who looked like him.

Then came more footsteps.

Cash turned around. Mr. Fuller stood there. "Sorry. We didn't know—"

"It's okay."

"There's food in the fridge for you."

"I'm microwaving it now."

Mr. Fuller walked to the fridge and grabbed a beer. "Someone was making copies of an article that was published about Emily. Our daughter. The article had the age-progression photo. They left a copy there, and the guy working the counter said the girl making copies looked like the age-progression photo."

Cash nodded as if he hadn't known. "What are the cops going to do?"

"Nothing. They are certain it's a con. And I'm so afraid of what this will do to Susan. She's going to crawl back into that dark hole."

Cash wanted to tell him. Tell him about Chloe. Tell him Mrs. Fuller wasn't crazy. To come clean. Confess he'd been the one to take down the photo and leave the copy of the article behind in the printer. However, it wasn't just about them. It was about Chloe now, too.

Mr. Fuller looked at Cash. "Before we took you in, she . . . All she thought about was Emily. She lost it again when the other asshole conned us. Because of you, she didn't . . . she got over it. I don't know if we'll get lucky this time!" Desperation sounded in his voice. "See you tomorrow." He walked out.

Cash watched him leave, and he felt the same helplessness in his chest as he'd heard in Mr. Fuller's voice. Curling his hands into fists, he wanted to hit something. No, what he wanted to do was fix it.

Surely if Chloe saw the truth, if she knew for certain she was the Fullers' daughter, she'd do the right thing. He'd called the nanny's phone again on the way to work, but no one answered again. Even if he talked to the nanny, would that really prove anything?

He needed proof. Solid proof.

Right then, Cash knew what he had to do. He had to get them. He had to get the adoption papers.

He pulled the plate out of the microwave and took it up to his room.

He and his dad had broken into museums. An adoption agency should be a piece of cake. In fact, he recalled how he and his dad worked the museum job. That's what he needed to do.

27

Saturday afternoon, Rodney pulled in front of Jack's house. He'd gotten the address from his ex-wife, Jack's sister. Jack had obviously done well for himself these past fifteen years, because he'd upgraded his lifestyle. The two-story brick home was in a nice neighborhood. It rubbed Rodney the wrong way. He should have profited as well. He'd helped the man build his business by supplying kids in the man's first years in the adoption business.

Having been raised by a Hispanic stepmom, he spoke Spanish since he was five. It hadn't been hard to pay needy families in Mexico and Central America to give up a kid for a better life in America, not if he funded them a couple of thousand. And since Jack earned five times that from families desperate to have a child, it was profitable.

Sometimes, Rodney didn't even have to pay the families, and he kept Jack's money. Poor people wanted a better life for their kids, too. Then he found the same type of families here in the States who were desperate enough to offer up a child. It had been easy money.

It all ended when that kid died. Jack blamed him. Then the man freaked out, saying the cops would be on their asses. Rodney assured him he could replace the kid. He even had a family in Mexico prepared to give up a child, but at the last minute, they changed their minds.

Desperate, and maybe a little messed up—those were his white powder days—he found another kid. He'd thought she was just an illegal kid. How the hell was he supposed to know that some nanny would bring some rich doctors' kid to the bad part of town?

Still staring at the house, he cut the engine off, got out of his Honda, and went and knocked on the front door.

Linda, Jack's wife, answered. The second her eyes met his, she frowned. "So you're the reason my husband's blood pressure is running so high."

"Nice to see you again, too." Rodney tried to step inside.

She didn't move away from the door. "Just leave, Rod. He doesn't need the likes of you in his life."

"Can't do that, Linda. Tell him I'm here!"

For a second, he thought he was going to have to push his way inside. But she relented.

He walked in; she took off out of the room. He stood there, checking out all the nice furnishings.

"What are you doing here?" Jack asked, walking in. Out of his business suit, wearing khaki shorts, he looked even more like an old fart. And damn, the man was only five years older than Rodney.

"Looks like you're doing well for yourself. Who you got doing my job?"

"No one. I'm doing things right. What do you want?"

"I thought I'd give you an update."

Jack's face grew red. "What update?" Fear made the old man's eyes go wide. "I told you I was handling this. I don't want any part of what you do."

"Calm down. All I wanted to tell you was I found the girl," Rodney said. "Unless . . . ? Has something happened? The kid come back?" He took a step toward Jack, studying him.

"No. I haven't heard a word."

"Then why are you shitting your pants right now?"

"I'm not. I've got the letter written and everything."

"What letter?"

"I told you. I'm giving her a letter that she'll think is from her mom. It says she doesn't want to see her. It'll work."

"Let's hope so." He started to leave, then stopped. "You got a couple hundred bucks?"

"What for?" Jack's expression went hard.

"Because I need it. And because from the looks of things, you got plenty."

Our double date on Saturday night was good, but Cash was quiet. Distant. He told me about hearing the Fullers' argument. And about Mr. Fuller saying the police weren't looking into Emily Fuller's case. While I saw that as good news, Cash didn't seem nearly so happy.

I know he's worried about the Fullers. Part of me worries he blames me for them hurting.

We didn't see each other on Sunday because he said Mr. Fuller wanted him to help do yard work.

So by the time school's out on Monday, I'm ready for some Cash time. And since today's Mom's first day at work, I ask him to come over.

He follows me home from school, but Lindsey is just walking away when he tells me, "I can't stay long. I'm picking up shifts at work this week."

"What about your class on Wednesday?"

"I'll miss one class. It won't matter."

Being an insecure twit, I wonder how much I matter. I start wondering if he just doesn't like me anymore.

"What's wrong?" I reach for his hand. "Are you mad at me?"

"No. It's just . . . Mrs. Fuller didn't go into work today. This morning she looked like she hadn't slept."

"Are they still fighting?"

"No. But they're not talking. She's sleeping in your room."

"What?" I ask, sure I misunderstood.

He frowns as if he said something he shouldn't have. "In Emily's room."

My mind races. "They live in the same house as . . . ?"

"No. But they have a room. It's painted pink and has all your . . . all Emily's things in it. Clothes. Toys. Books. Pictures. It's like a shrine. She's been sleeping in there."

Cash leaves shortly after that, but his mood stays with me.

Somehow, my concern over Mom overshadowed the whole adoption versus kidnapped thing. But it was just a temporary reprieve, because the thought of Mrs. Fuller sleeping in the room with nothing but things reminding her of her missing little girl who might be me brings it all back. And I hear the voice again, *Your mama and daddy don't want you anymore.*

But if I'm Emily, they did want me. They loved me. Loved me so much that even fifteen years later, they have a shrine for me.

I go drop on the sofa. I pick up my grandmother's photo album, and I flip through it until I find that picture of me. A picture of me with my doll Emily. I stare at the empty look in my eyes.

We left it at a park only a few months after you got it. We went back to get it, but it was gone. You cried for weeks, wanting Emily back.

I wonder if I was crying for the doll, or for everything else I lost. My parents. Maybe even myself.

I lost who I was. I lost Emily Fuller. Is that the empty spot I feel?

Mom walks in around six. "Man, that smells good."

After an hour of feeling sorry for myself, I remembered I'd wanted to surprise Mom with dinner.

On the sofa, I push Felix off my lap and meet Mom in the kitchen.

"How was it?" When I see her smiling, I force a smile, too.

She sets her bag on the table, then yanks her wig off. "It was exhausting. But good. Everyone was nice. The doctors were easygoing. I had an hour lunch, and I went to a café next door and I wrote and ate soup. That was the best part of the day."

She hugs me. I hug her back. When we separate, I look at her. "Wow, you got hair, Mom."

She touches her head. "I know, I noticed it this morning. Maybe in another week, I won't need the wig."

"I think you could pull it off now. Put some big earrings on and red lipstick, and go for it."

We laugh. We eat dinner. We talk about her book.

Afterwards, she grabs her laptop, sits on the sofa, and writes. I escape into my room to do my homework. Felix joins me. As I pet him, I think about the other Felix. About the Fullers. I think about Mrs. Fuller sleeping in the room of a missing little girl who might be me.

I wonder if I walked into that room whether I'd feel as if I belonged there? If the empty spot I still feel in my heart would go away.

On Wednesday, Cash comes over before he has to go to work. When he first walks in, I know something's wrong. His eyes are bright with anger. "I caught 'em."

"What?"

"That asshole, Paul. I have him on camera." He hands me his phone. The video shows Paul standing by Cash's Jeep with another football player with red hair.

Paul says, "Do you think he's even noticed we did it?"

"Probably not," the redheaded guy answers. "He's an idiot."

"Maybe he'll notice this." Paul shifts, and the noise of metal running across metal sounds.

"They did it again?" I ask.

"Yeah, but their asses are mine now!"

I study him. I don't think I've ever seen him so mad. "You're going to show the principal?"

"I'm gonna do better than that. He's going to wish he never touched my Jeep." Tension rolls off him

"You can't get into a fight. You'll get into trouble."

"Trouble's my middle name. It's bred in me. It's what people expect from me."

"I'm serious, Cash."

"So am I."

"Turn it over to the principal, and let him deal with them."

"No. He did this to me, not the principal."

"Cash, don't—"

"You're back to not wanting to break eggs, Chloe. Can't you see—?"

"Think about the Fullers. If you do something, it's going to hurt them."

"I'm not trying to hurt them." His tone cracks with anger. "But those assholes damaged the one thing I've allowed the Fullers to give me. It's the only thing I've ever had that was new. That was perfect. They ruined it."

His words come loaded with emotion. "But it'll hurt the Fullers. They've got enough on their plates right now."

His eyes get bright. "Which is exactly the thing I've been saying since they brought me home. I don't belong there!" Cash storms out.

I call him to come back. But he's not listening.

I go vent to Lindsey, who says all the right things, but it doesn't help. The more I think about what happened, the more I blame myself for not handling things better. I've known how much he loves his Jeep. *It's the only thing I've ever had that was new. That was prefect.* I hurt for him.

I text Cash. He doesn't answer. I call. He doesn't answer. I know he's at work, but couldn't he at least reply? I need to tell him I'm sorry.

I text Mom: *Going to see Cash. Be home in an hour.*

Because he showed me where he worked, I know the way.

While I drive, I try to come up with the perfect apology that says I didn't mean to make it sound like he was intentionally hurting the Fullers.

I get to the garage. The lights are on in the office, but the doors to the garage are closed.

I park. When I walk in, a guy steps into the office from a side door.

"Hey," I say.

"Hey." He's young. I remember Cash telling me he's friends with a guy, Devin, who works here.

"Is Cash around?" I ask.

He smiles. "Are you Chloe?"

I force a smile. "Yeah."

"He talks about you all the time."

"Thanks. Can I see him?"

Devin looks confused. "He only works on weekends now. I think he has school on Wednesdays."

"But I . . ." He told me he was missing school to work. "Right." I feel like a thousand ants are milling around my chest, creating holes of doubt. Eating away at everything I believe about Cash. About us.

I drive off, but I pull into a parking lot a block away to try to understand.

My phone dings with a text. I grab it. It's him.

Him: *Sorry. Just pissed at Paul.*

Me: *Where are you?*

Him: *At work.*

Me: . . .

What do I say? Why would he lie about being at work?

Then I remember Mom asking me that very question about Dad. And we now know what Dad was doing.

I remember Cash has been going to school with college girls. Girls he might've dated before. Now those thousand ants are eating away at my heart.

Cash waited for Chloe to reply. She didn't. He sent another text.

Can I come by later?

No answer.

Was she still pissed? Probably, he acted like an idiot.

He called her. Her phone went straight to voice mail. Should he leave now and go there? He looked up at the adoption agency. No, he needed to stay. He'd been here every night this week, and so far the maid service hadn't shown up. And to pull this off, without getting his ass in a jam, he needed to know when they came.

Surely the agency had a cleaning service. Every company had one.

He leaned back in his Jeep, parked in a drugstore's parking lot across the street. *The hardest part of the job is the prep work.* He remembered the nights he'd slept in the car while his dad cased his jobs

An hour passed. Two. His stomach grumbled.

Great. Now he was hungry, miserable, thinking of the piece of shit his dad had been, and pissed off at Paul.

He texted Chloe again. No answer.

He called her again. No answer. He left a message again, telling her how sorry he was.

An hour later, he saw a van pull up at the building across the street. He waited, and sure as hell, two women got out with brooms and a vacuum cleaner.

"Finally."

It was eleven when Cash left. He texted Mr. Fuller and told him he was helping one of the guys he was studying with change a tire. Then he raced to Chloe's.

The house was dark. Hopefully, that meant her mom was in bed. He went to the window and tapped it. He saw Chloe lying there. But she didn't get up.

He tapped again.

She sat up, stared at the window. He tried to open it. It was locked. Why had . . . ?

She finally got up, but when she opened the window, she stuck her head out. "I don't want to see you."

"I know I got mad at Paul and I took it out on you. I'm sorry."

"Leave." She started to close the window, but he caught it and climbed in. "You're nothing but a liar." Hurt radiated from her words and slammed into him.

"Liar?"

She stood so straight, so tight. He'd never seen her so angry. "I went to apologize to you at work. You weren't there. You said you've been working every night. Is it one of the girls at college?"

"Girl?" He finally got it. "No. There's no girl. You're

right, I wasn't at work. I lied because . . . I knew you'd try to talk me out of it."

"Out of what? Did you go get in a fight with Paul?"

"No. I've been casing the adoption agency. We have to get those files to prove you're Emily."

"'Casing'? Like you're going to break in or something?"

"Yeah, like that. But not really."

"Are you freaking nuts?" she hissed.

"No."

"That's illegal," she said.

"It's your paperwork. I'm just getting it."

"You could go to jail."

"I won't get caught. I'm not even going to steal anything. Just take pictures like I did with the Fullers' file."

"It's called breaking and entering."

"I'm not breaking in. Let me tell you what I'm doing."

28

"My chicken marsala is great," Dad says. "How's your meal?"

It's Thursday. I don't know how I managed to get through school so mad at Cash, but now I'm sitting at an Italian restaurant with Dad. My palms are sweating and I'm sure I have hives crawling up my neck. I'm scared. But I'm less scared of hurting Dad's feelings than I am of Cash's plan. So I came up with my own.

I'm getting Dad to go to the agency with me. The only terrible thing that could happen tonight, besides Dad saying no, is if he insists on telling Mom. But I have a plan for that, too. It might include breaking more eggs, but I'll do it.

"Where's your mom tonight?" he asks.

I fork a noodle. "At a writers' meeting."

"She's writing?"

"Yeah. She's better." I look up at Dad through my lashes. I notice something different. His hair. He's combing it back like his old style.

"I need to ask you for a favor," I blurt out.

Dad sets his fork down as if he can hear the seriousness in my voice. "What is it?"

I swallow. "You know how you and Mom said anytime I wanted to find my birth parents, I could?"

"Yes." He sits up. "You want to do that?"

"Yeah."

He stares at me. "Well, you're almost eighteen. It shouldn't be hard."

"I want to do it now," I say.

"Now?"

"Tomorrow."

He looks confused. "Do what tomorrow?"

"Go to the adoption agency with you and get my paper-work."

His mouth drops. "Well . . . I'm not sure that's the way it's done. I think we need to get a lawyer."

"No. I already went to the agency. They said they couldn't tell me anything because I wasn't eighteen, that I needed a parent's consent. We can do this."

He pulls his beer closer. "Is this . . . Are you wanting to find them because . . . of what I've done?"

I look at him. "No. I just need to know things."

He settles back in his chair. "What does your mother think?"

I inhale. "Mom doesn't know. And you aren't telling her. She's finally getting better. I can't risk this upsetting her."

"Then that's all the more reason to wait a few months," he said. "You'll be—"

"No." I slap my hand down on the table. "Tomorrow."

"Honey, I work tomorrow."

"So now work and Darlene are more important than me!"

"Chloe, you aren't being fair."

Probably not, but I'm going for it. And I'm going hard. "Is it fair what you put Mom through? What you put me through? I haven't asked you for anything since you ruined my life. And you can't do this for me? One thing!"

He stares at me. *Is it working?*

The guilt in his eyes says it's working. "It's that important to you?"

"Yes."

He sits there as if considering it, then shakes his head. "If I did this behind your mother's back, she'd hate me."

"Too late, Dad. She already hates you. She wants to pickle your balls. I'm the only one you have to worry about hating you now. And I will if you don't do this."

"How was dinner?" Mom asks when I get home.

I'd told her I was meeting Dad. I figured if I lied and she found out, it would've been worse.

"It was okay," I say. "How was the writers' meeting?"

"Good."

I smile. "How did it feel going without the wig?" I'd encouraged her to do it.

She grins. "One woman came up to me and said she'd been dying to get her hair cut that short. I told her I'd been dying to do it, too. I didn't say literally."

I laugh, and it's like a big weight off my chest, knowing she's not going to flip out about my seeing Dad. Maybe, just maybe, my life is going to be okay after all.

I head to bed, put on my sheep pj's, and call Cash.

"How did it go?" His tone is boyfriend-sweet and concerned.

"He's doing it."

"Seriously?"

"Yeah." Buttercup jumps up and curls up beside my leg.

"And he's not telling your mom?"

"He wanted to, but I threatened him."

"What did you threaten him with?"

"Just to pickle his balls."

"What?"

I chuckle. "Nothing. He's staying in a hotel tonight and picking me up in the morning after Mom leaves for work. I'll get up and pretend I'm going to school."

"Wow," he says. "Are you going to be okay?"

"Yeah." I smile. "How are things there?" The pause says it's not good. The thrill of my success fades. I run my hand over my dog, who looks up with complete love.

"They're still not talking. She didn't go to work today either."

"Did she sleep in my room?" Then I correct myself. "In Emily's room?" As sure as Cash is, and even as almost sure as I am that I'm Emily, I can't help but think how it's going to feel if I learn I'm not her. If I have to go back to believing I wasn't wanted.

"Yes." Cash pauses. "Oh, I've decided what to do about the video of Paul."

My gut knots up. "What?"

"I got Paul's number from Mike, the guy I know who's dating Paul's sister. I'm going to send Paul the video."

"What are you going to say to him?"

"Just that I know he did it and if he ever crosses me again or messes with anyone at school, I'll turn him in."

"You're . . . not going to turn him in?"

"No. When I talked to Mike, he told me some stuff."

"What kind of stuff?"

"Paul's got it bad with his dad. His mom died several years back. Mike said last year, CPS was looking at removing him from his home. His dad beat him up pretty bad."

"And he's still living with him now?"

"Yeah. If a parent goes through some classes, they don't take the kids away."

"That's wrong."

"Yeah. So I don't want to be the reason his dad jumps Paul's ass. I mean, the Fullers have insurance, and it'll pay to fix the Jeep."

My chest suddenly feels heavy and light at the same time. Part of me doesn't want him to go easy on Paul. Yet, I'm so proud of Cash for doing this. "I think I love you," I mutter. When I hear what I said, I palm-bump my forehead.

"What?" he asks.

I could lie, but . . . "I said, I think I love you." I hold in that gulp of air, afraid it's too soon.

He's quiet for a long uncomfortable pause. "You *think* you love me? But you're not sure?"

I breathe, and then I laugh. "I love you," I say. "Paul doesn't deserve that you do this, but because you are who you are . . . I love who you are."

He's quiet again. "I think I love you, too."

I clear my throat. "Think?"

"I love you." He sighs. "I'm not going to deny that I'm nervous about how all this is going to work out. But we'll manage, right?"

"You mean if I'm really Emily?"

"Yeah."

"It doesn't matter. We're not related."

"I know, but I think it might be weird . . . for them. The Fullers."

That piece of news cuts deep, because I know how much he loves the Fullers. Oh, he doesn't say it, but I know it. "I don't want to lose you. I don't care who I am."

"We'll work it out. That's what I'm saying."

"Promise?" I ask.

"Promise," he says. "Now, answer a question. And I want the truth, okay?"

"Okay." I'm nervous, unsure what's so important.

"What did you mean by 'pickle his balls'?"

We laugh at the same time.

Dad and I are led to the same room as before. While Mr. Wallace recommended I make an appointment, I was afraid of being turned down. So we just showed up. I sit down and hug myself from the cold and nerves. Not sleeping last night didn't help.

"You okay?" Dad asks.

"Nervous."

"It's all right." He puts his hand on my shoulder. His touch sends pain right to my heart. The pancakes I ate this morning are now sitting in my stomach, heavy, and no longer so sweet.

I smile because I know he's doing it because I asked, make that pressured, him. Either way, he gets brownie points.

The door to the room opens. I actually jump. Because we waited so long last time, I expected the same today.

"Hello." Mr. Wallace walks in. I swear he's wearing the same black suit and red tie. But I do notice something different. In his hand is a manila envelope. My paperwork? "Mr. Holden, I presume?"

Since Dad had to show his ID to the clerk, the man's not merely presuming.

"Yes." Dad stands and offers him his hand. "I believe we met before."

"You're right, we did."

I stand and offer my hand as well. I'm alarmed by how damp Mr. Wallace's palms are. Is he planning on lying again?

We sit down.

"Thank you for agreeing to meet us on short notice," Dad says.

"Not a problem." Mr. Wallace's gaze shifts to me. "I'm actually happy you stopped in. I tried to call, but the contact information we have is no longer current."

Thank God. "Anyway, after you left last week, Ms. Holden, I pulled your file. I was disappointed it was listed as a closed adoption."

"Closed?" Dad sits forward.

"Yes. It means . . ."

"I know what it means," Dad says, "but we were told if our daughter ever decided to look into it, she'd be allowed."

"It is allowed. We contact the birth parents and see if they're willing. Ultimately, it's the birth parents' choice. But since your daughter came from the state, all those adoptions are closed."

I remember Cash telling me this. So Mr. Wallace isn't lying. Not about that.

Dad shakes his head. "I could swear we were told this was considered an open adoption."

Mr. Wallace frowns. "I'm sorry you misunderstood. I

think I have a copy—" He reaches into the envelope and pulls out some papers. He pushes them across the table to my dad.

Dad leans in to read them.

"Look at the third paragraph on the second page."

Dad does. He reads it, then he turns to the last page, and I see him look at the signatures at the bottom.

"I guess we got it wrong." Dad looks at me with sympathy. "I could swear we spoke about it."

"The adoption process is such an emotional time, facts are often misconstrued. However, because I could tell your daughter was serious about needing answers, I—" His gaze shifts to me. "—I reached out to your birth mother."

I hear what he's saying and realize then that this means that I'm not Emily Fuller. I swear my rib cage shrinks and I feel different emotions vying for space. Regret. Resentfulness. So I *did* want to be Emily. I wanted to be her so I'd know I wasn't just thrown away. I wanted to believe that my parents still loved me. That they'd built a shrine for me.

Mr. Wallace pulls at his tie. "Unfortunately, she's not open to a meeting. However, she took it upon herself to write a letter in hopes of offering you some answers. I hope this will help you find what you think you need."

I don't know what I expected to feel, but it wasn't this. I'm suddenly angry, furious—so pissed, I want to scream. She gave me away at almost three years old, and she doesn't think I deserve to meet her! Five minutes. Ten tops. What would it cost her?

"That's not right!" I say. "I deserve to meet her!"

In about three minutes, we are out the door. I'm sitting in the bucket seat of Dad's sports car. I stare at the envelope in my hand. I even asked to keep the paperwork, and Mr. Wallace agreed. Surely if the papers were fake, he wouldn't have . . .

"Are you going to read it now?" Dad asks.

"No!" I stuff it into my purse.

"Do you want to get lunch?" His voice is gentle. He knows I'm hurting. He cares. Shouldn't that be enough? That I have a mom and dad who love me?

Why isn't it enough?

"No. I want to go home."

"I can stay until—"

"No. I'll be fine. Just take me home. Please." I look out the window so he won't see my tears.

29

When we get to my house, Dad hugs me so tight and tells me how much he loves me. I think he wants to be my superhero again, but he can't. He can't fix this. I'm not sure anyone can. Before he drives away, he makes me promise I'll call him after I've read the letter.

I walk into the house. I'm greeted by Buttercup and Felix. I recall how damning it seemed that the Fullers and I both have cats with the same name.

I go into my bedroom, followed by eight paws. I sit on the edge of my bed and stare at the letter.

I slide my finger under the flap and feel the raw sting of a paper cut.

"Shit." I put my finger in my mouth to suck the pain away. Blood spills onto my tongue. I tell myself I don't have to open it. Why should I care about her? My lip starts trembling, and I remember sitting there in that princess costume feeling so alone. Abandoned.

I don't have a clue what that letter says, but reading it can't hurt any more than I'm already hurting.

I pull out the letter.

Before I start reading, I see the sheet of paper soaking up my blood. For some reason, that seems poetic. We shared the same blood. Maybe the same smile, the same facial features, but I'll never know. Then I focus on the handwriting. It's soft and flowy. Almost beautiful.

I blink away tears and start reading.

Dear Baby Girl,

I have sat here in this hard wooden chair for over an hour trying to think how to explain things without telling you some of the ugly truths. And I have finally come to the conclusion that if I'm going to write this letter, I'm going to have to be honest.

I was eighteen years old. I was naïve and believed in the good of everyone. I had met a man at college and he asked me to help him move. I said yes. He seemed like a nice guy.

He wasn't.

I gasp and put my hand over my trembling lips when I realize what she's saying. I have to wipe my eyes to keep reading.

The bruises on the outside went away, but not the ones on the inside. I didn't tell anyone. I was ashamed.

I left school the next month and went back home to my family. Six weeks later, I learned I was pregnant. I did not believe in abortion. I didn't know what to do. I looked into adoption. But the closer it came, the more I wanted to believe I was better than that. I wanted to believe that it wouldn't matter.

When you were born, you were so beautiful. I wanted to love you. I did love you in so many ways, but sometimes when you looked at me, I could see him. I tried, Baby Girl, I tried to keep you. I fought the depression, the anger, the nightmares of reliving that terrible night.

I know you are not him. And you have no blame, please don't take that on, but because of what he did, I was damaged and . . . you had his eyes, and the shape of his lips, and I knew I would never love you like you deserved to be loved. It got so bad, I couldn't hold you.

I let out a sad sound, and Buttercup comes up and rests his head in my lap. Felix paws at my arm.

That man robbed me of the life I deserved, but I refused to rob you of the life you deserved. I hope your life has been filled with love and laughter. I pray you understand that giving you away was me trying to give you a chance.

I ask you to forgive me for being a weak person and not being willing to meet you. I know I ask you to forgive, when I couldn't forgive him. But I ask you to forgive me not for me, but for you. Bitterness is like a cancer. It can eat you alive. My life is sad. And when I think of you, and I do think of you, I imagine you full of happiness and dreams.

Sincerely,
Your Birth Mom

My phone dings with a text. I lean over and see Cash's name on the screen. I know he wants me to be Emily. Right now, I'd give anything to be Emily.

I start to pick up my phone, but don't. I don't want to talk. I turn my phone off. I lie back on my pillow and cry myself to sleep.

Three hours later, I'm awakened by the familiar tapping on my window.

I stand up. My face feels swollen, my chest and throat raw. I see the window open and I see Cash crawl inside.

"You're going to have to quit cutting off your phone. I can't handle it." He moves in, takes one look at me, and doesn't even ask. He pulls me against him and I go straight to more tears.

When I'm no longer making desperate sounds, he pulls back. "What happened?"

I bite down on my lip. "I'm not Emily. My father was a rapist. My mother couldn't bear the thought of touching me."

He just stares at me. "Who said that?"

"She wrote me a letter." I motion to the bedside table.

He stands there with disbelief in his eyes.

"They even gave me a copy of the adoption papers."

"Can I see them?" he asks.

I nod.

He picks up the letter. "Is that blood?"

"A paper cut." And I feel like I have one right across my heart, too. He reads. His jaw tightens with each word he takes in. Then he puts it down and looks at the other papers.

"It's a lie, Chloe. I don't believe it."

I shake my head. "The agency wouldn't have given me

all this if it was a lie. Dad's and Mom's signatures are on the paperwork. Her signature is on the paperwork, too."

"It could be fake."

"It's not fake."

He pulls me against him again. His arms are so warm. He leans down and says in my ear, "It's a lie, Chloe."

I look up. "Why would anyone lie about that? Why would anyone write such a terrible thing if it wasn't true?"

"To convince you to stop looking."

I shake my head. "Cash, it's over. I'm not Emily. I know you wanted me to be." I feel more tears forming. "I'd give anything to be her now. But it's not true. I'm a product of rape."

"No! Don't you see? They wrote a letter to keep you from trying to find out anything else."

I drop down on the bed. "Stop! Give it up! I just need to accept this."

I eventually talk Cash into leaving. I find my phone and realize I have ten messages from Dad. I text him and say I'm okay, and thank him for doing it. He texts back and asks if he can call me. I reply I'm not ready to talk.

I spend the rest of the afternoon with a cold rag on my face, so when Mom gets home, she won't know I've been crying.

Of course, that was futile. When she walks in the door, hugs me, tells me she loves me, I break down in tears. I blame it on being the new kid at school. I blame it on missing my old friends. I blame it on PMS.

She tries to blame Dad, then Cash.

"No. I swear."

We go outside to the porch swing. Mom sits down, and I stretch out, rest my legs on the arm of the swing, and place my head in her lap. She runs her fingers through my hair the way she used to when I was upset about something. In a calm voice, she talks about her day and her book. She laughs and smiles, and I realize how much I've missed her. How much I love her. And how deep down I'm still scared to death the cancer could come back.

I also realize that my birth mother had done the right thing. She may not have loved me. But I have a mom who does. Yeah, she's been through a rough patch, but everyone is allowed to screw up sometimes.

Tuesday was payday. And when Rodney saw his check, he realized he was going to be short two hundred to pay his bills. Luckily, he knew where he could get it. And since he'd wanted to check in with Jack anyway, why not make it a face-to-face.

He got in his car and headed to A New Hope Adoption Agency. When he walked in, there was a couple sitting in the waiting room. He walked up to the counter, where a middle-aged woman sat thumbing through some paperwork.

"Jack in?" He leaned against the counter.

"Do you have an appointment?" Her tone was uppity.

"I don't need one." He started down the hall.

"Sir?" she called out, but he ignored her.

He moved to the office in the back and opened the door without knocking. Jack, sitting at his desk, looked up. His expression went instantly to fear.

Rodney's suspicion rose. "She came to see you again, didn't she?"

"No," he said. But that one word had lie stamped all over it.

Rodney shut the door. He rushed to the desk, placed his hand on Jack's fat neck, and pushed him, chair and all, to the wall.

"Don't lie to me, Jack. I hate it when people lie!" He tightened his grip until he felt the man's neckbones were about to pop. "Now, I'm gonna let you go, but if you don't start talking, I'm gonna finish what I started. You understand!"

The man nodded.

God, he was easy prey.

Rodney let him go and gave the man three seconds to pull air in. "What happened?"

"She . . . ," his voice squeaked out. "She came here with her dad. I did what I told you I was doing. I gave her a letter that was supposed to be from her mother." He ran his hand over his neck. "She's not going to look into it."

"You don't know that!"

"You can't do anything," Jack said. "You can't hurt that girl, Rod. She didn't do anything."

"She can talk."

"And say what? She was three years old. She won't even remember you. It's my ass on the line, not yours. Just leave her alone."

Rodney stared at the old fart. Jack was right.

The girl might not remember him, but that just reminded him of someone who would. The nanny. He'd read in the newspaper the description she gave of the man she'd seen talking to the kid.

Holy hell! He was going to have to kill them both.

The question was, who was he going to kill first? He started out the door.

"Wait," Jack pleaded. "What if I gave you money. Ten thousand dollars. You could disappear. Forget everything."

Rodney stopped and looked back. "Twenty-five thousand."

Wednesday morning, Cash walked out of his bedroom with a backpack containing everything he'd need for the day and night.

Chloe had spent the last three days trying to pull herself out of a depression. He stopped trying to convince her she was wrong and pretended he was letting it go. But damn it, everything in his gut said she was Emily. He was going to prove it.

Only a few steps into the hall, he heard the Fullers arguing again. He stopped and his gut became knotted with guilt. Then a door slammed and he assumed it was safe to leave.

When he got downstairs, Mr. Fuller was in the living room. Recognizing it as an opportunity, he said, "Hey, a group of kids are getting together to study for the SAT retake, and we might just stay the night at Jack's."

"Not on a school night," Mr. Fuller said.

Cash flinched. "Look at my GPA. I don't think staying up too late one night is going to ruin me. Besides, I'm three weeks away from being eighteen. I'll see you tomorrow!"

He took off for the garage and was about to get into his Jeep when Mr. Fuller walked out.

Cash stiffened, prepared to argue, but then Mr. Fuller said, "You ask first."

"What?"

"I know you aren't going to study. So you ask if she wants to have sex."

Cash shook his head. "This isn't—"

"Just listen—"

"No," Cash said. "Stop worrying about me and worry about your wife." But damn, it hurt seeing them so unhappy, especially when he'd caused it. And if telling them the truth wouldn't completely piss Chloe off, he'd confess. But he couldn't. Not that he was giving up. And tonight he'd get the proof.

"I'm plenty worried about her," Mr. Fuller said, sounding offended. "She's going to have to pull herself out of this." Then he shook his head. "Look, in this day, you don't just let it happen. You ask. And for God's sake, use protection."

"This isn't . . . I've got to go to school!"

Wednesday afternoon, at almost five o'clock, Cash parked his car in the strip center's parking lot, a block down from the adoption agency. A gloomy day, night had fallen early. He grabbed the burner cell from his glove compartment. He'd bought the phone from a kid who used to go to the private school. The guy worked at a phone repair store and regularly made extra money by selling the older phones.

After checking the time, Cash climbed out of his Jeep and grabbed his backpack. He started walking down the block toward A New Hope Adoption Agency.

Yes, Cash still believed that Chloe was Emily. And it was past time for him to prove it.

He knew Chloe would be pissed, hence the reason he hadn't told her he was doing it. However, she was already pissed that he didn't believe the asinine letter had come from her real mom. Not that they were arguing about it, but he felt it between them. He also felt her pain at thinking that her real father was a rapist.

Yes, the reason he could sympathize was because he lived with knowing his father had been a worthless human being. Almost subconsciously, he touched the scar at the center of his chest. The scar from the bullet that almost killed him. The bullet from a gun that his father might as well have fired himself.

A blast of a car horn yanked him out of this reverie and back to the project at hand.

Standing at the pharmacy again, he moved to the side of the building to keep out of the direct view of anyone leaving the agency. When he saw the black SUV, which he knew was Mr. Wallace's, pull out, he knew it was almost time. If they kept to their regular pattern, Wallace's partner at the agency would leave in five to ten minutes. The desk clerk always stayed about fifteen minutes later. And that was when he had to go into action.

Sure as heck, Wallace's partner's tan Malibu pulled out. Cash put on his gloves and waited until he got down the block before crossing the street.

He moved to the back of the agency building, where the desk clerk parked her blue Cruze. From the street, you could see only part of her car. Looking around to make sure no one was watching, he pulled the slim jim tool from his backpack and went right to work. He'd already checked and knew she didn't have an alarm, which was greatly appreciated by car thieves.

In seconds, he heard the slight click of the lock. Good to know that breaking into cars was like riding a bicycle. He got in, released the trunk, then opened the passenger door as well.

Running on adrenaline, he got out of the car and headed to the back of the building. Pulling out the thick fiber-filled jacket and a ski mask from the backpack, he put them both on. Then he stuffed the backpack in the front of his coat—patting it down to give him the appearance of a man with a beer gut. Finally, he pulled out the burner phone and dialed.

He'd called several times to make sure she answered the phone after everyone left. She had.

The phone rang once.

Twice.

Three times.

If she didn't answer, this wasn't going to work. The muscles in his neck tightened.

"A New Hope Adoption Agency. Can I help you?"

Relief washed over him. "Yes, I'm Charles Tannon and I work next door to your agency. I just saw some guy in the back trying to get into a blue Cruze. I yelled out. He took off, but he left the car open."

"Oh no. Is he gone?" she asked, panicked.

"Yes. He got in another car and took off."

"Thanks! Can you meet me—?"

Cash hung up, moving to the opposite edge of the building from where her car was parked.

He heard the front door shoot open and hurried footsteps. Waiting for her to cut the corner, he ran for the door. Before he got all the way in, he slipped the ski mask on.

Without slowing down, he darted into the men's bathroom, right off the waiting room. The door had been open, so he left it that way. He moved into a stall, took the throne, and placed his feet on the stall wall.

He heard Mrs. Carter walk back in, and she was talking— on the phone? He listened.

"No. The guy scared him off. He didn't even get into the glove compartment. My twenty-dollar emergency money is still there." Pause. "No. I don't want to wait around for the police." Pause. "And say what? Someone opened my car? I'm coming home. Turn on the oven, and I'll put dinner in when I get there."

He could swear he heard the door open and shut, but he still waited almost an hour before stepping out.

Mask still in place, backpack still serving as a gut, he looked for cameras. He wasn't sure they had them, but because they had one in the meeting room, he figured they might. But if this played out like he wanted, they'd never even look at the tapes.

He slipped his gloves on and went to the file cabinet. There wasn't a Holden file. Shit! If they'd destroyed it, all of this was for nothing.

He stood there fuming, then realized the file could still be on someone's desk. He ran from behind the counter and entered the first office. There were stacks of files. He went through them. His breathing felt restricted by the ski mask.

One file. Two. Three . . .

Seven. It wasn't here.

He shot out of one office and into the other. And there, smack-dab on top of the desk, was the Holden file.

Because he'd cased the building for only one week, he couldn't bet that the cleaning company came at the same time every night. He took out his phone and, page by page, snapped images. While not taking time to read, he noted a photocopy of the letter they'd given Chloe.

His heart raced. He continued taking pictures. Every few minutes, he swore he heard something.

Don't panic. You always screw up when you panic. Remember, this is a game. It's fun.

It may have been his father's game, but Cash never liked playing it. And for damn sure, it wasn't fun.

Finished, he put the file back together and placed it right where it was before. Then he went to the front of the office to find the best place to hide and wait for the cleaning crew.

Because the lights in the back of the building had come on first when they'd been here before, he assumed they cleaned the back offices first.

He looked around. If he hid behind the counter and one of them stepped behind it, he'd be seen. If he went into the bathroom and they decided to clean the bathroom first, he'd be caught for sure.

His safest bet was behind the counter. He curled up on the floor.

He sat there, remembering similar jobs with his dad. Pushing those thoughts away, the desire to start reading files hit. He'd just gotten his phone from his pocket when a car's headlights flooded the front room.

Was the cleaning crew coming this early? They hadn't shown up till almost eleven last week. And it wasn't even nine yet.

Or was one of the employees coming back?

Breath held, he sat frozen, waiting, listening. If it was an employee, he was screwed.

The lock on the door clicked. The door swished open. The light in the front office came on. Voices filled the room along with the sounds of rolling wheels.

It was the cleaning crew.

"Vamos a terminar rapido. Yo quiero estar en casa pronto."

One of the foster families he'd lived with had been Hispanic. He understood one woman saying she wanted to finish quickly.

"Sí. Yo voy a limpiar los baños primero. Tu limpias las oficinas."

One was cleaning the bathrooms first, and the other offices.

Footsteps echoed. But not toward the bathroom or the offices. Toward him. He closed his eyes. Didn't breathe.

The sound of crackling paper echoed about him, and he remembered the candy dish on the counter. Great, a sweet tooth was going to be his undoing.

He stayed frozen. The need to bolt bit hard.

Stay calm, never react too soon.

The footsteps started moving the other way. He waited until he heard the bathroom door close. Telling himself it was time, he shoved his backpack under the jacket and shot up and around the counter.

He'd barely gotten into the front room when he heard a scream from the hall.

You can screw up a wet dream, kid. I can't believe you're my blood! He heard his father's words.

Shit!

30

It took him two seconds to turn the key they'd left in the lock before exiting the building. Time enough for the other cleaning lady to storm out of the bathroom and scream as well. When he got out of the parking lot, he tore off the mask but kept moving. It was almost dark. He darted between two businesses, caught his breath, yanked off the coat, and crammed it back into his backpack with the mask.

Then, with the backpack over his shoulder, he took off, trying to look calm. He never looked back, just kept walking, marking his steps to freedom and to his Jeep.

He got in. His T-shirt was soaked with sweat. He started the engine and drove off. As he pulled down the street, a cop car, sirens blaring, passed him.

Only then did he remember his phone. Had he dropped it in his backpack? Or had he really fucked up and left it in the office?

He pulled over, yanked his backpack open, and didn't

breathe until he found it. Panic still clawing at his insides, he resumed driving, listening to his wheels roll and his heart race.

Trying to control his breathing, he told himself it was okay. He'd taken precautions. He'd worn his mask, his jacket, the stuffed jacket that made him look heavier.

He kept driving for thirty minutes before he decided it was safe to pull over. He saw a Whataburger and turned in to park. Heart still thumping, he got out his phone to read the files.

He saw he had one call and two texts from Chloe.

He read one: *Where are you? Please tell me you're not doing it!*

The voice message said the same thing.

He texted her back. *I'm fine. Will call later.*

Then he swiped over to his images and started reading.

He read one page, then moved to the next. Each one had his gut clenching. There were signed documents with the Holdens' names and another one from a Marie Garza—the woman the agency claimed was Chloe's birth mom. The next image was a copy of the handwritten letter to Baby Girl. There was an envelope with only Maria Garza's name in the return address, and another handwritten letter to the agency.

Dear Mr. Wallace,

I am so sorry I got upset when you called. I realize it is not your fault that this child needs answers. Unfortunately, I am unwilling to divulge my information. I have, however, written a letter that I'm asking you to deliver to her.

I'm so sorry I am not now in a place, nor do I believe I ever will be, to meet her.

She signed the letter: *Maria Garza.*

Cash exhaled. Frustration swelled inside him. He swiped his phone, and on the screen was a birth certificate.

It named a child born on November 18, Christina Garza. If he believed what he was reading, then it was true.

Chloe wasn't Emily.

Shit! How could he have been so wrong?

His phone rang. Chloe's number flashed on the screen.

"Where are you?" she asked.

"I'm coming to your house. Can we talk?"

"About what? What did you do, Cash?"

"Meet outside. Wait on the porch. We'll ride to the park and talk. I'll be there in thirty minutes."

With his new stack of cash, Rodney had decided to skip work. Instead, he bought a gun off the street—no way was he using his own. He also picked up a hat. One of those sock hats people wore in the winter that went past the ears. One that would hide his graying red hair. He stole a car, too. A nice little black Corolla that wouldn't stand out. No use paying for that when so many idiots left them unlocked.

Hell, he'd made a good living snatching cars for a few years. Never mind that was what he'd been caught at, and what had gotten him nearly a year in prison.

Thankfully, he learned from his mistakes.

Jack was stupid to think he'd leave. He wasn't running, looking over his shoulder for the rest of his life. He took care of his problems. Always had.

He didn't like doing this, but it had to be done. Jack would thank him, too. That fat fart wouldn't last in prison.

With the girl out of the way, tomorrow he'd go to a library and pull all the old articles that had been published about the case. He remembered one had listed the nanny's name. Hopefully, she wouldn't be too hard to find.

He pulled his car over in front of the girl's house. Lights were still on. He cut the engine off and settled in.

He'd wait until she went to bed. Go to her window and—*bang*. Easy work.

Right then, the front door opened. She walked out. All by herself, too. He picked up his gun. Maybe he didn't have to wait after all.

I step onto my porch in the dark; the air smells like rain and fall. I'd told Mom I was going to ride to the store with Cash. It's almost eleven.

"Just fifteen minutes," I told her, reminding her I don't ask for much.

She nodded.

Headlights beam down the street. It's him. When he pulls up, I hurry to his Jeep and climb inside. "Did you break into the adoption agency?"

He starts driving, then looks at me. Guilt brightens his eyes. "Yeah." He takes a right like he's going to the park.

"I told you not to do it."

"I know. I just . . . I thought I was right."

I hear something in his voice. "And now you know you weren't, don't you?" I swear I'd stopped believing it, but maybe I hadn't. Because I feel another wave of disappointment fill my chest.

He pulls into the parking lot at the park.

"What did it say?" I ask.

He pulls over, stops the car, and hands me his phone.

"There's a birth certificate for a Christina Garza on November eighteenth."

I read the screen. "Christina Garza." I feel my lips quiver. "That's my name." My name before I became Chloe Holden. The father is listed as unknown. Of course, she wouldn't put his name.

I swipe the screen to see what else he got. There's a picture of an envelope addressed to A New Hope Adoption Agency with only the name Maria Garza on it where the return address would be. But there's no mailing address. I enlarge the image and look at the stamped seal. It reads NASHVILLE, TENNESSEE, and the stamped date is listed as four days ago.

I swallow. "So I'm really the daughter of a rapist."

"Just because he's a piece of shit, doesn't mean you are."

I hear his words and then remember. "You said trouble was bred into you." I breathe in, then out, and I realize how much Cash and I have in common.

"I was wrong. It isn't who our parents are that matters, it's who we are. But I was so sure." He leans in and kisses me.

"At least our dating won't be a problem with the Fullers," I say.

"Yeah," he says.

I kiss him. "Thank you for doing this. I know my name now. But if you'd gotten caught, I'd have felt like shit."

His gaze meets mine. He looks as if he's about to say something. I'm afraid he still wants to convince me this is a lie, so I kiss him again just so I don't have to hear it, but the kiss becomes warm, and I welcome the feel of his lips on mine.

He pulls back. "I found out that the Fullers' lake house is going to be empty on Sunday. We could go spend the whole day there. If it's warm enough, we could swim in the lake, cook hamburgers on the grill, just hang out."

I smile. "That'd be great."

"Yeah, it would," Cash says. Then, "Oh, I think I have some good news for you."

"What?"

"Darlene changed her status on her Facebook page. She's single now."

"Seriously?"

"Yeah, and she also posted that her boyfriend dumped her because her brother's a screwup. I think Darlene's brother stole your dad's credit card."

I grin. "Is it bad of me to think that's good news?"

"No."

When he pulls back, I say, "I love you."

"Not just think you love me?" he asks.

"Not just think," I say.

Right then, headlights pull in behind us. I hear a car door.

"What the hell?" Cash turns around.

Footsteps sound outside the car.

A man walks up to the Jeep. No, not just a man. A cop.

He taps on Cash's window.

"Fuck," Cash mutters under his breath, but rolls down the window.

"What you kids doing?"

"Just talking," I answer.

He leans in and lifts his face as if trying to test the air. Probably thinking we got weed or something. He looks at Cash.

I see Cash tense up, but I can tell he's trying not to act nervous. "We're just talking, Officer. Not doing anything wrong."

"Well, the park's closed. You should probably take this gal home."

Cash starts the engine, and we follow a black Corolla out of the parking lot.

"You okay?" I ask, seeing his profile and noting his frown.

"Yeah. I don't like cops."

"Why not?"

"I'm a foster kid. They blame things on us."

I shrug. "You really believe that?"

"I know it. The Fullers' neighbor had a car stolen. I'd been there a few months. They told the cops about me. The police came and talked to the Fullers and me. Accused me of stealing it. The cop was a real asshole. A week later, they found out the neighbor's daughter had taken it for a joyride, wrecked and left it at her boyfriend's house."

"I'm sorry." I reach for his hand.

"Me, too." I hear the emotion in his voice.

Damn it! Rodney was lucky he'd spotted the cop. He'd followed the Jeep here and saw it as a perfect opportunity. He was half out of his car when the damn cop pulled into the lot. Staring in the rearview window, he saw the Jeep pull in behind him to leave the parking lot. But the cop was behind them.

He turned at the first chance to get away. He didn't think the car would already be reported stolen, but he couldn't chance it.

Tomorrow was another day. Hell, maybe he should do the nanny first anyway. Like Jack said, the girl might not even remember him.

Thursday morning, Rodney went to the Joyful town library to see if he could hunt down the nanny. He started by searching for a kidnapping in Amigo, Texas. It came up. Even had a picture of the park where he'd snagged the kid.

It also had a picture of the girl. Cute girl. And she'd

grown up to be a damn pretty woman, too. Well, almost woman.

He started reading. *Carmen Vaca Gonzales, hired as a nanny for Susan and Anthony Fuller . . .*

Fuller? He kind of remembered that being the kid's last name. But why did it feel so familiar now?

Fuller? Fuller?

He reread the name. Anthony Fuller.

Shit! That was who co-owned the Jeep.

What the hell did this mean? It could mean only one thing. They knew. They knew who the girl was. That's what it had to mean, didn't it?

He read on. The next paragraph included a description of him that the nanny had given. It even included his tattoo. He slammed his hand down on the table.

He wasn't going to jail.

He wasn't!

Maybe he should do what Jack said and leave. But did he really want to be on the run for the rest of his life?

On Saturday after Cash got home from work, he planned on telling the Fullers the truth. About his being the one to take down the age-progression photo, about his being the one getting the photocopies, but when he walked into the house, they were cuddled up on the sofa, watching a movie.

They looked happy, and uncertainty hit. If he told them now, would that just cause more problems?

"We've got reservations at eight at Perry's Steakhouse," Mrs. Fuller said. "You coming?"

"No. I . . . need to catch up on some homework."

He sat down in a chair, still debating—tell them, not tell them. If he didn't tell them, was it because he didn't want to be blamed for causing all the hurt? Or was it because . . . damn it, he still didn't believe it?

Or maybe it's because of the text he got from the nanny today. She was supposed to be home tomorrow. Part of him still wanted to talk to her, but Chloe would flip. It's as if she wanted to pretend the whole thing never happened.

Mrs. Fuller got up. "Well, I'm going to shower." She walked over and ruffled his hair. "We're proud of you, Cash." Then she left.

Mr. Fuller sat up on the sofa. When he heard the door close, he looked at Cash. "She's better."

Cash just nodded.

Sunday morning, I'm standing at my bedroom window. A little anxious and a lot excited about spending the entire day with Cash. His Jeep pulls up, and I grab my backpack and head out.

"I'll see you later, Mom," I say. I go to the kitchen to grab the bag of groceries that I bought for our cookout. Of course, he insisted he'd buy them, but since he'd paid for the last few times we ate out, I called rank.

Mom doesn't answer. I walk back into the living room, where she's on the sofa with her laptop.

"Bye," I say.

She never looks up from the computer. Her hair is like an inch long now. She's not wearing the wig at all. She's even gained more weight. She looks healthier. Even happy.

As soon as I put the whole daughter-of-a-rapist thing behind me, then maybe my life will almost be in the normal range. Well, other than worrying that my mom's cancer might return.

"Mom?" I say. "Mom!"

She finally looks up. "What?"

"I'm leaving."

Right then, I remember Dad trying to explain the reasons he cheated. What was it he said? *Your mom had her writing.* Oh, it doesn't excuse anything, but maybe I can see how he might have been a tad lonely. "Mom?" I say. "Mom!"

"To go where?" Mom asks.

I frown. "To the lake house with Cash. I asked you about it Thursday night?"

"Oh yeah," she says. "Are his parents going to be there?"

Because I'm worried she'll disapprove, I lie. "Yeah." I feel a little guilty. Especially since . . . well, I'm thinking today's the day things get taken to the next level. Part of me is so sure it's right. I was ready two weeks ago, when I yanked my nightgown off, but another part is . . . well, nervous.

It may not be my first time, but it's my first time with Cash. And that seems big. It seems bigger than it was with Alex. Or bigger in a different way. Last time it was . . . a rite of passage. I'd cared about Alex, but I wasn't . . . in love with Alex. This time, it's because . . . I want to be with Cash.

"Have fun, and don't be late. You have school tomorrow."

I nod. As I step onto the porch, Cash is getting out of his car.

"Do I need to come in?" he asks.

"No. She's writing."

He takes the groceries from me. "I brought an ice chest to keep the meat and cheese cold. Did you bring your swimsuit?"

"Yeah." I motion to my backpack.

"Good. It's supposed to get up to eighty-eight so the water should be perfect." He sets the groceries down and looks in the bags to pull out the meat and other items that need to be kept cool. When he sees the bag of caramels, he looks at me. "Thank you."

We get into his Jeep.

"Have I told you how glad I am that you moved here?" he says.

"I think so," I say. "But you could tell me again."

He passed a finger over my lips. "I've never been this happy."

"Me, either." A warm feeling fills my chest.

It takes us almost two hours to get there, but the drive passes quickly. We turn on the radio, but talk over the music and discuss school. He hasn't sent the video to Paul yet, but he plans to do it tomorrow. I'm a little worried Paul will still go off on him. If he does, will Cash have the willpower not to get into it with him?

We talk about Lindsey and how she and David have invited us out next weekend to go shoot pool again. Cash tells me about his auto tech class and how they are finally getting to work on cars. We talk about everything but me not being Emily. I know we both still think about it. But since we met Wednesday night, we haven't mentioned it.

Cash finally pulls up to a gate and punches in some numbers, and the big wooden arm rises and we drive in.

"Screw it!" Rodney watched the gray Jeep drive off. He slammed his hand on the steering wheel. Another damned gated community.

He really hated rich people!

He should have taken the shot back on the road, but every damn time he almost did it, another car would show up.

He drove past the gate slowly. Watching which way the Jeep turned after entering the subdivision. At least it wasn't with a live guard.

He drove around another three minutes, then turned around. He'd spent the last two days at the nanny's house. She hadn't been home.

He needed to do this. Finish it. Since Wednesday, all he could think about was getting his ass caught. Spending the rest of his life in prison.

He pulled over to the side of the road beside the gated entrance and turned the air conditioner up. The damn thing was on the fritz. He sat there, sweating, waiting for another car to pull in. It didn't look like a big subdivision. He'd find the Jeep. Find them. Finish the job.

Then, hopefully, Carmen Gonzales would be home and he could take care of her. Afterwards, he'd get the hell out of Texas. Go somewhere nice. Somewhere it wasn't so damn hot.

Finally, a car drove in. Rodney pulled in behind him and made it through before the gate closed. Now all he had to do was find the damn Jeep and kill two kids.

When we arrive at the lake house, I'm shocked. I envisioned a small rustic place. It's not rustic. It's not small. It's three times as big as the house Mom and I live in.

Cash parks in a garage, and we get out and walk in through the kitchen. "It's huge."

"Yeah, it's more of an investment than anything else. They lease it out most of the time. We come here a week or two every summer and weekends when it's not booked."

He sets the cooler on the kitchen floor and empties it into the fridge. "Do you want to swim now?"

"Yeah, let me change." I look around.

"There's a bathroom right behind you," he says.

I step into the bathroom and slip on my suit. I bought a new one right before I moved here, so it's been worn only a few times. I stand in front of the mirror. The swimsuit is not super small. In fact, the bottoms are boy shorts, but there's still a lot of skin showing. Other than that one night

I yanked off my nightgown, Cash hasn't seen this much of me before.

It suddenly occurs to me that I haven't even seen Cash without his shirt, which for some reason strikes me as odd. Alex took his shirt off every chance he got. And he didn't even have half the body that Cash has.

I look at the bathroom door and wonder if maybe I should just slip on a shirt over my swimsuit before walking out, but it seems kind of stupid. I still grab the towel I brought and tie it around my waist.

Backpack on my shoulder, I walk out.

He's not in the kitchen, and I assume he went to put his own bathing suit on.

He walks in with his swimsuit and a T-shirt. Now I really wish I'd worn the shirt.

He stares at me and smiles. He comes over and kisses me. "I have towels outside. We can use those so you don't have to carry home a wet towel. And I have some sunscreen, too." He grins. "And I'll be happy to help you with your back."

"Only if I can do yours." I grin, but still feel butterflies.

"Yeah."

I set my backpack on a counter and toss my towel on top of it.

Cash does a double take. His eyes are all over me. "Wow," he says. "You are so beautiful."

He makes me feel beautiful—not vulnerable, like some guys do when they see you in a bathing suit.

We walk out the back door, which leads to a covered patio with a table and chairs, a grill and a couple of big hammocks. He snags two towels and some sunscreen from a cabinet.

"This is nice," I say.

His arm slips around my waist. The feel of his touch moving over my bare skin sends sweet shivers to my toes.

We walk to the end of the deck that leads out into the water, where he drops the towels and the sunblock.

Cash pulls his shirt over his head.

I try not to stare, but I can't help it. My eyes eat up all the bare skin. He has a line of dark hair that starts around his navel and trails down into the trunks. I lift my eyes, and when I do, I see a scar. Located almost in the center of his chest, it's about four inches long, straight, except in the middle of that linear scar, it's round, about the size of a quarter.

His shirt lands on top of the towels. "What happened?" I ask before realizing it might sound rude.

31

Cash knew she'd ask. In fact, he'd gone over the lie he told the three other girls who had seen him without his shirt. The lie that included a skateboard and a broken beer bottle. But he didn't want to lie to Chloe.

"It's not a pretty story," he said. He picked up the sunscreen. "Come here, I'll put some of this on your back."

She moved in. Her eyes met his, and he could already see the empathy there, as if she somehow knew it was hard to talk about. "I want to know," she said.

He nodded. "I was shot."

"Your dad?" Her eyes went moist.

He closed his eyes one second. "He didn't pull the trigger, but he might as well have." He forced himself to say it.

"I told you he wasn't a good guy." He had to still himself to say it. "He pulled cons. Stole cars. Robbed convenience stores. He preyed on the most vulnerable. The elderly. I faked having cancer, and people gave us money. I hurt parents like the Fullers. Dad saw an age-progression photo that kind of looked like me, and—"

He heard her intake of air. "That's why . . . ?"

"Yeah." He closed his eyes, praying this wouldn't change her mind about him. About them. But if it did, he couldn't blame her. "The last job he pulled was a convenience store. A cop just happened to pull up. I was in the car. I was the getaway man."

"You said you were eleven when he died."

"I was. He taught me to drive when I was eight. He taught me everything. How to pull a con, to cheat people, to steal."

She shook her head. "How did you get shot?"

"A cop walked in when Dad was robbing the store. He pulled a gun on Dad and Dad shot him." Cash inhaled, remembering sitting in the car and seeing it through the glass doors. "He normally never fired. He always said if a job was executed right, you didn't need a weapon."

Swallowing his emotions, he continued. "He jumped in the car and screamed at me to drive. We didn't get down the street when a patrol car was on us. I pulled over. I didn't want to die. Dad was screaming at me. I threw the keys out the window." Cash could still hear him, hear the anger in his voice. "Dad yelled out to the officers and told them he'd kill me if they didn't back off. Then he told me to go get the keys. They fired. Bullets went everywhere. They said they didn't expect me to be a kid."

Cash looked away from her. "I was shot. Dad took a bullet, too. He got the keys. I called out to him—I was laying there, bleeding, scared to death. He didn't even look at me. He drove away." Cash's eyes burned. "He made it only a hundred feet or so. He ran into a parked car, but it was the bullet that killed him. I know I lied about that, I just . . ."

Tears ran down Chloe's face.

Shame scratched at Cash's conscience. "I told you I was trouble. I've done terrible things. And I don't blame you if you want to walk away. I don't deserve someone like you."

She blinked, and a few tears webbed her lashes. "Stop saying that! You were eleven! It wasn't your fault." She clenched her fist. "I wish he weren't dead, because I want to kill him myself."

Cash shook his head. "You don't get it. I knew what we were doing was wrong, Chloe."

"He beat you, too, didn't he?" More tears ran down her face. "He broke your arm, right?"

"Yeah. But I should have—"

"I hate him, Cash! I hate him as much as I love you." She moved closer, and she touched his scar. "I can't believe I'm whining about my life when you went through that. I'm sorry." She hugged him then, and they stayed like that on the deck, just holding each other for a long time.

When she pulled back, he saw something he'd never seen before. Acceptance. Yes, the Fullers accepted him, but they didn't know the things he'd done. He'd never told them. Never told anyone. No one but Chloe. And she didn't blame him.

"Are we going to swim now or what?" she asked.

He looked at her. "You sure you want to be with me?"

"Don't be crazy," she said.

"No, listen to me, I get—"

"Are we going to swim or what?" she asked.

"I just want you to—"

She shoved him. He fell back into the water. When he came up, he couldn't help but laugh. She stood on the pier, all smiles and curves and bare skin. She was the most beautiful thing he'd ever seen, and she knew all the bad things he'd done, and she still loved him.

Maybe his life wasn't so damned after all.

They swam, raced, and splashed each other for an hour. When they got out, they fell into a hammock and made out. When things almost went too far, he stopped and untangled himself from her and sat up.

He raked a hand through his hair. "We could—If you want to, we could . . ."

"Go inside," she said.

He looked at her. "I was told I should ask . . ."

"Ask what?" she said.

"If you wanted to . . . you know."

She made a funny face. "Who told you that?"

He laughed. "Mr. Fuller."

"Asking makes it a little awkward, doesn't it?"

Still grinning, he said, "I thought the same thing. But it kind of makes sense. It should be a choice, not . . . an afterthought. I don't want there to be any regrets."

She nodded. "Okay."

He lifted a brow. "Okay . . . ?"

Her smile widened. "Okay, you can ask."

"Ahh," he said. "Do you want to . . . go inside?"

She bit down on her lip. "The girl you dated who had a lake house close to here, did you two, you know . . . go inside . . . here?"

"Not here," he said honestly.

"No one, here?"

"No one." He'd answered honestly, and he figured if she'd asked, he could, too. "Did you and Alex . . . ?"

"Not here," she said.

His lips tightened. "I don't like Alex."

She grinned. "I don't like *her*, either." She pulled her hair back. "Did you bring protection?"

"Yeah." Then he worried . . . "Not that I planned—I mean, I'd never have—"

"I know," she said, saving him from having to say more.

I wake up. It had been amazing and emotional. The words *I love you* were said a lot. I'd cried. He immediately thought something was wrong. I immediately convinced him it wasn't.

Cash put on some music, I borrowed his shirt, and we lay in bed for an hour, laughing, talking, holding on to each other until we dozed off. When I sit up, I see Cash sitting at a small desk with his phone.

He must have heard the mattress shift, because he looks back, gets up to kiss me. "You getting hungry?"

"I'm starving," I say.

"Me, too. I started the grill."

His hair is wet, meaning he showered. I can't believe I didn't wake up. "Can I clean up?"

"Yeah. I put out clean towels."

When I leave the bathroom, he's still at the desk. He looks at me. I'm back in my jeans and top. "I liked you better in my shirt."

I grin.

He looks at his phone.

"What are you looking at?" I ask.

He frowns. "Don't get mad?"

Just like that, I know. "The pictures of the paperwork from the adoption agency?"

He nods. "Did you bring the letter with you?"

"Cash—"

"Just answer me."

"Yeah. I didn't want to leave it in case Mom . . . It's in my backpack. Why?"

"Something's bothered me, and I couldn't put my finger on it, but I think I know what it is."

I digest what he's saying. "Cash, I don't want to start—"

"Can I just look at it?"

I relent. "Yeah."

He walks into the other room. When he comes back, he has the letter in his hand. "I was right, Chloe. The letter's a fake."

I shake my head. "How—? You don't know that."

"I do. Look." He grabs his phone from the desk and joins me in bed. "Your birth mom's name on the birth certificate is Marie. But in her signature, here, it looks like an *a* on the end. On the letter she signed to Mr. Wallace and on the envelope that was mailed, she signed it as Maria. Look at how she writes the capital *M* in 'Your Birth Mom.' It's not the same as the adoption papers. You can see it."

I don't glance down. "I can't do this, Cash. I've accepted—"

"Just look at it." He holds out the letter and his phone.

I do. And he's right, but . . . "My signature doesn't look the same all the time."

"But it has her name on the birth certificate. It's Marie, not Maria. And the name on the envelope is Maria, not Marie."

I hear him, but . . . When I don't say anything, he adds, "I got a text yesterday from the nanny. She's back from Mexico. I didn't text her back. But I think we should go talk to her."

My mind races, and my heart tries to keep up. "No. I'm not doing this again, Cash."

"Don't you want to know the truth?"

"I do know the truth."

"Give me this, Chloe. Go with me to see the nanny, and if we still feel that way, then I'll let it go. I promise."

Rodney parked in front of his hotel room and rushed inside to wash the blood off.

He had struck out finding the boy and girl. But not so much with the nanny. Her lights had been on. He hung out there, watching and waiting until the neighbors went to sleep.

It had been a piece of cake getting into her house. He eased in, quiet as a mouse, making sure she was alone. She had been.

Washing his hands in the bathroom sink, he watched the bloody water get sucked down the drain. He hadn't liked doing it. That just proved he wasn't all bad.

He kind of wished she hadn't woken up, though. Hadn't switched on her bedroom light. Then again, when she saw him, he knew she recognized him. "You!" she'd screamed.

He'd hesitated. And that gave her just enough time to come at him.

He'd shot her, close range. Then the damn woman fell on him. Bled all over him. He closed his eyes and reminded himself he had to do it.

It was that or jail.

He wasn't going to jail.

Now he had to take care of the girl. And the boy? He should probably take care of him, too.

On the way to school on Monday, Cash pulled over to get gas. Standing there, he hit send on the video to Paul's number. Still holding the pump, he realized he was smiling. Not because of Paul, but because he couldn't remember ever being so happy, or exhausted.

He'd barely slept last night. Reliving every moment of

Sunday, wishing she were in bed with him, and trying to figure out how soon they could do that again. This afternoon wouldn't work, because Chloe's dad was in town again, and tomorrow she'd agreed to go with him to see the nanny right after school.

She'd made him promise a dozen times that if they didn't learn anything, he'd drop it. He promised. But damn if he didn't believe he was right. Chloe was Emily.

After hearing the pump click, telling him his tank was full, he went in to buy Skittles. On the counter, they had roses for sale. He got a red one.

Walking back to his Jeep, he saw a man leaning against the front passenger door. A big, burly guy, balding gray hair. He watched Cash with purpose. Cash approached with caution.

His father's words rang: *Never let your guard down. Everybody wants a piece of you. Everyone is out to get you.*

He pulled his keys out of his pocket and wished he weren't holding a red rose. "Can I help you?"

"Ain't that sweet." The man motioned to the flower.

"What do you want?" Cash asked, happy when another car pulled in to the pump next to him.

"I think I'm the one who can help you. Name's Ken Jennings." He held out his meaty hand.

Cash didn't take it. The hairs on the back of his neck stood at attention, telling him this guy was trouble. "I don't know you, so I don't have any idea of how you could help me."

"You see, people come to me to fix their problems."

"I don't have any problems." He motioned for the guy to move away from his Jeep.

The man didn't move. "Yeah, you do. I got a videotape of your car parked at a dry cleaner in Fort Landing. Amazingly, it's the same time someone broke into A New Hope Adoption Agency."

Cash's muscles tensed. Damn! Had he even looked for a camera before he parked?

"And here's the thing," the man continued, "I happen to know you come from trouble. With just a few phone calls, I think you'd be wearing some handcuffs, trying to explain a lot of shit. Do you want that?"

Cash's heart thumped, but he dared not show it. "Get your ass off my Jeep."

"Now, boy, listen to me. Just drop all this. Leave it alone. The guy who hired me doesn't want trouble. But there's someone else who doesn't feel that way. Your girlfriend needs—"

"You lay one hand on her, and I'll kill you. Get out of my way," Cash seethed. The man stepped away from his door, but it took everything Cash had not to put his fist in the guy's face.

Instead, he got in his Jeep and drove off. What the hell was he going to do now?

32

I get to school a few minutes early. I park, get out, and look around to see if Cash is there. David picked Lindsey up for school, so I'm on my own. I see Cash's Jeep pull in, and I start that way.

"What the hell is your boyfriend up to?" a voice says behind me.

I swing around. Paul, fist clenched at his side, storms toward me. Cash told me he was sending the video, so I know what this is about. "I'm pretty sure he explained it in his text," I say, and I know that, too, because I helped him write it.

"He's trying to mess up my chances at a football scholarship, isn't he?" He gets in my face.

I take a step back.

"Get the hell away from her." I hear Cash, and he's running toward us.

"What are you trying to pull?" Paul yells at Cash.

"Not a damn thing. Read the damn text. Now, get lost," he says. Cash's expression is rock hard. Anger tightens his face. He looks ready to fight.

"What are you going to do? Take it to the coach?" Paul moves closer.

Cash takes my arm. "Come on."

I start walking with him.

Paul bolts in front of us and takes a defensive stance.

Cash releases me and grabs Paul by his shirt and slams him into a car. "Listen to me. I know your father is a piece of shit. I had one like that, too. I'm giving you a fucking break, but it wouldn't take much to change my mind. Now, get the hell away from me! And stop trying to be like your damn father! Got it?"

Paul's face goes white.

Cash lets him go and grabs me by the arm. "We gotta go."

I let him guide me. "Go where?"

"I screwed up, Chloe. I gotta fix it."

"Fix what?"

We get to his Jeep. "Get in. I'll explain as I drive."

"Explain what?" I see his knuckle is bleeding. "You're hurt."

"Please. Trust me. Get in?" He sounds desperate.

His tension is contagious. I get in, but as soon as he's behind the wheel, I start again. "What's going on, Cash?"

"They know I broke into the adoption agency." He drives off.

"What? You said you weren't caught."

"I kind of was. They know I was there."

"Did they call the police?"

"I don't think so."

"But I don't understand. Why would—?"

"They're trying to hide the fact that they kidnapped you. They want us to drop it. And they threatened you. You are Emily." Fear brightens his eyes.

My mind's spinning. "We don't know that."

"Do you think they'd do this if they didn't have something to hide?" His hits the dashboard with his palm. "Damn it. You're Emily."

My chest tightens, my head spins. "What are we going to do?"

"We're going to the police. No. First I'm getting the paperwork, then we'll go. We'll show them everything."

"Wait. Stop. Let's think about this. They'll arrest you for breaking into the agency."

"I'm fine with that. As long as they catch that asswipe."

Emotion makes it hard to breathe. "I told you not to break into that agency. I told you. Now look what's happened."

"I know!" he says. "I'm sorry." He keeps driving.

I keep trying to make sense of this. We are about a mile from his house. But all I can think about is the mess all of this will cause. Mom. Cash. Dad.

"Dad?" I remember he's supposed to be in town. I remember I used to go to him for all my problems. He was my superhero.

"What?" Cash says.

"I'm calling my dad." I grab my phone and find his number and hit dial. "Dad?" I say when he picks up.

"Yeah."

Cash speaks up. "Tell him to meet us at the police station."

I look at Cash. A sob escapes my lips.

"Chloe? Is everything okay?"

"I need you. Can you come to my house?"

"What's wrong, baby girl?"

"I can't explain it now, just come. Please."

"Is this about the adoption?"

"Yeah," I say. "Just come, okay?"

"I'm on my way," he says. "I'm about two hours from town. I'll be there as soon as I can. You sure you're okay?"

"Yeah." I hang up and look at Cash. "Take me home."

"Let's get the papers first," he says.

"No!" I yell at him. "I want to go home. Damn it. I told you not to do it! Now look what happened."

All of a sudden, I hear a big bang. I hear glass shattering.

Cash slams on his brakes.

"Get down!" he screams. When I don't do it, he grabs my head and pushes me down.

I start to fight him, but then I hear another pop. Then a thud on the side of Cash's car.

"Please tell me someone isn't shooting at us!" I scream.

Cash doesn't answer—he is too busy driving.

The car swerves and I hear another pop.

Cash turns the wheel, and the car jolts like he hit something. I'm jerked around, and the seat belt cuts into my side. I scream again.

The back end of the Jeep swerves. We start spinning. Cash never stops fighting the steering wheel. He finally gets the car straight—then he floors the gas. He's white-knuckling the steering wheel.

"Is he gone?" I ask.

"Stay down!" Cash yells, and he's looking behind him. "I knocked him off the road."

I close my eyes and pray. Seconds inch by. Then a minute. I don't hear another pop. I don't hear the car, just the sound of my own breath. But I don't sit up; I'm too scared to move. Suddenly, Cash takes a sharp right and comes to a screeching halt.

I open my eyes and see the horse statue. Then I see a man looking at us from a booth. "Slow down, Cash!"

"Call 911!" Cash yells. "Someone's shooting at us. Send the police to my house. And if a black Corolla tries to get by, stop them! He's got a gun. Now, open the damn gate!"

The man starts moving. Cash slams his foot down on the gas. We race forward. A minute goes past.

I watch as he reaches up and hits a garage opener attached to his sun visor. Then he takes a sharp right again.

I hear the sound of a garage door opening. He drives inside and then starts hitting the garage button to close.

He looks over his shoulder. "Come on!" he orders me. "Let's get inside!"

"I'm scared!" I cry out.

"Come on, Chloe."

I manage to undo my seat belt. He rushes around the other side of the Jeep and practically yanks me out.

He has me by the arm and bolts inside the house. His house. The Fullers' house. He stops in the kitchen and looks back. "Follow me."

"Where?" I ask.

"Mr. Fuller has a gun in his weight room."

"You think he's still coming?"

"I don't know, but I'm not waiting to see."

My insides are trembling. I follow him upstairs to a home gym.

He runs to a cabinet and opens it. Then he pulls out a gun.

Seeing it brings on another wave of fear. "Do you know how to use it?"

"Yeah," he says.

And I don't know if that makes me feel worse or better.

"Follow me," he says.

I do as he says and we move down the hall. He opens a door and rushes to a window.

I stand there. My heart's thumping. I hear it in my ears, feel it in the base of my neck.

Then I hear a meow. I look down, and an old red tabby is standing at my feet. He rises up and sniffs the air. As if he's sniffing me. Felix. My heart clutches.

Tears fill my eyes. I look around. The room's pink. There's a trundle bed with a rainbow bedspread. There're cabinets lined with pictures, toys, and books. I walk over to a shelf and touch a teddy bear—my heart stops. Everything is familiar. Everything is . . . mine.

"Shit!" Cash says.

"Is he coming?" I manage to ask.

"No, it's not him. It's Mrs. Fuller."

I hear a door slam downstairs.

"Damn it!" Rodney rammed his fist into the dashboard and tried again to start the engine. It rolled over, but didn't catch.

Blood rolled down his brow where he'd hit his head when the kid slammed his car with the Jeep. He drew in air, trying to think what to do. His gut burned with the need to start the car and find them and take care of his problem once and for all.

He turned the key again. It started. Aching to finish this, Rodney was about to pull into the street, but then he heard sirens.

"Shit!" He gripped the Glock in his hand.

He wasn't going back.

Then, much to his amazement, the two patrol cars hurled past.

He sat there another few seconds, his own blood stinging his eyes; then he realized he had to get the hell out of here.

I stand there, hearing what Cash just said, but praying it isn't so.

"Cash?" I hear a woman yell from downstairs. "Cash, where are you?"

He looks as panicked as I feel. "What do I do?" he asks, and puts a hand to his head.

Footsteps tap up the stairs. "Cash!"

He rushes to the door. I stay there—my feet feel nailed to the floor.

"I'm here," he says.

"What happened?" Panic echoes in her voice.

He clears his throat. "The police are on the way. George was supposed to call them."

"They've been looking for you. Where have you been? Tony's on his way. I've been calling you. Why didn't you answer?"

"I cut my phone off. I can . . . explain," Cash says.

"The police, they've been looking for you."

"I know," Cash says. "I told George at the security gate to call them."

"What? No. They came to my work."

"But I just called them." Confusion sounds in his tone.

"Did you hurt . . . someone?" Mrs. Fuller asks.

I can see Cash standing in the hall. His shoulders are tense. He has the gun behind his back. "He was shooting at us," Cash says. "I knocked him off the road."

"The police think you shot her?"

"What?" Cash asks. "Shot who? I haven't shot anyone. He was the one shooting."

"Why aren't you in school? Oh God, Cash. What have you done, son?"

"I haven't done anything. What are they saying?"

I hear the panic in his voice, and then I see her move to stand closer to Cash.

I don't move. I feel numb. My insides are quaking. I'm cold. So cold.

Cash looks back at me. I'm not breathing. I'm dizzy. I force myself to pull in air.

She sees me. Her eyes widen. She takes one step, then puts her trembling hands over her mouth. "Oh my God!"

She takes a step closer. I can't breathe.

She takes another step, and I lurch back. I don't know why, but I don't want her to touch me. I'm afraid. Afraid of what I'll feel. My vision is watery. I suddenly see black spots in my vision.

"How?" She looks at Cash. "I don't understand."

A phone rings. It's hers. She's holding it. Then a doorbell chimes.

She shakes her head. "Cash? How . . . ?" She rushes me. My knees give. She catches me.

A soft cry spills from my lips. She pulls me toward her. I'm surrounded by her scent.

I'm suddenly young. And she's my mom. I'm Emily Fuller. I know her smell. I know her touch. I know she's my mother.

Your mama and daddy don't want you anymore.

I'm sitting on that dirty brown sofa. *I want my mama. Yes they do! They do love me!* I screamed.

I feel the hand across my face. Feel my jaw jerk back. Feel the sting. Feel myself fall against the sofa.

"Emily? Emily." I hear her voice. I start sobbing on her shoulder. My knees completely give, and I crumple to the floor. She comes down beside me. "Oh, baby. It's okay."

The doorbell continues to chime. A phone continues to ring. I see Cash move to the window again.

"It's the police," I hear Cash say. "Mrs. Fuller, what is it they think I did?"

She looks up at Cash. "They think you shot Carmen Gonzales."

33

"The nanny?" Cash asked staring at Mrs. Fuller. Everything happened so fast. The gunshots. The car spinning. Nothing was making sense.

Mrs. Fuller nodded. "How do you even know—?"

"I was trying to find out what she knew about Chloe. About Emily," he said.

The doorbell rang again, followed by knocking. The knocking grew louder. "They found your number on her phone. Found messages. They wanted to know where you were yesterday. I told them you were at work. They called back and said you weren't at work. Where were you?"

He stood there, feeling a thousand different emotions. "I was at the lake house."

"With me," Chloe said in a weak voice.

"Okay." Mrs. Fuller stood up. He noticed her hands were still shaking. She reached down and offered Chloe a hand. "Let's go open the door."

He looked down at the gun he held and set it on the bedside table. Mrs. Fuller saw it and gasped.

Did she think he did it?

She turned and started down the stairs. He followed her. Chloe moved beside him, one step at a time. He reached for her in case she fell. She jerked back. And the look of terror on her face made him want to kick himself.

Damn it. I told you not to do it! Now look what happened. He recalled her anger at him earlier. And he knew he deserved it. He remembered seeing the guy holding up the gun. Remembered seeing it pointing right at Chloe.

He'd caused this. He almost got her killed.

When they got to the foot of the stairs, Mrs. Fuller stopped. "Go in the living room. Both of you."

Cash led Chloe there; then he went back and stood in the entryway.

Mrs. Fuller looked back at him. "Go into the living room! I'll talk to them. When Tony gets here, we'll all go down to the station."

Cash did what she asked.

When she opened the front door, her words carried into the living room. "We'll take him down to the police station."

"Sorry," a deep voice said, "there are multiple things going on right now. There's the issue about Carmen Gonzales. Then the security guard at your gate said your son pulled in, saying someone was shooting at him, and he had a girl curled up on the floorboard. If I can just see him, speak to him and the girl for one minute, I'll leave and let you bring him down to the station. But I need to see them."

Cash stepped out. The cop standing there was the same asswipe who'd accused him of stealing a car. The same guy who'd treated him like trash because he was a foster kid.

"I'm here," Cash said.

The man's frown found Cash. "Care to explain?"

"A man was shooting at us." Cash squared his shoulders.

"Someone tried to shoot you?" Mrs. Fuller asked, panic in her voice.

"I'm fine," Cash told her.

"And where did this alleged shooting take place?" the officer asked.

"'Alleged'?" Cash spit out. "You're a prick, you know that?"

"Cash," Mrs. Fuller said.

Cash ignored her. "My Jeep's in the garage. It has bullet holes in it. And is wrecked where I knocked him off the road. Go look, and then let's talk 'alleged.'"

The cop beside that man moved forward. "I'll go check the garage."

The first officer still stood there, staring. "What do you know about Carmen Gonzales?"

"I've never met the woman. I texted her and spoke with her niece."

"About what?" the officer asked.

When Cash didn't answer, the cop piled on another question. "Where were you yesterday?"

"I think you can wait and talk to him at the station," Mrs. Fuller said.

"You think I hurt her?" Cash asked the officer. "Why? Because I'm my father's son? You think I'm just like him? What do you want to do? Shoot me? It's not like it would be the first time a cop did that!"

"He's telling the truth." Chloe walked out of the living room. "I was with him all day."

"What's your name?" the officer asked Chloe, and looked at her as if her association with him somehow made her guilty. Made her trash. And, damn it, maybe it did. He'd almost gotten her killed. Just like his dad did with him.

"I said you can talk to them later!" Mrs. Fuller said again. "I'm getting both of them a lawyer."

"I don't need a lawyer!" Cash said. "I haven't done anything. I don't have anything to hide."

The other officer walked back in. "The Jeep's been shot up."

I stand there as Cash starts trying to explain.

"Wait." The officer with an attitude says, "Take her out of the room." He motions to the other policeman.

I start to argue but realize it won't help. I move into the kitchen. The officer motions for me to sit at the table. My knees nearly buckle before I sink into a chair.

"We didn't do anything wrong," I say. "We were together all day yesterday."

Mrs. Fuller walks into the room. "You don't have to talk to him."

The officer's gaze shifts to Mrs. Fuller. "Are you her mother?"

Mrs. Fuller hesitates—then her voice catches when she says, "Yes!"

Tears fill my eyes.

Mrs. Fuller moves to stand beside me. "It's going to be okay."

Right then, my phone rings. I pull it out. I swipe tears off my cheek and catch my breath. "It's my dad. Can I answer it?"

Dad's still an hour away. I tried to explain, but I know I just confused the hell out of him.

He made me promise him that I was okay six times. But nothing sounds okay when you end it with *They're taking me to the police station.*

A door into the kitchen opens. Mr. Fuller walks in. When he sees me, he stops dead in his tracks.

I get a knot in my throat. I want to cry. Drop my head on the table and just sob.

Mrs. Fuller says, "She's alive," and she starts crying, and the two of them hug.

Mr. Fuller keeps staring at me, and I feel as if I'm about to fall apart. Then it's time to go to the police station. The cops don't want Cash and me together. Mrs. Fuller refuses to let them take me in a police car. She drives me, and Mr. Fuller is driving Cash. She also tells me Mr. Fuller is getting a lawyer to meet us there.

I start to remind her that we didn't do anything, but I don't have the strength. We get into her SUV.

She looks at me. "Can you explain anything?"

I swallow the panic still crowding my throat and tell her about meeting Cash. About how he thought I was trying to get money from them. "Then, when he learned I was adopted—"

"Adopted?" she asks.

I tell her about my parents. About the adoption agency.

She tears up some more. When she stops at a red light, she looks at me again. "You don't remember me?"

I hesitate. I bite down on my lip. "Not . . . When we hugged, I recognized your smell." I start crying again.

She reaches over and takes my hand. "It's going to be okay. You're home now."

The way she says that one word, *home,* should make me feel good, but instead it sets a fear in my belly. I swipe at the tears on my face. "I love my parents."

She looks almost offended and stares back at the road. "We'll figure this out."

When we walk into the police department, a man wearing a black suit is standing at the door. "Mrs. Fuller?"

"Yes. You must be Mr. Jordon."

"Yes, ma'am." He looks at me. "Miss Holden?"

I nod.

"I got a room for us to talk." He motions us inside.

"Can you please get Mr. Carter here? He's the detective who worked my daughter's kidnapping."

"I've already spoken with him," Mr. Jordon says.

The room with only a table and chairs in it reminds me of the adoption agency, but instead of smelling like air freshener, it smells like sweat. Like fear. And it might be my own.

We sit down, and Mr. Jordon says, "I spoke with Mr. Fuller, but I'm still confused."

"Where's Cash?" I ask, remembering how the cop treated him. "Does he have a lawyer?"

"Of course," Mrs. Fuller says, sitting beside me.

Mr. Jordon pulls out a pen and paper. He looks at me. "The police believe Cash, and possibly you, went to see Carmen Gonzales."

"We didn't," I say. "I swear."

He nods, then says, "I'm told your father is on his way. We should wait until he gets here to talk."

"We didn't do anything wrong," I say and I repeat the story of how I met Cash.

He nods. "I think we need to wait until we can get Miss Holden's adoptive parents here."

"We'll pay for representation," Mrs. Fuller said.

The man frowns. "She's a minor, and before I can look into her case, I need their permission."

"She's my daughter," Mrs. Fuller says.

The door to the room opens, and my mom walks in. "Oh God. Chloe. Your dad called and said you were here. What's going on?"

I stand up. She rushes past Mrs. Fuller and hugs me. I tear up again, and my insides start shaking like before.

Mom pulls back and says, "What happened?"

"Someone tried to shoot them," Mrs. Fuller says.

"What?" Mom looks at her, then back at me. "Are you okay?" She runs her hands up and down my arms.

I nod.

Then Mom turns back to Mrs. Fuller. "Who are you?"

Mrs. Fuller's shoulders stiffen, and she stands up. "I'm her mother."

Mom doesn't move. She just stands there as if the words need to soak in. "The hell you are," Mom says, and looks at Mr. Jordon. "Who is she?"

The man stands up. "Let's let Chloe and her mom have some time."

Mrs. Fuller flinches, but she moves to the door. Then she stops, turns, and I see fire in her eyes. She stares at Mom. "If you are responsible for this, I'll find out. And I won't rest until you're locked in jail!"

"What are you talking about?" Mom says.

Mr. Jordon moves in front of Mrs. Fuller. "We'll be back in a few minutes."

The door closes. Mom looks at me. "You have some explaining to do, young lady."

I drop down in the chair, and for the third time, I start the story of meeting Cash.

"I knew I didn't like that boy!" Mom snaps.

"Cash didn't do anything wrong," I insist. "But they think Cash, and maybe even I, shot a woman."

"What?" She frowns and her hands are shaking. "This isn't making sense."

I try to explain about the nanny.

"You are not her! We adopted you."

"We think the adoption agency did it."

"You believe this?" She stares at me.

I want so bad to protect Mom, to close the floodgates, but it's too late. It's the truth; I know it. I feel like I'm drowning in it. And I might have to watch Mom drown, too.

"That's the most ridiculous thing I've ever heard. We'll get in touch with the adoption agency. They'll put a stop to this."

I swallow. "I've already been there."

"To the adoption agency?"

I nod.

"And they told you it was a mistake, right?"

For the life of me, I don't even know where to start.

"What did they tell you? They denied it, right?"

"They lied, Mom. To me and Cash and even Dad."

Mom's eyes round and then tighten into slits. "Your dad? He went with you?"

"I begged him to. You were depressed and—"

"He has no right to do that without consulting me! Where is he?"

Freaking great. I just started World War III! "He didn't want to do it, I made him."

"We'll deal with that later," Mom says, anger adding snap to her words. "How do you know they lied?"

"Because someone went to Cash and threatened him and me if we didn't stop looking into it. Then they started shooting at us." My heart goes back to pounding. "And I just know, Mom. I remember things." Tears fill my eyes.

She puts a hand over her mouth and takes in some shaky breaths. "Did Cash shoot the woman?"

The anger simmering inside me spills over. "No!" I yell. "Have you heard anything I said, Mom? He was trying to help me. Someone shot at us."

Right then, the door opens and Dad walks in.

"We need to talk!" Mom slaps her hand on the table.

"Who are you letting her hang out with?" Dad spits out.

"Stop!" I jump up so fast, my chair clatters to the floor. "I am not going to listen to you two argue. I have had a really bad day! This is about me now. I'm the kid here. And if you don't want to act like my parents, then leave!" I put my hand over my mouth and sob.

Mom jumps up and hugs me. Dad shuts the door.

34

"Don't worry about me," Cash told Mr. Murphey, the lawyer the Fullers hired. "Worry about Chloe."

"Emily," Mrs. Fuller said. "Her name is Emily."

Cash sat in an interview room, flanked by the Fullers. He couldn't blame Mrs. Fuller for feeling like she does, but she couldn't expect Chloe to forget about the last fifteen years of her life.

"She goes by Chloe," he said. "She doesn't remember—"

"Look," Mr. Murphey said. "I don't want to interrupt, but I need to get to the facts of what happened between Cash and Carmen Gonzales."

"He's right," Mr. Fuller said.

Tears filled Mrs. Fuller's eyes. "Those people kidnapped my baby."

"They didn't," Cash said. "I'm telling you the agency is behind this. If you try to make her parents out to be the bad people, this won't work. She loves them. They love her. She's had birthday parties with clowns and jumping houses. They aren't the ones who took her from you."

"How do you know?" she asked.

"Her father went to the adoption agency to try to get information. If they were behind this, he wouldn't have done that."

"So he knows they kidnapped her, and he didn't—"

"No." Cash leaned back in his chair. "It's not like that."

"Again," Mr. Murphey interrupted. "Can we get to Carmen Gonzales?"

Mr. Fuller set his hand on his wife's. "Susan, we need to deal with other stuff first."

She nodded.

Cash told the lawyer about contacting the nanny.

Mr. Murphey nodded. "Detective Logan noticed you have an injury on your hand. How did—?"

"I never saw the nanny," Cash said. "I had words with a boy at school in the parking lot."

"Did anyone see it?" Mr. Murphey asked.

"I don't know."

The lawyer frowned. "Be prepared to answer those questions. Now, how did you find the nanny?" Mr. Murphey asked.

Cash swallowed and didn't look at either of the Fullers when he answered. "I got the file from Mr. Fuller's desk.

The nanny's name was in there." He went on and told them about the man who found him at the service station.

"Okay." Mr. Murphey tapped his pencil on the paper. "One thing I'm not clear about: Why did the man threaten you and not the girl?"

Cash exhaled. "Because I broke into the agency."

"You did what?" Mr. Fuller asked.

"I broke in and took pictures of all her files."

I go through the how-I-met-Cash story one more time for Dad. My throat's raw from crying and talking. A knock sounds at the door.

Mr. Jordon sticks his head in. "Is it a good time to talk?"

"Yes," Dad says.

He walks in.

"Who are you?" Mom asks.

"I'm Mr. Jordon. The Fullers have hired me to represent Chloe."

"Leave," Mom said. "We don't want you here. We'll get our own lawyer. They'll try to take you away."

"I'm almost eighteen," I say. "They can't do that."

Mom slaps her hand on the table again. "She threatened to have me thrown in prison."

Mr. Jordon speaks up. "I'm not here about a paternity case. I'm here about Carmen Gonzales."

"I don't care. We'll get our own lawyer," Mom insists.

"Wait," Dad says. "I'll pay him. He works for us now."

"No!" Mom snaps.

"Our daughter might be in trouble. We need him."

"I didn't do anything," I say. "And Cash was with me all yesterday."

Mr. Jordon sits down. "The police are wanting to talk to you."

Ten minutes later, we're waiting for the officers. Dad went out and got me a drink and a pack of crackers. When he comes back in, he has a Diet Coke for Mom, too.

When he hands it to her, she looks like she's about to say something nasty. I clear my throat that's already too raw.

She accepts Dad's offering.

I scoot back, pull my legs up in the chair, and drop my head on my knees. I sit there and worry about Cash. I don't talk. I don't move. Neither do Mom or Dad.

In a few minutes, Mr. Jordon walks in, accompanied by two officers. There's just enough chairs for everyone. They sit down. I've never been claustrophobic, but now I think I am. There just doesn't seem to be enough oxygen in the room.

"I'm Detective Carter," the officer I've never seen introduces himself. I recall Mrs. Fuller asking for him, and I can feel him staring at me. I can't help but wonder if he still thinks this is a scam.

The bigger officer, Officer Logan, the one who was so rude at Mrs. Fuller's house, looks at me. "Where were you yesterday?"

"At the Fullers' lake house."

"All day?"

"Yes. We didn't get back until after seven."

"She's telling the truth," Mom says. "I was home."

"How is she?" I ask. "The nanny?"

"She's in a coma, but still alive." The officer shifts in his chair. "Did you see the man shooting at you today?"

"No." Tears fill my eyes. Dad grabs my hand. "Cash pushed me down in the seat."

"Did Cash say who he thought it was?"

I try to think. "I don't think he said, but he'd just told me that a guy had threatened him that morning about us not looking into the adoption. So I think we both assumed it was him."

He nodded. "Mr. Colton has an injured hand. Do you know how he did that?"

"Him and a kid at school argued this morning. He thought the guy was hurting me. He didn't hit him, just pushed him against another car."

The officer nodded once again. "And the name of this guy?" he asked, but I could tell he was just testing me.

"Paul Cane. Cash never even saw the nanny. We were going to talk to her tomorrow. We were the ones getting shot at."

"Have you found the man who did that?" my dad asks.

"We found a black Corolla that fits the description of the car, but, no, we have not located the man."

"Ms. Holden," Detective Carter says, and places his hand on the table. "Do you believe you are Emily Fuller?"

I feel Mom and Dad staring at me. "Yes," I say, and my tonsils shake.

"Do you remember anything?"

I nod. "For years, all I remembered was sitting on a dirty sofa. There was a dirty carpet, and I was holding a tiara and wearing, like, a princess dress."

The man's eyes widen. "And have you remembered more?"

Again, I nod. "A face. A man with red hair. He told me . . . that my mama and daddy didn't want me anymore." A knot forms in my throat. "He hit me."

Mom makes a scratchy noise and reaches for my hand.

Now Detective Carter nods. "We would like to run a DNA test."

"No," Mom says. "They'll try to take you."

"No one is going to take me." I focus back on the officer. "Tell me where and when I need to do it."

"Actually, I already have two here. The Fullers have requested one. They have access to a lab that will come back quicker than ours." He gives me instructions on preparing a DNA sample.

I swipe my cheek twice with what look like Q-tips. The detective seals them up. Then he hesitates. "One other thing," he says. "The Fullers would like to speak to you. All of you."

"No. Chloe's tired," Mom says.

Mom's right, I'm exhausted. So much so that I almost give in—then I realize Mom needs to know this is my call. "We'll see them." I turn to Mom. "And we'll play nice."

Time passes, and finally Mr. and Mrs. Fuller walk in. Everyone is gone but Mom, Dad and me, but the Fullers don't sit down. They just stand there.

They both look at me and then focus on Mom and Dad.

"Is Cash okay?" I ask.

"As good as can be expected," Mr. Fuller says, and the way he stares at me makes my chest hurt.

"Can I see him?" I ask.

Mr. Fuller speaks up. "They still don't want you two talking until things are cleared up."

"We didn't do anything," I say.

"It's protocol or something," Mr. Fuller says.

Mrs. Fuller steps forward. "I need to apologize." She looks at Mom. "What I said earlier about you and jail. I wasn't thinking straight. If what Cash believes is true, then you aren't at fault. He tells me . . ." She tears up and her voice cracks.

My own tears well up again. I remember how she smelled like . . . like home. I ache to stand up and hug her again, lose myself in that smell, but I know it'd hurt Mom. And, like it or not, right now I have to think of her.

Mrs. Fuller continues, "I'm sorry. I . . . I needed to blame someone."

Mom nods, but she doesn't look all that forgiving.

"One other thing," Mr. Fuller says. "We're worried that whoever shot at Chloe and Cash earlier might return. We want to make sure that she'll be safe." I hear a crack in his voice, and my heart cracks, too.

I see their side of this. They just found their daughter, who had been stolen from them, and they have to walk away. My chest burns with the injustice of all of this.

"Don't worry," Dad says. "I've got this."

The Fullers leave. It's still a few hours before we are told we can go. We walk out to the parking lot. It's only the afternoon, but it's cloudy, the sky is dark, and I feel like it's midnight. I crawl into my mom's backseat and curl up into a ball. I hear Mom and Dad arguing over something, but I'm too tired to referee.

I hear Mom opening her door. "You want to put on your seat belt, hon?" Mom says.

"No," I say. "I'm lying down." I know it was stupid, but I can't be nice anymore. I just want to go to sleep and for just a little while forget all of this.

The next thing I know, Dad's waking me up. "Come on, sleepyhead. I don't think I can pick you up anymore."

I lift up. He helps me out of the car and puts his arm around my shoulder. "I'm so proud of you."

I look up. "For what?"

"For how you handled everything. I can only imagine how hard today's been on you."

I lean against him and let a few more tears leak out. "I love you."

"I love you, too. And so does your mom. This is hard on her, but she'll come around. I promise."

We get to the porch. "Are you hungry? I can order a pizza or something."

"No, I just want to go to bed."

He nods. "I'm staying here," he says. "So don't worry about anyone hurting you."

I look at him. "Mom's okay with that?"

"She's going to have to be."

I keep looking at him. "Hide the kitchen knives before you go to sleep."

He smiles. "I've already thought about that."

We walk into the house. Mom rushes over and hugs me. I purposely inhale her scent, thinking it will smell like home, too. And it does, but it's not the same as Mrs. Fuller. More tears sting my eyes. I hug her tighter because I feel disloyal.

"Can I get you something to eat or drink?" Mom asks.

"No. I want to go to bed."

"I love you," I say before I walk into my room and fall onto my bed. I'm certain I'll be dead asleep in five minutes. But I'm not. I'm back on the dirty brown sofa. I'm scared. I'm lonely. I want my mama. I remember being hit. Then time seems to jerk, and I remember hearing the gun popping off.

I roll over, sure that I don't have more tears in me, but I find a few. I think about Cash. And how hurt he seemed when the cop didn't believe him about being shot. Felix and Buttercup come and curl up beside me.

When I wake up, it's dark. Mom brings me soup and insists I eat. I manage a few bites. Dad tries to get me to come out of my room and watch television with him, but I refuse.

I curl back up in my bed and sleep some more. A little

later, I hear Dad in my room. "Sorry," he says. "Just checking to make sure your window is locked."

"It's probably not," I say, too emotionally sunk to care that someone might be after me.

The bright sun wakes me up and yanks me into the past. Not too far back, just a few years. To the sleepover days when Cara and Sandy and I'd stay up all night, talking about boys, college, and our grand plans for our lives. Funny how fast your own past starts feeling like it belongs to someone else. I can't help but wonder if I felt like that when I was three.

I lie there for a long time without moving. I remember Dad's here. In the same house as Mom. I don't recall hearing them arguing during the night.

If I'd known all it took was to get accused of attempted murder to make them cordial, I might have considered it earlier. Then the sarcastic thought bumps against my conscience, and I think about the nanny. I wonder if she's okay.

I sit up. When I do, I see pillows and blankets on the floor. I instinctively know Dad slept there. Probably scared of Mom.

I throw my covers back, but see my phone on the bedside table. I know I'm not supposed to, but I can't help it. I grab it, look at my closed bedroom door, and text Cash.

Me: *You okay?*

I hold my breath and wait. Three dots appear. Then . . .

Him: *We can't talk.*

Me: *Since when are you a rule follower?*

Him:. . . . . . .

Nothing. Five minutes later. *Still nothing.*

I see Lindsey texted yesterday. Like, five times.

Her: *You okay?*

Her: *What's going on?*

Her: *I'm worried about you.*

"I'm worried about me, too," I mutter.

I force myself out of bed. I smell coffee. I seldom drink it, but I will today. I go pee and move into the kitchen.

Dad's on the phone. He looks at me and smiles. "Yes. I moved the meeting to next week," he says as if he's talking to his boss.

He hangs up. "Good morning."

I move to the cabinet to get a cup for my go-juice. "Where's Mom?"

"I convinced her to go to work. She's called three times to check on you."

I see the clock. It's ten, and—*bam!*—I remember. "I was supposed to drive Lindsey to school."

"Your mom drove her."

I pour coffee in my cup and lean against the counter. "You slept on the floor in my room?"

"Yeah. Finding your window open got me worried about . . ." He doesn't finish, but I get it.

I put the cup to my lips and talk through the steam. "You sure you weren't just scared of Mom?"

"Well, there was that." He smiles, then doesn't. "I don't blame her for hating me, Chloe."

Before I can stop them, the words come out. "Me neither."

He wipes a hand over his face. "I don't expect this to change what I did, but just so you know, Darlene's gone."

"I should hope so, after her brother stole your credit card."

His brow creases. "How did you—?"

"She posted it on Facebook. Cash friended her." I take my first real sip of hot, bitter caffeine. "She thought he was a hot soccer player."

He turns his cup. "I'm not surprised."

"Me neither." I sit down.

"Oh, I do have some good news."

I look up. "What?"

"A detective called. The nanny woke up. He was going there to talk to her."

Mr. Fuller tapped on Cash's bedroom door, then stuck his head in. "You up?"

Up? He hadn't slept. But he answered, "Yeah."

"Can we talk?" Mr. Fuller said.

"I'm talked out." How many times had he told the same story? How many times had the cops looked at him as if he were his father?

"Well, you can just listen, then."

Mr. Fuller walked into the room and sat down in a chair by Cash's desk. "Detective Logan called this morning. Carmen Gonzales woke up. They think she's going to be okay. This whole thing is getting cleared up."

Cash slumped back against his pillows. "Yeah, cleared up after they talk to her, because they wouldn't believe me."

"They're just doing their job."

Cash's gut twisted. All night long, he kept hearing Chloe's words. *I told you not to break into the agency. I told you.* But damn, he'd almost gotten her killed.

Remembering Mr. Fuller was still in his room, he looked up. "Did they find the guy who shot at us?"

"Not yet. They're trying." He hesitated. "Mrs. Fuller and I want to say thank you, again."

"Why? I screwed everything up. That guy almost killed Chloe. That bullet went through the passenger window." His chest clutched.

"None of that is your fault."

"Yeah, it is. I'm the one who took down the flyer. I was the one who made the photocopies. I hurt Mrs. Fuller. And when I was young, I helped my dad con people like the guy who conned you guys out of money. I did terrible things."

"That has nothing to do with this. And, yes, perhaps the thing with Emily could've been handled differently, but—"

"Maybe that cop's right. I'm going to screw everything up because I'm just like my old man."

"Stop!" Mr. Fuller said. "You know what I don't get? You get so angry because people judge you, but then you judge yourself harsher than anyone. Give yourself a break, son."

I don't deserve one. "Can you leave so I can get up?"

Mr. Fuller frowned. "I'm leaving, but we hired a security guard. He's out front in a car."

"I don't need a babysitter! If you want to hire someone, hire them for Chloe."

"I did. But don't say anything. I think Mr. Holden might be insulted."

I'm planted on the sofa, staring at the television but not really watching it. Dad's in the kitchen, working on his computer. A knock comes at the door. I haul ass off the sofa.

"Stop." Dad steps out of the kitchen. "Go back in the living room."

I stop, but I don't move. My heart's racing. I'm praying it's Cash. I'm already figuring out what I'm going to say if Dad won't let him in. I'll break eggs left and right. Even scramble a few. I need to see Cash.

Dad moves to the dining room window, peers out, then glances back. "It's Mr. Fuller."

Bam! I get a lump in my throat.

Dad opens the door. "Come in."

"Thank you." Mr. Fuller walks in, his gaze finds me, and he smiles. "I just wanted . . . I got word that Mrs. Gonzales cleared Cash and Chloe of any wrongdoing."

"That's good," my father says.

"How's Cash?" I take a step closer.

"He's coping." Mr. Fuller's gaze stays on me.

Coping doesn't sound good.

My dad looks back at me. "I . . . need to make a call." He holds up his phone and walks into my mom's bedroom.

Mr. Fuller moves a little closer. "I like . . . your father."

I get how hard it must be for him to say that. I also get how hard it is for Dad to leave the room. It's all hard. Everything. I force myself to say, "He's a pretty good guy."

"The DNA test should be done tomorrow, but . . . I think we all . . ."

"I know," I say.

He drops his hands in his pockets. "I'm aware that this is difficult on you."

I nod.

"I just . . . Susan and I want you to know that we're working on accepting that you don't know us. And I know Susan kind of had a chance to talk to you, but I didn't." He looks away for a second. "I wanted you to know that . . . I loved you, too. You were a daddy's girl. Your moth—Susan used to say that you had me wrapped around your little finger. And you did."

When he looks up, his eyes have tears in them and my own follow suit.

"Losing you nearly killed us." He passes a hand over his mouth. "I gave up that you were alive. But not your mom."

I take in a shaky breath.

"Not because I loved you less, I just . . ."

"I understand," I say.

He nods. "We want you to be a part of our lives. And we

realize that it's not going to be easy to work all this out. But we are determined to find a way."

"Me, too," I say.

He pulls his hands out of his pockets. "Would it be too much for me to ask for a hug?"

My breath catches. I walk into his arms. When my cheek lands on his chest, his smell, like Mrs. Fuller's, is so familiar, and it feels safe, little-girl safe. And there's something else, too. When my cheek lands on his chest, my heart says, *You know this place. You've been here before.*

When the hug ends, I wipe the tears from my eyes. "Did the police say it would be okay now if Cash and I spoke?"

"They didn't, but I'm assuming it's okay."

Dad comes back in, and he walks Mr. Fuller to the door. Mr. Fuller offers Dad his hand. "Thank you. Thank you for raising a perfect girl."

35

Dad and Mr. Fuller stand on the porch and talk. I'm curious as to what's being said, but I take advantage of the time to go into my room and call Cash. His phone goes straight to voice mail.

"Hey," I say. "We can talk now. Can you come over?" I don't know why I'm feeling insecure about us, but I am. "I love you. And I don't just think that. I do . . . love you." I hang up. My eyes get moist again, and I don't know if I'm crying about Mr. Fuller or just missing Cash.

"Hey," Dad says.

I look up. He sees my tears and walks right over and puts his arms around me. Between the love I feel for him and the feeling I just had with Mr. Fuller, I'm pretty sure I'm getting emotional whiplash.

"It's like a freaking movie of the week!" Lindsey says when I finish my thirty-minute story of what happened yesterday. She came over as soon as she got home from school.

"Yeah," I admit.

"Has Cash called you yet?"

"No. I'm scared that . . . Why hasn't he called me?"

She frowns. "Don't worry. I know he's crazy about you." Then her eyes tighten. "You don't think the Fullers told him he couldn't . . . date you, do you?"

Hearing that sends a wave of pain to my mangled heart. "I don't know. I don't even know if they know we're together."

Lindsey drops back on my headboard. "And I thought I had a messed-up day yesterday."

I fall back on my pillow. "What happened?"

"A shit storm," she says. "Lunchroom brawl. Food throwing and everything."

"Seriously?" I ask.

"Yeah." She smiles. "It was crazy."

"What happened?" I'm happy to concentrate on her problems to escape mine.

"I found out that Jamie is dating Jonathon."

I lean up on my elbow. "You're kidding me! That totally breaks the girlfriend code."

Again, Lindsey frowns. "I don't think she's my friend anymore. In fact, I know she isn't."

"You confronted her?"

She nods. "You remember Amy? She's in my history class."

"Tall girl?" I ask.

"Yeah, she told me about the dating. During lunch, I asked Jamie—and at first she denied it, then she got all pissy. She called me a freak because my mom is gay. She said it loud, as if trying to embarrass me. I seriously don't know why I ever liked her."

"I'm sorry," I say. "What did you do?"

"I called her a prejudiced prick."

"And then . . . ?"

"I didn't have to do anything," Lindsey laughed. "Jamie didn't realize we were sitting one table from Shawn, the nice guy who always tells you he loves your hair."

"Yeah." Then I realize. "Oh. He's gay."

She nods. "I talked to him about Mom last year. He's nice. Anyway, he always sits with his LGBTQ friends."

My mouth drops open. "And?"

"Shawn stood up and real calm-like asked Jamie, 'Why does that make her a freak?' It was like the whole lunchroom was dead silent and everyone heard it. Jamie got pissed and called him some really ugly names. And you know everyone at school loves Shawn. So someone, I don't even know who it was, told Jamie to stop being a bitch. Then she got hit by a slice of pizza. It was so powerful, as if . . . I don't know, I felt like I didn't have to worry about what people thought anymore."

I smile, knowing what a relief that would be for Lindsey. "I'm sorry I wasn't there. I'd love to have seen that."

She laughs. "The pizza got Jamie right in the face. It, like, stuck to her. She got mad at me, as if I'd done it. She tossed her salad at me. Before I knew it, food's flying everywhere. A teacher stopped it. But she'd heard everything, and the only one to get in trouble was Jamie. She's suspended for, like, forever."

We lie there and watch the ceiling fan turn. Lindsey finally speaks up. "I didn't realize what a bad friend Jamie was until I met you."

"I'm sorry I wasn't there to give Jamie hell, too. I'd have thrown my pizza at her."

She smiles. "I know you would've. We make a good team." She bumps my shoulder with hers. "Can we, like, be friends forever? Like, after college? And when we get old, like our parents?"

"Yeah," I say.

She squeezes my hand. "Do you want me to call Cash and talk to him?"

"No. I'm sure he's just still dealing with things." I really want to believe that.

Right then, my phone dings with a text. I roll over to get it, sure it's from Cash. It is.

My heart's in my throat. There's eight words. Eight. *I think we need to take a break.*

When Mom comes home that night, she scowls at Dad, sees my puffy face, and hugs me. "I'm so sorry. I shouldn't have gone to work."

"No. You should have." I can't imagine being in the house all day with them. But yeah, I kind of cried off and on this afternoon. Part of me wants to call Cash and give him hell, but I don't even know what to say. Was this his plan all along? To dump me when the truth came out? My gut says it wasn't. He told me he loved me, and I believed him. But I'm too hurt to give him that much credit.

Dad orders pizza. I see Mom listening to him order. She gets up and goes to the bathroom, but not before I see the beginning of tears in her eyes. I know what caused it, too. It's the normalcy of him calling in pizza, ordering one with half pineapple and Canadian bacon. Ordering it because he knows she likes it.

I realize how hard it is on her to have him here. I really need to ask him to leave. But I also know as long as he feels I'm in danger, he won't. He loves me, too. And maybe he even still loves Mom. Now I want to tear up.

Mom comes back out. Dad puts the news on and sits in the chair farthest away from Mom. Tension is high, and Dad reaches over to the end table and picks up the family photo album.

He starts flipping through it, then stops and frowns. It takes me a minute to realize the issue. Mom's edited photos. He's been cut out. I almost feel sorry for him, but I realize he did this to himself. And while I think I've pretty much forgiven him, Mom's not there yet. She may never be there.

He puts the album back down. Thirty minutes later, the doorbell rings.

"That's probably the pizza." Dad jumps up.

"I can pay for my part." Mom grabs her purse.

I see the look in Dad's eyes, he wants to argue, but he knows he deserves Mom's ire, too. "Give it to me later." He moves to the door.

Mom pulls out a twenty and puts it on the coffee table.

I hear Dad at the door, and it doesn't sound like a delivery person. Dad moves into the living room, followed by Detective Carter, who spoke with us last night.

He nods at us. "I just wanted to come and let you know we pretty much wrapped everything up. You're no longer in danger."

"The agency confessed?" I ask.

The detective nods.

"Have a seat." My dad moves to sit beside me on the sofa.

The man takes the chair. "Things ended up being uglier than we thought. Mr. Wallace claims he wasn't behind the kidnapping. But he and his brother-in-law, Mr. Davis, were . . . basically buying babies to adopt out. Fifteen years ago, Davis had attained a child who was originally supposed to be adopted by you." He looked at my parents. "But before he got the child to Wallace, she died—supposedly of natural causes—but we are looking into that."

"Christina Garza," I say.

He looks at me. "Yes. That's the name we were told. Afraid that the illegal dealings would land him in jail, the brother-in-law buried the child and brought a different child. According to Mr. Wallace, he recognized you were not Christina Garza, but was told by Davis that Mrs. Garza had decided to keep her daughter and gone and gotten another girl from a mother who'd recently agreed to give up her child as well.

"When Mr. Wallace saw the news about the missing Fuller child, he realized what had happened and he went to his brother-in-law. Supposedly, Mr. Davis confessed about the child dying, saying he kidnapped a child to take her place. Mr. Wallace realized he'd go down with him, so he kept his mouth shut. Which makes him just as liable as his brother-in-law."

"So it was Mr. Davis who shot at us and who shot Mrs. Gonzales?" I ask.

"Mr. Wallace had contacted him when you showed up at the agency. Because the papers had said Ms. Gonzales gave a description of a possible kidnapper, Davis knew she could identify him. He wanted to make sure she didn't talk.

Mr. Wallace was the one who hired someone to talk to Mr. Colton. He swears he was trying to protect you, not threaten you."

"You caught Mr. Davis?" Mom asked.

"Yes. We picked him up at the Houston airport, trying to fly out to Mexico using his ex-wife's new husband's passport about two hours ago. Luckily, she realized he'd taken it and reported it."

I sit there, my hands locked in my lap as I try to take it all in. I'm shocked that in a matter of minutes, and without emotion, the man has detailed how my life, and the Fullers', had been ripped apart.

I see the look of dismay on both my parents' faces. Mom takes my hand and squeezes. "Is it clear that we weren't aware that the agency was doing anything illegal?" Mom asks.

"No one suspects that." Mr. Carter stood up. "I'm just thankful that things turned out." He looks at me, and I know he means that I'm alive.

Dad sees the man out the door. When he walks back into the living room, he has the pizzas. He puts them on the bar between the living room and kitchen.

Mom looks up. "That means you can leave."

Dad drops his hands into his pockets. "Yeah, it does."

He starts gathering his stuff. I hear him moving around, and my chest grows tighter.

He comes over and kisses me. "I'm going to stay at a hotel just until things settle. I'll see you tomorrow."

I nod. My chest is so tight, I think my ribs might crack. Between everything that's happened with the Fullers, Cash, and now this, I know my heart is truly broken.

He looks at Mom. "Can we talk a minute?"

"I'm not interested in anything you have to say," Mom says.

I get up and go to my bedroom. I shut the door, but I stand there and listen.

I hear Dad say, "I don't blame you for hating me. If I were you, I'd never forgive me either. But I just want you to know I realize what I lost. You deserved so much better."

I wait to hear what Mom says. There's a tiny part of me that longs for her to say she forgives him.

She doesn't. Mom never says anything. I hear Dad leave.

Later, Mom and I eat pizza alone. I try to hide the fact that I'm dying inside. And I can tell Mom's dying a little bit inside, too.

We go to bed early. I'm still awake, staring at my phone, praying Cash will call—when Mom walks in with her pillow and blanket.

"Can I sleep with you?" she asks.

I smile. "Yeah."

She crawls in bed beside me. "I'm scared."

"They caught him," I say.

"No. Not of that. I'm afraid you'll love her more." Tears fill her eyes.

"Not true." I lean up on an elbow.

"I don't know," she says. "They have money. They can buy you nice things. You"—her voice shakes—"look like her."

I brush a tear from her face. "I want to get to know them. I want to spend time with them. But remember in second grade, when my teacher was pregnant? You told me that a person loves with their heart, and you don't have to be in someone's belly to be in their heart."

Mom takes in a tight breath and nods.

"Love doesn't come from money or bone structure. Do you love me less because I don't look like you?"

Cash had deleted Chloe's message without listening to it. Detective Logan came by the house yesterday and informed them that Mr. Wallace and his brother-in-law had been arrested. There would be no charges filed for his breaking into the agency.

"We should celebrate," Mrs. Fuller said when the police left. "Go out to eat."

"Sorry." Cash had bowed out.

He went up to his room and spent the night and this morning coming up with his plan. Now all he had to do was execute it. It was going to hurt. They weren't going to understand. But it was the right thing.

He closed his suitcase and left it at the bottom of the stairs. When he heard them in the kitchen, he walked in.

Mrs. Fuller smiled and stood up. "Pancakes?"

"I'm not hungry." He sat down in a kitchen chair. "We need to talk."

"Sure," Mrs. Fuller said.

The lump in his chest swelled bigger. "I don't know if I've ever really said thank you for everything you've done for me."

"You don't need to say thank you. We're family."

He wasn't going to argue that point now.

"Is this about you and Chloe?" Mr. Fuller said. "We pretty much know that you two are . . . close."

"No, it's not that." He swallowed, preparing himself to hear Mrs. Fuller's sigh. "I've been thinking about this for a while and now an opportunity came up."

"What opportunity?" Mrs. Fuller asked.

"Devin, the guy I work with, his roommate moved out last month, and I think it's time for me to go ahead and move out."

"Move out?" Mrs. Fuller said. And there it came. The long heartfelt sound that shot right to Cash's gut. "You can't!"

"I'll be eighteen in two weeks. And we both know I could be declared an adult right now."

Mr. Fuller shot up from his chair as if too angry to stay seated, then dropped back down. "You told me you'd wait until you graduate."

"He told you that?" Mrs. Fuller asked, her words an accusation.

Cash took in a deep breath, hoping to break up the knot of pain. "I'm not doing this to hurt you."

"Well, it hurts," Mrs. Fuller said. "And you can't do this."

"I want to be on my own. I can't breathe here."

"You don't make enough money!" Mr. Fuller said.

"I talked to Mr. Cantoni, my boss, this morning. He's agreed to hire me full-time."

"What about school?" Mrs. Fuller's voice is pure pain.

"Tomorrow I'm going to talk to Ms. Anderson, my counselor, about taking the GED. And next semester, I'll start college."

"Is this because of . . . Emily? We love you, Cash. Just because we're thrilled to find her doesn't mean we don't love you."

Emotion knotted his throat. "It's not her. Like I said, I need my space." He stood up. "I'm sorry if this hurts you." His eyes stung. "But I'm doing it."

He started out of the room.

"You come back and sit down," Mrs. Fuller said, and she was crying.

He didn't stop. He picked up his suitcase and the pain he carried, the pain he'd carried since his father left him on the pavement to die, and he left. He wished he'd left years ago. It wouldn't have hurt this much then.

On Thursday, still not a word from Cash, and he's not even been at school. I sit in the living room, waiting for Mom to leave for her writers' meeting so I can go. Dad came by on Wednesday on his way back to El Paso after the Fullers had called and said the DNA test was positive. They asked if I would call them. That afternoon, Buttercup and I took a walk to the park. I found a quiet spot, leaned against a tree, and I called them.

They both got on the phone. They were so nice. Mrs. Fuller asked if I could come over sometime. I suggested tonight since Mom would be at her writers' meeting.

They seemed happy with that. I ended up telling Mom before she left for work this morning. I didn't want there to be lies between us. She said she understood. But instead of going straight to the meeting from work, she came home.

She hugs me. "Are you nervous?"

"A little," I tell her.

"Don't worry. There's no way in hell they aren't going to be thrilled with you." Then she hands me a thick envelope.

"What's this?"

"Photos. I made copies. You might explain why some of them have cutouts. But I just thought they'd want them."

I squeeze her hand. "Thank you for making it easy for me."

She no sooner gets out the door than my phone rings. I pray it's Cash, but it's not. It's Dad, wishing me luck.

"Are you okay?" His love sounds in his voice.

"Yeah," I say, but it's mostly a lie. I'm broken inside. I can't understand why Cash is doing this. And I can't help but worry if they told him I'm coming tonight. Does he not want to see me?

As I drive to the Fullers', I think about what Lindsey asked: *Did the Fullers tell Cash he couldn't date you?*

My gut says it isn't that, but I'm hoping to find out. Not that I want this night to be about Cash. I know it's about so much more. It's about the first three years of my life. It's about filling that empty spot I've carried in my heart most of my life.

I have to get passed through at the gate. But they told the guard I'm coming. I park in front of their house, and before I get to the door, they're on the porch.

I notice something right away: Mrs. Fuller's eyes. She looks hurt.

They both hug me. Tight and long. But it's okay. I kind of needed it.

Cash isn't there. I wonder if he's upstairs. But I do everything I can to push him out of my mind.

We sit down at their dining room table. I give them the pictures. They are so grateful to Mom. We ask each other questions. Several times, Mrs. Fuller and I start crying. Mr. Fuller works extra hard not to. But I see him passing a hand over his face every now and then.

They want to know everything about me. From my favorite color to my driving record. They have a sandwich tray of every meat, every cheese, and every different kind of bread known to mankind. Then different chips and desserts. I'm so nervous, I don't eat much. Neither do they.

I'm there several hours before I relent and ask about Cash.

The moment his name leaves my lips, tension fills the room.

"He moved out," Mr. Fuller explains.

I'm floored. "But . . . but he's not eighteen," I say.

They tell me Cash's plan.

"Why's he doing this?" I ask.

Mrs. Fuller says, "That boy can be stubborn sometimes. We're planning on going to see him this weekend. Check out where he's living. And try to talk him into coming back."

I don't know how to broach the subject, so I just ask. "Is this because . . . because he and I like each other?"

"No," they both say at the same time. "We thought it might be why he felt he needed to do it, but he swore it wasn't."

Mrs. Fuller adds, "Chloe, he had a rough childhood. I sometimes think he pushes people away because he's scared to care too much."

I nod, and I realize how right she is. I knew he didn't feel as if he deserved the Fullers, but I think maybe it's even more than that, he was afraid that people will abandon him like his father and all the other foster parents.

I'm hit with how sad it is, but then that sadness turns to anger. Anger at Cash for abandoning me and the Fullers. But I don't want anger building inside me. I push it aside, to concentrate on the Fullers. But it stays in my chest the rest of the evening. Building. Burning. What gives him the right to just walk away from people who care about him?

Then I suddenly realize it's after ten. "I should call Mom."

"Yes, don't worry her," Mrs. Fuller says.

It's eleven when I get home. Mom and I sleep together again. I tell her about the night. But I'm careful not to say anything that might make her feel like she's second fiddle.

36

Friday morning, Mom's alarm goes off at six. I lie there another ten minutes; then I get up. I have things to do. I get ready and let Mom think I'm going to school. I'm not.

I have eggs to buy. I have eggs to break. An omelet to make.

At the store, I get two dozen. Hey, if you're going to break eggs, you might as well do it right.

I'm not sure what time Cash goes to work. I drive by the garage at nine. He's not there. I drive by at ten. He's not there.

I worry he doesn't work on Friday.

I go to a restaurant and order . . . You guessed it—eggs.

When I drive by the garage at eleven, his Jeep's there. It's been repaired. No bullet holes.

I pull into the other side of the parking lot.

I'm shaking. I grab my two dozen eggs and walk over to his Jeep. I look around and see someone's in the office. I think they see me, and that's exactly what I want.

I set one carton down at my feet. And I stand up, open the other, and I throw my first egg. It lands with a *thud-crunch* against his windshield. In the corner of my eye, I see movement through the glass walls.

I throw egg number two. This one hits his passenger door. I watch the yellow yolk burst and ooze down the side.

"What are you doing?" someone yells out from the office door.

I don't say anything. Egg three hits the windshield.

I'm up to half a dozen when I see Cash, wearing navy coveralls, walking out of the garage.

"What are you doing?" he asks.

I ignore him and go for two more eggs. Then I look at him standing there, just staring. Just staring at me. I'm so mad, tears hit my eyes.

I can't read his expression. Not that I care. I throw another one.

"What are you doing?" he asks again.

"I'm breaking eggs."

He crosses his arms. "That's bad on the paint job."

"Yeah, I heard that once." I throw another one. Then I reach down and pick up the second carton.

He unlocks his arms and takes a few steps closer. "Listen. It's better this way," he says.

I throw an egg at him.

He dodges it and frowns. "You deserve—"

"Better than you? You're right. I deserve better than someone who isn't scared to care for someone. Who isn't scared to admit he cares for them."

He doesn't say anything.

"People care about you, and you don't even have the decency to admit you care about them!" I throw another egg at him. Then I throw another at his car, and then when I'm out, I throw the carton at him. That's when I see people standing in the parking lot, watching me.

Suddenly what felt like such a good idea seems foolish. I run for my car and reach for the door handle. It's locked.

"Stop!" he yells. "You can't just come here and say what you want to say and leave. We're not done arguing."

"Yes, we are!" I reach in my pocket for my keys, but they aren't there. I yank at my door as if it will magically open this time. It doesn't. I look in the window to see if I left them in the ignition. They aren't there.

I hear him walking toward me. "You're wrong."

I swing around. "About what?"

"I did admit it! I told you I loved you."

"Yeah, but then when I really needed you, you were gone." Tears fill my eyes.

"You were so mad at me, Chloe."

"When was I mad at you?"

"When I told you about being caught at the agency. And I couldn't blame you. I messed everything up."

"I wasn't so mad as upset. And you messed up when you walked away!"

"I nearly got you killed. They accused you of being part of shooting Mrs. Gonzalez. Because of me. My past is never going away. It's going to come up, and it's going to hurt anyone who's around me."

I take a few steps forward and poke him in his chest. "You're an idiot! None of what happened was because of your past. It happened because of mine!"

"You could have been killed!" he says.

I realize he's not listening to anything I say. I'm wasting my time. And more people are now standing around.

I remember setting the egg cartons down and realize I probably dropped my keys, too. I run over there.

His footsteps fall in cadence with mine.

I see my keys on the asphalt. I snatch them up.

I'm halfway to my car when suddenly he's in front of me. "Can we please talk?"

"I didn't come here to talk. I came to break some eggs. And I'm all out of eggs." I move around him.

He shoots in front of me and blocks me from my car door. "Okay," he says. "I was wrong!" There's a tremble in his voice.

I cross my arms. "Move away from my car."

"Let me explain!"

"There's no explaining. You turned your back on me."

"Give me a second chance?"

"So you can leave again the next time some trouble arises? No thank you! Like you said, I deserve better."

"Please. I've been miserable, Chloe. I can't sleep. I can't eat. Well, I can't eat anything but—" He pulls out a crumpled-up, half-empty packet of Skittles from his pocket. Then he pulls out another one. He sets them on the top of my car. "But I can't eat the red ones, because . . . because I know you like them so much."

He digs in his other pocket and pulls out two more crinkled packages of Skittles.

I take in a breath. "You hurt me!"

He nods. "I know. I'm sorry!"

I tilt up my chin. "You hurt the Fullers. They've done nothing but love you, and you just left. You don't care what it does to other people. You push people away."

"You're right. I do. And I'm tired of pushing. And you're right that I'm scared. Everyone left me—my mom, my dad. The foster parents. But if you'll give me a chance . . ." He takes a step toward me.

I hold out a hand. "You'll move back in with the Fullers and go back to school."

"If they'll let me, but like you said, I hurt them. And I didn't mean to." Pain echoes from his voice.

I shake my head. "They love you."

He takes another step toward me. This time, I don't back up. He reaches for me. And I fall against him. He pulls me in, and I cry on his shoulder. Then he pulls back and kisses me.

I kiss him back. He smells like oil and grease, but he tastes like Skittles and he feels like love.

I hear people whistling and clapping. But I don't care. Because right now, right here, I think that empty spot in my heart is finally filled.

Epilogue

Christmas music seeps out of the house stereo system. A real Christmas tree twinkles in the corner of the Fullers' living room. The scent of pine and the warm smell of turkey and dressing flavors the air. I'm caught in a moment of nostalgia. Not the bad kind, but the kind that says this is right.

I peer around the corner into the dining room and listen to all the chatter. Dad and Mr. Fuller are talking about football. Mom and Mrs. Fuller are arguing with Brandon and Patrick, Dad's cousin and his husband, over which is better, corn bread dressing or bread dressing.

Brandon and Patrick had come down for Thanksgiving and met the Fullers, who invited them over for Christmas. They'd agreed on the condition they could cook everyone's dinner. I can tell it's hard for both my moms to stay out of the kitchen. But what's getting a little easier is them being together. I still feel a little like I'm walking on eggshells, not wanting one to feel more important than the other. I love them both. But I think they know it, and it's not nearly so difficult as I thought it would be.

"Oh," Mrs. Fuller says, "Chloe told us you think you sold your book! We have to have a champagne toast for that."

"More than sold it," my dad spoke up. "It's at auction now. Several New York publishers are bidding for it."

"Wow," Cash whispered, stepping beside me, "your dad seems awful proud of your mom."

I look up at him and kind of smile. "Yeah. He knows how much she wanted it all those years."

"Are they actually talking now?"

"Some," I say. "Well, you saw them at Thanksgiving. And they talked about what I needed for Christmas. He came over last night. Mom even waited until he got there before she left for her writers' group Christmas party. I think she wanted him to see her all dressed up. When she left, Dad asked me if she was dating someone."

Cash slips his hand on my waist. "Did you tell him the truth?"

"Yeah. He looked hurt. Jealous."

"He kind of deserves it," Cash says.

"I know," I say.

"You want them to get back together?" he asks.

"I just want them happy."

"Susan and JoAnne," Brandon calls from the kitchen. "We need some tasters in here."

Cash leans a little closer. "Did the Fullers tell you that they bought the house in Houston?"

"Yeah." Cash applied and was accepted to go to the University of Houston, so we're both going there. He still refuses to let the Fullers pay for his college, but they've been looking for a property near the school so both of us can live there. Separate bedrooms, of course. That's been said several times.

I figure what they don't know won't hurt them.

More laughter leaks from the dining room.

I look at Cash. "You know I've thought a lot about how things would have been in another life if I hadn't been kidnapped."

"Yeah," Cash says.

"Well, I'm not sure it would have been all that great. All of them are my family. I wouldn't have wanted to miss out on knowing any of them."

"I agree," he says. Then he reaches in his pocket and hands me a bag of red Skittles. "Merry Christmas."

I grin and pull out the caramel candy I picked for him. Then I lift up on my tiptoes and kiss him. "Merry Christmas."